THE ORDER

Book #1 - The Nina Chronicles

Stan Morse

Published by Stan Morse

All prose and artwork: © 2016 Stan Morse

ISBN: 0989851354
ISBN: 9780989851350

Thanks to the following who read early drafts of this novel and offered their comments, or who helped with technical details: Robert Bettis, MD, Chris Bigelow, Emma Crowe, Joy Crowe, Kaitlyn Crowe, Ruby Eckert, Collette Felton, Amy Holmes, Kya Holmes, Nick Moran, Theresa Moran, Earl Papac, Nicole Porrovecchio, Ray Sandidge, Doug Sandvig, JoAnne Strandberg, Olivia Strandberg, Cameron Walter and Gaylen Willett

Thanks to graphic artist Ashley Goff for the excellent book cover artwork

OTHER BOOKS BY STAN MORSE
Circling the Earth in a Wheelchair
Brothers of Summer
Goering's Gold

For Nina

PROLOGUE

They faced each other across an oak conference table crafted from an Ardennes Forest log harvested in the year 1692. Making the table slightly younger than the graceful, brown-haired German woman, who looked to be in her late twenties. And a few years older than the equally youthful-appearing Austrian, whose face vaguely resembled a Van Gough self-portrait.

"Clarissa may have found *The One*," Liesel said, knowing he would be upset upon hearing the news.

Pieter ran one palm up his forehead, pushing back his blonde hair. Open conflict with the Order's oldest living member had long been expected. And now, it had finally arrived. What rankled most was that it had come during *his* watch as chairperson of the Council.

"Are you certain?"

"I believe it to be so," came her steady reply.

Pieter's anger swelled, and his face began to turn red. "Then we should consider taking immediate action!"

"Why?" Liesel pleaded. "This is our opportunity to learn exactly what she intends. We may even have a chance for a compromise if we play it right."

"The only thing she intends is our ruin!" he shot back. "Just a quick *poof* and there we go, with the whole world suddenly on our backs." He shoved his leather armchair away from the table and stood. Down came his palms flat and hard on the golden-grained surface. He leaned forward, fixing her with a look that said: *End of the World Now in Progress.*

"I don't believe she intends to ruin us," Liesel insisted, staring back into those unflinching blue eyes.

"Of course you don't," Pieter replied, almost mocking. "You and she have been friends for decades, so you *would* believe her. But why should *we* take that risk?" His lips were now pressed hard, leaving no doubt.

Liesel wasn't willing to yield. Not when the stakes were so enormous. "It certainly presents a risk for us," she conceded. "But what about the bigger picture? What about the future of humanity?"

"Hah! What a joke you make." He lifted his hands from the table and stood up straight, arching his back, as if recoiling from the absurdity of what she'd just said. "Do you really believe humanity is even *worth* saving these days?" He squeezed his eyes shut, as if a headache had erupted. They opened slowly, painfully. "So let's talk about the facts, not about this fantasy you and she seem to have about saving the human race. Do you actually know anything about this person she has found?"

And here was a possible opening. A slim chance to buy some time.

"It's just a girl," Liesel said. "She would be about thirteen years old."

"Thirteen?" Pieter was amazed. "How could she have possibly managed to find someone so young?"

Liesel chose not to answer. She couldn't lie to another member. The truthing skill precluded it. An honest answer might easily lead to a betrayal of Clarissa's earlier confidence about the mother, and that was something Liesel wasn't willing to risk. At least not yet. She folded her hands on the table, demurely waiting for his anger to subside.

He glanced up at the ceiling, frustrated. "Do you think she has already told the girl *what* she is?"

"No, of course not. Someone so young would never be able to handle that kind of knowledge. I believe she will keep her in the dark for a good while longer."

Pieter turned, took a few steps away from the table until he faced the leaded glass windows. He stared out through one of the diamond-shaped panes.

From three stories up there was a sweeping view of red- and gray-tiled roofs and narrow cobbled streets. And further down, the steep-walled banks of the Limmat River as it bisected the heart of Zurich. On the far side of the dull green swiftly moving water lay the Banhofstrasse, where Liesel had recently purchased the cream-colored dress and jacket she now wore. And on the far horizon, the white peaks of the Alps.

He took a deep breath, as if inhaling the history embodied in the room. The sixteenth century light oak paneling. Beeswax-and-resin polish on the dark pine floor. The musty smell of leather from the bound folios shelved along the back wall. The burnt smell of charcoal from the green-tiled, fifteenth century German *Kachelofen*—a stove they still used to heat the room on those rare winter days when the Council was called into session.

With hands now crossed behind his back, fingers interlaced, he grumbled, mostly to himself, "If she's that young, we may still have a bit of time."

It was the best Liesel could have hoped for, and she fought to suppress a smile.

Pieter turned from the window, hands gesturing to empha-size the continuing force of his displeasure. "But we can't just hope it will magically turn out for the better. If Clarissa is left unfettered and allowed to develop this girl as her tool, it will be on all of our heads when it goes wrong."

"Of course," Liesel agreed. Knowing that a few months could make all the difference.

"We must discuss this with the full membership at this fall's gathering," Pieter continued, beginning to sound more confident. "And then we will need to have the Council vote on an appropriate action."

"Of course," Liesel said. Knowing she had won the day with the warrior. A small miracle!

Now would come the far more difficult task. There was only one action the Council might be expected to approve, and she feared for the future of this teenage girl, living in the far reaches of the American Northwest. Wondering how she might help to protect someone whose name she didn't even yet know.

CHAPTER ONE

Nina's hopes for finding morel mushrooms were dashed when a gust of spring wind startled her into looking around. Surrounded by old growth forest, her usually reliable sense of direction suddenly went missing.

I'm lost!

The towering pines swayed and a flurry of cones rained down. A large and especially prickly one stung her left shoulder. As she rubbed the tender spot, a raven landed on a nearby branch, stared at her, and gave a loud *Cawwww!*

Nina stared right back into its black eyes. The bird took a challenging hop towards her, and was tensing for another when a bolt of lightning sizzled above the treetops, close enough to leave the tang of ozone in the gloomy air. As thunder pounded the ground, the raven launched into flight and vanished into the trees.

Nina shivered, clutching her arms to her chest as a chill wind bit through her jeans and cotton jersey, wishing she'd brought a jacket. And wishing even more that she'd left a note to tell her foster parents where she'd gone. If she didn't find a way out, the searchers wouldn't even know where to begin looking.

As the wind calmed, Nina began turning around, searching for clues. And then she heard a most peculiar sound.

Pop!

She was thinking it must be a snapped limb, when it came again, this time insistent, and ominous.

Pop! With a bit of a *crunch* at the end.

Could it be a bear?

Her heart beat faster.

And then she realized this wasn't an animal sound. It was too crisp. More like the sound a tool might make. Her curiosity took over, and her heartbeat eased.

Gripping the handle of her red mushroom bucket, fingers damp, she crept through the trees, careful not to step on any dry sticks that might crack and betray her presence.

Ahead she saw a place where the light shone brighter. Within the great pines lay a tiny glade. What she glimpsed amongst the slivers of light shafting down through the hazy air sent tingles along her spine.

Sitting on a log was a very prim and proper lady who looked to be in her forties. She wore an old-fashioned dress of blue and white checked gingham that fell to the tops of her leather boots. Neatly tucked on her head was a gray felt hat with a narrow silver band.

Beside her on the log, within easy reach, sat two plump gray squirrels, upright on their haunches, alert in attendance. In her right hand the lady held a rock the size of a goose egg. In her left she held a walnut, which she now laid on the log and held firmly between her index finger and thumb. She brought the rock down solidly on the nut.

Pop!

The squirrels glanced at each other before one of them took a short hop to the cracked nut, which the lady released. The squirrel gathered up the shattered pieces in its mouth, returned to its companion, and politely shared half. Tiny claws began to dig nutmeat from crevices, nibbled as if this were a party and the squirrels its honored guests.

Nina was wondering whether to stay or flee when the lady's head tilted just a little to the left. "Ah!" she said, as if speaking to the squirrels. "I believe we have a guest." She smiled and looked directly at the tree behind which Nina hid.

"Please do join us, won't you dear?"

Nina considered running away.

But where would I run to?

She swallowed hard, and then began to edge along the massive reddish-brown trunk. For a few seconds her right hand clutched at a slab of bark. She finally let go and stepped from behind the tree, carrying the red plastic bucket with barely a handful of morels shifting nervously in its bottom.

"Welcome to our little gathering," the lady said, laying the rock down amongst the shell fragments. "Are you hungry?"

It seemed like a strange question, given the circumstances, and Nina wanted to say, "No." She just wanted to ask if the lady knew the way out of the forest. But she'd only eaten a single bowl of cereal for breakfast, and that now seemed as long ago as yesterday.

"I guess I'm a little hungry," she confessed, still nervous, glancing again at the squirrels.

Nina had expected them to run away when they saw her. But they now sat, passively watching, attentive to each word. It was a curious thing. So much so, that her concerns about talking to a stranger began to fade. There was a great puzzle here, and Nina loved puzzles.

The lady reached behind the log and lifted a wicker picnic basket and set it down at her feet. She raised the flap and pulled out a sandwich wrapped in waxed paper.

"I hope you like wild strawberry jam and peanut butter." The corners of her mouth lifted in a careful smile.

"Yes, thank you," Nina replied, as her stomach grumbled loudly, and then grumbled once more. She'd never had jam made from wild strawberries. She stepped forward and took the sandwich the lady held out, unfolded the waxed paper to find whole wheat bread cut on the diagonal. Thinking it might be the lady's only lunch, she said, "Would you like half?"

"No, but thank you for asking." The lady reached into the basket and lifted out a second sandwich. "I much prefer pickle sandwiches. And today I have my absolute favorite: sliced cornichons with watercress plus a touch of mayonnaise and a spoon's worth of Dijon mustard." She peeled the waxed paper from her sandwich, and looked up.

"I imagine you might prefer a glass of milk with a peanut butter and jam sandwich, but I have no milk. Would you like a cup of tea?"

Nina said, "Yes, please." Swept up in the magic of a most remarkable moment and no longer the least bit afraid.

The lady lifted a green thermos from the basket and set it on the log. The squirrels were still perched nearby, looking back and forth between the lady and Nina. The lady briefly shifted her attention to them and said, "I think it's time for you to go so this girl will have a place to sit."

The squirrels glanced at each other, and then turned and scampered down the log and launched off the end and bounded to the edge of the clearing, where they climbed the trunk of a huge pine. At the first large branch they paused for a quick glance back. And then, with a twitch of their tails, they rounded the trunk and were gone.

The lady brushed away bits of walnut shell from the log and reached into the basket and lifted two teacups with purple violets on white porcelain. She set these on the weathered bark and poured a light green tea from the thermos. "I hope you like mint," she said, as she replaced the cap and set the thermos on the ground. She patted the log on the other side of the teacups. "Why don't you sit here?"

Nina sat, too amazed by what had happened with the squirrels to think of much else for a moment.

The lady handed her one of the cups, and lifted the other to her lips and took a sip. She took a bite of the cornichon sandwich and chewed and swallowed and then took another sip of tea. She looked at Nina and said, "Please tell me what brings a girl like you so deep into the forest."

There seemed no harm in telling. She was, after all, lost. And her best hope for directions out of the forest was sitting beside her.

"I came to find mushrooms."

"Are you looking for any particular kind of mushrooms? Or just mushrooms in general?"

"Morel mushrooms. The ones with caps that look like honeycombs."

"Ah, yes." The lady's face held approval. "Those are one of my favorites. I prefer them sautéed in butter with tarragon and freshly ground pepper."

The sky rumbled, and the earlier urgency Nina had felt about the possibility of a downpour now returned. Even after she got back to the ski lodge and her bike, it was at least twenty minutes of pedaling to reach Portage and the safety of the house.

"Do you know the direction to the ski hill?" she blurted out, immediately embarrassed by her abruptness.

"Of course!" The lady laughed, as if this had been understood.

"I'm worried I won't get back home before it rains."

"I don't think you have to worry," the lady said. "It's still a while before the storm arrives. But just to be sure, I'll check." She lifted her left hand and touched the tips of her middle and index fingers to her tongue, and then raised her arm straight up with her fingers in a "V." She held it for three or four seconds, and then down came her arm. "We have a bit of time left before it rains," she confirmed. She reached for her teacup and calmly took another sip.

Nina just stared. How could anyone tell when rain would come by holding two fingers up in the air? "Are you sure?" she asked.

"Of course, dear. It's easy to tell once you know how. Perhaps someday I will have the chance teach you how to do it." Another smile, and the lady put her teacup on the log, and in a very practical voice said, "We have not yet formally introduced ourselves. My name is Clarissa. What is yours?"

"Nina."

"Just 'Nina'?"

"Nina Beatrix Haas," she confessed, followed quickly by, "But I don't use Beatrix. Most kids think it's a weird name."

"I disagree," Clarissa said. "Beatrix is a wonderful name." She took a bite of pickle sandwich and chewed thoughtfully.

Nina took a couple gulps of tea, and said, "What is your full name?"

Clarissa swallowed, then chuckled, as if the idea of her having a full name was funny.

"I've had different names at different times. But those which have been most important in my lifetime would include, Clarissa Julia Antonia Alexandria Cumberland."

Nina had ever met anyone with five names, and it made her wonder how someone got that many. "Did your parents give you all of those?"

"No," Clarissa said, and for a moment the smile was gone and her eyes were distant. "My father named me 'Clarissa' and I acquired the other names as I needed them." The generous smile returned.

"Should I call you Mrs. Cumberland?"

"That is far too formal. 'Clarissa' will be just fine." Then she added, "I would like to call you 'Nina Bea.' Is that alright?"

Nina liked the ring of it. No one had ever called her *Nina Bea*. "Okay," she agreed.

"Good. If in the future I get in touch with you, you'll know it's me if 'Nina Bea' is on the return address of the letter."

"Or on the Internet?"

"I don't use the Internet," Clarissa said flatly, as if the Internet was upsetting. She offered no further explanation, taking another bite of sandwich and looking off into the forest.

Nina was about to ask why Clarissa disliked the Internet, but a strong roll of thunder came pounding through the forest. It was definitely time to start for home.

"Yes," Clarissa said, as if she had read Nina's mind. "It's time to get you to your bicycle."

It occurred to Nina that she hadn't told Clarissa she had come on a bicycle. Clarissa was already busy gathering up the teacups and sandwich wrappings and pushing everything back inside the picnic basket. A little bit of the fear Nina had first felt now returned.

Before lifting the basket, Clarissa took two steps away from the log and closed her eyes and began to pivot clockwise. When she stopped she was facing almost the same direction from which Nina had first entered the glade. Pointing, she said, "That is the way." And without delay she lifted the basket and marched into the shadows. Nina followed close behind.

As they walked it seemed as if a secret path had opened up. No deadfall branches or snaking roots reached out to trip a foot. No bushes pulled at jean cuffs or scratched at her jersey.

Clarissa spoke without looking back. "Nina Bea, why were you so intent upon searching for morels?"

"I was going to sell them to the health food store."

"And why do you need to sell mushrooms, rather than take them home for your family to eat?"

A warm flood of embarrassment rose in Nina's throat. The words seemed to stick.

"I have foster parents and . . . if I want something special . . . I have to pay for it myself."

"Special like what?"

Nina felt her throat constrict a little more, but felt obliged to answer. Clarissa was, after all, leading her out of the forest.

"Lots of things. I wanted to go snow skiing last year, but I didn't make enough money to buy skis and boots. But I was able to buy a bicycle!" She was proud of that purchase. She had saved two hundred dollars and found a used mountain bike in the *Langston Herald*.

Still, it was an embarrassing confession. Most kids at school didn't struggle with money—or more precisely, the *lack* of money. Many even had their own cell phones. Her foster dad insisted Nina wouldn't be texting or surfing the Internet on a smart phone. She didn't even have her own computer. Dan Torgerson told her she was lucky to have an hour each evening for schoolwork on the computer in his home office.

Clarissa's next question carried a little concern.

"How many jobs do you have?"

"A bunch."

"Like?"

"We have a strawberry patch and I sell the berries. Last winter I scooped snow from walks. A man in a wheelchair pays me to pick up fallen pine cones from his yard."

Nina could have gone on. She'd found ways to make money doing things other kids never wanted to do. Raking leaves. Weeding gardens. Even scraping the wads of chewing gum from beneath the seats at the Ruby Theatre in Langston.

As she thought about how many odd jobs she'd done since coming to live with Dan and Evelyn two years ago, she heard

Clarissa say in a cheery voice, "I believe we've found the edge of the forest."

And sure enough they had. Within seconds they emerged from the tall trees and walked out into an area that had burned off the year before. It was now covered in new grass, burned stumps, and a scattering of seedling pines. Nina spied the distant support poles for the rope tow at Kearney Ridge. She turned to Clarissa and said, "Thank you!"

Clarissa set down the picnic basket. "You are welcome, Nina Bea." She paused, as if thinking something over, before she said, "I want to give you a gift, but you must promise not to tell anyone who gave it to you."

The offer sounded a little creepy.

"Why?" Nina challenged.

"You'll have to trust me as to why. Can you do that?"

Nina considered the unusual request. "I guess so," she said, uncertain how to handle such an offer, prepared to run if the "gift" was something bad.

"Alright," Clarissa said, as if she understood Nina's uncertainty. She reached into the picnic basket and pulled out a stuffed bunny with long floppy ears. Its fur was short and golden brown and its feet were padded in dark leather. The bunny's eyes had enormous black pupils set against sapphire blue around the rims. On its chest was sewn a round badge with five golden waves, five blue waves, and in the middle a red heart and a silver star. The bunny looked old fashioned and handmade. The badge seemed almost like a piece of jewelry.

She held out the rabbit, and said, "Nina Bea, this a very special bunny. It was given to me by my father when I was your age."

Nina sat her bucket down and took the bunny. The fur was silky soft. As she squeezed the bunny she felt a lump in its chest, where a heart might be. No adult had ever given her a gift like this, and it made the bunny seem very special indeed. She looked at Clarissa and said, "Are you sure?"

"Yes," Clarissa said. "It's yours to keep."

Nina studied the bunny. "Does it have a name?"

"Well," Clarissa said carefully. "I had a name for it when I was a child. But I think you should give it a new name." A smile traced her lips. "Do you have any ideas?"

Nina stared into the bunny's blue-rimmed eyes. "Is it a boy or a girl?"

"Most definitely it's a boy."

Nina tried to imagine what he might be called, but the "right" name wouldn't come. She looked back at Clarissa. "Must I name him now?"

"Of course not. You may take as long as you like."

A fierce rumble came tumbling out of the darkening clouds.

"Time for your bicycle," Clarissa said. "Hurry now, or you and the bunny will get soaked."

Nina picked up her bucket. Holding the bunny tight, she said, "Thank you for the present. And thank you for showing me the way out of the forest."

Clarissa smiled. "You are most welcome, Nina Bea, and thank you for your company. It was not unexpected. Now please hurry home before the rain arrives."

Nina started for the ski lodge. After she had taken a few steps, it occurred to her that Clarissa must also need to escape the rain. She stopped and looked back, but Clarissa had disappeared! And that seemed impossible unless . . . but she couldn't think that. Meeting Clarissa today *had* seemed magical. But real magic? Nina was too practical for that. She nearly called out, but lightning again slashed through the clouds and thunder rolled.

Nina turned and began to run.

She found her bicycle exactly where she had left it, leaned up against the wall of the lodge. "I'm sorry," she said to the bunny, as she pushed him into the red bucket. "But I need to go fast and I can't hold you." She grabbed her helmet off the rack above the back fender and strapped the bucket onto the rack.

Twenty minutes later Nina turned up Mellison Street, pedaling hard the last two blocks. In the driveway fat raindrops were starting to splatter onto the asphalt.

As she pushed the kickstand down, she decided it was a bad idea to tell Dan or Evelyn about the bunny. How could she explain talking to a strange woman in the forest? And besides, she had promised Clarissa not to tell. If they saw it, she would have to lie and tell them she had found it. And then they might insist upon turning it over to the police if they believed it was some child's lost toy.

Over in one corner of the garage was a stack of empty boxes Dan used as sample cases for his wine distribution business. Nina found a battered carton at the back and knew it was one he probably wouldn't ever use. So into this box she placed the bunny, making a promise, "I'll come back for you tonight after they have gone to bed." She folded the flaps and crossed the corners so they wouldn't spring back up.

As she pushed open the door leading from the garage into the living room, Evelyn's anxious holler came from the kitchen, "Nina, is that you?"

Nina hollered back, "Yes, Mom." And even as she said the word "Mom" she felt a stab of guilt. She wished she didn't feel that way. But she did, just the same.

Her real parents had died in a car accident in Spokane when she was a baby. Although they remained a mystery to her, she still felt a strong loyalty. It seemed like a betrayal to call some other adult "Mom." But Evelyn insisted that's what she wanted to be called. And Nina suspected she might be the only child Evelyn would ever have calling her "Mom." After two years it nearly felt right.

Nearly.

It was different with Dan. She never called him "Dad." She called him "Dan" and he seemed perfectly fine with that. Nina knew this bothered Evelyn. But it had been silently arrived at between the three of them that this was how things would be. Evelyn got a daughter, of sorts. Dan dodged the bullet of starting a real family. And Nina got a chance at growing up in a more-or-less normal home.

After two years with the Torgersons, Nina figured the chances for an adoption were practically zero. She felt totally okay with that. Adoptions were permanent and forever. And "forever" scared her, although she couldn't explain why. It just did.

The aroma of tuna casserole filled the air. Her shirt and jeans were damp, but instead of immediately changing, she walked straight through the living room and into the kitchen.

Evelyn came over and kissed her on the forehead.

"Where have you been, sweetheart?"

A glance at the smiley-bear-face clock on the wall beside the refrigerator showed it was a quarter past six. For a moment, Nina was asking herself that same question. *Where have I been for eight hours?*

In answer to Evelyn's question, she held up the red bucket.

"I went mushroom hunting, but I only found a few." Nina turned the bucket so Evelyn could see the brown morels in the bottom—three fat ones, and five nubbins—not anywhere near enough to sell to Mr. Beardsley at the health food store.

Evelyn took the bucket and scooped up the mushrooms and laid them in the sink and rinsed them with cold water. "They'll be wonderful in a breakfast omelet," Evelyn said over her shoulder. And then, with a hint of concern, "Where did you find these?"

Nina was tempted to lie. Having turned thirteen last August, she now enjoyed greater freedom to go off exploring, particularly on Sunday mornings while Evelyn was in church and Dan was usually off golfing or shooting at the gun range. But the ski hill was still a place beyond Evelyn's comfort zone. Nina had never felt right about telling a lie, so she chose the truth.

"Up at the ski hill," she confessed. "Where the fire burned last summer."

Evelyn's brow pinched with concern as she stepped to the oven and pulled out a glass baking dish filled with tuna casserole with a crispy breadcrumb crust. As she set it on the metal drainer rack by the sink, she said, "Did you go up there alone?"

"Yes, Mom." Her apologetic-yet-hopeful tone, plus the use of "Mom," had the desired effect. The pinch on Evelyn's brow relaxed a little, but there was still concern in her voice.

"Honey, you know how I feel about you going beyond the Portage area by yourself. You never know what might happen."

"I'm sorry, Mom," Nina said, trying to make "Mom" sound casual, not calculated.

The kindness in Evelyn's eyes confirmed it was working.

"Well, the next time you feel the need to go mushroom hunting, please let me know and I will be happy to drive you."

"Okay." Nina returned a girly grin.

Evelyn's smile broadened. Her eyes now held a bit of mischief, as if there was some surprise she hadn't yet shared.

"Dan's trade show in Yakima went longer than he expected. He called an hour ago to say he was going out to dinner with a corporate buyer from back East, and that he'll be spending the night at a hotel in Yakima." Evelyn's face was aglow with excitement. "We can have a girls' night. I rented a movie and there's a quart of ice cream in the freezer."

Ordinarily, Nina would have been excited by both ice cream and a movie. But her thoughts turned for a moment to the bunny. A bunny that would now have to wait in a crumpled box.

I'll just have to be patient.

She smiled, and said, "Great, Mom. What movie?"

13

"It's a secret," Evelyn said, and then she winked.

This didn't surprise Nina at all. Whenever she had the chance, Evelyn liked to play what Nina called "The Secrets Game." It was as if Evelyn yearned to be a child again. For a woman who was thirty-seven it came off as goofy. Still, it was a part of Evelyn which Nina had learned to accept, and to go along with.

"Can you at least please tell me the ice cream flavor?" And now she was playing the game. Evelyn loved it when Nina shared her drama.

"Rocky Road," Evelyn said. Her left eyebrow lifted and her face grew mock serious. "With hot fudge sauce."

The moment dissolved into laughter for both.

"Why don't you go and change out of those damp clothes, sweetheart. When you get back I'll have dinner all ready."

"Okay, Mom."

As she left the kitchen Nina realized she had called Evelyn "Mom" at least four times, maybe five, in the space of three minutes. It had to be some kind of record. She felt guilty, knowing she had only repeatedly said "Mom" to defuse Evelyn's reaction to her ski hill trip. But it had made Evelyn happy, and that was okay too.

As she pulled on dry jeans and a shirt, Nina briefly studied herself in the mirror. It reflected an athletic girl with a polite nose and brown eyes with long lashes. Ninety-five pounds of tomboy energy, with a few sun freckles on otherwise flawless skin. Straight brown hair cut short.

As she stared into the mirror she wondered what Clarissa had seen in her. A brave girl out for an adventure? Or a child who had foolishly gotten lost!

She now remembered something Clarissa had said as they were parting. *It was not unexpected.* What had she meant? Had Clarissa expected to find her in the forest? Or, had she simply expected a lost girl to be happy to find help?

Nina decided it must be the latter, because the idea of Clarissa waiting for her out there among the trees was too strange. It would mean Clarissa had watched her from the time she parked her bike, anticipated where she would go, and found a convenient log to sit on and wait. And then for entertainment she had attracted two squirrels. That all seemed just plain scary.

Thinking about the squirrels made Nina wonder if maybe there had been some kind of magic. She'd never seen squirrels act like that. Almost as if they were Clarissa's pets. Nina could invent logical reasons for Clarissa being in the forest. But the squirrels were something else.

Once more, Nina puzzled about how much time she must have spent up at the ski hill. Had she really wandered around in the forest for nearly seven hours? She tried to remember, but found it impossible to recall most of the afternoon. It seemed as if a lot of what had happened had been deleted from her memory.

She pushed the thought of lost hours aside. Her stomach felt empty, and she now wanted a big scoop of casserole and a tall glass of milk. And afterwards, ice cream with hot fudge sauce.

Most of all, Nina imagined the time when Evelyn was in bed, and she could go out to the garage and bring the bunny back to her bedroom. Poor bunny, stuck inside a dusty old box.

A bunny with no name.

Later that evening, when she was in bed, lying on her side with one arm draped over the bunny, Nina again wondered why so much of her afternoon was missing from her memory. A memory that was usually perfect. It took her a long time to fall asleep.

As that night's dream began to unfold, Nina was sitting beside the bunny. They were in a grassy field. The bunny was talking, occasionally nibbling a blade of grass. It spoke in a voice similar to Clarissa's, yet softer, and quite innocent.

"Are you okay?" the bunny asked, looking up with wide eyes.

"I don't know," Nina replied.

"What don't you know?"

"The future, I guess. Sometimes it seems impossible that things will ever work out right for me."

The bunny nibbled more grass. Nina wondered if he was through talking, but then his head came up, his eyes seemed even bluer at the edges, and he smiled. "Don't worry. The future will come quickly enough. And for you, Nina Bea, it will be filled with wonder and adventure."

"Promise?"

"Yes," the bunny said. "I promise. With all my heart, I promise."

Just before dawn, and with the bunny now cuddled up in her arms, Nina dreamed she was sitting at the edge of a mountain meadow, looking out across a scattering of colorfully striped tents.

CHAPTER TWO

Charlie Dozen was born a full-blooded Shoshone of Wyoming's Wind River Tribe. His Indian name, given at birth, was Little Twelve Toes, because each of his feet had six perfectly formed toes. The extra toes greatly bothered his father, Charging Buffalo, who asked the tribe's medicine elder, Four Winds, for help so his newborn son could grow up to be a proper warrior. Four Winds met the request with a blade of razor sharp obsidian.

The toes grew back before a second full moon had passed.

Again, there was a cutting.

Once again, the toes returned.

Four Winds climbed the high ridge above the encampment, smoked a pipe of visioning herbs, and studied the ravens as they roosted in the branches of an ancient pine while the sun fell beyond the western mountains. When he returned to camp the following morning, he told Charging Buffalo that the Raven Spirit had said to accept his son as blessed in some different way, which would in time become apparent.

Neither man could have known how truly prophetic this was.

After he grew up, Little Twelve Toes took the white man's sur-name of "Charlie" and the last name of "Dozen." But in his heart, he would always be *Little Twelve Toes.*

On a muggy New Orleans morning, Charlie Dozen was dressed in black leather: biker jacket, slick pants, and high-top boots. A braided ponytail fell behind his pork pie hat. A black string bolo tie, fixed with a cabochon of turquoise set in silver, hung loosely around his neck.

His long legs were comfortably stretched out under a patio table, beneath the white-and-turquoise awning of the Café Du Monde at the edge of Jackson Square. He contented-ly sipped at a mug of French roast coffee, eyeing two beignet doughnuts on a plate, dusted with powdered sugar, crisply hot from the deep fryer.

Beyond the street and the railroad tracks, the muddy Mississippi flowed at a sluggish pace. The clicking and buzzing of insects drifted up from the direction of the brown water.

Tourists wandered around in the damp heat, wearing sou-venir tee shirts, Mardi Gras beads, straw hats; a few posing for cartoon caricatures drawn of themselves at one of the umbrella-shaded handcarts jumbled along the perimeter of the Square.

Charlie was enjoying a fresh start in New Orleans. His last residence had been on a bleak stretch of dusty ranch land in the South Dakota badlands. A place populated by coyotes, scorpions, and bearded men who treasured guns, pickups, and privacy most of all. A place where work for Indians was scarce.

When the time came for a move, Charlie decided it would be to somewhere with no dust storms, better food, and more toler-ant neighbors. He was now perfectly happy to be sitting in the heart of Cajun Country, drinking coffee that didn't taste of dirt, and eating pastry that wouldn't leave a thick film of lard in his mouth.

Charlie's newfound serenity was about to be challenged.

He sensed her approach long before he heard the slap of her sandals on the pavement. It was her *resonance* that he felt—a "presence" that members of the Order shared with each other.

Several seconds later, her smooth voice came from behind his chair.

"Hello, Little Twelve Toes."

Charlie stared for a long moment at the coffee mug he held. "Hello, Clarissa," he finally said, in a careful voice. He set down the mug so it wouldn't reveal his hand was trembling just a little. "It's been a while."

She moved to his right, and he saw she was dressed in a yellow cotton shift, open toed sandals, her hair in a bun beneath a gray felt hat. Looking much like she had the first time they met in Germany so many years ago. And still beautiful in all the ways that mattered.

He waived at a chair on the opposite side of the table and Clarissa settled gracefully. Charlie pointed to his beignets.

"No," she said, with an appreciative smile. "But thanks for the offer. I've already eaten breakfast."

If any of the Café Du Monde's patrons had been watching carefully, they would have seen brief confusion sketch the face of the strongly built Native American in his mid-twenties. They might also have noticed Clarissa acknowledging Charlie's confusion with pursed lips and a slight tilt of her head, an apology of sorts.

Calm begin to settle upon Charlie's heart. "So," he began anew, "to what do I owe the pleasure?"

"I need to ask a favor."

"And that would be?"

"I may be headed for a problem with the Watchers."

Charlie let that last word settle in the warm morning air, trying to imagine what strange set of circumstances might have led

Clarissa to have a problem with anyone or anything. Still . . . if she was going to have a problem, the Watchers were certainly capable of being problematic.

"Why?"

Uncertainty—bordering on fear—troubled her face, which surprised Charlie even more than her unexpected visit. This problem wasn't going to be something simple to fix. He looked past Clarissa, to customers sitting around nearby tables. A few were by now throwing them casual glances, as if they might be local celebrities.

"Do you want to share the particulars here?"

"No," Clarissa said. "May we go for a stroll?"

Charlie looked at his coffee, knowing he couldn't take the stoneware mug. He spread out a napkin to wrap up the warm beignets. "Certainly," he said, reaching into his pocket for a few dollars to slide beneath the mug before pushing back from the table.

They ambled along with her arm now lightly held in the crook of his bent elbow, up a narrow one-way street lined with red brick and painted stucco three-story buildings. Baskets of flowers and ferns hung from wrought iron balconies. From a storefront restaurant came the mouth-watering smells of jambalaya, gumbo, and freshly baked cornbread.

After a few blocks the tourists thinned out and Clarissa began to explain.

"Do you remember the first time I contacted you?"

"Of course."

"How old were you?"

"Forty-five."

"Even at that age, wasn't it was a shock to learn what you were?"

"Certainly."

Charlie knew from early childhood that he would grow up to be a warrior. He'd always assumed his talent in combat was a natural part of his Native American heritage. Later, after he met Clarissa, he discovered those skills sprang from a source far beyond the accident of being born a Shoshone.

"What would that revelation have been like if you were thirteen years old?"

Charlie considered the question. Finally, he said, "I doubt I would have believed it. And if I did, it would have frightened me."

"Precisely," Clarissa said. They paused at an intersection to let an aging white Cadillac with red upholstery and a failing muffler rumble past. She stepped off the curb with Charlie at her side and crossed to the opposite corner, and then stopped and turned to face him.

"What if you had been told you didn't have the potential for just the warrior skills? What if someone told you in your early teenage years that you had the potential for the whole package? What if someone told you that you were going to be—"

"Like you?" Charlie finished her thought.

Clarissa smiled. "Yes," she confirmed, with eyes that were kind and momentarily powerful. "You do have a clear idea of what it means to be like me, don't you?"

"Of course."

It was that knowledge which had eventually driven them apart. Their affair had also set Charlie on a course of avoiding other members of the Order. Yet his loyalty would never flag, because of what she had meant to him during the few months they had lived with each other and traveled across Europe.

Clarissa continued quickly, as if time now mattered very much.

"Thirteen years ago, I found a woman who held the promise of attaining my level. She and her husband had a baby daughter. This couple died in a car accident soon afterwards, but luckily the baby wasn't in the car.

"I've checked up on the girl from time to time, but always from a distance, never making direct contact. As I watched, I saw hints of the same kind of power her mother had begin to emerge."

Clarissa paused as a group of middle-aged tourists crowded down the sidewalk, led by a guide who was explaining how the city was rebuilt after Hurricane Katrina. Clarissa waited until they passed.

"I finally decided to meet the girl and learn firsthand what her true potential was. That meeting took place yesterday." Remembering the meeting in the woods brought a shiver. Afterwards, she'd flown by private jet through the night to meet with Charlie.

"She's incredible, Charlie. Simply incredible. She has all of the potential her mother had—perhaps more. And, of course, she still has no idea of what she is—or what she might become."

"So what's the problem?"

"I believe my contact will remain unknown to the Order. But if the Watchers do somehow connect me to her, they will step in and she will be taken away."

"Have they been nosing around?"

"I don't think so. But I can't be certain." Clarissa was tempted to explain why the Watchers might be interested in keeping tabs on her. But that would necessitate disclosing facts she still wanted to keep secret. At least until she had a better sense for how everything might unfold.

He was watching her, wanting more of an explanation, and when she didn't choose to elaborate, he asked, "So what do you need me for?"

"This girl—I call her 'Nina Bea'—needs a warrior to force the Watchers to step back and leave her alone if they show up."

"Does she live near New Orleans?"

Clarissa chuckled politely. "Oh, Charlie. I wish it were so. But I'm afraid not. She lives in a little town out in the middle of nowhere."

"Please tell me it's not in the Dakotas!"

"No," Clarissa laughed, this time more freely. "She's in Washington State, east of the Cascade Mountains, in a town called Portage. It's on a lovely lake, in evergreen country not unlike where you were born on the Wind River."

Charlie looked up the sidewalk to a restaurant with a chalked reader board advertising the daily special of crawfish gumbo. He sighed. "I don't suppose they have any fabulous restaurants in this little town of Portage?"

Clarissa smiled an apology.

Next on the list was money. South Dakota had been tough near the end, and he'd left with little more than his clothes. In New Orleans, he'd spent his few remaining dollars renting a small room above the bar where he presently worked as a bouncer. It was embarrassing to admit poverty to someone who lived on the opposite end of the financial spectrum. But there was really no choice.

"I'm not presently in a position to pay for the trip out west," Charlie confessed.

"I'm sorry," Clarissa said. "If I'd known that, I would have brought more cash with me." She reached into a pocket of her dress and withdrew a gold coin. "I always keep one of these on hand in case of an emergency," she said. "I think this qualifies as one. Selling it should cover your expenses for a while." She handed Charlie the coin. "Let me know when you need more."

He studied the shiny disc in the palm of his hand. The bust of the Roman emperor was crisp. Around the edge were the Latin words: MAXIMIANVS AVGVSTVS. Charlie turned the coin over. On the reverse side, the words: CONSVL III P P PROCOS surrounded the embossed image of an emperor seated on a curule chair.

Charlie looked up. "Is it real?"

"Oh yes."

"And valuable?"

She smiled. "Please find a reputable dealer if you want a reasonable price."

"Which would be?"

"Maybe fifteen."

"Thousand?"

"Yes. It's literally in mint condition."

Charlie slipped the coin into a pocket of his jacket.

"When should I leave?"

Her face grew serious, the smile now gone. "Sooner would be better, but it'll probably take you a day or two to sell the coin. There's a bed and breakfast in Portage called the Bosecker Inn. Get a room when you arrive, and I'll come and find you."

CHAPTER THREE

Nina waited for the school bus on Monday morning, struggling to remember the details of last night's dream. She usually remembered dreams, or at least bits and pieces. But not this time.

She was also still missing big chunks of what had happened yesterday after she left the house. What she did remember, like pedaling up the dirt road to the ski hill, meeting Clarissa, and seeing those amazing squirrels, wasn't nearly enough to fill up eight hours. The gaps were puzzling, even a little scary. For a moment she wondered if she might have some kind of brain disease, maybe a tumor.

Sitting in the shade of the big oak near the highway, while the other kids crowded the sidewalk where the bus would stop, she shifted her focus to what had happened at the house last night—relieved to find she had no problem remembering those events.

Evelyn's mystery movie turned out to be *Maleficent*. They popped corn, and enjoyed bowls of ice cream.

When they finally said goodnight, Nina waited until Evelyn's bedroom light went out. A few minutes later she crept into the hallway, pausing at her foster parents' bedroom door. Upon hearing Evelyn's gentle snoring, she walked down the hallway to the garage, eased the door open, and was finally able to retrieve the bunny.

She retreated to her bedroom and snuggled beneath the covers with her arms wrapped around the soft fur, falling asleep completely happy for what seemed like the first time in a very long while.

After waking up in the morning, she looked for a place to hide it. Her room had a closet, and at the back on the right side was some narrow shelving. The shelves were all but invisible behind shirts and pants and two dresses that hung from a chrome bar. She nestled the bunny beside her winter boots and pushed the clothes back into place.

Now, as she waited for the bus, Nina found herself wanting to tell her best friend, Chantha Miller, about yesterday's strange events. Chantha lived across the lake in Dartmouth Village, and boarded the bus twenty minutes ahead of Nina.

Frank and Anna Miller had been unable to have their own child, so they used an agency that arranged adoptions from Cambodia to find their adorable baby girl. Friendship came easily between two girls who had an orphan past. Because of this bond, there was absolutely nothing Nina hadn't shared with Chantha.

Until now.

One of the things Nina did clearly remember from yesterday was her promise to Clarissa not to tell anyone *who* the bunny came from. It felt like a promise she must keep. So if she was going to tell Chantha anything about the bunny, she had to figure out something short of the full truth. But how could she possibly lie?

When the yellow bus came barreling down the East Lake Road, she shouldered her backpack and lined up behind the other kids. She now reluctantly decided she wouldn't tell Chantha anything at all.

As she climbed aboard she saw Chantha four seats back. As always, Chantha had saved her a seat. As the bus driver, Mrs. Kennedy—smelling of musky perfume and cigarette smoke—pulled the lever to shut the door, Nina pushed her backpack beneath the seat and sat down beside Chantha. The bus rumbled away from the curb.

As Nina settled in, Chantha started to look at her in a strange way. Nina returned a puzzled look, feeling her ears beginning to grow warm. Chantha cleared her throat, as if prompting. Nina stared down at her lap.

"So?" Chantha finally challenged.

Nina looked up, confused.

"So . . . what?"

"You're different," Chantha said. And there wasn't any wiggling around.

"How?" Nina's ears were now burning.

The bus slowed for its last pick-up, brakes wheezing. The door swished open and a draft of diesel and musky perfume floated through the cabin. Three more kids climbed in.

Chantha studied Nina's eyes. "I don't know, exactly," Chantha said. "You just seem . . . mysterious." A nervous uncertainty entered her voice. "You look like you got two years older over the weekend. Are you okay?"

Nina thought she understood what had Chantha worried. She knew about Dan's unpredictable temper from what Nina had told her. Dan was capable of spectacular meltdowns, and it didn't take much to tip him off. When he came apart, the fallout was usually directed at the nearest soft target. And that often ended up being Nina.

"I'm fine," she said. "It's still okay at home."

Chantha gave a big sigh of relief. Then she came back with the same question.

"So why do you look so different?"

"Well," Nina began slowly, knowing she had to tell Chantha *something*. "I went mushroom picking up near the ski hill . . . and I found a stuffed bunny."

Chantha gave her a funny look. "That's all?"

"It's a very special bunny," Nina defended, wishing she hadn't made that promise to Clarissa. Wishing she could tell Chantha about the meeting in the forest, and especially about the squirrels.

"I guess it must be if it makes you look so different. When do I get to see it?"

Maybe she couldn't tell Chantha *who* had given her the bunny. But Clarissa hadn't told her not to *show* it to anyone, had she?

"Can you do a sleepover this weekend?"

Chantha thought for a moment. Saturday was the annual blossom festival. Everyone would be in Langston for the carnival and the parade. After the festivities, her parents would probably okay a sleepover. They liked Nina. "She's a great little girl," Frank Miller had proclaimed to his daughter, after first meeting Nina. Chantha hadn't corrected her dad about the "little" part. Nina was four inches taller than her, and the gap just kept getting bigger. Her height wasn't something Nina made a big deal of. And in turn, Chantha never talked about her parents having more money. The two girls simply supported each other. That was what "best friends" meant.

"I'm sure my folks will say okay," Chantha said. "How about yours?"

"Evelyn's in charge and I'm sure she'll say yes."

When the bus pulled up in front of the brick school building, another seventh grader was waiting for them.

Selena Hernandez was nearly as tall as Nina, with wavy brown hair that fell to her shoulders.

As they stepped down onto the sidewalk, Selena said, "Work it, girls!" She did a quick twist of her hips, broke into a big grin, and turned to lead the way to the main entry doors.

Chantha glanced at Nina and silently mouthed two quick words, "Sleep over?"

Nina gave a slight shake of her head. You simply couldn't tell Selena something in confidence and expect it to remain a secret. Selena would share "secrets" with anyone she wanted to impress. And Selena was set upon impressing the world.

Chantha's curiosity grew stronger. Why was secrecy about a lost-and-found stuffed bunny so important?

Selena glanced back as she hurried towards the doors, oblivious to their silent exchange, and said, "Come on . . . we'll be late for algebra!"

As the girls hurried to Mr. Nott's math lab, Dan Torgerson was pulling into his driveway. During the four-hour drive back from Yakima he had thought about nothing but new job options.

He had worked construction in the Seattle area before he met and married Evelyn. Both had vacationed at Lake Cascade while growing up, and they loved the rural feel of the valley. The opportunities for hunting and fishing especially appealed to Dan. In 2003, they decided to move east of the mountains and buy a house in Portage, where Dan would open his own construction business.

At first, Dan's new business flourished. There was a building boom going on and Cascade County had its fair share of the pie. At the peak of the rush, Dan employed fourteen carpenters, often working overtime to build what seemed like an endless run of new houses.

For three years Dan made terrific money, and he was finally able to afford some of the things he'd always wanted. A bass boat; oak-and-leather furniture; two limited edition shotguns; a high-powered rifle. He and Evelyn began taking vacations to Cabo San Lucas each winter.

And then Evelyn started to talk about having children.

Dan had been raised with two brothers and three sisters and he remembered the sacrifices his parents were forced to make. At thirty-one, he figured there was plenty of time. He listened, patiently, whenever Evelyn brought up the subject. But he always found some way to shift any definite planning into the future.

Then, in 2006, the economic boom stalled. Dan was forced to start firing employees. It was only a couple of the younger guys at first. But after several months the business began to chew up more and more cash and the layoffs multiplied.

So, Dan thought, *I'll just shut it down until the economy recovers.* He had a tidy retirement account, no debt, and forty grand secretly stashed in a Montana bank. And there was a side benefit: the slow-down was a perfect excuse for putting off any serious talk about having kids.

But as one year stretched into two, and then three, the economic recovery was slow to arrive. It became clear that construction might never be as good as it had been—at least not for many years to come.

Dan saw his savings steadily dwindle and was unwilling to wait.

Even though the construction industry in Cascade County was practically dead, more and more people were coming to visit a growing number of boutique wineries. The local chamber of commerce promoted it as "Ag Tourism." On any particular weekend there were now long black limos cruising up and down the county roads, filled with bachelorette parties, girlfriend get-aways, or friends who just wanted to party in style with no risk of a drunken driving ticket. Wine sales were booming, and Dan was certain he could take it to the next level.

But he had overlooked three crucial facts: First, there weren't enough grapes grown in Cascade County to support a profitable flow of prestigious "estate grown" wines beyond the vineyard tasting rooms. Next, the high mark-up for boutique wines made them a harder sell to supermarkets, most of whose customers were content to pay seven or eight bucks for a bottle of Australian or Chilean wine. And finally, wine club members bought up most of the truly premium wines that did make it out of the tasting room.

Dan once again pictured himself slipping towards poverty.

He slammed the pickup door and walked into the house. Evelyn saw his grim face when he entered the living room, his shoulders seemingly bent under the weight of the world.

"Was it that bad?"

Dan all but threw himself onto the couch. "I could have sold two hundred cases if I'd had them to sell." He closed his eyes and rubbed the lids with his palms. Evelyn sat down next to him and stretched an arm around his shoulders.

"I should have gone into beer. With a micro brew you can make enough to meet any demand, and you don't need a bunch of lousy grapes!"

Evelyn was hurting for him. *With him.* He had worked so hard, first with contracting, now with wine. She'd recently seen him begin to lose hope of ever making it big again.

Even more troubling was what this might mean for the foster daughter she was beginning to love very much. A girl who had finally started to call her "Mom" on a regular basis.

Dan finally thought to ask how her weekend had gone.

"It was fine," she said. "Nina and I watched a movie. We had ice cream. She really is a lovely child." Evelyn's voice turned almost desperate. "Dan, she actually called me 'Mom' half a dozen times before dinner."

"Really?" His eyes were now wide with suspicion, and he straightened up on the couch. He had grown tired of Evelyn's complaints about being called "Evelyn" by someone he still privately thought of as "The Experiment."

He now countered her hopefulness with, "Do you think maybe there was some special reason? Like maybe she's angling for us to buy her something?"

Evelyn wanted to say "No." She desperately wanted to believe that Nina was finally coming around, responding to the love she'd shown. But as much as she wanted to think that a special bond had finally formed, Evelyn wondered if he might be right. Something had changed in Nina over the weekend. It was almost as if a different child had come back from mushroom hunting. And as much as she wanted that difference to be Nina's attitude towards her, she feared that it might be something else.

Still . . . Evelyn clung to the hope that Dan was wrong.

CHAPTER FOUR

When Nina's school bus pulled to a stop on Monday afternoon, she was surprised to see Evelyn standing under the big oak. Chantha also saw her, and turned to Nina with sudden concern. "Do you think something's wrong?"

Instead of saying yes, Nina said, "Sometimes she goes for a walk along the beach. She probably came by here and decided to stay and meet me." But that wasn't what she believed. She could count on her fingers the number of times Evelyn had come to meet her at the bus. Those had mostly been when there was heavy rain or snow and Evelyn came to pick her up in the car. After all, it was just a little more than a block from the bus stop to the house.

The girls hugged, and Nina shouldered her backpack. With each step up the aisle she grew more nervous. Mrs. Kennedy already had her hand on the lever to shut the door. A hurry-up grimace confirmed she was behind schedule, and probably overdue for a cigarette.

Nina paused and looked back at Chantha and said loudly, over the chatter of the other kids, "I'll let you know tomorrow about the sleepover."

But when Nina reached Evelyn she knew a sleepover would be a problem.

"Hi, sweetheart!" Evelyn said brightly. But her eyes were red from crying.

"Hi, Mom," Nina said. "Is everything okay?"

Evelyn's shoulders sagged a little, even upon hearing "Mom."

"Dan had a difficult weekend," Evelyn said.

"Difficult" meant Dan was in a bad mood. It meant she should say as little as possible, finish her chores early, and then either retreat to her room or go outside to play.

The reason for Dan's current troubles would at least not be a topic for family discussion. Evelyn worked hard to shield Nina from being drawn into Dan's dramas.

Not that figuring out what had Dan upset was much of a challenge. Nina knew Dan's current turmoil must have something to do with his wine business. She'd noticed how few sample cases had come through the house since January. The stack of boxes in the garage hadn't grown during that time. And boxes at the back of the stack had begun to collect a thick coat of dust.

As they left the shelter of the oak, Evelyn searched for something safe to talk about.

"How was your day at school?"

Nina gave the answer most kids give when parents ask how school went. "It was okay."

"Did you learn anything new?"

Evelyn was trying to direct the conversation to a safe topic. And Nina did appreciate the effort. Still . . . of course she had learned "new" things at school. That's what school was for: learning new things. But the "new" things were usually basic and boring. The really interesting parts of her day were what she shared with her friends. Nina felt no desire to report on most of that stuff. Still, Evelyn was trying, so Nina attempted to make her day sound interesting.

"In English class we worked on writing sentences using noun adjuncts."

Evelyn looked puzzled, but still tried to sound interested. "What's a noun adjunct?"

"That's where you use a noun to modify another noun."

"Oh." Evelyn remained puzzled.

Nina now recited what her English teacher, Mr. Preston had told the class.

"Like instead of writing 'big' train, you write 'freight' train. The word 'big' is an adjective, but 'freight' is a noun since it describes a person, place or thing. It's also something a train might carry. Since it's more specific, it's a more powerful way to create an image in a reader's mind. So 'freight' becomes a noun adjunct." Nina could have given the names of several authors who were good at using this technique, but she knew Evelyn wasn't really interested. Evelyn had probably learned about noun adjuncts when she was in school, but that was a long time ago.

Evelyn put on a happy face that really meant *please change the subject,* and said, "That sounds interesting."

"Chantha and I also talked about the blossom parade this weekend."

There was finally a look of real interest.

"Are Chantha and Selena going?"

"Yes, and we also talked about meeting up at the carnival grounds afterwards." Nina sounded hopeful. "That is, if I have permission—"

"Of course you do, sweetheart! How were you planning on getting to the parade?"

"I thought I'd just catch the transit bus. Mr. Miller said he'd drive me and Selena home afterwards."

Evelyn looked suddenly eager, and offered, "If you need me to take you just let me know."

"Okay," Nina said. Feeling relieved when Evelyn didn't insist.

When they reached the house, Dan's black pickup was parked in the driveway. The hood was up, and Dan was bent over in front, doing something to the engine. As Evelyn and Nina walked past, he looked up, a wrench in one hand, both hands grimed with grease. "Hi, Nina," he said in a polite voice that didn't invite a conversation.

"Hi, Dan," she replied with equal politeness. Dan looked back to the engine, and Nina and Evelyn walked in through the front door.

Dinner that night turned into a *let's get through this without an argument* ordeal. Evelyn's pan-fried chicken and mashed potatoes with garlic toast garnered a belch or two from Dan, but those were practically his only audible contributions. He did make a couple off-hand comments about the weather, and how the tourists had finally begun arriving in the valley. Nina cleared the table and volunteered to do the dishes with Evelyn.

Dan retreated to the basement den with a bowl of the Rocky Road ice cream left over from what Nina and Evelyn had enjoyed the previous evening. He planted himself in the black leather recliner and turned on the wide-screen television he'd bought for two grand—a price he now resented because it had nowhere near the sharpness of the newer models. Just three years old, and today you could pick up a larger and better set for half the price.

And ain't that the story of my life!

When the dishes were done, Evelyn turned to Nina and said, "Why don't you go and do your homework, sweetheart. I'll take Dan a beer and try to get him into a better mood."

Which suited Nina just fine. After she had taken out the garbage—her last chore of the evening—she went to her room and shut the door.

She read the geology assignment, finished a book report, did her algebra, and finally went to the bathroom and brushed her teeth.

From beside the boots in the closet, she pulled the bunny and sat him on her bed. She undressed and climbed into blue pajamas, pulled back the sheet and blanket, and while holding the bunny she pulled the covers up over her head.

There had been no chance to discuss the subject of a sleepover, and she was now certain she'd have to tell Chantha it wouldn't work for this weekend. She wrapped her arms around the bunny and said, "Why does life have to be so hard?"

Finally, she kissed the bunny's nose, and drifted off to sleep.

CHAPTER FIVE

On Thursday morning Dan made a surprise announcement at breakfast.

"I'm going to take my boat to the Potholes Reservoir this weekend and do some thinking. You girls will just have to live without me for a day or two."

Evelyn's face softened like play dough left in the sun.

To Nina it sounded just fine. She knew her foster parents were arguing about keeping her, and guessed that Evelyn was losing. It was obvious from her increasingly frequent and more powerful mood swings. Now it seemed Dan would go off, catch a few bass, and arrive at some final conclusion without even allowing Evelyn an opportunity for further protest. But at least there wouldn't be open warfare inside the house.

After breakfast Dan went out to his pickup, revved the engine, and churned gravel as he pulled out of the driveway. Off to pick up his aluminum boat, already on a trailer, at the "dry" marina four blocks away.

"I'll walk you to the bus," Evelyn said quietly, struggling to mask the hurt.

Nina wanted things to be okay for Evelyn, but it was an adult matter and beyond her control. The signs were impossible to deny. She wouldn't be staying much longer in the Torgerson household. A reality she had faced before with other foster homes, and would somehow again survive.

Nina gathered up her books, and with Evelyn in tow, stepped out into a beautiful spring morning. The air was crisp. Fine beads of dew slickened the metal handrails on the front steps. In the yard, a robin was busy poking the grass and eying sideways in search of worms. When Nina and Evelyn walked out, it flew up into a neighbor's tree. As soon as they reached the street it flew right back down.

As they walked, Evelyn knew it wasn't a good idea to confess to Nina that she and Dan were fighting. But how could she not tell? How would keeping it a secret be fair?

Nina sensed the tension, and knew if Evelyn started talking it could easily snowball, with Evelyn saying things she couldn't later take back. She decided to make the first move, and at the same time take advantage of an opportunity that she hadn't expected to have.

"Mom," she said carefully. "Chantha and I were talking about maybe doing a sleepover this Saturday after the parade. I didn't want to bring it up, but with Dan out of town, do you think it would be okay if she came over?"

Evelyn felt a weight lift, as if by magic. Instead of what she had almost confessed—that things with Dan weren't going so well and she didn't know what the future might hold—she said, "That would be wonderful, sweetheart!" After a moment she added, "Is Selena coming too?"

Nina almost said "No," but reconsidered, and improvised. "We haven't asked her yet. I didn't know if it was going to be okay, and I didn't want to get her hopes up."

"Well, you know she's always welcome."

Words now poured out of Evelyn with what sounded like admiration, and even a little envy.

"You care so much for other people's feelings, Nina. It makes you special that you *care*. Don't ever forget how important it is to care about how other people feel."

Nina thought Evelyn might hug her right there on the street, or maybe even cry, but the moment passed. They arrived at the oak and Evelyn gave her a light kiss on the forehead and walked back up the street.

The bus arrived five minutes later. Nina climbed the steps and smiled at Mrs. Kennedy, whose left eyebrow lifted skeptically before she eased the door shut.

Nina settled in next to Chantha near the middle of the bus. "We're on for Saturday," she said.

"Great!" Chantha's face was radiant. "What about the parade?"

"For sure."

"Do you need a ride?"

"No, I'll take the bus so your dad won't have to drive all the way around the lake to pick me up."

"He wouldn't mind," Chantha insisted.

"It's okay."

"Then I'll meet you at nine at the main entrance to the fairgrounds."

"I'll tell Selena in second period gym class that she should meet us there," Nina said.

"Is she still out of the sleepover?"

"Yeah," Nina said reluctantly. She was remembering Evelyn's warning not to forget people's feelings. If Selena found out she'd been cut out of a sleepover, Nina wasn't sure she could find a way to make it right.

"Why don't you want her to see the bunny?"

"Because once she knows she'll tell everybody. I want to keep the bunny a secret for a while. I'll tell her later."

"Okay." Chantha looked out the bus window, once again puzzled about why the bunny should be such a big deal. Why did it need to be a secret? It was just a stuffed toy . . . wasn't it?

Nina settled back in her seat, satisfied for the moment. She would only need to share the bunny with Chantha, at least for now.

CHAPTER SIX

Six days after meeting Clarissa in the forest, Nina caught the 8:30am bus from Portage into Langston.

The streets were streaming with people headed for the parade route, carrying folding chairs, blankets, coolers, backpacks, picnic baskets, and clutching the hands of little kids who were determined to test their limits . . . and their parents' patience.

The fairgrounds were in the opposite direction from where everyone was headed. As Nina walked against the tide, she was met with happy "Good mornings!" and excited smiles, plus a few quizzical looks for why she was headed in the wrong direction.

The people gradually thinned out and were gone before she finally reached the edge of a field where the lush grass had recently been mowed.

The Cascade County fairgrounds spread out across a broad bench of land on the northern edge of the city, close to where the East Lake Road entered town. On the far side of the bench stood several corrugated tin sheds that housed animals during the autumn fair. Beyond the sheds was a rodeo arena. Past the arena the rocky ground climbed into brown foothills.

The Fontina Brothers Carnival had taken over the fairgrounds for the blossom festival weekend. Newly erected rides were now scattered across the field: a Ferris wheel, Rock-a-Roll, Spinbuster, Cup-and-Saucer, and a miniature railroad—always popular with the youngest.

Several booths lined the perimeter of the field, where carney gypsters would soon be touting how easy it was to toss rings onto pegs, pitch quarters into Depression glass, throw baseballs to knock down the dummy clowns, and beat the Whack-a-Mole. But for the kids who lined up to, as the barkers put it, "Try your luck for a measly buck!" there was rarely a stuffed animal carried away. The carnival was temporarily shut down for the parade.

From the edge of the field, Nina gazed out across Lake Cascade to where a breeze rippled the steely blue water. Langston's downtown, and its surrounding rural neighborhoods, lay spread out on her left. A few miles up the shoreline, to her right, was the much smaller town of Portage. Beyond Portage the foothills rose to meet the mountains that held the dark forest where she'd met Clarissa. As she wondered where that lady might be today, a colorful banner atop the spire above the Ferris wheel whipped a couple times, snapping sharply, before falling limp.

Nina felt a tingle of awareness, as if someone were watching; but when she looked around, there were only two men hard at work on the far side of the carnival, erecting a tent by pounding stakes into the turf, and then pulling heavy ropes to stretch the brown canvas. Neither seemed interested in the girl who sat at the edge of the grass over a hundred yards away.

She turned her attention to the new dandelions poking up. There were honeybees moving among the yellow blossoms. Again, there was a peculiar tingle. She picked one large bumblebee and wished it to land on a certain dandelion, and sure enough, it did land on that dandelion!

She concentrated on attracting more bees, picturing them landing on the dandelion the first bee had just left. As she tried to imagine a swarm of bees, her eyes closed, and what she saw in her mind's eye was not bees, but the bunny Clarissa had given her. Then the bunny sat up on its back legs and winked!

Nina's eyes flew open. There was no bunny sitting on the grass in front of her. But the image of its winking was vivid. Nina kept her eyes wide open, afraid of what she might see if she closed them again.

In two minutes, Chantha and Selena came walking hand-in-hand up the road, talking, smiling and waving when they saw her.

Nina stood, brushed bits of grass from the bottom of her jeans, and when the two girls reached her she gave each of them a hug.

"What do you want to do after the parade?" Selena asked, as they hurried back into Langston.

Nina said, "I thought we could get something to eat and then come back to the carnival." What she didn't say was that she also hoped she and Chantha could split from Selena early and head back to the house.

"Okay," Selena agreed, perfectly happy.

⇌ ⇋

After the girls left, the men erecting the tent took a break, poured coffee from a thermos, and lit cigarettes. The one whose name was Tony stretched his tanned arms, for a moment admiring the rattlesnake tattoo spiraling around his right bicep. He gazed out across the field to where the girl had been sitting.

"Hey Joe," Tony said. "Look at that." He pointed at what he'd seen.

"Holy crap!" Joe said. "Are those cats?"

"No," Tony said. "I think they're rabbits."

Joe whistled in amazement. "There must be a hundred of 'em!"

"At least," Tony agreed. "Maybe even two hundred."

Dozens of gray rabbits now huddled together at the edge of the grass, and many more were bounding across the ground towards them from every direction. Congregating in the very spot where Nina had sat daydreaming.

"What the heck is that all about?" Joe said.

"I dunno," Tony replied. "But they sure came in a hurry. That girl couldn't have left more 'n five minutes ago."

"You want to go take a look?"

"Nah," Tony said. "We got too much work to do."

The girls found a spot to sit on the lawn near the courthouse steps. They settled in beside a young family with three boys, including a two-year-old who was constantly running and tumbling and hollering, but still shy enough to not stray too far. A few restless teenagers roamed through the crowd.

Within minutes came the rat-a-tat-a-tat of a snare drum. A military honor guard marched into view, soldiers proudly holding an American flag, a Washington State flag, and banners for the Army, Navy, Marines and Air Force.

Following the soldiers was a float covered in apple blossoms and bearing the festival queen and her princesses, wearing poufy black gowns with glittering tiaras and white-with-sequins elbow-length gloves.

Selena was already looking bored by the time the third float had passed. She turned away from the parade for a moment, and spotted a group of teenage boys standing near the vendor carts. "I'll be back in a minute," she said in an excited voice. Before Nina or Chantha could stop her, she was running across the courthouse lawn, dodging people, leaping a cooler, and jumping across blanket corners. She quickly reached the boys, all of them at least two or three years older than herself. In a few minutes she came prancing back through the throng.

Chantha said, "Selena, you shouldn't do that!"

Selena faked innocence. "Do what?" she asked.

Chantha shook her head, knowing Selena was well aware that the boys were too old for her.

Nina agreed. "Chantha's right, Selena. You'll get into trouble flirting like that."

Selena looked hurt. "You both sound like my mom. And besides, I didn't do anything wrong."

"You should know better than to tease those boys," Chantha insisted.

This heated exchange drew looks from nearby spectators. The father of the three boys, sitting on the blanket beside them, give a brief nod in agreement.

Selena lost her joyous smile. "I was only trying to have a little fun," she said, pouting. "They promised I could meet up with them later." Her pout intensified.

Chantha gave Nina a look. *What are we going to do about this?*

Nina imagined the worst. Selena's parents expected her to be with her and Chantha. Otherwise, they would have arranged to pick her up at the carnival. In a moment Nina would later regret, she came up with the only solution she could think of to keep Selena out of trouble.

"We were hoping you could come to a sleepover at my house tonight."

"A sleepover?" Selena looked surprised. "Why didn't you tell me earlier?"

Selena wasn't the only one who was surprised. But Chantha recovered fast. And now, she saved Nina from embarrassment.

"Nina's foster dad only decided this morning to head out of town for the weekend. Until we found out he was going to be gone, there was no chance for doing something at Nina's house. We were going to ask you right after the parade."

Selena's eyes flashed anger upon hearing mention of Dan Torgerson. "No offense, Nina, but your foster dad is a real—"

"Selena!" Chantha interrupted. "Not here!"

"Oops!" Selena said, grinning. "Sorry about that."

After the parade, Chantha called her father and told him they were headed for the fairgrounds. He agreed to meet them at the entrance after they finished with the rides.

With chicken burritos and orange sodas in hand, the girls walked through the thinning crowd. By the time they reached the fairgrounds, the carnival was flooded with kids. They bought tickets and stood in line for the Ferris wheel.

While they were on the wheel, it stopped while their cage was at the very top. They gripped each other as it rocked wildly, screaming almost as much for attention as for fear the cage might break loose and plummet to the ground.

The rocking stopped and they could now spy down on the crush of kids eating carnival food, boarding rides, shouting and laughing. The air was redolent with the smells of bearing grease, fresh-spun cotton candy, deep fried onion rings, and corn dogs.

They next boarded the Rock-O-Plane, which lived up to its name as the bullet-shaped cage flung them around. Nina now regretted how much food she'd eaten. But she survived both this ride, and the Tilt-A-Wheel.

Selena tried to win a jeweled tiara by pitching quarters into a shallow bowl from ten feet away. After eight tries, and watching the quarters spin and dance and leap out to land worthlessly on the black felt, she finally gave up. "How about the ring toss?" she said, eyeing the next booth.

"Nah," Nina replied. "It's just another gyp joint. Do you see anyone walking around with one of those big stuffed animals?"

Selena looked around and none of the kids held even a middling-sized stuffed pet.

The red-haired pitchman in the ring toss booth was eyeing the girls, expecting them to play. He now gave Selena a half-smile full of yellowed teeth. Selena gave him a "yucky" look. "I guess I'll save my money," she said, turning away from the leering carney.

When they reached the main gate, Selena said, "I need to call my parents about the sleepover."

Chantha reached into her back pocket and pulled out her cell phone. She handed it to Selena, and after a minute of talking to her mom, Selena touched the screen to end the call and handed the phone back. "Thanks," Selena said. "I'm supposed to check in when I get to Nina's house. Can I borrow a pair of pajamas from you for tonight, Nina?"

"Of course," Nina said. "Do you either of you want to do anything more here?"

Both Chantha and Selena shook their heads.

"Anything else we need to do in town?"

The answer was "No."

It was nearing 3pm, and Chantha said to Nina, "Is it too early to head for your house?"

"No," Nina said.

Chantha called her father, and Frank Miller arrived fifteen minutes later and loaded the girls into his green Volvo wagon.

As they drove up the East Lake Road, Nina let the other two tell Frank all about the parade and the carnival. She was thinking how best to ensure Selena would keep the bunny a secret. Not that she expected Selena to keep a secret for long. Hopefully, it would at least be a few days.

That still left the problem of explaining how she'd gotten the bunny. The story of "finding it" had begun to seem lame. But coming clean meant confessing to Chantha that she'd lied. Nina wasn't looking forward to owning up to the only lie she'd ever told her very best friend.

But what exactly was the new story? Nina searched for a solution, found nothing good, and decided to let things happen as they happened. Maybe she would even get lucky, and Selena wouldn't think the bunny was all that special.

When Frank pulled up in front of the Torgerson house, Evelyn's car wasn't in the garage, so they went straight downstairs.

After washing up in the bathroom, they pulled out the hide-a-beds from both couches and made them up for sleep later that evening.

Finally, Nina decided it was time. Evelyn still wasn't home and Nina didn't want her to see the bunny.

"I have a surprise," Nina said. "And a confession."

Chantha returned a strange look.

Selena said, "A surprise and a confession?" Her face lit up with excitement.

"Wait here," Nina said.

She sprinted up the stairs and went to her room and pulled the bunny out from the back of the closet. She was momentarily afraid the bunny might wink at her. But he just stared back with wide, sympathetic, lonely eyes. "I wish I could keep you a secret," she said to the bunny. "But I can't. I'm sorry."

When she reached the bottom of the stairs, Chantha and Selena were waiting. The moment Selena saw the bunny she said, "Wow! That's like totally retro. Where did you get it?" Followed by, "I want one."

It was Nina's moment of truth. She said, carefully, "I can't tell you where I got it, because I promised to keep the person who gave it to me a secret."

Chantha had expected her to say "I found it." So when Selena's back was turned for a moment, she gave a fierce look at Nina which demanded an explanation.

Nina returned the briefest *I promise!* look.

Selena was reaching for the bunny and missed the exchange. She wrapped her arms around it in a hug so tight Nina felt like she herself was being squeezed out of breath.

When Selena finally let go, Chantha said, "Let me," reaching expectantly. When she held the bunny, instead of hugging it she studied the strange crest sewn on its chest. "What's this?"

Selena volunteered, "It's probably from the company that made it. They must have these on all of their stuffed animals."

Chantha looked doubtful. "I've never seen something like it before. Have you, Nina?"

Nina shook her head. More than that, Nina didn't think it had come from a company. She had looked for a manufacturer's tag, but found none. The longer she thought about it, the more she believed someone had sewn this bunny by hand and that it was one of a kind.

Selena wasn't ready to give up. "I have to have one of these, Nina. You have to tell me where you got the bunny from. Whoever gave it to you would know where to get another one."

"I can't tell you. Like I already said, I promised to keep it a secret."

"Will you ever be able to tell me?"

"I don't know." Certainly not until she saw Clarissa again and could ask permission. And when might that happen?

Selena said, "Then I'll find the company myself." She turned to Chantha. "Can I use your cell phone to take a picture of the bunny and then email it to myself? I'll get on the Internet and find out where I can buy one."

"No!" Nina shouted.

Both Selena and Chantha were stunned.

"Why not?" Selena pleaded.

"Like I already said, I made a promise to keep the bunny a secret," Nina insisted.

Selena hunched up her shoulders and fell silent.

It might have turned into more than just a very awkward moment, but the girls heard a car pulling into the garage. A door opened and closed, and Evelyn's voice came at the top of the stairwell.

"Nina? Are you and your friends in the den?"

"Yes, Mom," Nina called back. She gave Selena a pleading look.

"Well, okay," Selena said, disappointed. Chantha nodded in agreement. Evelyn's footsteps sounded at the top of the stairs.

Nina grabbed the bunny from Chantha and pushed it under the blankets on the nearest hide-a-bed.

As Evelyn came down the steps, she saw three faces which did not look happy. Mistaking the reason as being her sudden appearance, she quickly said, "I didn't mean to interrupt whatever you girls were doing. What time would you like to have dinner?"

Nina said, "Whenever you want will be fine, Mom."

"Then let's eat at six. And if you want to watch a movie later, we have several DVDs you can pick from. Would you girls mind if I came down and watched a movie with you?" The question hung in the air like thick morning fog. It was Chantha who finally replied.

"Of course we wouldn't mind, Mrs. Torgerson."

Evelyn looked relieved. "Well, then," she said, "I'll get up to the kitchen and start working on sauce for the spaghetti. Does spaghetti and meatballs with garlic bread sound okay to you girls?"

A sound round of "yeses" smoothed the tension even further. Evelyn retreated up the stairs. The girls looked at each other. Finally, Chantha said, "Truce, okay?" And Selena said, "Yeah, truce." Nina agreed with a simple "Sure." Still unhappy that things had gone so sideways.

"What do we do with the bunny?" Chantha asked.

"I don't want to risk taking it back to my room while Evelyn is around. Can we hide it in your knapsack?"

"Sure," Chantha said. She reached under the covers and pulled out the bunny and carried it to her knapsack, pulled out a pair of white pajamas to make space, and tenderly pushed the bunny inside.

Nina said, "Let's go upstairs and help with dinner." The controversy over the bunny seemed settled, at least for the moment.

But as they headed for the stairs, Selena said, "I almost forgot to check in with my mom."

"You can use my cell phone if you want," Chantha said, pulling it from her back pocket. "We'll be in the kitchen." Nina and Chantha headed up the steps.

Selena was about to ring her mom when she felt the temptation of Chantha's knapsack against the wall. She almost decided to do the right thing.

Almost.

Instead, she walked over to the knapsack and pulled the bunny out and used Chantha's phone to take a picture of the badge on its chest. Then she took a selfie holding the bunny, and emailed the photos to herself before calling her mom.

As she shoved the bunny back into Chantha's pack she felt a little guilty. But she was also certain that when she found the company that had made the bunny, and reported the discovery to Nina and Chantha, everything would be just fine.

CHAPTER SEVEN

The sun beat down on the misty bayous as the privately chartered Citation jet lifted off from New Orleans' Lakefront Airport. Only Clarissa and the two pilots were on board for the non-stop flight to California. A curtain shielded her from contact with the crew, who had been instructed to ensure the lady her privacy.

As the jet climbed and turned westward, Clarissa looked down on the Pontchartrain Causeway. Charlie would soon be crossing the miles-long bridge by train, headed first for Chicago, then to Washington State. She felt a stab of guilt for how she was now using him.

She had discovered Charlie in 1891 while attending Buffalo Bill's Wild West Show in Berlin. Despite a promise she'd made to herself many centuries before, to never again become romantically involved, she did just that.

Out of jealousy for his company, she suggested he not contact any other member of the Order. This left Charlie invisible to the Watchers; he simply wasn't on their record books. And that was what now made him so valuable. If they sent someone after Nina, Charlie would be a totally unexpected defender.

The "in love" part of the relationship soon faltered. But neither Charlie nor Clarissa had lost the most important component of love: respect. They made a pact to post coded ads in the New York Times to let the other know where they were currently living. Occasionally they met, although the intervals between those meetings were now measured in years.

Protecting and nurturing Nina would bring them back together, at least for a while.

The Order had traditional rules concerning contact with new members. Anyone who was still young would be monitored until they were mature enough to handle the stress of knowing they would eventually have to leave their parents, their friends, their communities, and begin new lives.

New members most often showed up "on the radar" between the ages of forty and fifty, when someone who should have at least a few gray hairs and wrinkles would appear to still be in their early twenties. The Watchers remained on the alert for the signs: A newspaper publishes an article about how "youthful" someone looks. A doctor submits a paper to a medical journal reporting about someone who appears to have slowed the aging process. There had even been a supermarket tabloid which ran a story about a woman aged fifty, who looked twenty. Fortunately, no one really believed the reporter's claim to have found an immortal. The woman who was the subject of the story was contacted by a Watcher and helped to disappear.

And now there was Nina.

If she had been a regular new member, Clarissa might have simply alerted a Watcher in Zurich, who in turn would have set a timetable for future contact.

But Nina was unique in two ways.

She held the potential to be like Clarissa—someone with all of the skills a member might possess. And this made her the perfect tool for Clarissa to use in gradually bringing the Order to the attention of the "right" people in science and government.

More importantly, she had been born to another member— her mother—and that was a first. The genetics of membership had always been a roll of the dice. It was *the* great frustration for members that their children lived normal lives, had normal medical problems, and died long before their member-parent looked even a year or two older.

But if Nina's children continued to carry the trait, they would also live the long life spans of members. Her descendents would grow in number at an exponential rate. And within decades, the human race would begin to change.

As she gazed out the window at the horizon, now shading into the blackness of space, there was one more thing on her mind. For the first time in her very long life, Clarissa was uncertain how much longer she had to live.

CHAPTER EIGHT

Charlie wasn't fond of trains.

Early in his life the wood burning steam engines, pulling boxy coaches and red cabooses, had transported everyone from Army troops to pioneer families across the Great Plains and over the Rockies. At first, the iron horses were declared off limits to the heathen natives. Years later, when Indians were finally allowed to board, Charlie was forced to sit with the Negros in a special car, where the benches were unpadded, and with no easy way to relieve yourself until the train stopped. He once nearly punched out a porter after being told he could not pee into a can at the end of the segregated coach. He was instead told to step out into the freezing winter slipstream between two cars, straddle the drawbar, and whiz down onto the creosoted ties and crushed rock rushing beneath the train.

By the time jet aircraft came along in the 1960s, travel restrictions for minorities were gradually ending. If you could afford a ticket, you could now move by bus, train or airplane nearly anywhere in the world.

Four decades later, a few angry men flew two airliners into New York skyscrapers. The security response was a move towards the intensive screening of passengers, including things like retinal scans, finger prints, and facial recognition imaging; all of it kept in ultra fast computer memory, and easily available to security workers for confirming someone's identity. For a person like Charlie, that spelled an end to air travel, unless you wanted to risk being questioned about your birth date, your social security number, and where you came from. If someone probed too deeply, your most recent fake identity would fall apart.

Train security was also becoming stricter. But so far it hadn't progressed to where it made Charlie nervous. Bombing a train just didn't have enough appeal for terrorists, because no one had as of yet figured out the equivalent of flying a train into a building. Charlie thought it was only a matter of time.

So instead of catching an easy flight to Seattle, Charlie walked to Union Station in the central business district and boarded the City of New Orleans, bound for Chicago. From the Windy City, he would catch the Empire Builder for passage across the northern states. He would eventually debark at the city of Wenatchee in central Washington. That was as near to Portage as trains got. Charlie figured he could catch a bus for the last few miles of his journey.

He was leaving later than he had hoped. If Clarissa had truly desired him to be out of town within a day or two, she should have found some way to give him cash instead of that miserable Roman coin.

The reputable dealers had shied away. Some didn't believe it was real. Others figured an Indian with a coin of that value must have stolen it. One dealer wanted it but didn't have ready funds on hand, so he offered to take it on consignment. Charlie said he'd get back to the man, left the shop, and hoped the fellow didn't think he'd not returned because the merchandise was hot.

In the end, Charlie managed to negotiate a price of six thousand with a collector who was recommended by the only rare coin dealer in town he hadn't yet met in person.

As he now watched Lake Pontchartrain slide by from his private compartment, he pondered Clarissa's instructions. He was to locate the girl, but not approach her unless she was in trouble. In which case Charlie was to trust his warrior instincts and do what was necessary.

Otherwise, he was to be on the alert for the appearance of a Watcher. If possible, he should prevent the Watcher from making contact with the girl. Exactly how he was to do this was left open. As he considered the many possibilities, he began to like what he was doing less and less. His only real advantage was that he was still unknown to the Order. If he intercepted a Watcher, that advantage would end.

Clarissa had given him a most unusual tool to potentially use in any confrontation.

He reached into the pocket of his leather pants and withdrew the disc of gold. It was a bit larger than a silver dollar and twice as thick. The face was a glazed swirly five-point, golden-yellow star-wheel set against turquoise-blue. Centered in the wheel was a heart the color of blood. And in the center of the heart lay an eight-point silver star.

The Crest of Clarissa.

"Carry this with you, and show it to a Watcher if you come face to face," Clarissa had told him. "It will confirm you as being on my side, and it might give you an edge."

Charlie slid the crest back into his pocket and felt the weight of it, lying warm and smooth against his thigh. Perhaps it would bring luck. And three ounces of gold was always going to be of value. But he seriously doubted it would ever slow down anyone from the Order.

He looked out the window and saw the train had nearly completed its slow crossing of the Pontchartrain. He now imagined how much nicer it would be to be back in the Café du Monde, with a fresh plate of beignets and a steaming cup of French Roast, watching seagulls wing low and fast across the muddy waters of the Mississippi.

CHAPTER NINE

Frank Miller's blue Volvo pulled up in front of the Hernandez home on Sunday afternoon. Selena quickly hugged Chantha goodbye, practically jumped out onto the sidewalk, and sprinted for the front door.

Maria Hernandez was running a vacuum in the living room, expecting her daughter. When she saw the Volvo pull to the curb, she shut off the Hoover. When Selena yanked opened the door, Maria was waiting.

"How was your sleepover?" she asked. Not that she actually needed to know. Maria had spoken with Evelyn by phone for updates on the girls, and the reports were positive. Nevertheless, if you were a mother you still asked. Sometimes important information came because you cared enough to pry, even if they protested. Girls her daughter's age nearly always objected. Maria cared very much about everything her daughter—who seemed to be growing up so quickly—was up to these days. So despite any amount of protest Selena might make, Maria insisted upon details, and expected full and honest answers.

"It went fine," Selena said, waiting for the question she knew would come next. The one her mom always asked her on Sunday afternoons.

With the predictability of a proud mother's expectations for a bright but precocious daughter, Maria asked, "Have you done your homework for school tomorrow?"

"No," Selena conceded. "I was going to do it this evening."

Maria looked at her watch. "It's only four o'clock. You have two hours until dinner, so why don't you make good use of the time and get your studies done." Maria paused, "Or, I could find some chores if you would prefer—"

"I'll do my homework," Selena quickly agreed. "But can I use the computer first?" The desire to begin searching for a bunny like Nina's had grown into an obsession.

"Do you need it for your homework?"

Selena wanted to tell her mother yes; but her homework for tomorrow was all algebra and those problems had to be hand-written. Her mom seemed to be able to read minds when it came to lying, so Selena begrudgingly said, "No."

"Then please do your homework first. After dinner, if you've done all of what you need to do for your classes tomorrow, you can have some time on the computer."

Selena went to her room and threw her jeans jacket into a corner, wishing she had her own computer. She grabbed her math book, a sheet of paper and a pen, and flopped down onto her bed and began to solve the equations her teacher had assigned.

It took a little over an hour to complete the math. With the hope she might still be able to begin her bunny search before dinner, Selena rolled off the bed and walked to the family room, only to discover that her ten-year-old brother was on the computer playing some stupid combat game.

"Benny," she pleaded. "I need to use the computer."

Her brother ignored her.

"Benny!"

On the screen, a sudden burst from a black robot's machine pistol struck a soldier in the chest and it went down. A message in flaming yellow letters read: *YOUR CAPTAIN HAS FALLEN.* Benny finally looked away from the screen.

"Do you see what you've done? You made me lose."

"Benny," Selena pleaded. "I need to use the computer for something important."

"This is important!" Benny screamed back.

"No it's not! It's just a game!"

"Mom!" Benny hollered at the top of his lungs.

Maria heard the argument escalating as she grated cheese onto a pan of enchiladas. She lifted the pan and walked over to the oven and slid it onto the wire rack and closed the oven door. After she'd set the timer, she walked from the kitchen, past the dining area and into the family room, where her two children were now solidly squared off in front of the computer desk. Benny got in the first salvo.

"She's interrupting my game!"

"No shouting," Maria cautioned, before looking to her daughter. "Selena?"

"I just asked if I could use the computer. He's only playing some dumb war game."

Benny looked ready to explode.

"Alright, children," Maria said sternly, with a sharp glance at both. "If there's any more arguing, neither of you will have computer privileges for a week."

From the stunned looks, Maria knew she had made her point. She continued while the shock still held their attentions.

"I told Selena she could use the computer after dinner if she finished her homework. Have you finished your homework?"

"Yes," Selena said proudly, followed by a defiant glare at her brother.

"Good. But I said you could use the computer *after* dinner. So you need to let Benny do whatever he's doing on the computer now."

Benny grinned and was ready to say something mean to his sister, but Maria was having none of that.

"Son, you will not bother your sister this evening when she uses the computer. And that includes watching television." Maria glanced at the wide screen TV that hung on the far wall.

"But Mom! My favorite program is on—"

"If you hadn't yelled at your sister, I would have let you watch TV while she uses the computer. But since the two of you can't seem to behave when you are together, my only alternative is to separate you."

Benny looked ready to launch a protest, but when he saw his mom's face, he thought better of it.

Maria turned to Selena and said, "Come and help me make a salad." She turned for the kitchen, and both kids knew there would be no further debate. Selena followed her mother, throwing a dagger look at Benny, who stuck out his tongue in reply. Maria knew some kind of silent exchange was happening but chose to look straight ahead as she walked out. You could only do so much.

After dinner, Maria enforced the "no TV" ruling. Ernesto was home from work, and Benny made a brief attempt to persuade his dad to intervene. The response he got was, "Your mother was here and saw what happened. I'm not going to argue whether or not it's fair that you don't get to watch TV. Now go to your room and do homework, or whatever." Ernesto had a sudden inspiration. "Better yet, I think you should help your mother with the dishes."

Done deal.

Benny was silent—but steaming—as Maria led him to the kitchen.

Joyous in her triumph, Selena headed for the family room and sank into the swivel chair in front of the computer. She pulled up her email and downloaded the images she had taken with Chantha's cell phone.

Now . . . how do you find out where a bunny is made?

She began with stuffed toy makers, in particular those selling plush pets, and discovered there were actually dozens of companies. After running through what seemed like a bazillion bunny images, and finding nothing that came close to matching Nina's bunny, Selena realized it wasn't going to be as easy as it had seemed.

She shifted her focus to the badge on the bunny's chest. The first words she typed for the search were "blue earth heart star" which yielded mostly environmental and psychic stuff.

Next she tried "heart inside circle with star" and came up with a bunch of mystical and superstitious mumbo jumbo.

When other word combinations brought nothing even remotely close to a match, Selena began to suspect the badge was unique. Maybe it wasn't even a commercial logo?

Time to try something different.

Selena had found several websites offering to design and produce custom stuffed animals. If she couldn't find who had made the bunny, then she would find someone to make one for her.

As she began to revisit those sites, she discovered that creating a plush pet from scratch was not cheap. Design services easily ran into hundreds of dollars. If you wanted to make just one bunny, it would cost a small fortune. Of course, if you ordered a thousand, the price per bunny dropped to easily affordable. But Selena didn't need a thousand bunnies. She just needed one.

As she sat in front of the screen, entirely frustrated, she hit upon one last idea. She had hundreds of friends on Facebook. One of them—a girl from Michigan—was continually posting pictures of unusual stuffed pets. Would she recognize the bunny or the strange badge on its chest?

When she opened the girl's home page, she pasted the photo of herself holding the bunny, then the separate image of the crest, and wrote: *I want to find a bunny like this one. Do you know where it might have been made? Or where the badge on its chest comes from?* ☺

Satisfied, she logged off. It was nearly ten o'clock.

Selena went to her room, pulled on pajamas, and climbed into bed, all the while hoping her distant friend in Michigan would be able to help her get a bunny of her own.

The response would be far different from the one she hoped for.

CHAPTER TEN

It was Wednesday afternoon when a very puzzled Nina met Chantha in the school hallway at her locker, and asked, "Have you seen Selena?"

They usually saw her when she and Chantha got off the bus in the morning. And then in the school hallways. But Nina hadn't seen her since the weekend sleepover. Selena had somehow even managed to avoid the one class the three girls took together: Mr. Nott's algebra lab.

"I saw her this morning," Chantha said, grabbing her history textbook, and shoving her English workbook onto the top shelf.

"Is she okay?"

"I think so."

"Did you talk to her?"

"No. It was between classes in the hallway. We barely had time to say, 'Hi.' I think she was headed to choir practice and she seemed in a big hurry."

That didn't sound like Selena, a pure chatterbox whenever she had the chance.

"I've got to run," Chantha said, as she slammed her locker shut. "See you on the bus."

"Okay."

Nina's last period was 'independent study' so she headed for the library, hoping to find Selena there. No luck.

She settled into a chair at one of the study carols and opened her biology book, but her thoughts turned to what had become a stressful time at home.

Dan had returned from the Potholes Reservoir late on Sunday afternoon. She expected a pronouncement about her future that evening, but Dan gave no clue as to whether he would agree to keep her in the foster arrangement, or return her to the state for placement elsewhere. As the week progressed, he continued doing things as if nothing had changed. He worked on his pickup. Mowed the lawn. Made the rounds to local winery customers. In the evening he planted himself in front of the television until he was ready for bed. Sometimes Evelyn sat with him, but mostly it was Dan by himself.

If he'd said anything to Evelyn about the future, she hadn't chosen to share it with Nina.

She decided the best plan was to keep out of Dan's way. So her life had settled into an uneasy waiting game. After chores and dinner, she retreated to her room, did her homework, and finally cuddled up with her bunny.

As for the bunny's name, she decided that since the bunny's fur was the color of honey she would temporarily call him "Honey Bunny." She hoped for a better inspiration, but the names that came to mind—Roger, Buddy, Brownie, Lodestar, and many others—all sounded wrong. It didn't seem right to deprive the bunny of his dignity by calling him 'Bunny,' so *Honey Bunny* it would be, at least for now.

In the library, Nina now felt more tired than ambitious. She crossed her arms atop the open biology text and laid her head down with her right cheek pressed against her left forearm. As she drifted off to sleep and her mind uncoiled, a recurrent dream she never quite managed to remember when she was awake came spinning up out of the darkness.

She was walking out from the old forest with Clarissa. Instead of parting near the edge of the burn, Clarissa continued to walk with her until they reached the lodge. When they arrived at the big log building, a car was parked alongside.

"This is how I got here," Clarissa said, when they reached the car. Clarissa opened the driver's side door and pulled the trunk release lever. "I'll make sure you get home, so let's put your bicycle into the trunk. But first, I want to tell you some important things."

Once the bicycle was loaded, Clarissa led Nina to the lodge door and reached for the heavy iron handle, pushing it open. They went inside and Clarissa lit a fire in the open-faced stone fireplace. They talked for hours as the rain fell outside.

As she floated along in her dream, Nina heard Clarissa's words and knew they were important. At some time in the future she would remember them when she was awake, but only when it became necessary. The bunny would be one of the keys to remembering. He would serve as a bridge between her conscious and unconscious worlds. For now, Clarissa's words in the dream were soothing and reassuring. Nina knew everything was going to work out. Clarissa made her that promise.

Later on, when there was a break in the rain, Clarissa drove Nina to the bottom of the ski hill road, right up to where the graded dirt gave way to asphalt. Together they lifted Nina's bicycle from the trunk. Nina swung one leg over the bar and sat on the seat, grabbing the handgrips of the bike.

"Just a moment," Clarissa said. "There is something you may need to remember very soon, if it becomes necessary."

"What?"

"I'm sending someone to help you in case of an emergency."

"An emergency? What kind of emergency?"

"Don't worry. I doubt there will be trouble. But remember, if it becomes necessary, I am sending you a warrior. His name is Charlie."

"Charlie?"

"Yes, Charlie."

"How will I know who he is?"

"If you need him, he will find you and come." Clarissa reached out and placed a hand on Nina's wrist. "Remember . . . Charlie."

"Charlie." It felt good to say the name, and she repeated, "Charlie."

Now, the warm hand on her left wrist was tugging, and—

"Nina! We're going to be late for the bus!"

Nina's eyes fluttered open and for just a moment she was still half-asleep and she murmured, "Charlie?"

Chantha's yell brought her fully awake. "*Nina!*"

And now she saw it was Chantha tugging at her wrist.

"*We're going to miss the bus!*"

Nina looked at the wall clock and it was thirteen past three. The bus left at fifteen past three. Mrs. Kennedy was not one to hang around waiting for some kid who hadn't bothered to show up on time.

Nina slammed her biology text shut, grabbed her knapsack off the floor, and ran with Chantha from the library, down the long hallway, past lockers, dodging kids, blasting through the front doors and sprinting down the sidewalk.

Mrs. Kennedy's bony hand was already reaching for the lever as they pounded up the steps and found seats. They had barely sat down when the engine revved and the bus lurched away from the curb.

"Whew!" Chantha said. "That was a close one."

Nina was panting to catch her breath as she shoved her knapsack under the seat. "Yeah," she agreed, fighting to regain her wind. She took several deep gulps of air. "Thanks for finding me. I guess I fell asleep."

Chantha looked puzzled. "When I woke you up you said something funny."

"What?"

"You called me 'Charlie'."

"What?" Nina didn't remember saying that. "Are you sure?" she asked.

"Of course I'm sure." Chantha squinted her eyes, confirming, "For sure you said 'Charlie'."

Nina shook her head. "Well, if I did, I don't remember it."

Chantha just stared back in disbelief. "Well you said it."

"Okay, calm down," Nina said. "If you say I said it, then I guess I said it." She thought about the name. *Charlie.* She didn't know anyone by that name. But now that Chantha insisted, it did seem just a little bit familiar.

CHAPTER ELEVEN

Clarissa expected the owner of Chun Li Information Systems, LTD to be in San Jose when the cab delivered her to the downtown office building. So when the receptionist in the fourth floor suite said, "I'm sorry. Ms. Li is in China until the nineteenth." Clarissa was dismayed.

The slim young woman, with short spiky hair fringed in red and orange, politely asked, "Would you like me to try and set up a video conference with her in China?"

Clarissa shuddered at the thought of her image and voice going out into a world where entities like the NSA roamed. "No," she insisted. "I prefer a personal meeting."

"I could email her," the receptionist said, hopefully.

Clarissa looked directly at the woman in a special way that commanded attention. The receptionist's animated face now smoothed and relaxed. Clarissa said precisely, carefully, "Make an appointment for me as soon as she returns. Do not under any circumstance send her an email or make a telephone call or in any other way contact her using my name." As an afterthought

Clarissa added, "It will be alright. She expects to see me when she returns."

It took several seconds before the young woman's face began to reanimate. "Yes, ma'am," she said, pulling up the appointment calendar on her computer and typing *Clarissa* in the 8am slot for Monday the 19th of May.

"Thank you," Clarissa said, with a smile. This brought a smile from the receptionist, who was once again the cheerful and helpful face at the front desk.

"Do you need a cab?"

"Yes. Thank you. And can you recommend a good hotel?"

"The Hyatt is nice," the girl said. "Do you want me to call for a reservation?"

"Yes, please."

With a room booked, Clarissa took the elevator back to street level. By the time she reached the double glass doors, a yellow Checker taxi was already pulling up outside. It delivered her a few blocks to the modern nine-story Hyatt Hotel.

After freshening up, Clarissa left the hotel and walked along Park Avenue, where she bought an iced Americano at the Crema Coffee Company, before strolling over to the Plaza De Cesar Chavez. Still feeling the disappointment of Valerie not being in her office, she found a bench beneath a large jacaranda tree in full purple bloom, fronting a shallow pool. Two young boys and a girl were dashing through water jets erupting from the concrete. She sipped her coffee and watched the children, envying their innocence.

Clarissa's thoughts now turned to Charlie. She had expected to reach Portage long before his arrival. It would now be the other way around, with Charlie arriving first. She hoped he was already on the train out of Chicago. *And if he's not yet left?* For a moment she considered taking a cab to the airport and flying back to Washington.

But I need Valerie Chun Li, and this meeting must happen as soon as possible.

She thought about Nina Bea, hidden away in a small mountain town, completely unknown to the Order. *How could they possibly learn of her existence?*

Clarissa settled back on the bench to watch the children play.

CHAPTER TWELVE

A gust of wind swirled the scent of diesel across the Union Station platform. Charlie hugged his arms against the chilly breeze blowing in off Lake Michigan.

The City of New Orleans had arrived in Chicago two hours late, leaving him just three hours before the Empire Builder left for Seattle. It was still enough time to find something good for dinner.

At different times in his life, Charlie had spent time in Chicago. During more recent stays, he'd come to especially like the local specialty of deep-dish pizza. There was a Giordano's nearby, and Charlie set off on foot to find out if it was open.

Pizza had arrived in Chicago around the time of his first visit to the city, in 1882, after he'd fled his ancestral home on the Wind River in Wyoming. Tribal members had begun to notice—and resent—how youthful he looked. Too youthful for it not to be some kind of evil enchantment.

Charlie hadn't come to Chicago looking for pizza. He was chasing the possibility of employment with Buffalo Bill's Wild West and Congress of Rough Riders of the World. Charlie figured the show, which toured eastern America and Europe, would take him far enough away from Shoshone country to let everyone back home forget he existed.

Bill hired him straight away. Charlie gratefully sank into obscurity, just one more Indian brave amongst the dozens of natives in the show. Spectators paid to see the famous stars like Sitting Bull and Annie Oakley. They hardly cared about the regular Indian braves—unless they were being shot at. And even that bit of attention was fleeting.

Charlie was careful not to draw attention to himself. He kept a low profile by downplaying his abilities with weapons and on horseback. As one of the savage horde he was hardly noticed, at least at first.

But as the years wore on, long-time employees began to see what the Shoshone on the Wind River had noticed. Between the travel and the physically demanding performances, several years of hard work should have begun to wear lines into Charlie's face. Deep lines. But he still looked like the fresh-faced, early-twenty-something kid who had signed up in '84.

Charlie's stage name was Comanche Dan. But behind his back they had begun calling him *The Ageless Indian.* He didn't understand his seemingly perpetual youth, but he knew what it meant. It was time to disappear again.

He was ready to leave Bill's show and return to America at the end of the '93 European tour, when the troupe arrived in Berlin at the end of August. It was here that a woman approached Charlie on the street and offered a reason why a man in his midforties might look so many years younger.

That woman had been Clarissa.

The revelation that he might live for hundreds of years came as a shock. It didn't matter to Charlie that there were a few others who shared what he immediately began to call *The Curse.* Charlie was an Indian. He and his people had already been culled out of "decent society." Now he knew for certain there was no way he could ever return to the Indian way of life. And no matter how much society progressed in accepting Indians, he would also never be able to enter the mainstream of American culture. He felt impossibly alone, when all he truly wanted was to belong. And he didn't want to belong to a tiny band of long-lived freaks.

It took Clarissa days to convince Charlie that he should even want to continue to live. What turned the trick was falling in love. But a romance between near immortals proved to be more of a challenge than Charlie would have imagined. The parting came just months later, in Paris.

"Have faith," Clarissa reassured him, as he boarded the train that would take him to Le Havre, where he would catch a ship for the Atlantic crossing back to America.

"I'll try," he promised. "But only if you come and visit me once in a while."

"I will. I promise."

Charlie returned to the American shore, and settled into a routine that required a move every few years. And he came to cherish those lovely visits from Clarissa, usually in New York or Boston.

Now, as Charlie sat aboard the Empire Builder in a first class cabin, watching the rolling hills of Wisconsin's Dells lake country pass by outside his window, he thought about the girl Clarissa had asked him to protect.

Charlie was forty-five when he first met Clarissa in Berlin. He had been stunned when Clarissa explained just how different he was. It had taken time to accept the reality of his future. But this girl . . . only thirteen years old . . . how could she possibly be expected to handle the news?

The sun was late in the sky. Charlie pulled the window curtains and went out into the hallway, turning left towards the dining car, still thinking about the girl. And wondering what she was doing at that moment.

CHAPTER THIRTEEN

As Charlie settled in for a meal aboard the train, two thousand miles away Nina and Chantha finally caught up with Selena in a school hallway. There was a wild look in her eyes, as if she had been caught doing something bad. To their great surprise, she burst into tears.

Nina hurried to put an arm around Selena's shoulders, thinking something terrible must have happened, maybe a death in her family. The loving arm, meant to comfort, only made Selena cry harder.

Chantha stood looking on, suspecting it was not something that had happened to Selena or her family. There was too much guilt in her tear-stained face.

Kids in the hallway stared, then turned away after a brief shake of the head from Nina or Chantha said the situation was being handled. Fortunately, no teacher came along before Selena's eyes finally began to dry.

"What's wrong?" Nina asked.

"I'm so sorry," was all Selena could gulp out before more tears streaked her cheeks. She coughed. When the tears again ceased, she said, "I was only trying to find out where I could get a bunny like yours."

Nina and Chantha exchanged puzzled looks. "What do you mean?" Nina asked.

The buzzer sounded for the next class period. "There isn't enough time to explain," Selena pleaded. "But I promise I'll tell you at the end of school. Can you meet me outside before the busses leave?"

"Sure," Nina and Chantha said together. With much confusion, they left Selena in the hallway and hurried off; Nina to biology, Chantha to history. Selena stood alone in the hallway looking scared and very miserable.

That afternoon, Nina and Chantha stood on the sidewalk waiting. For a while it seemed Selena might not show, but she finally appeared at the main doors.

Nina had given a lot of thought to what Selena had said in the hallway. And what started as a nibbling concern eventually blossomed into fear. When Selena walked up with a guilty face, Nina crossed her arms, and said, "So what's this about you wanting to find a bunny like mine?"

"I thought it would be easy," Selena began, her face a mask of unhappy. "It's so beautiful, and that badge on its chest is so unusual, it seemed like it shouldn't be hard to find one like it on the Internet."

Nina's stomach did a little somersault, but she said nothing, just clung a little tighter to her two homework books, and waited for Selena to continue.

"At first I looked on websites that sold plush pets to see if I could find a bunny that looked the same. But there weren't any. So I searched for anything that looked like the bunny's badge, but there wasn't anything like that either. I thought I'd never find out where your bunny came from, and then I remembered a friend of mine on Facebook who's always posting photos of plush pets. I thought she might know where the bunny or the badge came from, so I sent her a picture of the bunny and asked her if she had seen either one before."

Nina held up a hand to stop Selena. "You sent her a picture of my bunny?"

"Yes."

"Where did you get a picture of my bunny?"

Selena took a long, deep breath before the confession rushed out. "When we were there for the sleepover, I used Chantha's cell phone and took a picture of the bunny and then I emailed it to myself."

"Selena!" Chantha practically shouted. "I didn't give you permission to do that!"

"I know," Selena said, tears threatening to come again. "I'm sorry. It was wrong. Only, I thought it wouldn't do any harm."

Nina knew there was more. Was a photo of her bunny now circulating out there on the Internet? How many people had seen it? Even though Clarissa hadn't specifically told her not to take a photo of the bunny, or not to put a photo of it on the Internet, she remembered her saying that she herself never used the Internet. If Clarissa discovered the bunny's photo was floating around in cyberspace, might she possibly ask for it back? Or be angry?

"So what *exactly* has happened?" Nina demanded.

Selena looked down at the sidewalk as she spoke. "My friend didn't recognize the bunny or the badge. But she liked the bunny so much she decided to ask some of her friends if they had ever seen a bunny or a badge like it. And some of those friends asked their friends. And . . . I started getting posts on my home page, and emails from girls, all wanting to know about the bunny and where it came from. And a lot of them want one for their own." What Selena didn't reveal was that she'd also gotten lots of requests from girls wanting to be added to her friends list. She liked that. But now wasn't the time to be bragging about new friends.

Nina was furious, but also curious. Furious because Selena had violated her trust. The curiosity came in wanting to know just how strong the interest was for the bunny. Curiosity could wait. She first had to learn how much damage had been done.

"How many emails and Facebook posts have you received?"

Selena slowly said, "As of this morning . . . maybe two thousand."

Chantha cut in, astonished. "Holy crap!"

Selena's head came up and her eyes briefly met Chantha's before they turned back down towards the pavement. "I'm sure it's more by now," she mumbled.

"And you said some of them want a bunny like mine?"

Selena's reply was barely a whisper. "Yes."

The bus pulled up to the curb and students began to climb aboard. Nina said, "I want to see those posts. Can you come to my house right now and log onto your Facebook page so I can see them myself."

"I guess so. But I'll have to call my mom to get an okay."

"Chantha?"

Chantha pulled out her cell phone, shook her head in disapproval, and begrudgingly handed it to Selena. Within a minute she had the okay.

But as the girls went to board the bus, Mrs. Kennedy took one quick look at Selena and said, "She's not on my route."

Nina spoke without hesitation, in a voice that sounded more like a command than a request. "She has her mother's approval. We can call her mom on the phone if you need that."

This seemed, quite remarkably, to convince the tough old lady bus driver, who was always in command and who never let anyone get out of line or do anything funny, to let Selena board the bus. "Okay," Mrs. Kennedy said. And with a smile even! "If her mom says fine, that's good enough for me."

As the girls settled into seats, Chantha turned to Nina and said in a hushed voice, "I don't believe you got old lady Kennedy to take your word like that."

Nina just shrugged. There was something much more important to think about. Over two thousand girls had shown an interest in the bunny.

The ride up the Eastlake Road seemed like forever. Selena's head stayed down most of the way. Nina tried not to stare at her, instead mostly gazing out the window and wondering just what all of those Facebook postings actually said. Chantha remained upset that her cell phone had been misused, frowning whenever she looked in Selena's direction.

When the girls stepped off the bus in Portage they practically ran up the street to the house. Nina found Evelyn in the kitchen.

"Mom, Chantha and Selena came for a visit. Can we please use the computer for a few minutes?"

Evelyn had just finished mixing chopped garlic, onions, and ground beef for a meatloaf. As she washed her hands and wiped them on a towel, she said, "I thought I heard some extra feet come in the door. I don't see any reason why not. Dan won't be home for at least two hours." She smiled as she put the towel back on the rack. "Did you have a good day at school?"

Nina forced herself to be patient, when all she really wanted to do was run out of the kitchen and go to her father's home office and start up the computer. "Yes. It was fine."

"Good," Evelyn said. An understanding look came to her face. "You look like you've got a fire to put out, so why don't you and your girlfriends go use the computer. And if you want, you can ask them if they would like to stay for dinner."

"Thanks, Mom." Nina rocked on the balls of her feet for just a second as she considered giving Evelyn a hug. Realizing it might draw more interest than she wanted, she instead gave Evelyn a big smile before turning away.

They had the computer up and running within two minutes. Selena pulled up Facebook and typed in her user name and password, and when the screen opened there were 354 new posts in just the past hour. The latest, made just twenty-two seconds ago, read: *What a wonderful rabbit!!!!! Please let me know where I can buy one!* Another message was posted as they watched. *Love the rabbit. Let me know if you find out where it came from. And that really is a cool badge on its chest. XOXO!*

"I don't suppose we also need to check your emails, do we?" Chantha said solemnly.

Selena stared at the keyboard. "They're pretty much the same," she said. "Everybody wants one."

"It's a real hit," Chantha said sourly. "Too bad it's not your bunny."

Nina's eyes closed for just a moment, before she said, "I've been calling him the Honey Bunny, but if everyone wants to buy one maybe I should be calling him the Money Bunny."

"What do you mean?" Chantha asked. Both she and Selena looked at Nina, not understanding what she was getting at.

"What I mean is that if so many people want to buy this bunny, and if we could figure out a way to make them . . . I'll bet we could sell a million."

Chantha gave her a look which said teenage girls don't get into the business of selling a million plush pets.

"Well, maybe not a million," Nina conceded. "Maybe just a few thousand."

Chantha and Selena laughed. For them it was now a joke. But not for Nina. Selling stuffed bunnies might be *the* opportunity. She didn't have a clue where to begin, but she could learn. If it didn't work out, then it didn't work out. But what if it did work?

"Selena, may I have access to your Facebook? I want to read more of what kids are saying about the bunny."

"Sure," Selena said, immensely relieved that Nina wasn't by now screaming at her. She readily gave Nina her password, and Nina saved it on the computer.

The girls tromped back out to the kitchen and told Evelyn that Chantha and Selena had decided to catch the public transit bus and they wouldn't be staying for dinner.

"What a shame," Evelyn said. "I was looking forward to you girls being in the house just like last weekend."

"Sorry, Mrs. Torgerson," Chantha said.

"Yeah, I'm sorry, but my mom's expecting me," Selena added.

This seemed to appease Evelyn, who said, "Well, you both know you're welcome here anytime." With a smile, she shooed them out of the kitchen.

The girls walked back down the street to wait for the bus. When it finally pulled up, Nina gave Selena a hug and said, "Don't worry. I forgive you for what you did. Maybe we *will* find you a bunny like mine." And to Chantha, "Give me a call this evening."

After the girls were gone, Nina lay on her back on the grass to think. There was nothing she could do about the bunny's photo being spread across the Internet. And if Clarissa never used the Internet, how likely was she to find out?

Besides . . . if everyone who had seen the photo of the bunny wanted one, and if she could figure out a way to make copies, it wasn't going to be just a few dollars, like for picking up pine cones or selling raspberries or mushrooms. It would be real money. The kind of money where it wouldn't matter if Dan decided to pack her up and ship her off to a new foster home.

But there were things Nina needed to know first. Some of which, Chantha's lawyer father would be able to tell her. When Chantha called back later that evening, she would ask her to ask her dad for a few minutes of his time.

Nina finally began to relax, letting the sun warm her body. She stared up at the sky. And dreamed about a world where she had enough money not to have to ever worry about anything ever again.

CHAPTER FOURTEEN

Angled light poured in through the crystal-cut leaded glass, throwing little rainbows of color across the purple-and-cream Persian rug that lay on the Order's Zurich conference room floor.

Pieter Silberhof was pacing back and forth in front of the windows, manicured hands clasped behind his back, suit coat nervously unbuttoned, gray herringbone slacks neatly creased where they brushed the tops of his brown Gucci wingtips. "He's late," Pieter said, for what seemed like the hundredth time.

Liesel sat at the conference table, in one of the leather armchairs, and held her silence. Just two weeks had passed since their awkward discussion about Clarissa and the girl. And now, information received the previous day had caused this emergency meeting of the Watchers. Their third member, Sandro, lived in Rome. His train through the St. Gotthard Tunnel had been delayed. Pieter's agitation was understandable, but there was nothing that could be done except to wait.

"He should have taken a jet. We have one stationed in Rome. Isn't this the kind of emergency they're supposed to be available for?"

Liesel gazed out the windows at a single small cloud that punctuated an otherwise blue sky. "He couldn't have known the Gotthard would be slow today," she said, calmly. "Usually the Swiss are good about their trains running on time." The corners of her mouth lifted slightly. The Swiss could be arrogant over such things as their trains always being on schedule. That one was now running late was pleasantly amusing for a German who had chosen to drive from Munich to Zurich for this meeting, even thought it had consumed several precious hours in heavy traffic on the autobahn.

"That is no excuse!" Pieter snapped.

He gave up his pacing and sank into a chair on the opposite side of the table, reaching to pick up one of the two photos, the one of a girl holding a stuffed rabbit doll. He stabbed a finger at the circular crest on the doll's chest. "This!" he said in his stern Austrian accent, "This should not be there." He slammed the photo back down on the table.

"Agreed," Liesel said. "But it is. And we will deal with it."

At that moment the door to the room burst open and a winded Sandro Alighieri entered. He tossed his finely woven straw Panama fedora onto the conference table, wiped beads of sweat from his forehead with a shirtsleeve, and hiked up his loose-fit pants before collapsing into the nearest chair.

"*Madonna! It's a long climb up that hill!*"

Pieter stared for a second at the fedora. It was making a fine sweat-ring on the polished oak. He thought for a moment about asking Sandro to remove it, decided it was unimportant, and instead said, "Let's get started."

Sandro picked up the photo that showed a girl holding a bunny with the Crest of Clarissa on its chest. "So this is what has caused the big fuss," he said, studying the image. "Where did our I.T. service pick it up?"

"Facebook," Liesel said. "Apparently this child, whose name is Selena Hernandez, sent out a request to her friends trying to find out where the bunny comes from. She says she wants to buy one. What do you think about that?"

Sandro puzzled over the photo, and then looked up at Liesel. "Do you think she may be of the Order?"

"Doubtful," Pieter cut in, fuming with anger. "But not impossible. It seems more likely it belongs to someone close to her who has come into contact with Clarissa. Otherwise, why would she want to buy one if she already has one? But that's all speculation at this point. For all we know, she could have bought it at a second hand store and now wants another, perhaps to give as a gift." He continued quickly with, "What we need to do is get someone out there as soon as possible to—"

"Figure out if Clarissa is up to something?" Liesel interjected.

"Exactly," Pieter said. "And if necessary . . . damage control. We can't have Clarissa sharing information about the Order with . . . with children!"

"Agreed," Sandro said.

The three Watchers settled back in their chairs, and for a long moment the room was silent.

Pieter and Sandro had always been in agreement that what Clarissa had proposed nearly twenty years ago was not in the best interests of the Order. Liesel was less certain. As the Internet grew in power and influence, she had begun to make inquiries of members to determine if support might exist for pulling Clarissa back in to negotiate some middle ground. Interest had so far fallen short, and Liesel knew she might soon face a choice: split from the Order, as had Clarissa; or continue to work from the inside to find some way to defuse the crisis. So far she had chosen to remain embedded within the Order. But now . . . this.

Liesel finally broke the silence. "I agree we need to send someone. I suggest Sandro." She waited to see if Pieter would protest. Putting a warrior like him on the ground in America wasn't an appealing prospect. Much better it be the charming Sandro.

Pieter's right eyebrow lifted in protest. He gave both Liesel and Sandro long looks, but eventually said, "Agreed."

"Fine," Sandro said. "Do we have an appropriate jet here in Zurich?"

"There's a Gulfstream in our hanger," Pieter said.

"I'll need to pick up a few clothing items. I didn't take time to pack before I left Rome."

Liesel cautioned, "Before you rush off, I think we should agree upon some ground rules."

"Such as," Pieter challenged, frowning.

"No direct contact if it turns out the child is a potential new member. Absolutely no confrontations with Clarissa. And Sandro must fly back for a full Council meeting immediately after he has the facts."

Pieter's frown deepened. "What about the crest? Shouldn't Sandro try to retrieve Clarissa's stuffed rabbit?"

"No," Liesel insisted. "That's the kind of confrontation we need to avoid. After all, the damage is already done. These images," she pointed to the prints on the table, "are already spread around the globe. There's really no point in taking an added risk by trying to gain possession of the toy at this point."

"I don't like it," Pieter said. "But I will accept this approach, for now."

"Anything else?" Sandro asked. Both Pieter and Liesel shook their heads. "Good. I'll hit the Bahnhofstrasse for a couple shirts and a pair of pants, and then head out to the airport. How soon will the Gulfstream be ready?"

Pieter said, "The pilots have already been informed and will have the jet fueled within the hour."

Sandro grabbed his fedora from the table and set it at a slight angle on his head. "*Ciao!*" he said, as he breezed out the door.

Pieter and Liesel sat and stared at each other. It was Pieter who eventually broke the silence.

"You wanted to go, didn't you?"

This came with an accusatory tone Liesel didn't particularly like. But that was Pieter's way. Always to the point, even if it was brutal. You at least knew where he stood.

"I'd be lying if I said 'No'," she confessed, adding a slight shrug of her shoulders.

"Then why didn't you ask?"

"Because I knew you would disagree."

Pieter nodded slowly. Then, "Do you still have some sympathy for what Clarissa wants to do?"

"Possibly."

Pieter's anger immediately surfaced. "We've existed in secret for this long! Why should that change?"

Liesel's face became animated with frustration. "Because the *world* has changed, Pieter. And in particular, the Americans' obsession with collecting information and analyzing everything they get their hands on has become so much more determined."

"You mean the NSA."

"Yes, of course the NSA. And the CIA. The FBI. And if it isn't the Americans, then it will be the Russians. Or the Brits. Or the French. We can't even be sure they don't already know we exist."

"But we can hope."

"Yes, of course. We can hope. But that's gambling, isn't it?"

"I suppose so. But if we come right out and make it known to one and all what we are . . . how would that be a good move?"

"We'd at least have an opportunity for controlling how the information is released."

"But they would still come after us, hoping to find the secret we already know doesn't exist. They would capture our members and have their DNA picked apart, hoping to discover the secret of eternal youth."

"We could assure them we're just a random luck of the draw, and not something that can be replicated."

"But that's not what they would want to believe. They would insist upon trying to find a way to live for centuries."

Liesel had to admit, at least to herself, that Pieter was right. The drive would be strong to find an answer to the question of aging somewhere in members' DNA. And the world's discovery that a handful of people had lived for a very long time, and enjoyed perfect health, would most certainly rip apart the peaceful existence that members of the Order enjoyed.

But Clarissa's plan wasn't a simple tell-all disclosure. She had shared a few details with Liesel thirteen years ago, including her discovery of a woman whom she felt she could groom for the transition. Someone very special. Someone unknown to the Order.

And then came the car accident and the woman's death. After reporting that the woman's baby daughter still lived, Clarissa had slipped out of sight. That is, until the letter she had received several days ago, in which Clarissa asked Liesel to keep an eye out for anything "suspicious." Clarissa hadn't elaborated what that meant. But Liesel realized it had to concern the child, who would just be entering her teen years.

She looked down at the image of the bunny with the Crest of Clarissa on its chest. A quite famous bunny among members of the Order. And for the first time, she began to speculate whether or not a worldwide disclosure on the Internet of this most ancient of personal crests was entirely an accident. And with that suspicion beginning to blossom, she also began to wonder if placing her trust in Clarissa had somehow been a mistake.

CHAPTER FIFTEEN

Sandro's Gulfstream landed at the East Wenatchee airport at nearly the same moment as Charlie's Empire Builder train pulled into the whistle-stop station across the Columbia River in the city of Wenatchee. Separated by miles, neither man had the slightest chance of sensing the other's resonance.

Unaware of the Watcher's arrival, Charlie found an espresso café, ordered a croissant and a latte, and sat down to wait for the next transit bus.

Clarissa had given him some uncomfortable advice.

"When you go out to Washington, I suggest you lose the biker look. Try to blend in a little better."

So Charlie was now casually dressed in blue jeans and a striped gray and teal cotton shirt. The golden crest was safely tucked into the watch pocket. He still wore black leather boots. And cut the ponytail? Get real! There were limits to what a warrior would do.

Three miles away, Sandro was dressed in white-and-tan Italian summer wear, plus his straw fedora. He was pleased to find the cab he had ordered waiting at the curb just beyond the tarmac where the Gulfstream now sat.

By the time the sun flooded the valley with the reluctant warmth of a late spring morning, Sandro was headed north on Highway 97, along the eastern bank of the Columbia River.

Sandro's skill set was *charm*. The combination of a smile, kind words, a pleasant look, and a warm and enveloping *presence*, resulted in someone you just naturally wanted to please. Simply put, this man—who had been born eighty-one years before Columbus discovered America—could talk you into taking off your shoes and walking on broken glass.

His plan was simple. With a name like Selena Hernandez, he assumed her family was Hispanic. They were likely to be Catholics. If he could manage to meet alone with the local priest, finding Selena should become simple. He would turn on his charm, and the priest would tell him whatever he needed to know.

He watched out the cab window as fields of sagebrush slid past, wondering about the girl—this *Selena*. Was she of the Order? If she was, and if Clarissa continued to control her, then she would remain unschooled in the Order's etiquette of secrecy. They couldn't risk such a person on the loose. She would need to be kidnapped, flown out of the US, and relocated to the enclave far up in the Alps.

Sandro had never met a young person who was a member, and he now wondered what her resonance might feel like. *It's probably weak. She's not much more than a child.*

He stared out the cab's window, watching a flight of Canadian geese gliding above the surface of the river in a "V" formation. They began to splash down in a smoothly coordinated landing.

Back in Wenatchee, Charlie left the cafe, crossed the street, and boarded the bus for Langston.

CHAPTER SIXTEEN

When Valerie Chun Li pushed through the double glass doors of her San Jose office on Monday morning, she was pleasantly surprised to see the remarkable woman she had met a year ago. There sat Clarissa Cumberland, wearing a light blue dress and a gray felt hat with a silver ribbon. Despite her surprise, Valerie still felt the same effusive warmth she had experienced during their accidental meeting at the museum. So instead of immediately questioning her receptionist about why no one had informed her of Clarissa's presence, she approached and held out her hands.

"Clarissa! What an unexpected pleasure."

"The pleasure is equally mine," Clarissa said, standing and reaching to hold Valerie's hands in her own, feeling the warmth, the vibrancy of true youth.

Without turning to look at her receptionist, Valerie said, "Tina, do I have anyone else scheduled this hour?"

"No one other than Ms. Cumberland, Ms. Li."

Valerie turned and gave her receptionist a quick look. The spiky haired twenty-two year old, who had always been reliable, seemed oblivious to the lack of warning she'd given the boss. Valerie would need to discuss this with Tina later. But for now, she turned back to Clarissa. "Please," she said, gesturing past the reception desk.

Valerie's corner office looked out through tinted windows across the sprawl of downtown San Jose. A stand-up desk was placed against one wall. There were four comfortable chrome-and-leather chairs arranged around a low red-lacquered, Ming-Dynasty-style table with a glass top.

Valerie gestured towards a chair.

"Thank you," Clarissa said, taking a seat.

"Would you like anything to drink?"

"I'm fine," Clarissa replied, although she felt anything but fine.

She had discovered Valerie by accident while on a walk through the L.A. County Museum of Art's Asian collection. She first felt the resonance of a member of the Order upon entering the museum. As she searched through the galleries, she finally saw a tall and athletic Chinese woman who was studying a painting on loan from Shanghai. She approached, introduced herself as someone who also appreciated that particular painting, and as they shared impressions about the work it became clear that Valerie had no idea of what she was.

Later, as they chatted in the museum's coffee bar, Clarissa realized Valerie's skill set might be of great use to her. She had taken her gift for mathematics and turned its power upon the Internet. Chun Li Data Solutions analyzed information, performed statistical sampling and forecasting, and created cryptographic algorithms to protect data. This left Valerie uniquely positioned to mix things up in the cyber world if Clarissa ever needed to go on the offensive against the Order.

Valerie now sat sipping tea from a delicate porcelain cup with a glazed red dragon on the side.

"So . . . what brings you to San Jose?"

Clarissa had laid her handbag on the table, and she now reached for it and pulled out a disk that fit neatly in her palm. She handed it across the corner of the table. Valerie's eyes grew wide as she took it. "It's heavy. Like it's made of—"

"Gold. Yes, it is solid gold."

Valerie let out a long, soft sigh of appreciation as she studied the glazed side of the disc. A radiant silver star inside a blood red heart inside a yellowish glazed star with bluish-green blades interspaced. Her eyes came up to meet Clarissa's. "It's beautiful," she said. "Do these markings have a special meaning?"

"Blue is for the Earth. Yellow is for the sun. The heart is love. And the silver star is in memory of my father. Together they form my crest."

"It's beautiful," Valerie said, reaching to hand it back to Clarissa.

"No, please. It is yours to keep."

Valerie was stunned. "But it must be valuable." She hefted the disc. "It has to weigh at least three, maybe four ounces. And solid gold . . ."

"Please accept it in payment for the favor I came to ask." Clarissa folded her hands in her lap as if to signal a done deal.

Valerie again studied the disk, turned it over to look at the plain gold back, and then returned to the glazed side. And finally she said, "What do you need?"

"I want to know if, and when, that crest ever shows up on the Internet. Are you able to set up such a search?"

Valerie shrugged. "Sure. I can get somebody working on it right away."

Clarissa cleared her throat, nervously, and said, "I'd truly appreciate it if you could do the work yourself. You see, there are very few people who know this crest exists. I wish to keep it a secret. Would it be possible for you to not share it with anyone?"

Valerie paused, thought of a reason or two why she might disagree, and finally decided it would be an interesting challenge. Creating an algorithm to search for this set of symbols wouldn't take long. And there was no real need to show it to any of her staff, although it was tempting to brag on what was the most unusual form of payment she had ever received. She finally said, "Sure. I can do that for you."

"Thank you," Clarissa said. "I appreciate your help."

Valerie laid the crest on the table, momentarily thrilled by the soft *chink* of gold on glass. "How do I get in touch with you?"

"I'm not a cell phone user and I'm not on the Internet, so finding me might be a chore. I'll get in touch with you from time to time, by regular phone, if that's okay."

"No Internet? No cell phone?" Valerie was surprised. "I couldn't do that."

"I'm old fashioned. I like the peace of not having people bothering me on a constant basis."

Valerie laughed. "That would be a bonus once in a while. You can certainly call me whenever you feel the need." She glanced at her watch. "Speaking of which, I've been gone for two weeks and I have some phone calls I need to answer, and several meetings I need to attend outside the office. I hate to rush you out the door, but would you mind?"

"Of course not." Clarissa stood.

And suddenly, Valerie felt guilty for so abruptly ending what had been a very pleasant few minutes at the start of what was going to be an extremely busy and stressful day. "Please, let's have breakfast tomorrow morning," she said. "There's a restaurant at the Hyatt. Would seven work for you?"

Clarissa hadn't intended to do anything other than head out to the airport. She was tempted to decline the invitation. But would one more day really make such a difference? She would need this woman on her team at some point. So after a brief pause, she said, "Of course. Seven it is." After a thoughtful pause, she added, "Please don't be too hard on your receptionist. I insisted she not contact you to let you know I would be here this morning. I also told her a small lie, that we were good friends. So it's not really her fault for me being a surprise when you walked in."

Valerie appeared to accept the explanation, and said, "As far as I'm concerned we *are* good friends." But she would still have that chat with Tina. No sense in letting sloppy procedures become entrenched.

She saw Clarissa to the reception desk and then returned to her office. At the standup desk she laid out a single sheet of paper, picked up a pencil, and began writing a string of numbers and commands, more comfortable with the mathematical expressions than she was with writing in English. Within minutes she had completed the algorithm. She went over to her computer and translated it into binary code. A few minutes later the office's powerful main server was out on the web searching for something that looked like the Crest of Clarissa.

It didn't take long for results to start pouring in. By then, Valerie was out of the building with meetings for the rest of the workday. It wouldn't be until near dark that she returned to her office for a surprise.

CHAPTER SEVENTEEN

Chantha's father agreed to meet with Nina, and suggested it take place at his law office on Saturday. Then he strongly hinted that any further assistance might be conditioned upon involving her foster parents.

For a chance to explain, Nina didn't immediately protest about involving Dan or Evelyn in future meetings.

Still . . .

When Frank Miller let her in the front door and led her back to his office, Nina was prepared.

As Frank settled into his chair and looked across his desk, he saw a focus and determination more expected from a seasoned business client. The chair suddenly felt a little less secure than it usually did.

"So please tell me Nina, what's on your mind?"

Nina had thought a great deal about this moment, and launched without hesitation into the straight-up truth about her foster parents.

"I'm just an accommodation in the Torgerson home," she said bluntly. "I've come across something that could make a real difference in my life, and I need adult help to make it happen. But neither Dan nor Evelyn are capable of giving me that help."

Frank leaned forward, not having expected such a tough-as-nails assessment from someone so young. "An accommodation?"

Nina got looks like this from kids at school, and even from adults, when she used big words. They were thinking, *Stop acting like such a smarty-pants!* But *accommodation* was the correct word, and Nina wasn't backing down.

"Dan's only concerned about what *he* wants, which is mostly grownup toys like trucks and snowmobiles and hunting rifles. He loves Evelyn, but Evelyn has always wanted a child. Dan doesn't want a child, but in order not to lose Evelyn he finally agreed she could have a foster kid. He figured that when Evelyn saw how much time and money went into raising children, she'd agree with him it wasn't worth it. Except it turned out Evelyn really enjoys having me around. The problem is she's not very mature. It's almost like she gets to escape into being a child herself and I end up being her playmate." Nina paused to see if Frank understood. He nodded for her to continue. She relaxed just a little.

"Dan demands complete attention, and he's starting to resent Evelyn spending so much time with me. So, either their marriage is going to fall apart, or Dan's going to make things so unpleasant that Evelyn will be forced to turn me back over to the state."

Nina waited for Frank's reaction, hoping he wasn't going to freak out; maybe even call the foster placement office and ask for state intervention. To his credit, Frank absorbed the rather amazing statement with a face that was outwardly calm. What he thought of as his *Lawyer's Game Face*. It did, however, take a good long while before he spoke. And when he finally did speak there was more respect in his voice.

"Well . . . you certainly used the word 'accommodation' correctly. That is, if what you say about Dan and Evelyn is true." Frank paused, and seemed to come to some conclusion about where the interview should now go.

"Let's say you are correct, that your foster placement isn't going to work out. Chantha showed me a photo of a stuffed pet—a bunny rabbit—and said you think it's important. How does that come into play?"

Nina explained how Selena had taken photos and posted them on Facebook, and the huge reaction after a viral sharing of the bunny images. Most girls who saw the bunny photo wanted one of their own. Nina wanted to find a way make bunnies and sell them. The money, she said, would give her "options." What those options might be she didn't elaborate. But Frank guessed they had to do with the "accommodation" situation.

"So there's a lot of interest," Frank conceded. "And I'll even admit that if I could find one in a store, I'd buy it for Chantha. It's adorable. But to get copies of the bunny into stores you'll need to form a business, find funding, identify a manufacturer, create a distribution network, and many more things. Even after all of that, there's still one big problem."

"What?"

"Someone created this bunny, including the circular crest on its chest. And the law says whoever did that owns the copyright. Once you create a pattern and fix it in a tangible medium, which means—"

"I know what 'tangible' means," Nina said, "and I assume 'medium' means a physical substance like cloth or fur."

"That's correct," he said, reminding himself to be patient— this was, after all, a thirteen-year-old girl. Even if she had an impressive command of English.

"To market the bunny you still must have a written agreement with the person who made the bunny in the first place. So my next question is . . ."

And Nina was thinking: *Here it comes. The one thing I can't reveal.*

"Where did you get the bunny?"

"I can't tell you that," she said. And there it was. Even to Nina it sounded unreasonable.

Frank shifted uncomfortably in his chair. "Nina, please understand that anything you tell me is protected by the attorney client privilege. If you tell me not to reveal who gave you the bunny, I'm bound not to tell anyone. But for me to help you, I need to know where the bunny came from."

"I promised the person who gave me the bunny that I wouldn't tell anyone who I got it from. So before I can tell you, I'd need her permission first."

"So it was a woman?"

Nina hadn't meant to use the feminine pronoun. She continued as if the slipup had been intentional.

"Yes, it was a woman."

"Does she live here in the valley?"

"I think she lives somewhere else." She was struggling not to sound defensive, and losing the battle.

Frank heard the disappointment, and reminded himself this was his daughter's best friend. He added hopefully, "Are you able to get in touch with her? If she could come and meet with me maybe we could work something out. At least she could tell us where the bunny was made and we could then make appropriate inquiries."

Nina didn't think Clarissa would want to come to a lawyer's office. "Isn't there some other way?"

Frank settled back in his chair, finally seeing a way to get himself off the hook. He hoped it wouldn't be completely upsetting for Nina.

"If you bring me proof of who created the bunny, we can talk about the next steps for manufacture and sale. But unless you have that in place, I'm afraid there's no way you can go into business. Even if every girl in the entire world wants to buy one, companies who make these kinds of toys will require proof that you have the legal rights to the design. If you launched a product without having the rights, and if it were wildly successful, even if the true owner didn't object, there's a likelihood that companies who are less than scrupulous—" Frank paused as he used the word, but one brief look from Nina assured him she knew exactly what it meant "—would copy the bunny and soon you would have lots of copycat bunnies out there in the marketplace. And since you can't prove you have the copyright, there is no way to defend the exclusive right to manufacture the bunny."

Nina hadn't thought about copycats. With the bunny's image floating around the Internet, companies in China or India might start selling cheap knockoffs at any time. What would Clarissa think when she saw her bunny on shelves at discount stores?

Frank saw panic flash cross Nina's face. "Don't worry," he said quickly. "Any foreign company would face the same copyright barrier. Whoever owns the rights to this bunny could sue to stop any unauthorized manufacture."

What had seemed like a real chance, suddenly seemed hopeless. Nina wasn't even certain she would see Clarissa again, much less be able to get her permission to copy the bunny. That was, if she even owned the copyright to that bunny! "Thanks for meeting with me," she said. "I guess I was just dreaming."

Hearing this hurt Frank nearly as much as if she were his own daughter. "Nothing should ever stop you from dreaming, Nina," he said. "It's just that the adult world is far more complex than kids your age understand. There are lots of rules that don't seem to make much sense until you learn why they came about in the first place. That's why education is so important. It gives you the knowledge to do the things you want to do."

The last thing Nina wanted was a lecture on the value of education. But she resisted the urge to defend herself. Getting mad solved nothing.

Frank shifted to what he considered to be the greater problem. "I'm concerned about what you've said about your foster parents. If things break down please call me. I'll do whatever I can."

Nina felt a little better on hearing this. At least something positive had come out of the meeting. "Thank you," she said. "I guess I'd better get home. Evelyn will be expecting me for dinner."

She accepted Frank's offer to drive her back to Portage. As his car pulled up in front of the Torgerson house, he again told Nina he would do whatever was in his power to help her if things turned bad. Still, he felt nothing but guilt as he watched her climb the steps, push open the front door, and disappear inside.

CHAPTER EIGHTEEN

With the help of Father Thomas Clark, identifying Selena became easy. Just before the start of Sunday morning Mass, Sandro slid into a pew three rows behind the Hernandez family. It was readily apparent there was no resonance coming from her. This was just an ordinary girl, no different from millions of other thirteen-year-olds.

When the service was over and the last of the parishioners had departed, Sandro again approached the priest, knocking on the door of the vestry which was immediately behind the church. He was now free of his robes, dressed casually in slacks and a black shirt but still wearing a white collar. They shook hands and stood on the front lawn, under a hot sun and with the scent of lilacs in bloom on a light breeze.

"That was a fine service you gave, Father Clark."

Tom felt a pride that was almost sinful. To have praise coming from such a gentleman! "Thank you, Mr. Alighieri," he said, with a self-satisfied look. "Were you able to meet with the girl and her family?"

Sandro had made up a story that Selena's family might be the same one he'd had the pleasure of giving directions to in Italy two years ago. He now shook his head, and said, "I sat behind them, but when I was able to take a closer look it was clear this is not the same family I met in Venice."

"I'm sorry. Perhaps the family you met will be at another service. You are most welcome to come back to our church and participate in Mass."

"Thank you, Father. Perhaps if I remain in Langston the full week I will have that opportunity." But Sandro had no intention of staying. He now fished for the last bit of information he needed.

"Selena and her family may not be the ones I met in Italy, but she is a lovely child just the same. She must be very popular with other children in the church."

"Oh yes," the priest agreed. "She has many friends."

"I imagine she might even serve as a contact for reaching out to non-Catholic children in the community?" Sandro's charm was now in full force, radiating, irresistible. The priest responded.

"She has friends at school from all walks of faith."

"Wonderful! That is so different from Italy. We Catholics are so many back home, and those without the true faith are so few."

"What a shame. Here, our Selena is a treasure. She is very popular in school."

"Has she ever brought her friends to church?" *Tell me about those friends!*

"Not yet. Someday she may, God willing. I know she has two close girlfriends her own age; their names are Nina and Chantha. She even mentioned one of them recently, during confession . . ." The priest hesitated, knowing how completely wrong it was to repeat anything said in confession. Still . . . "Just yesterday she mentioned Nina. She was very troubled by something she had done."

"I'm sorry to hear that," Sandro said in his most soothing, most charming way. It had the exact effect intended, and the priest continued.

"Yes," the priest said, almost as if it were now he who was confessing, compelled to unburden his own soul. "She felt she had betrayed this girl."

"At that age, children are so sensitive, but it's usually not something truly important," Sandro said, prompting the priest for more.

"Yes, of course, you are right. It involved some kind of doll or stuffed animal. I think it was a rabbit. Selena wanted one for herself. She apparently took a picture without permission, but was unable to find a similar one on the Internet. She felt she had betrayed a trust and committed the sins of pride and envy." The priest paused, realizing he had gone well beyond where he should have stopped.

Sandro quickly said, "Well, I'm certain it will work out for the child. It seems a very common and easily forgivable mistake for someone of that age."

"Yes," the priest readily agreed, relieved and again feeling comfortable. "It was nothing extraordinary."

Sandro was careful to hide his excitement. There was now one final piece of information he needed to extract from the priest.

"Do you have a parish school?"

The priest looked skyward as if in both apology and prayer. "We are too small of a congregation to afford a parochial school. The only option for children here in the valley is a secular education. But," he added, with the same insistence as when he spoke to any person who might suspect the Catholics felt above the rest of the population, "our public school system is quite excellent."

"I'm glad to hear that. Is it near the church?"

"It's not far," he said. "Just a few blocks in that direction." He pointed down the street.

"Thank you, Father." They shook hands, and again the priest invited Sandro to attend church for Mass. Sandro again thanked him, and left with a final smile that made Father Clark feel like he'd just had a visitation from the Pope.

Sandro took a cab to confirm the school's location, and then checked into a hotel to wait for Monday morning.

Charlie arrived at the bed and breakfast around the same time Sandro was checking into his hotel. He'd spent nearly two hours on the bus, then had to wait an extra half hour to catch a connector from Langston up the east shore of Lake Cascade to reach the town of Portage.

The Bosecker Inn turned out to be a three-story, hundred-year-old New England style mansion. It was a block off the main highway, fronted by a white picket fence and a long bed of pink and purple petunias. Charlie climbed the three steps to the wide porch, noticed several comfortable wicker chairs scattered on the pine decking, and pushed open the door.

A slim blonde was sitting behind the reception desk, reading a magazine and looking bored.

Seeing her first customer of the day, Iris smiled at the man, who looked to be perhaps no more than two or three years older than she. He was attractive in a rugged and different sort of way that made her sit up a little straighter. She told him there were six guest rooms, but it was too early for the tourist season to have gotten into full gear, so Charlie could have his pick.

"Do you have something on the third floor?"

"Certainly. How many nights will you be staying with us?"

"I'd like to keep that open, if possible," Charlie said. "Can I reserve my room indefinitely?"

A look of surprised pleasure told him the answer was "yes." And beyond her obvious happiness at having made a substantial booking, there was also a shy flirtation as she asked for a deposit. Her interest spiked when Charlie pulled out a wallet packed with hundred dollar bills. She accepted a thousand dollars and handed him a receipt.

Charlie now decided it was wise to discourage any interest from a woman who probably had a high degree of success in dating men she was interested in.

"Does the room have a queen bed? It's possible my girlfriend might be joining me later on."

"Oh . . ."

Iris's voice had lost most of its sparkle.

"The upstairs only has a double. I can put you in number one. It has our largest bed and a bigger bathroom. It's twenty-five more per night and it's on the first floor, if that's okay?"

"Sure." Charlie handed back the brass key and picked up the replacement Iris laid on the counter.

The new room was located just off the dayroom. Once inside, he stashed the contents of his suitcase in the antique dresser and washed his face.

A few minutes later, Charlie headed for the Torgerson home, just three blocks away. When he walked past the house he felt a resonance coming from inside. It was so strong Charlie would have thought there was a gathering of members inside, and not just a single child.

He didn't linger. The girl would no doubt feel some measure of unease at his presence, even at this distance. For Nina, not yet trained to recognize it for what it was, it might feel like déjà vu, or a meal that hadn't settled well. Maybe a touch of dizziness, unexpected and unexplainable.

For the next hour, Charlie walked around, taking initial stock of the neighborhood. Most of the houses were modest. A community dock and a few boat slips on the waterfront. On the main highway there was limited business activity—a bar, a gas station, two restaurants. Beyond the town, apple orchards and vineyards reaching into the hills.

Satisfied that the neighborhood presented no unusual challenges, Charlie returned to the Bosecker.

CHAPTER NINETEEN

On Monday morning Charlie earnestly began the job of watching Nina. He posted up with a triple latte in hand, behind the window of a cafe two blocks down the street from where her school bus stopped. From his earlier experience of walking by her house, Charlie figured this was about as close as he dared come without risking a resonance reaction. He watched her sit beneath the oak and read a book until the bus arrived.

Half an hour before Nina boarded the bus, Sandro Alighieri was seven miles away, working his singular magic of charm on the vice principal of Langston Middle School.

At the age of 31, Boyd Nedrickson was the youngest employee ever hired for an administrative position by the Cascade County School District. His hiring had less to do with academics, and more to do with Boyd's college years as a starting defensive tackle for Oregon State. Langston High needed a line coach, and the vice-principal's job was the only budgeted slot available for a new hire.

Sandro had been scouting for an opportunity to watch kids as they arrived when Boyd came bounding up the sidewalk from the employee parking lot. Sandro intercepted him as he made the turn towards the front doors.

"Scusi me, sir," Sandro said.

Boyd paused, intrigued, having no clue he'd just come under the spell of Alighieri's charm. "Yes? May I help you?"

Sandro extended his hand, working a crude English heavily inflected by an Italian accent. "My name Guido Androcelli. I am from Roma, and am visit your beautiful town. Back in Roma I am teacher, and I was wonder if possible to see how your system work so I can make compare with ours. I hope be better teacher if I learn from American school system." A beaming smile of straight white teeth, hopeful wide brown eyes.

Boyd was hooked. "It would be an honor to show you around, Mr. Androcelli." He shook Sandro's hand, and then escorted him into the building, taking him first to the teachers' break room where a pot of coffee was already brewing.

"Would you like a cup of joe?" Boyd asked.

"Joe?"

"Oh . . . I mean coffee. We've also got cream and sugar if you want."

"Si . . . I mean, yes. 'Joe' is 'coffee!' How wonderful! Please, both cream and sugar." He sounded happier than a kid standing at the front gates to Disneyland.

After filling a Styrofoam cup and plopping in two sugar cubes, plus a dollop of imitation cream from a plastic mini-cup, Boyd escorted "Mr. Androcelli" to his office, where two assistant coaches were waiting. While they discussed summer recruiting for next fall's team, Sandro sat quietly at the back, managing to look happy, while suppressing a gag reflex as he sipped the rubbery brew. Fortunately, the meeting was short. Sandro threw the cup of now lukewarm coffee into a garbage bin as they walked down the hallway, explaining, "I like drink while hot."

"Would you like another cup?"

"No, Please. I already have coffee this morning at hotel." Sandro held out his hand and his fingers trembled. "Even my age, I get funny fingers if too much caffeine."

Boyd considered this for a moment. The Italian looked maybe thirty-five. Boyd could easily drink three cups before mid-morning without feeling more than a little surge. Oh well. He was, after all, an athlete!

"Mr. Androcelli, would you like to perhaps sit in on a class or two?"

Sandro shook his head. If he entered the same room as the girl it would likely cause her some discomfort. She wouldn't know the source, but in time she would see him again, in Europe, and she would most certainly remember. The consequences were potentially ugly. "No," Sandro said politely. "I think if I just see students as they come it would be fine."

"Great," Boyd agreed. They reached the front door as the first bus pulled up.

It all went fine until Nina's bus, one of the last to arrive, edged up to the curb. Even from as far away as the double doors Sandro felt her resonance as she stepped off the bus. As she came up the walkway it felt like a tidal wave making a run for the lee shore.

His instinct was to run. But the hallway behind was now filled with students. And with Boyd standing at his side there was no way to politely escape. So Sandro stood beside the vice principal and felt very much like a scarecrow watching wildfire roar in his direction.

She had come off the bus with an Asian girl. Sandro now saw the Hispanic girl he'd sat behind in church come skipping down the sidewalk to join the other two. After a few words they began to walk together towards the open doors.

Sandro now felt physically ill. As the girl approached, her attention momentarily shifted away from her two friends, first to the vice principal, and then to himself. As her eyes took him in it felt as if they stood alone in the middle of a desert.

Such power!

The moment mercifully passed. Nina's attention returned to her girlfriends as they walked in through the open doorway.

Sandro took off his hat and wiped the sweat from his forehead with the back of his shirtsleeve.

Boyd gave him a strange look. "Are you alright, Mr. Androcelli?"

Sandro fought to regain his balance, settling the hat back on his head. "Yes," he said, sounding shaky. "I think coffee maybe stronger than I need!"

"Well," Boyd conceded. "We do brew a strong pot to start the morning." But he sounded less than convinced.

The last of the students were crowding through the double doors and a buzzer sounded inside the building. "I'm sorry, but I've got another meeting," Boyd said. "Is there anything else you want to know about our school? Can I introduce you to our office staff, maybe the principal?"

Sandro turned to the vice principal, outwardly calm, inwardly fearful the girl would return and confront him. "No, I think I see enough. I much appreciate kindness you show."

"Alright," Boyd said, responding to Sandro's unspoken message. *Time to end this. Don't tell others about it. Our meeting was not important.* "Have a great time on your visit to the U.S." Boyd reached to shake the Italian's hand.

"*Ciao*—I mean, goodbye," Sandro said, quickly releasing Boyd's hand, and then hurrying out to the street. He wanted to sprint down the sidewalk, but forced himself to walk, feeling her presence slowly recede, grateful when, a block-and-a-half away, it was finally gone.

From a second floor classroom Nina watched the man in the tan trousers and white shirt and wearing the funny hat, the same man who had been standing with the vice principal, scurry down the sidewalk. A fragment of a dream, forgotten since she had awoken that morning, came to her. It was of Clarissa sitting inside the ski lodge, telling her about a special kind of danger. Telling Nina something of great importance might be about to happen. Telling her to be wary and careful because . . .

Others may come.

CHAPTER TWENTY

Mrs. Kennedy was in an unusually cheerful mood as Nina and Chantha climbed onto the bus for the ride home on Monday afternoon. "Hello, Nina!" she said as they reached the top of the steps.

"Hello, Mrs. Kennedy," Nina said. This simple recognition brought a triumphant grin from Mrs. Kennedy.

Chantha gave Nina a sideways glance as they walked back to their seats.

Nina just shrugged in reply. There was something far more important on her mind.

As the bus pulled away and headed up the Eastlake Highway, Nina turned to Chantha and said in a hushed voice, "Do you remember that strange man standing with the vice principal when we got to school this morning?"

"Kinda," Chantha said. "Wasn't he wearing a hat?"

"Yes. And tan colored pants and a brown leather belt that matched his dress shoes. Remember those shoes? They had sort of pointy toes."

Chantha gave Nina a straight-on stare. "You really sound a little freaked out about how he looked."

"It's not just how he looked or how he was dressed. He was . . ." Nina struggled to find the right words, and that was a rarity. She finally said, "It was like I was supposed to know him. Do you remember ever seeing him around the valley?"

"No. I just remember the vice principal standing there with some guy wearing a funny hat."

Could it have been so different for Chantha? How could a guy in such weirdly fashionable—and what looked like really expensive—clothes, not have impressed her as hugely as he impressed me? And why hadn't she picked up on his freaky vibe?

Chantha gave her a quizzical look, followed by a *whatever* roll of her eyes. But Nina wasn't quite ready to give up.

"I watched him when he left the school."

Chantha looked at her for a long moment, beginning to be concerned. Nina had a look on her face she'd never seen. *Spooked* almost.

"How did you manage to do that?"

"My first period classroom is on the second floor facing the street. I could see him when he left."

"And?"

"It looked like he was practically running down the sidewalk."

"That's really strange, Nina. Are you sure you're feeling okay? Because what you're saying doesn't make any sense. This guy is . . . like, running away from the school?"

"I guess," Nina said. And for the first time, a bit of doubt crept in. Could she have it entirely wrong? Was it just her imagination— the feeling of a stranger somehow being connected to her? Like he was some kind of lost relative? But "relative" wasn't quite right, was it? The connection seemed . . . and that was the problem: there was nothing to compare it to. Still . . . Chantha was right. When Nina thought about what she'd just said it did sound a little nutty. So maybe it was just one of those funny feelings you sometimes get?

By the time the bus pulled to a stop in Portage, Nina had decided it must be her imagination playing tricks.

As she passed Mrs. Kennedy, on sudden impulse she paused and volunteered, "Have a nice day, Mrs. Kennedy," before exiting the bus.

Doris Kennedy sat up straighter in her seat. When she pulled the lever to close the door, she didn't even feel the urge for a cigarette. As she shifted the bus into second, and then third gear, and motored down the East Lake Highway, she felt positively perky.

Dan's pickup stood in the driveway. Nina softly pushed the front door, so as not to draw attention. But as the door swung wide, she found both Dan and Evelyn sitting in the front room, Evelyn on the sofa and Dan at the dining table. And square in the middle of the table sat the bunny.

Both Dan and Evelyn stared at her. Nina stared right back, first at Evelyn, then more of a glare at Dan, and finally a nervous glance at the bunny.

Dan leaned a little forward in his chair. "Young lady," he began, and Nina was instantly nervous. Dan only called her *young lady* when something important was at stake. Usually something he thought she'd done wrong. Dan continued, "I think you have some explaining to do." He glanced at the bunny.

Nina wanted to grab the bunny and run. She was still holding onto her book knapsack, and she now dropped it at her feet. The sound of it hitting the floor was like a bomb had gone off. There was a heavy silence.

Evelyn suddenly looked nervous, and volunteered, "Honey, we don't think you've done anything wrong. It's just—"

Dan cut her off. "It's just that I discovered you and Selena used my office computer to get onto Facebook."

Nina saw the look on Dan's face and realized he wasn't mad. He was curious. And he looked . . . greedy. Nina felt anger begin to blossom. Her lower lip firmed up, and a small wrinkle formed in the space between her eyebrows.

Dan backpedaled. "Don't get me wrong, Nina. When I say it wasn't right for you and Selena to get onto Facebook with my computer, I really do mean it was wrong. We have house rules for good reasons. But," and now Dan's intent became perfectly clear, "I was surprised to discover how many people were interested in this bunny."

Dan had been far more than surprised. When he turned on his computer that morning and booted up Firefox and typed in the first three letters "f-a-c" to open his Facebook account, he'd hit the enter key without looking to see if it was his own account being opened. He was surprised to see the home page for Selena Hernandez pop up on the screen. There was only one way for that to have happened. Nina had permitted Selena to use his computer. He became instantly furious.

Then curiosity took over as he saw something strange: a series of comments and requests concerning a stuffed rabbit toy. There was even a photo of the rabbit, held by Selena. The selfie included a wall Dan recognized as being in his den. This got Dan to wondering why the photo had been taken there.

He went searching, and it wasn't long before he found the bunny hidden at the back of Nina's closet. He returned to the computer, and as he scrolled through the comments he began to realize there was a business possibility here that totally blew away what he was doing with wine. Hundreds of girls—no, *thousands of girls!*—had posted about the bunny, most of them wanting one of their own. Dan had no idea how you went about manufacturing stuffed toys. But how hard could it really be? You just hired a company and gave them the design. All he'd need was pictures of the bunny, and maybe to unravel the seams to see what was inside, trace a pattern for each piece of fabric, and voila! If you sold ten thousand units at thirty bucks apiece with a five dollar profit, that was fifty grand.

What if you sold a million!

Dan discussed his discovery with Evelyn and found her not only in agreement; she was absolutely excited. It meant she'd be able to keep Nina.

"Nina," Dan now asked. "Is this yours?" He nodded towards the bunny.

"Yes," Nina said, feeling her resistance begin to ratchet up like a clock spring wound too fast.

"Where did it come from?"

And this time she knew a lie was her only possible defense. "I found it," she said.

"Where?"

"Up at the ski hill while I was hunting for mushrooms."

Dan chewed at his lip, a habit signaling he was as deep in thought as his mind permitted him to go. "Was it, like, out in the open?"

"No," Nina said, framing an answer that wouldn't leave Dan wanting to turn the bunny over to the police. "It was buried under a bunch of leaves. It was dirty so I had to clean it up. I think it was up there for a long time."

This appeared to please Dan. "How long do you think it might have been there?"

"Maybe years," Nina said.

"Huh!" Dan said. "Well, I guess by now whoever lost it has forgotten it."

That was a relief! It wouldn't be turned in to the lost-and-found at the sheriff's office. She expected him to ask more questions about the bunny, but Dan now went off in a completely unexpected direction.

"Nina," he said, trying to sound sincere. "Evelyn and I have been talking about you, and we've come to a tentative conclusion." Dan looked at Evelyn, and Nina saw how excited she was— her face beaming with happiness. "It's time we considered your long term future. Evelyn and I agree that we'd like to move towards working on a permanent custody order. Maybe even an adoption. How would you feel about that?"

Several thoughts collided in Nina's brain. It would mean a home for the next five years. No more uncertain foster placements. She'd keep Chantha and Selena as friends.

But accepting Dan as her dad? How could she possibly do that? And with that look on his face, how could she even believe he was really sincere?

Evelyn now cut in with, "You don't have to make up your mind right away, sweetheart. I know it's a big decision for you."

"Right," Dan added. "Take your time." And the way he said it sounded all wrong.

Nina looked back and forth between the hopeful Evelyn and the determined Dan, realizing there was no comfortable way out.

"It's really up to you," Dan continued, in a voice that insisted there was only one logical choice for her to make. "You should let us know if you have any questions. We just want to be here for you, Nina." But it didn't sound right.

She looked at the bunny sitting on the table, and everything fell into place.

That is what he really wants.

"Can I take my bunny to my room?"

Evelyn was up off the couch without so much as a glance at Dan. She lifted the bunny from the table, under the now watchful eyes of Dan, who seemed to want to grab it from her. But he made no move. Evelyn handed Nina the bunny. "It's yours, so of course you can take it to your room."

Dan stood up and stretched, as if he'd been sitting in the chair for too long. "I've got some work to do out in the garage. We can talk more later." And with that pronouncement, he left.

Evelyn looked at Nina and the bunny, her smile uncertain, but still hopeful. "Sweetheart, I just want you to know that I love you and whatever you decide to do will be the right thing, and I'll support you in your decision."

But Nina knew there was just one decision that would make Evelyn happy. She tried hard to bring herself to use the word *mom*, but it just wouldn't come. So she finally said, "I'm glad you both want me." Evelyn gave her a hug and Nina returned the hug and felt sorry for Evelyn.

And then she was free to go to her room, where she collapsed onto her bed and curled up with the bunny. She looked into the bunny's blue-rimmed eyes and finally said, "What are we going to do?"

As Nina talked to her bunny, Dan was out in the garage fighting down his rage. He gave one of the empty wine boxes a solid kick and it flew across the cement in a brief cloud of dust and collided with the corner of his workbench.

It had been hard to even use the word *adoption*, much less sound sincere. He'd had to say it like he meant it or otherwise Evelyn would have begun to realize he wasn't at all interested in Nina. Now he'd have to endure a home study from a state caseworker, and make it appear he was truly interested in permanently taking on a child. When all he really wanted was the Facebook names list and getting that stuffed rabbit into commercial production. But adoptions didn't happen overnight. With a bit of effort Dan could stretch the process into months. And long before he had to pretend that he'd gotten cold feet, he'd have the bunny project up and running. A foreign firm with cheap labor would be churning out bunnies by the truckload.

"I'm gonna be rich," Dan confided to the stack of empty wine boxes. "And then I'm gonna be free!"

CHAPTER TWENTY-ONE

On Tuesday morning, Clarissa sat in the Bakery Café at the San Jose Hyatt. She had dreamt of Nina Bea, and the lingering images were unsettling.

They had walked on a beach along the Mediterranean Sea, talking about the history of the Order, and about Clarissa's past. Nina Bea asked question after question, and Clarissa gave full and frank answers, unable to deny her fledgling protégé, but still concerned about the damage she might be causing.

Her musings about the dream ended when Valerie appeared promptly at seven. Clarissa had an immediate and strong sense that something was wrong.

"Good morning," Valerie said, as she sat down across from Clarissa. She quickly added, "You were expecting your crest to show up on the Internet fairly soon, right?"

"Why?" Clarissa asked, cautiously.

"A girl named Selena Hernandez posted an Internet inquiry about the origin of a stuffed toy bunny which bears the crest. She's searching for where the toy was made so she can purchase one for herself. I'm not sure why she would want another when she already has one. Her query drew a lot of interest, and within a short time the response went viral."

"Viral?" Clarissa had heard the term, and knew it couldn't be anything good. Valerie confirmed her fears.

"Thousands of Facebook members have responded, nearly every one of them asking where they can buy one. They're mostly kids near her age. This girl must be completely overwhelmed."

Clarissa sat stunned. It was too soon! And who was Selena Hernandez? And why did she have possession of the bunny?

Valerie was waiting for a comment.

Clarissa pushed aside the temptation to tell her everything. But now a foundation needed to be laid, and time was suddenly no longer a luxury

"I don't know who Selena Hernandez is, or how she got the bunny. I gave it to a girl named Nina Beatrix Haas—I call her 'Nina Bea'—and she must have lent it to this girl Selena." Clarissa paused, searching for the right words. Valerie needed to understand the importance of the girl.

"Nina Bea is a very special child who is part of a small group of people because of her birth. In one sense, this group would think of her as a kind of royalty. She will eventually hold a very unique leadership position in this . . . society. They don't yet know she exists, but with my personal crest now being paraded across the Internet I'm certain they will detect its presence and begin to make inquiries that will lead to her.

"Unfortunately, I'm not in good standing with this group. They are going through an internal struggle. Many of them desperately want to keep the group—we call it 'the Order'—a secret. But a few, including myself, think we should be less concerned for our privacy, and more concerned about offering a certain kind of knowledge we have for the betterment of mankind."

"Knowledge?"

Clarissa rolled on, realizing how strange she was sounding, struggling to walk the line between what could—and what could not yet—be told.

"Do you remember that book *The DaVinci Code?*"

"Yes," Valerie said, now wondering if this might turn into a surprise *gotcha* moment. That's what she almost wanted it to be: a joke. Because the alternative was that Clarissa wasn't what she had appeared to be. And that was more than bothersome. It bordered on scary.

"The Order could be compared to what the author wrote about in his novel, except there's no religious element."

Valerie's uneasiness jacked up a notch. She barely managed to ask the next question without sounding incredulous.

"So you're a member of this Order?"

"Yes. In fact you might call me the senior member."

Valerie looked at Clarissa for a long moment before she said, "But you only look to be maybe forty-five."

"It's kind of you to say that," Clarissa said. "I'm a bit older."

"Fifty?"

Clarissa just smiled.

"So this girl?" Valerie prompted, hoping to wrap up the conversation. Wanting an opportunity to digest what she'd already heard.

"She needs protection. I've been working on that for the past few days. Only now I'm going to have to speed up the process."

For someone exceptionally talented at solving puzzles, this one now had Valerie stumped. If Clarissa had not already handed her three ounces of pure gold, she might have bailed right then. Still . . . it seemed like a marvelous puzzle.

Clarissa saw Valerie's confusion, and realized she was on shaky ground. "I'm going to need help in monitoring the Order's response to the crest. Would you be willing to do that for me?"

"Maybe," Valerie said. "But I'd like to know more about this group you belong to."

"You'll learn everything you need to know. I promise."

"Okay. We can take it one step at a time," Valerie said, adding, "Does this girl Nina Bea know about the Order?"

"No. She has absolutely no clue about who she is or what she represents to us. And if I tell her now, before she's mature enough to understand, it won't just upset her, it will entirely change her life."

"Is she in danger?"

"Maybe," Clarissa said. Then she reconsidered her hopeful assessment. "Probably."

CHAPTER TWENTY-TWO

The full Council gathered in Zurich.

Liesel and Pieter were still there. Sandro's Gulfstream stopped at La Guardia Airport to pick up the only American currently sitting on the Council, Trisha Peterson. The warrior Isaac Onejeme flew in from Nairobi. Francois DeVaux took the TGV from Paris.

The seventh member, Hiroshi Nishikura, currently lived in a sparsely populated mountain region on the southern island of Kyushu. It took a full day for him to receive the message, and then another day to drive to the international airport at Fukuoka to catch one of the Order's long range jets.

On a Thursday at noon, the full Council finally sat listening to Sandro in the boardroom.

"The girl's name is Nina, and she has the potential to become another Clarissa." All faces were grimly attentive. "She's only thirteen years old, but even now, just coming close to her is . . . frightening."

"Did she recognize you?" Pieter asked. There was apprehension, bordering on fear.

"It was obvious she felt something when she walked past, but I doubt she yet has the ability to identify someone of the Order."

"But you cannot be certain?"

"True. But if she already has that level of perception, I doubt we could stop her from doing whatever she wishes."

Hiroshi lifted his hand and Pieter nodded. The Japanese was one of the gentler members of the Council, a man whose skill was plants and their uses, particularly in medicine. "Shouldn't we let her develop as we have the others? Can she really be that much of a danger? She is, after all, just a young girl."

Isaac spoke without asking Pieter for recognition. "It's not her we are concerned about. It's Clarissa and her desire to reveal the Order to the rest of humanity. If Clarissa has chosen to groom this girl as her tool, we must move immediately to isolate the child from her influence. Only after she is safely in our custody will the danger from Clarissa again be manageable."

A warrior himself, Pieter agreed with Isaac that there was only one solution. Before anyone could respond to Isaac's comments, he said, "We must fetch her to Switzerland and place her into the compound. Immediately—"

"I disagree," Liesel interrupted. "This child has a right to her freedom until she is of an appropriate age—"

"But she is not being given that same right by Clarissa!" Pieter shouted, pounding a fist on the polished oak. "She is being manipulated!"

"Everyone please calm down," Sandro cut in. The tenseness in the room had become painful. "Let's get back on track. What do we do next?"

"Right," Pieter said, glancing from face to face, regretting his outburst. He would not win the day with a display of anger. "I agree we need to be calm. And we need consensus. Francois, we haven't heard from you yet. What are your thoughts?"

The Frenchman had been listening closely. Like Sandro, his skill was charm, but he was more reserved than his Italian counterpart. He took a moment to brush back his moustache with a thumb and index finger. Then he spread his hands wide, signaling his surrender to whatever the group's majority decision might be.

Pieter turned to the final member, the American. "Miss Peterson?"

Trisha Peterson was the youngster on the Council, having been born in 1911. She was still in awe of Isaac Onejeme, born in the year 912. A man who'd managed to survive eleven centuries in the rough and tumble of Africa. She looked around the table and saw others who should outrank her. Hiroshi was 414 years of age. Francois was 301. Sandro, 605. In the face of this accumulation of wisdom and knowledge, her personal opinion seemed insignificant. But the Order was a true democracy. Everyone was allowed—and expected—to express their opinions. A unanimous vote was always the goal. Today was no exception.

Content to go with the flow, Trisha said, "Whatever the group decides, I'll be fine with it."

"Do we need further discussion?" Pieter asked. When he saw no one wanting speak, he said, "A show of hands for sending someone to retrieve the girl."

Six hands went up.

Liesel's hands remained flat on the table.

Pieter said, "It is noted that Liesel votes not to retrieve the girl." He looked at her. "Or do you wish to simply abstain?"

"You were correct the first time," Liesel replied coldly.

"The motion carries, six to one. So now the question is, who do we send?"

"A warrior," Isaac said, his deep voice certain, uncompromising.

"You?" Pieter asked.

"No. I am a black man and that is a very white community where I would be too obvious and . . . memorable."

"Who then?"

"I think we should consider sending Gunther," Isaac said.

Liesel's shock was shared in varying degrees by everyone except Pieter, who appeared to have known this was coming.

Gunther was a northern German born in 1744. What separated him from the handful of other warriors in the Order was that he enjoyed—and actively sought out—physical combat. Hand to hand, preferably. Having volunteered to fight in every major European war, he seemed not to care which side he fought for. It was not a wise lifestyle for someone who might expect to live for centuries, barring something like a bullet in the head, or close contact with a hand grenade, nerve gas, or a mortar shell. But no one had ever accused Gunther of possessing wisdom. Having been gifted with an extended life and perfect health, Gunther was the only member who chose to risk death for the thrill of it. It was a miracle he was still alive.

Pieter now asked Isaac their prearranged question.

"And the reason for sending Gunther to capture a girl?"

No one in the room was fooled. This had been carefully planned.

Liesel knew she had been betrayed in her earlier confidence to Pieter, and silently vowed to find a way to get even. But that would have to wait. She was probably going to lose this battle. The only question was: how much dignity could she salvage?

Isaac looked from face to face and spoke slowly to convey the weight of his conclusion. "Clarissa has been alive much longer than myself. To live for so long takes great foresight and much caution. She will have prepared a defense of this child, and we cannot know what that defense might be. But I guarantee you it will be in place, and to send someone other than a warrior would be foolishness. Gunther is somewhat primitive in his methods, but if he encounters another warrior—someone we are unaware of whom Clarissa has placed to defend the child—he will have the greatest chance for success. If we send someone less powerful, and he is prevented from taking the child, it will only serve to alert Clarissa. Any subsequent attempt will be all the more imperiled. That is my reasoning, but I am prepared to hear objections." The black pupils and wide whites of his large and expressive eyes moved from face to face, measuring their reactions.

Pieter nodded in agreement, and looked around the table. "Any comments?"

Liesel had become progressively more upset as Isaac spoke, and was quick to respond.

"If this child is as special as Sandro says, she might someday be of enormous benefit to the Order. That Clarissa has chosen her speaks for itself. How many other members with Clarissa's abilities do we have recorded in our histories?" She pointed at the bound volumes filling the bookcases along the back wall, containing the handwritten history of the Order. "I know of only three. There was Eustachus of Athens, who passed during the fifteenth century. He was reported to have lived for fifteen hundred years. The Egyptian, who was sometimes called Amon, was rumored to have lived for over three thousand years, dying shortly after the Roman Empire fell. And of course, there was Livia . . ."

The woman known as Livia had never accepted the offer to join the Order. She had lived in seclusion in Spain for seventeen hundred years, before entirely vanishing in the middle of the eighteenth century. During her lifetime, she had used her total command of the powers to enforce her isolation, apparently wanting nothing to do with others of her own kind. No one knew why. Most members thought she must have died.

Liesel looked at each of the Council members and her face pleaded for understanding. "Can we truly risk someone as precious as this child to the brute force of Gunther?"

There was silence. A stalemate. Until Trisha finally spoke up.

"I'm an American. So is this girl. Maybe it would be best if I made the attempt. I would certainly be less noticeable than Gunther. The girl may be comfortable with me if I approach her slowly and try to first make her my friend."

All of them stared at the slim, pretty blonde from New York. There were gradual nods of assent from all except Isaac and Pieter.

Silence hung like a gallows noose until Isaac finally conceded.

"I accept what our American member has offered, and withdraw my suggestion of Gunther." He quickly added, "But in case she fails, we should be prepared to immediately send the German to complete the task."

This time there were quick nods of assent around the table.

⊷⊶

Later that day, as a Gulfstream jet carried her across the Atlantic, Trisha sat alone in the cabin, thinking about something Liesel had said when they were alone together on the drive to the airport.

"Do you remember when you were thirteen years old?"

Trisha considered the question as she gazed out the window. The limo was speeding along the A-1 freeway, past woods, farms, cows, and the occasional cornfield. She did remember being thirteen, back in 1924. It was the year her family had moved from Carbondale, at the southern tip of Illinois, north to the metropolis of Chicago, hard against the shore of Lake Michigan.

Suddenly, instead of a rural life in the Corn Belt, where a train passing through town was often the day's great thrill, she lived in a world of tall buildings, streets bustling with automobiles, the racy undercurrent of speakeasies and gangsters.

There was also plenty of racism—not just against blacks, but focused hatred for Asians, Indians, the Irish, and anyone else who sounded or looked "different." Everyone belonged to a clan—whether racial, religious or cultural. It was a matter of survival for most.

Trisha's young world now expanded beyond her wildest early small town dreams. She read of Einstein's discoveries, and wanted to be a scientist. She went to the movies, and yearned to be Gloria Swanson all wrapped up in the arms of Rudolph Valentino. She saw young women "flappers" in their stylish clothes, and imagined swirling on a hardwood floor to the driving beat of a jazz band. And more than anything else, Trisha dreamed of a world where women were treated equally with men.

Trisha turned to Liesel in the speeding limo, distant memories of the golden age before the Great Depression still clear in her mind's eye.

"Everything was magical," she said wistfully. "Everything seemed possible." She gazed past Liesel, out the window. "My parents were alive. I had a precious little brother who loved me. I dreamed of growing up and having a career, of raising my own family, owning my own home. Of belonging to a community where I would be safe and accepted."

"Would you go back?"

Trisha wanted to say "No." She had lost her parents. Her brother died of lung cancer at sixty-two, long after she'd broken off contact, but still secretively following his life. When she reached 40, her skin was still smooth, there were no gray hairs, and rumors about her strangeness began to turn vicious. She felt progressively more lost. Had it not been for her discovery by the Watchers, and being assigned a mentor to ease her into a new way of life . . .

Haltingly, Trisha said, "I wouldn't want to go back if I knew I was going to become what I am today. Not if I knew that everyone around me would die. But if I could be innocent again . . . sure, I'd go back."

"This girl you are going for," Liesel said, in a steady voice. "You are going to steal all of that away from her."

Trisha looked at Liesel, now with a pained acceptance clouding her vision. "I know," she said. "But I will be easier for her than Gunther. And we *must* take control. There is no other choice. We can't let this girl grow up to become what Clarissa wants her to become. The Order is going to fetch her to Switzerland regardless of how you or I feel about the fairness of it. At least in me she'll have someone who cares about her emotional state."

Liesel nodded, almost imperceptibly. In the distance a jet could now be seen roaring off into the sky. "Yes," she finally agreed. "At least she'll have someone sympathetic to hold her while she cries."

Both women fell silent, staring out the limo's windows as the green Swiss countryside swept by.

CHAPTER TWENTY-THREE

Having to maintain a distance from Nina shackled Charlie's protection plans. But Clarissa had been clear and certain about avoiding direct contact.

Portage now became the focus of his attention, especially the area within four blocks of the Torgerson house. After five days, he knew every hedge, rooftop, fenced backyard, and shadowy place where someone might hide.

He occasionally saw her from a distance, usually when she boarded the school bus or was riding her bicycle.

There was one telling moment that stuck out. One day after school, she walked down to the boat dock and stood for a long time, gazing out across the water, looking very lonely. Charlie felt a sudden urge to go and tell her about the Order. To give this solitary girl a big hug and tell her that everything was going to be alright.

The urge passed. Clarissa was right. You can't shatter the reality of someone that age and not expect enormous damage. Still . . . Charlie was tempted.

On Friday afternoon, Charlie took the bus into Langston. He strolled past the large brick school and walked the nearby streets. Which left only the bus pickup routine to learn.

In small towns, strangers stand out, especially near schools where teachers and parents are on the lookout. Charlie couldn't just post up across the street and wait for the end of the school day. That was begging for a chat with a deputy sheriff.

He went searching for the bus garage, and found it six blocks away from the school. There was an espresso stand across the street, where he bought a latte, settled down at a small table where customers ate lunch or enjoyed a drink, and waited. For a brief moment he thought about beignets and the Café du Monde.

Half an hour later, a line of boxy yellow busses rolled out of the garage.

Charlie set off at a trot for the school. When he reached the end of the last block, his fears about not being able to spot her vanished. She was standing on the sidewalk, talking with an Asian girl. A bus pulled up, and they climbed aboard.

As he walked along the opposite side of the street, he caught a glimpse of the two girls sitting together near the middle. He could clearly feel Nina's resonance.

There came a nervous moment when he thought she glanced out the window and looked directly at him. But then she immediately returned her attention to her friend, and Charlie decided it was just his imagination.

After the bus left, Charlie walked three blocks to the local transit stop.

He arrived back in Langston at 4:30. As he approached the Bosecker, Charlie finally felt what he'd been hoping for: Clarissa's presence. He skipped up the steps and pushed open the front door.

Iris greeted him from behind the desk with, "Charlie, there's a woman in the dayroom who's come to see you."

"Thanks, Iris," Charlie said. From the questioning look on her face he realized she thought this might be the girlfriend he'd mentioned.

He walked into the dayroom.

"How's my favorite warrior," Clarissa said with relief, standing to take his hands in hers.

She looks older.

Clarissa saw his concern, and acknowledged the strain. "It's been a challenge," she confirmed. "Is there a better place we can talk?"

"My room," Charlie said.

Once the door was shut he offered her a chair, and asked, "Where are we at?"

"There's trouble. I'm not certain when, but it may come soon. Is Nina Bea alright?"

"As far as I know. She goes to school on the bus each morning, returns every afternoon around three forty-five, sometimes plays near the house or rides her bike."

Clarissa sensed there was more. "And?" she prompted.

"I'm no expert with children, but—" Charlie gave a nervous cough, "—she spends a lot of time alone. It must be a lonely life she's leading."

"What about the foster parents?"

"She and the woman drove off together once. The foster dad always comes and goes by himself in his pickup. They don't appear to do much together as a family."

This didn't surprise Clarissa. A girl with her massive potential would easily intimidate and overwhelm kids her own age. She undoubtedly had a similar impact on her foster parents; particularly the man. As for loneliness? It was a burden no matter how long you lived or how bright you were.

"You said trouble was coming?" Charlie was standing, hands loose at his sides.

"I gave Nina Bea a stuffed bunny with my personal crest on its chest. Somehow, a girl named Selena got hold of it and posted a

135

picture of it on Facebook. It went viral, and I have no doubt the Order will eventually pick it up. They'll send someone to check out this Selena, and when they find out she isn't one of us, they will look further and eventually find Nina Bea. Then they'll try to take her out of the country."

"Would the Order consider the possibility of having her killed?"

Clarissa shuddered, remembering that Charlie had lived outside the Order for his entire life. "No," she said, solemnly, "Maybe I never told you, but we have a rule. Any member who kills another member is hunted down and eliminated. The most recent person to violate the rule was a woman in fifteenth century France. She was tracked down by a team of five members, and when they caught her they burned her at the stake as a lesson to any who might feel inclined to repeat the crime."

Charlie shuddered. "So what's next?"

"It's time for you to get to know Nina Bea. I haven't seen her since three weeks ago in the forest. Let me contact her first. I'll say I have a friend that I want her to meet. We can set up a time and a place."

"And until then?"

"Keep alert."

"Where will you be?"

"I'm going to take a room here at the Bosecker," she said, with a satisfied look.

Charlie led her out to the reception desk, and said, "Iris, I'd like you to meet my aunt Clarissa."

"Please to meet you, Ma'am," Iris said, with relief in her voice. This older woman wasn't the girlfriend!

"The pleasure is mine," Clarissa replied, her message of charm so strong that Iris felt a little giddy. "I was wondering if you had another room to let?"

Iris would have evicted someone if there hadn't already been a vacancy.

CHAPTER TWENTY-FOUR

Dan Torgerson got busy following the living room confrontation with Nina.

With a little finagling, a woman from Evelyn's church—who was crafty with sewing projects—agreed to take the bunny apart and make a pattern. More importantly, for the hundred-dollar bill Dan waived in her face, she agreed to keep her mouth shut. He would come and take pictures and cut samples from each different bit of fluff and fabric before the woman sewed it all back together. Then he would replace it on Nina's closet shelf, and she would be none the wiser.

The patterns and samples would be express mailed to an Indian company that specialized in the wholesale manufacture of plush pets. Dan had found the company on the Internet. During his first phone call, the rep identified himself as "Thomas."

"Come on 'Thomas'," Dan said sarcastically. "You're in India, right?"

"Yes, I am in the city of Jaipur."

"So tell me . . . *Thomas* . . . is there really anyone from Jaipur who names their son 'Thomas'?"

There was a long pause on the other end of the line. Dan imagined "Thomas" was weighing the benefits of telling the truth versus trying to convince him that his name really was Thomas. Finally, the man confessed, "My Indian name is Amit."

"Well, Amit," Dan said gleefully, "let's get down to business."

Amit asked where the bunny came from and what it looked like. He sounded relieved when Dan described how the bunny was found, apparently abandoned, and looking well used and very old fashioned. "Primitive" was the word Dan used. "Like someone made it at home."

"We can make a little change here and there," Amit said. "We should be fine on any copyright issue."

Dan hadn't been too worried. Was a copyright owner really going to sue someone in India? Good luck on that one! He planned to form a limited liability company in the U.S. to handle any potential legal challenges at home.

"We will need a deposit," Amit said towards the end of the conversation.

"How much?"

"For minimum design and setup, five hundred."

"And what do I get for that?"

"You get a first bunny doll. After that, we quote you a price based upon design and materials, and depending on how many dolls you want to order. I would think a cost to you of not more than five dollars per unit is possible."

It was a far better margin that he'd first imagined. Dan figured that if he placed an initial order of a thousand bunnies, and they sold for thirty bucks apiece, that would yield a twenty-five thousand dollar profit. He could pad the shipping charges and squeeze out a few more dollars from all those teenage girls. Even the five-dollar-per-bunny price might be negotiable. After all, what were the women and children in India who did this type of work going to be paid? Maybe a buck an hour?

"Okay," Dan agreed. "We can talk more about the price after I've sent you the design info."

"Good," Amit said, and hung up.

This left Dan wondering when he could get his hands on the bunny without alerting Nina. He fretted about it all week, until on Thursday afternoon Evelyn came to him while he was on the computer.

"Honey," she said in her *Please don't be too upset with me* tone of voice. "Nina asked if she could sleep over at Chantha's on Friday and Saturday. Do you have any objections?"

Objections? It was perfect! Dan's face went Hollywood for a moment, as if he really was thinking whether or not this presented a problem. He finally looked up at Evelyn, smiled, and said, "Oh . . . I think that should be fine."

"Thanks, dear!" She gave him a kiss on the cheek before she hurried out to tell Nina that she could go.

Dan returned to working on a spreadsheet for the project's finances. He'd found the perfect name for the file: Billionaire Bunny Project.

CHAPTER TWENTY-FIVE

Nina and Selena arrived at the Miller's on Friday afternoon to spend the weekend. That evening, Frank and Anna laid out a picnic-style dinner on the back deck, with German sausages, Anna's family recipe for potato salad; and for later, Hershey's chocolate, marshmallows and graham crackers for smores. Nothing short of grand!

By six that evening, Frank was keeping an eye on the wood blazing down towards a thick bed of coals, occasionally checking on the girls inside, presently tangled up in a game of twister. Chantha and Selena were all shouts and giggles and seemed not to have a care in the world—regular thirteen-year-olds on a sleepover.

Nina appeared to have moments when she was struggling with some inner emotion. Twenty years of lawyering had taught Frank to look for signs of unhappiness in his clients, and he now saw a red flag with Nina.

She would occasionally glance around the room, as if checking for something the other girls didn't—or *couldn't*—see. She would throw a wary and almost fearful look, sometimes towards a corner of the room, out a window, or off into empty space. These distracted moments would quickly pass, with Nina again looking happy as she twisted her body to angle a foot onto a different green, red, blue or yellow circle. When she smiled and was involved, she looked like any thirteen-year-old. But in those wary moments, she seemed *ageless.*

A glance at the glowing pit of coals told Frank it was time for dinner. And maybe also time to relax his focus on Nina. She wasn't his immediate problem. And it really wasn't necessary to get all worked up and *make* her his problem. "Girls!" he shouted through the open door. "Grab your roasting sticks!"

The girls untangled and scrambled out the door to select long willow whips from several Frank had cut earlier. The sausages slid easily onto the sharpened ends, and if they weren't entirely straight on the sticks it didn't really matter. The girls crowded up to the fire, holding their dogs over the coals while they sizzled and popped, dripping fat, the skins bubbling up black spots, until they were nicely charred and ready to slide into buns.

Anna joined the party, and soon all five sat on folding chairs pulled up around the teakwood table, gobbling down sausages, with an occasional squirt of ketchup or mustard dribbling down chins. A few corn chips and baked beans fell onto the deck, where ants and birds would later have a feast of their own.

When it came time for smores, Frank and Anna watched with pride as Chantha waited until Selena and Nina each selected marshmallows and pushed them onto their sticks.

The girls were allowed two graham cracker slabs, two large marshmallows, and half a bar of chocolate. They sat around the fire ring, waiting until blue flames licked the marshmallows before blowing them out and smashing the gooey blackened puffs and chocolate squares between graham crackers.

As the girls enjoyed their campfire desserts, Frank and Anna worked to clear the table. When they were finally together in the kitchen, rinsing dishes and loading the dishwasher, Frank turned to Anna and asked, "Does Nina seem a little distracted tonight? Or is it just my imagination?"

Anna had also noticed something was amiss, and had good reason to believe there was trouble ahead because of an earlier telephone call from Evelyn. As they talked details for what Nina should bring, Evelyn shared something, while her voice held an edge of uncertainty.

"We're going to go for an adoption," Evelyn confided. "We just told her, and I think it took her a little by surprise."

Anna had endured the bureaucratic dramas of Chantha's adoption, and knew it wasn't as simple as just deciding to do it. State caseworkers and a court-appointed guardian ad litem would thoroughly scrutinize prospective parents. Anna wasn't too worried about Evelyn passing the scrutiny of a home study. It was her husband Dan who raised concerns. He didn't strike Anna as the fathering type. Still . . . Nina would soon be turning fourteen. She had bounced between foster homes since her parents died. Lack of stability was tough for a child. Maybe adoption wasn't such a bad idea. And if things got rough, Nina seemed capable of speaking up for herself.

"I'm happy for you," Anna told Evelyn. "Have you thought of who you want to hire to help you with the process?"

Evelyn's voice turned apologetic. "Dan's already found a lawyer. I didn't get a vote on that. Otherwise, I'd have wanted your Frank."

"Don't worry," Anna comforted, "Frank's up to his ears with clients these days. I'm sure whoever Dan has picked will be fine."

But even as she offered encouragement, Anna wondered why Dan had excluded Evelyn from choosing a lawyer. Adoption was a huge step for any couple. Including Evelyn on critical decisions, like the choice of a lawyer, would have made good sense from a relationship point of view.

Now, standing in the kitchen with Frank, Anna shared what she had learned.

"Really?" Frank said, surprised. He would have liked to report about his meeting with Nina. Her complaints about the Torgersons didn't square up with the prospects for an adoption. But Frank took his vow of attorney-client confidentiality seriously. He was ethically bound not to share what he learned behind closed doors, even from a person as young as Nina, and even with his wife.

Anna waited for a comment, and when none came, she did a little prodding. "Chantha told me you met with Nina at your office. Is there something you know?"

"Yes," Frank said carefully. "But I need to keep it under wraps."

"Is there going to be trouble?"

"I'm afraid so." And now Frank was replaying that earlier conversation with Nina, measuring it against what he'd just seen in her. Maybe her uneasiness did signal she was going to become his problem.

Anna looked at Frank, trusting he would do what was necessary. "Okay," she finally said. "Let me know if there's anything I can do to help."

Frank kissed her on the cheek. "I do love you so much," he said. And then he took her in his arms and gave her a hug.

While the Millers worked in the kitchen, the girls finished their smores. Afterwards, they poked at the fire with their willow sticks, watching sparks blaze up into the air, pretending the orange swirls were fairy spirits set free to glide through the night sky. A gentle breeze blew in from the hills and brushed their faces with the scents of sagebrush and dry leaves. A spiraling column of sparks fled dangerously across the lawn, but fell harmlessly on the green grass before it could reach wild plants beyond the yard that might burn.

Sunset brought a chill, and the gradual death of the fire finally moved them back inside.

By the time Frank and Anna came to check, the girls had loaded a DVD and were lying on the sofa beds watching *Percy Jackson: Sea of Monsters*. Chantha hit the pause button on the remote control.

"Do you girls need anything else?" Anna asked.

The chorus of "No's" was immediate.

"Then good night," Anna said.

"Have fun," Frank added.

"Thanks Mom, Dad," Chantha said quickly, in a way that really meant: *Hurry up and leave so we can watch the rest of the movie!*

Once her parents were gone, Chantha hit the pause button, and the fantasy world of mythical creatures with magical powers returned.

After the movie, the girls lounged on the sofa beds for a while, talking about school and the coming summer break.

By ten o'clock, it was finally completely dark outside. They walked out onto the deck and stared up at the sky, in search of constellations.

"That's the Big Dipper!" Selena said proudly.

Chantha pointed to another grouping. "Isn't that Centaurus?" It did look a little like the mythological man-horse creature— that is if you had a really good imagination.

"It is," Nina confirmed. "And over there, that's Virgo. And that one over there," Nina said, pointing, "is called *Canes Venatici* after the hunting dogs used by another constellation named *Bootes*." She pointed to a jumble of stars that looked more-or-less random to Chantha and Selena.

Earlier in the day, Chantha had spent time on the Internet learning what constellations were visible this time of year. Still, she was no match for Nina. She just stared, and said, "Where did you learn all those from?"

Nina's embarrassment was immediate. It was a feeling she was no stranger to, having been called "smarty pants" and "know-it-all" plenty of times, and not just by kids. "I saw them in a book at the library," she said.

In truth, she had once leafed through an astronomy text during study hall. From that, she could picture in her mind every constellation in the northern sky, plus their Latin names. She didn't have to work hard to memorize them. She just remembered. It didn't make her feel particularly special. Just different. On this particular night, she could have easily named a dozen other constellations.

"Let's go back inside," Nina said, wanting to end the uncomfortable moment, a little worried that Chantha might ask her to name more star groups. And then resent her for knowing so many. "It's too cold out here."

Once through the French doors, they decided it was late enough to call it good. Selena took one hide-a-bed for herself. Nina and Chantha snuggled under a quilted comforter next to each other on the second bed.

After a few minutes they got over the giggling and the whispering and saying silly things and drifted off to sleep.

Around three in the morning, Nina awoke from the nightmare of riding a raft with Dan in a river filled with bunnies, while he tried to push her overboard. Fearful of returning to sleep, she slid to the edge of the mattress, gently lifted the comforter, pushed it from her body and stepped out onto the floor.

Light was softly edging through the windows from a crescent moon that hung low on the horizon. *An aching moon* she thought. *Aching just like me.*

She eased the handle to one of the French doors and stepped out onto the deck, hoping the cold night air would banish the lingering fear from her dream. Her bare feet made light tracks in the dew that had fallen on the deck. She pulled one of the chairs away from the table and sat facing away from the house, the wooden slats cold against the backs of her legs. With so much uncertainty, especially about the adoption, she fantasized for a few seconds about running away. Sadly, there was no place to run to for a girl her age. They would find her and return her to Evelyn and the awful Dan. Or, maybe the state would finally give up on home placement and send her to an orphanage. And then she would forever lose the friendship of the two girls inside.

She was on the verge of crying when she heard Chantha's voice.

"Are you okay?" Chantha had awoken and realized Nina was no longer in bed. She got up and pulled on slippers, silently pushed the door to the deck, and now stood behind her.

Nina pulled back a little sniffle before she said, "I don't know."

Chantha slid a deck chair over next to Nina's, sat down, reached an arm around Nina's shoulders, and they sat together in silence for a while.

Chantha finally asked, "What's the matter?"

"I think Dan is going to steal the bunny and make a bunch of them to sell."

"Can he do that?"

"He can and he will because he's a creep, and he doesn't care about anybody except himself."

"Can I do anything to help?"

Nina thought for a moment, and then said, "If he can't get his hands on the bunny, then he can't copy it. At least not very well." She looked into Chantha's face with sudden hope. "Would you be willing to hide the bunny at your house for a while?"

"Of course! When can you bring it over? Or, do you just want to bring it to school on Monday?"

Nina put a finger to her lips to signal silence, stood and took Chantha's hand, tugged her through the French doors, and crossed the room to where her backpack lay against a wall. Nina reached in and pulled out the bunny.

With wide eyes, Chantha whispered, "Why didn't you show us earlier?"

Nina whispered back, "I didn't plan to bring him out at all. I just didn't want to leave him where Dan could find him." She handed the bunny over to Chantha. She took him gently, as if possessed of a treasure. As she held the bunny close she said, "I feel a lump inside his chest. Have you felt that too?"

"Yes," Nina whispered back. "I think it's his heart."

Chantha ran her fingers across the bunny's chest. The lump was in the same place as a heart might be. "I'll protect him," Chantha said. "I'll find the perfect hiding place."

Suddenly, the sleepy voice of Selena came from across the room.

"What are you two doing?" There came the ruffle of bedding being pushed aside. Chantha quickly shoved the bunny back into Nina's knapsack.

Selena walked over to where the two girls stood.

Chantha said, "We went outside to look at the moon. It's up now. Do you want to go and see?"

Selena was still very sleepy. "No," she said. "I'm going to get a drink of water, and then I'm going back to bed. Are you two going to stay up?"

"No!" Nina and Chantha said in almost perfect unison.

In the morning, while the girls devoured scrambled eggs and English muffins with hot cocoa, Frank decided to pry a little, no longer satisfied that he could blindly let events play out in the Torgerson house.

"Selena, Nina, do either of you have any special plans for the summer?"

Selena jumped right in with, "Our family may be driving to California in August to visit relatives. We may even get to go to Disneyland."

"What about you, Nina?" Frank hoped to hear about the adoption.

Nina shrugged. "Nothing special, I guess."

Anna was listening, and had an inspiration. "The school sent out an email to parents this week. They've got some interesting summer courses."

Chantha realized what her mother was getting at. *Why didn't I think of that?* She pushed back her chair, and without a word ran to her room, returning with a printout.

"Mom showed it to me before you two got here." She handed the sheet to Nina. "Look at the third one."

It read: *BASIC BUSINESS PRINCIPLES - Learn the steps for starting a business. Course will emphasize use of the Internet. Each student will choose a hypothetical business product and create a marketing plan. Three weeks, on Mondays and Wednesdays from 9am to noon.*

Chantha said, "We can use the bunny for our product!"

Nina remembered the warning Frank had given about copyright protection. She looked at him, but he didn't appear to protest. Instead, he smiled with approval.

"C'mon, Nina," Chantha insisted, "it'll be fun."

Selena added, "We can use the list of all those girls who contacted me. That'll really impress the teacher."

Nina found herself caught up in the sudden enthusiasm. *Why not?* "Okay," she said. "Let's sign up and see what happens."

Anna felt relieved, as did Frank. Not only would it give Nina a positive direction for the summer, but with Chantha working closely with her on the project, it would be that much easier to glean information about how Nina was handling the impending adoption.

CHAPTER TWENTY-SIX

Charlie and Clarissa sat on the back porch of the Bosecker Inn, she with a cup of mint tea and he with a latte. The massive weeping birch on the lawn blocked all but a few beams of sunlight shafting through the gently stirring leaves, painting the edge of the porch in dancing pools of yellow.

Clarissa said, "You know her schedule. When and where do you think would be best?"

Only one option made sense to Charlie. "When she gets off the school bus in the afternoon. If you wait for her under the big oak, you could bring her back to the Bosecker to meet me."

"Good." Clarissa had hoped for sooner. Monday was three days away, and in that span of time a lot could happen—*if* the Order chose to act. "Can you keep an eye on her house in the meantime?"

"Sure," Charlie agreed.

But as dusk fell and Charlie walked past the Torgerson home, Nina's resonance was missing. He reported back to Clarissa, and there was a tense moment. "Try again in the morning," she finally said. Charlie couldn't ever remember her sounding so nervous.

149

Early on Saturday morning the pickup was still parked in the driveway. Evelyn's car was still inside the garage. The Torgersons were at home. But there was no trace of Nina's powerful resonance.

Charlie and Clarissa spent the day searching Portage, but with no luck. At sunset they again sat on the porch of the Bosecker.

"If she doesn't show up by Monday I think we have to presume something bad has happened," Clarissa said. "If she's gone, we'll need to make contact with the Torgersons. It should be me who goes. I'll be able to question them more effectively."

Charlie knew Clarissa would use the full extent of her powers to interrogate the adults.

And God help them if they have turned her over to the Order.

Mid-morning on Sunday, Charlie was sitting in the restaurant on the East Lake Road, enjoying his usual triple latte, when he felt a resonance. It came at first like a ripple across a pond, but quickly rose to the power of a tsunami. Charlie looked out the window and saw a Volvo driven by a middle aged man. In the back seat were Nina and the Asian girl. As they passed the restaurant, Nina looked nervously out the car window.

Her resonance quickly faded as the car moved on up the street. Charlie grabbed his latte and practically sprinted back to the Bosecker.

CHAPTER TWENTY-SEVEN

There were plenty of wealthy investors in America who hated paying what they thought of as unfair income taxes. The boutique investment firm Trisha Peterson worked for handled financial transactions that paid generous broker's commissions to those willing to take the risk of hiding massive assets, and the income they generated. With Trisha's charm, it proved easy to convince the rich to move their money "offshore" where large sums could be shielded from the IRS. Using her European contacts from the Order, she transferred fortunes into secret accounts, which kept both her clients and her partners very happy.

This cozy and lucrative arrangement had worked well until recently, when the U.S. Treasury began punching holes in the secrecy dikes of banks in tax haven countries. With new regulations that focused greater scrutiny on money transfers, who knew when the Feds might show up at Trisha's door with a subpoena! And then she would have to make a frantic dash to the airport for a flight to a country with no extradition treaty. Which meant being stuck in a place like Argentina for a very long time. Not an exciting prospect for a woman who enjoyed Broadway theatre, shopping on Madison Avenue, and skiing in the French Alps.

Heightened enforcement of the rules on foreign banking wasn't the only reason to move on. Coworkers had begun to compliment her a little too often on how young she looked. The praise from women, in particular, was more often than not laced with jealousy. Cosmetics could only make you look so old. It was all but impossible to hide a youthful and perfectly fit body.

New York had been kind to Trisha for eleven years, and that was enough.

So on a sweltering afternoon near the end of May, she walked into the managing partner's huge corner office and announced she was taking a long vacation. He grumbled, but Trisha was the firm's star and what Trisha wanted, Trisha got.

The next morning, she loaded those few possessions which mattered into the trunk of her powder blue Mercedes SLS coupe, turned the key to her apartment for the last time, and drove through the city streets until she reached the Holland Tunnel. By nightfall she had crossed the border between Indiana and Illinois.

It was a great relief to finally be on the road.

Since the meeting in Zurich, Pieter had been on the phone far too often, pestering her about when she might finish "the project." With the NSA—and who knew how many others— monitoring foreign calls, everything had to be discussed in code. Conversations were couched in generalities like "the project" or "our friend."

There was no safe way to share the details of her plan by phone, so she simply told Pieter she would be driving out to Washington State. He argued that he could provide a quicker way, implying a jet. But the Mercedes was an important element of Trisha's plan.

When a member of the Order disappeared, it was highly desirable for ordinary folks to believe they had died. Trisha had devised a scheme to make that seem to have happened. After she drugged the girl and stashed her somewhere near the airport, she would drive the Mercedes into the nearby Columbia River. Not at a spot where it was too deep. She needed the police to eventually find her car. When she didn't show up at a local hospital, or return to work in New York, the coroner would rule it a death by accidental drowning, with a footnote that no body was found. Since there was no spouse, child, or relative to argue the matter, there would be no pressure for a lengthy search. And who would possibly believe that someone would stage their own death by driving a Mercedes worth two hundred grand into a river! It was sweet. So she needed the car out West.

There was one other piece of the plan she would have loved to tell Pieter. A serendipitous thing had come her way, almost as if by magic. But she couldn't risk disclosure over the telephone. When he found out, even the conservative Austrian would think her brilliant. Until then, she had grown tired of him pitching her crap, even if it was phrased in the simple code they used.

So on the last phone call, when Pieter began to sound more like a whiney child than a centuries-old warrior, Trisha simply hung up.

CHAPTER TWENTY-EIGHT

Clarissa stood beneath the oak, glancing around to see if anyone was watching, knowing how out-of-place she would seem to parents at a place where their children were delivered daily.

A couple minutes later a dark blue Dodge minivan pulled to the curb and a woman in her early thirties got out. After receiving several suspicious glances in her direction, Clarissa called out, "Hello. I'm waiting for my niece Nina Haas. Are you also here for someone on the bus?"

"My two little ones," the woman replied briskly, followed by a shallow smile. She walked to join Clarissa in the shade of the oak.

"How old are they?" Clarissa asked, trying to sound interested, but not *too* interested.

"Billy is eight and Alice is ten." The woman spoke carefully, as if even this might be too much information to give a stranger.

"Those are wonderful ages," Clarissa said, with the kind of enthusiasm one might expect from anyone who truly cares about kids. "Children have so much curiosity and energy at those times in their lives." But her happy attempt at signaling safety still fell short of convincing the mother.

"Yes," the woman hesitantly agreed. "I didn't catch your name . . ."

"Clarissa," she said. "And yours?"

"Doris Troxler. I didn't know Nina had an aunt. I thought she was in foster care."

Clarissa didn't have to read Doris's mind to know what she was thinking: *I'm not certain you are who you say you are.* It was time to put an end to her fears. Clarissa focused her ability to control, and sent a message: *I am safe, and no threat to your children.* Then she offered a simple reason for her presence.

"Our family's had a rough time over the years and I'm now the only one who's left for her, and she's the only one who's left for me. I came to Portage to make sure she's doing okay."

And one final nudge: *You must have struggled with tragedies in your own life. Won't you please feel a bit of empathy for me now?*

Doris nodded, suddenly sad. From seemingly out of nowhere had come a memory, of when she was eleven, when her dog "Poochie" was struck and killed by a car. And then another memory, six years later, of her dad dying from cancer. And just three years after that, a college friend who suffered a stroke from a drug overdose. Doris was by now nearly in tears.

The troubling moment began to fade a few seconds later, as the school bus appeared on the highway.

When the doors whooshed open, first out were the Troxler kids, who ran towards their mom, the boy clutching a Spiderman lunchbox as it banged against his leg, the girl pumping hard to keep up with her little brother.

Nina stepped off the bus behind a teen-aged boy, and turned to wave to an Asian girl whose face was framed behind one of the bus windows.

Then she turned and saw Clarissa.

For an uncertain moment she stood still on the sidewalk. After the big yellow bus rumbled away, she began to walk towards the oak, slowly at first, and then more quickly.

"Well," Doris said to Clarissa, "I hope you have a wonderful visit with your Nina." She turned to her children. "Come on, you two. Daddy's home early and we're going out for pizza." Both kids yelled, "Yeah!" and they were already climbing into the minivan by the time Nina reached the oak.

Clarissa felt the warm flood of resonance. Nina also felt it, but had no way to interpret it, other than as being happy to see Clarissa.

"How is my lovely Nina Bea?" Clarissa asked, spreading her arms wide.

"I was afraid I'd never see you again," Nina said, emotion welling up inside. She dropped her book bag and wrapped her arms around Clarissa, burying her face against one shoulder.

"You never should worry about that," Clarissa said, holding Nina tight. She smoothed Nina's hair with one hand and Nina sighed and relaxed. The warmth of the sun and the chirping of birds and the sound of cars on the highway faded, until all Nina could sense was happiness. She reluctantly let go and reached down to pick up her bag.

"There's someone I want you to meet," Clarissa said. "But first, do you think your foster mom is expecting you?"

Nina usually found Evelyn at home after the bus dropped her off, working on dinner, always on the lookout for her arrival. "Probably," Nina said.

"Then you should go and tell her you want to go out to play."

"Where do I meet this person?"

"Do you know the Bosecker Inn?"

"Yes." Nina nodded, picturing the three story mansion, less than a minute away by bike, three minutes on foot.

"He and I are both staying at the Inn. Would it be possible for you to meet us there?"

"Yes," Nina said, instantly curious. Was this her husband? Would he also seem magical? And then she remembered the bunny was still at Chantha's. Would Clarissa want to see the bunny? Nina felt a sudden fear. Maybe Clarissa already knew about the bunny being on the Internet! She shouldered her book bag and said, "I'll be there as quick as I can," and ran off up the street.

Clarissa turned and walked back towards the Bosecker, puzzled about what she had just missed. *Why was Nina Bea so worried in those last few seconds?*

Dan's pickup was parked in the driveway, and it reminded Nina of how strange he'd acted after Frank Miller had dropped her off on Sunday morning. Dan avoided her all day long, running errands in the valley, and otherwise mostly holed up in his study with the door closed.

At dinner, Dan didn't look across the table at her even once. The only words he spoke, other than asking for food to be passed, was, "I'm going to do some work in the garage tonight," and this was directed solely at Evelyn. He left the table looking like a grumpy little boy who has been denied a new toy.

As Nina now entered the living room she heard Evelyn in the kitchen. Dan was nowhere in sight. Nina went to her room and dropped her bag on the bed and then came back out.

"Hi, Mom," she greeted Evelyn. This brought a smile to an otherwise stressed face.

"Hello, sweetheart," Evelyn replied, giving her a quick kiss on the forehead, before returning to the counter where she was chopping cabbage for slaw. "How was school?"

"Everyone's excited about getting out for summer break," Nina said, beginning to suspect something had happened. Evelyn was usually far more upbeat upon her arrival. "Otherwise, there's not much going on. I don't even have any homework assignments."

"Did you see your girlfriends at school today?"

"Yes," Nina replied. "We had lunch in the cafeteria."

Nina was now certain something was troubling Evelyn. Dan seemed the likely source. And as much as she wanted to take off for the Bosecker, she knew Evelyn was her best defense against Dan. Anything she could do to shore up support would be time well spent. So she gathered up a moment of patience, and instead of asking if she could go out to play, she said, "Do you need any help with dinner, Mom?"

Evelyn smiled, and her mood seemed to brighten a little. "No, sweetheart, I've got it handled."

"Are there any chores you need done?"

Evelyn turned and gave Nina a modestly suspicious look. "Well aren't you the helpful one."

Nina chose her next words carefully, trying not to sound too calculating. "You just look a little tired, and I thought you might want some extra help."

Evelyn appeared to relax a little. "It was a challenging day," she confessed. "But we'll have a nice dinner, and I'll get some good sleep tonight and be right as rain tomorrow."

Nina didn't believe Evelyn would be right as *anything* tomorrow. There was a storm approaching and his name was Dan, and both she and Evelyn were in his path.

She continued to stand, as if prepared to help should Evelyn think of something for her to do. But in her head the words *Please let me go outside* repeated over and over. And as if by magic, that's what Evelyn said.

"Why don't you go outside, sweetheart. Dinner's not going to be ready for a while."

"Thanks, Mom!" Nina flashed a grin and practically ran from the kitchen.

A minute later, Dan appeared and planted his hands on his hips. "Well?" he demanded. "Did you ask her about the bunny?"

Evelyn lifted the bowl of coleslaw and walked to the refrigerator. Without looking at Dan, she said, "No, I did not ask her. And you will not ask her either."

Dan hated being told what to do. Flustered, he left the kitchen, thinking how nice it would feel to take his 12-gauge shotgun, load it with buckshot, and go blast a bunch of quail to smithereens up by the old irrigation ditch.

Nina stood on the porch of the Bosecker and braced her hands on her knees and took a moment to catch her breath. When she pushed open the door she found Iris at the front desk, reading one of those tabloids you see in supermarket checkout lines. There was a two-headed dog on the cover. Iris looked up. "Yes?"

"I'm here to see Clarissa Cumberland," Nina said in her politest voice.

"They're in the day room." Iris pointed towards the open door beyond the desk.

Nina walked through and saw Clarissa seated in a wicker chair. And then she froze when she saw the man. It was the stranger she had seen out the bus window at school.

Clarissa stood up and so did the man. He was muscular, over six feet tall, and this made him seem even more threatening.

"Nina?" Clarissa said, seeing her hesitation. Nina cautiously took a step forward.

"This is—"

"Charlie," Nina interrupted.

Both Clarissa and Charlie lost their easy smiles.

"How did you know?" Clarissa asked. *Have I so underestimated her?*

The name had just popped into her head and went straight out her mouth before she could try and stop it. She had no idea how she *knew.*

The man now said, "My name *is* Charlie. Have we met before?" He sounded puzzled. Almost afraid.

"I don't think so," Nina replied.

"Then how did you know my name?"

"It just seemed right," she said. Almost adding that she had seen him at the bus stop, and had possibly seen him somewhere else—*or felt his presence?*—in Portage during the past few days.

"Well," Clarissa began again. "This is my friend Charlie Dozen." She looked at Charlie. "Charlie, this is Nina Beatrix Haas. I call her 'Nina Bea'."

"Nice to meet you, Nina Bea," Charlie said, with a smile that was at once charming and vulnerable. It made Nina feel a little more comfortable. A flicker of an almost-smile crossed her face. Clarissa gestured towards the padded wicker chairs, and they all sat around the small glass-topped coffee table.

Nina tried not to stare at Charlie, although she couldn't help taking little glances out of the corners of her eyes, trying to piece together what she knew.

Clarissa was still recovering from the shock of Nina knowing Charlie's name. She remembered telling it to her up at the ski lodge. But she'd been using her power at full strength to block its memory, and there was simply no way Nina Bea should now be able to dredge it up. There was certainly no emergency to have triggered its recall. And even if she had somehow dislodged the memory of the name from her subconscious, there was nothing to attach it to the man she had just met.

But nevertheless she knew!

"Charlie is an old friend of mine. I've known him since he was . . . quite young."

Nina stared for a long moment at Charlie. He appeared to be in his mid-twenties, and that didn't match up well with "old friend."

Charlie nodded, and said, "I *was* young, wasn't I." He looked at Clarissa, as if remembering a time long ago.

"Like me?" Nina asked.

"Yeah," Charlie said.

But Nina sensed he wasn't telling the truth. "Do you live near here?" she asked, trying to sound polite. But it sounded more like a lawyer cross examining a difficult witness.

"No," Charlie said, growing more uncomfortable.

Nina thought it was the truth this time. *But how could I know?*

"I live in Louisiana."

Clarissa cut in with, "I asked Charlie if he would like to spend some time with me. It's been quite a while since we've visited, and I thought it would be nice. He agreed to come up to Washington. While he was here, I thought it would be nice to introduce the two of you." Suddenly, she wanted to reveal everything. *But I can't do that.*

Nina sensed Clarissa's unease. And for the first time the lady seemed vulnerable.

Charlie tried to save the moment. "I'll be here for several days," he said. "I hope we have a chance to do some visiting."

"Okay," Nina said, reluctantly. She now wanted the conversation to end. She mostly wanted Charlie to leave so she could talk with Clarissa. But there was no obvious way to make that happen.

Clarissa saw Nina beginning to withdraw, and knew it would do more damage than good by continuing what had become a surprisingly awkward moment. "Well," she said. "I'd guess you'll be expected for dinner soon. I just wanted you to meet Charlie. How would it be if just you and I have tea here tomorrow after you get home from school?"

"Okay," Nina readily agreed. And then she looked at Charlie and attempted to be more polite than she felt. "It was nice to meet you, Mister Dozen."

"Likewise," Charlie said. He smiled. Nina smiled. And that was that.

After Nina left, Clarissa and Charlie sat in the dayroom. Neither was smiling.

"That didn't go as well as I'd hoped," Clarissa confessed.

"Agreed," Charlie said, his mind still spinning from the encounter. "She's got this power inside of her, and she senses it but she has no idea what it's all about. Did you see how quickly she figured out we weren't telling her everything?"

"Yes. I believe that I have severely underestimated her abilities." *And how many times do I have to tell myself that before the reality of it sinks in!*

"My name!"

"I know. That was stunning. I told her your name up at the ski hill, but I thought I'd entirely blocked it from her conscious thought."

"Obviously not."

Clarissa was discovering a new fear. *It was necessary to reveal nearly everything to her up at the ski lodge, just in case I'm no longer around. But the triggers for bringing it to the surface aren't meant to be pulled so easily. She remembered his name!*

"Clarissa?" Charlie said, bringing her back to the moment. "Are we sticking with the plan?"

"We have to," she said. "There's no other choice." But making Nina Bea and Charlie friends would now be far more difficult. *And maybe it won't work at all.*

With all of this came a truth. A switch inside Nina Bea had been inadvertently tripped. She was growing. *Emerging like a flower on a hot spring day.* Managing her would be more difficult . . . but also more promising.

She has the potential to grow into a leader, and not just of the Order.

<hr>

Nina had retreated to the waterfront, and now sat on the old Portage boat dock, her feet dangling inches above the water, replaying the meeting in her head. Charlie Dozen wasn't what she had expected. She had imagined a man near Clarissa's age, maybe a few years older. A best friend; a traveling companion; perhaps a husband. But this man looked half Clarissa's age. Nina was having a hard time figuring out why the two of them would be lodged together at the Bosecker. The way they spoke, the way they looked at each other, none of it added up to marriage, or even romance.

So why did Clarissa ask Charlie Dozen to come, and why was it necessary for her to introduce him to me? And what was he doing at the school?

Nina thought back to the moment when she had first seen Charlie from the bus. She had not so much seen as *felt* his presence. When she looked out the bus window directly at him, he had turned his head away. The revelation came that it hadn't been an accident he was there.

Clarissa sent Charlie Dozen to watch me!

Nina's head hurt at this thought. She wanted to believe she was imagining it. Because if she wasn't, it meant Clarissa had more in mind than just being her friend. But what? And why?

I'm a thirteen-year-old orphan. Who would care?

Another connection now jiggled into place.

The man who was standing with Vice Principal Nedrickson. I felt something similar with him to what I feel around Charlie and Clarissa.

Nina stood up and kicked at the planking with the toe of her left sneaker, working free a large splinter. When it broke off, she picked it up and hurled it out into the lake. It landed with a small splash, scaring two ducks into flight.

Enough thinking for today. It was dinner time.

Nina left the dock and headed home. She wasn't excited about facing Dan across the dining room table, but there was no avoiding it. There was also no avoiding the questions she would need to ask Clarissa at tomorrow's tea. She just hoped Charlie Dozen wouldn't be there to complicate things.

CHAPTER TWENTY-NINE

Liesel found Pieter Silberhof brooding in the Zurich conference room. Sitting at the table with his head bowed, almost as if in prayer. As she closed the door and walked to the table, his head came up like a sleepy cobra.

"Where have you been?" he demanded.

"Shopping," Liesel said. She turned on the ball of her left foot in a little pirouette to show off the charcoal gray English tweed suit she'd purchased that morning. "Do you like it?"

"It's lovely," Pieter said dismissively. "And how nice to know you have nothing better to do than to go shopping for clothes." He rose from his chair and walked to the window and looked down at the river, clasping his hands behind his back and pretending to ignore her for the moment. As if speaking only for his own benefit, he said, "Maybe that's what the American is doing even now. She's off shopping for some pretty bit of skirt. How else can one explain the delay?"

"Pieter, it's only been three days."

He spun around. "I offered her a jet and she turned it down. She's driving across the entire country to get to where she needs to go!" His hands were now flung up in wild exasperation. "Does she not understand the importance of what we are doing?"

Liesel pulled a chair from the table and sat down. "We have to trust her, Pieter. And I'm certain she understands how important this is."

He stood with his back to the window, momentarily steeled into silence. Unable to comprehend how she could be so patiently accepting of this incredible turn of events.

Liesel made one last attempt at reason.

"We have asked her to kidnap a thirteen-year-old child. That's a serious crime, and if she is caught she'll go to prison for a long time. Where she won't age. How well do you think that would turn out for the Order?"

Pieter stubbornly continued to vent his frustration. "I just wish we knew what her plan was. It would make me a great deal more comfortable."

Liesel silently agreed. The only thing they knew for certain about Tricia's plan was that she was driving across the country. Such an effort seemed inconceivable to most Europeans, who considered a trip lasting over an hour to be something of a journey. Driving three thousand miles was nothing short of bizarre. But . . . she was an American, and Americans sometimes handled situations differently. *Very differently*, in this instance. They were stuck with the mystery of what she was up to, at least for the moment. It was that simple.

"Pieter, she will call soon—hopefully—and we will send the jet for her and the girl and everything will be fine. Now, if you don't need me for anything other than to listen to you complain, I'm going to walk up to the Kunsthaus and check out the Giacometti exhibit before it closes."

The Kunsthaus was Zurich's modern art museum. Located near the hilltop above Old Town, it was within easy walking distance of the Order's building.

Pieter raised a skeptical eyebrow, and gave a slight headshake of disbelief.

"This is the last day for the exhibit," Liesel insisted, hoping to lighten his mood. "You should walk up with me, if for no other reason than to get some air."

"No," Pieter replied stubbornly. "But please, by all means, take yourself up the hill and enjoy the exhibition. Heaven forbid you should miss the watercolors of a second class painter. Be sure to have a nice lunch in the museum cafe." He turned again to face the window. In a few seconds he heard Liesel's chair pushed back and then the door to the conference room open and softly close.

As Pieter gazed out across the river at the jagged horizon of the Alps, he finally committed to a decision he'd been struggling with. Just because they'd handed capture of the girl over to the American didn't mean he couldn't arrange for a back-up plan in case she failed. There still was time to make special arrangements.

Pieter descended the stairs to the basement where his suitcase was already packed, then ordered a cab to take him to Zurich's main train station. When he arrived, he went to the Reisebüro travel agency beneath the high arched roof of the main hall. A middle-aged man with close-cropped blonde hair waived him over to a desk.

"May I help you?"

"Yes," Pieter said. "First class ticket to Wilhelmshaven, please."

The port city was Germany's largest harbor on the northern sea. The docks district had a dicey reputation; a place where someone wanting to mix things up could always find willing participants. It was the perfect place for the Order's most inglorious member to now be living. Someone Pieter urgently wanted to talk to in person.

As he stepped aboard the DB Bahn first class passenger car, Pieter wondered what it would be like to see Gunther again.

CHAPTER THIRTY

As Pieter's nighttime train sliced northward through the heart of Germany, Nina, Chantha and Selena sat in a triangle facing each other on the school lawn, beneath a towering weeping willow. It was "summer celebration week" and students had the option of the cafeteria or a sack lunch on the lawn. Nina wanted to talk business and didn't want the cafeteria's distractions.

"Selena, did you change your password on Facebook?"

"Yes," Selena said. "And I blocked Dan like you asked. But he's just going to get friended on someone else's page, and he'll still be able to follow the bunny requests. It's crazy who some people let into their circles." Her words practically oozed with disgust.

Nina was tempted to remind Selena of her own huge Facebook following. It seemed foolish to open your life up to that many people. And for that very reason, Nina didn't have a Facebook account. But sometimes you just accepted things your friends did, even if you wouldn't do them yourself. *You take the whole person.*

That is the true meaning of friendship. Besides, all of those friend links were now going to come in handy.

"Good," she said, turning to Chantha. "Your dad said there were legal problems with copying the bunny. I may have a solution."

Chantha and Selena scooted in closer, to where their knees almost touched.

"What?" Chantha asked, excited.

Nina's voice dropped. "I can't tell you yet."

"Please!" Selena pleaded.

"Shush!" Chantha scolded.

"Just give us some idea," Selena said, now much softer. She still felt terrible about putting the bunny up on the Internet, and desperately wanted to make up for her "greatest mistake ever."

Nina decided maybe giving a little information wouldn't hurt. "Well, first of all, remember me telling you that I promised the person who gave me the bunny I wouldn't tell who gave it to me?"

Both girls nodded.

"She returned yesterday, and I'm meeting with her after school today." Nina looked at Selena. "You can't tell anyone about this, Selena. Do you understand? Absolutely nobody."

Selena nodded solemnly. Even as her head bobbed up and down, she remembered telling the priest about the bunny during confession. *But he can't tell anyone what I said, so that doesn't count . . . does it?* She hoped her face wasn't turning red.

"I promise too," Chantha said.

Nina already trusted Chantha, but she gave her a nod of approval just the same. She turned back to Selena, and said, "I need you to create a list of the email addresses for everyone who is interested in buying a bunny."

Easy enough for Selena. "I'll have it ready in a couple days," she said.

"Good." Nina turned back to Chantha. "Would you please ask your father if I can talk to him again?"

"Of course. When?"

"Tomorrow after school if he has the time."

"Okay." Chantha eased back, aching to share her own news. She'd found the perfect hiding place for the bunny. But she didn't want to tell Nina in front of Selena.

On the bus ride home. That's when I'll tell her.

With their business now completed, the girls relaxed. Nina reached for a carton of chocolate milk. Selena tore open her bag of chips. Chantha crunched into an apple.

In the tree above, a Goldfinch clutched at one of the stringy branches, its yellow feathers brilliant against the willow's spring green. A bumblebee landed on a nearby dandelion and began working among the delicate filaments. The girls grinned at each other. The game was on!

For the rest of the day Nina found it nearly impossible to focus on what her teachers were saying. One part of her mind insisted there were mysterious things afoot, and that she was at the center of some massive struggle. Another voice insisted that she was completely imagining all of this. She was, after all, only a girl of thirteen, who didn't even have real parents. So what possible interest could Clarissa—a woman who charmed squirrels!—or Charlie—a strange Indian!—have in a foster child? But still, they did seemed *very* interested.

When the final buzzer sounded, Nina sprinted down the hallway and out to the sidewalk. Chantha joined her a minute later.

When Mrs. Kennedy pulled up, the girls were first onboard. The bus was barely half-full, and they sat in the back, away from prying ears.

"I want to tell you where I hid the bunny," Chantha said, as the bus pulled onto the East Lake Road.

Nina leaned in close.

"You know that maple tree with the swing in our back yard?"

"Yes." Nina pictured the old maple with its four huge branches spreading above the ground. A thick rope with a round wooden seat hung from the largest branch.

"Right beneath the swing there's a rough patch of dirt."

"Yeah."

"I took a gallon jar with a metal lid and put the bunny inside and then I dug a hole directly under the swing and buried the jar." She had been careful to pack down the dirt so it looked exactly like it was before she dug.

Nina pictured the bunny, inside a jar, alone in the dark. For a second she felt his loneliness. But then . . . maybe it wasn't so bad. Bunnies slept underground in burrows. And even if the Miller's house were to burn down, the bunny would be safe. Besides, who would think to dig in Chantha's back yard?

"It's perfect," she finally said.

Chantha smiled, relieved. She had been worried that her choice might not be quite what Nina imagined as an ideal hiding spot.

When the bus stopped in Portage, the girls hugged and Nina promised to report about the meeting with Clarissa.

The problem of making up an excuse to go out and "play" vanished when she found that Dan's pickup and Evelyn's car were both gone. She ditched her knapsack in her room and ran out to the garage, saddled onto her bike, and pedaled over to the Bosecker, hiding the ten-speed behind a massive lilac bush alongside the Inn.

Clarissa was waiting in the same wicker chair she'd sat in the day before, sipping an iced mint tea.

"Hello, Nina Bea," Clarissa said. "Would you like a tea?"

"No, but thank you." Nina sank nervously into a chair. The moment she had both hoped for and dreaded had arrived. "I need to tell you something about the bunny."

"What is that?"

"One of my friends, her name is Selena, took a picture of the bunny and put it up on the Internet on her Facebook page. She wanted to find out where the bunny was made, because she wanted one of her own. But everyone started to share the image of the bunny, and now thousands of people have seen it."

Clarissa took a sip of tea, happy Nina had chosen the truth. She nodded for her to continue.

Nina dreaded the question she now needed to ask, because if Clarissa said "Yes" it would put an end to any hope of selling bunnies.

"Is there a company that made the bunny?"

"No," Clarissa said. "This one was made a very long time ago, by hand. It's one of a kind."

"Whew!" Nina said. And then, realizing how quickly she had said *Whew* without any explanation as to why this was important, she felt embarrassed.

"Is that all you needed to know?" Clarissa asked.

"No," Nina said. But the next question made her just as nervous as the last one had.

"Most of the kids who saw the photo of the bunny want to buy one. I think selling copies would be a good way to make money. But I was told by a lawyer—he's my best friend Chantha's dad—that you can't copy and sell something unless you have permission from the owner of the copyright." She swallowed hard. "Since it's your bunny, I need to ask if it's okay for me to copy it." There. She had gotten it out.

Clarissa replied calmly, as if only the smallest of favors had been asked. "You are now the owner of the bunny. If you feel you need to ask my permission, you may certainly have it. But the bunny is yours to do with as you wish." From the happiness in Nina Bea's eyes, Clarissa knew she had won points. *And isn't it ironic that I feel I must win points. But I know I must.*

"If I needed something in writing, for where the bunny came from, and giving me the right to make more, would you be willing to sign a legal paper?"

"Of course," Clarissa said, suddenly uneasy. But she would still sign whatever she was asked to sign. *So I won't* lose *points.*

The bunny issue decided, Nina now had a more delicate question. As Clarissa took a sip of tea, Nina asked, "Who is Charlie?"

Clarissa's teacup rattled nervously as she set it back on the saucer. The answer had to be as much of the truth as possible. Nina Bea would sense an outright lie. And later on, she would remember this conversation.

"Charlie is a warrior," Clarissa said, watching Nina Bea's intensity turn to confusion.

"A warrior?"

"Yes. He was born a Shoshone Indian, and he grew up learning to be a warrior."

"Why is he here?"

"Because I invited him."

"Because of me?"

And now the truth revealed its thorns.

"Yes."

"Why?"

Clarissa thought she saw an opportunity, and made a mistake.

"This all began thirteen years ago when I met your mother."

Nina's eyes grew wide.

Clarissa instantly knew she'd said the wrong thing. She attempted to cover with an explanation.

"When she and your father died, I made a commitment to find you and help you, if I could, when you were older."

This only dug a deeper hole. And now, a flood of questions rose in Nina's mind. She held her silence, mostly from shock.

Clarissa continued while she still had the chance, hoping the excuse she now invented would work.

"When I finally met you three weeks ago, and learned you were having trouble with your foster father, I decided to ask for assistance from someone who could come to your rescue if necessary. That someone is my warrior friend Charlie. You don't need to ask him for help if you don't want to. But he's there if you need him."

Nina barely heard a word Clarissa was saying.

"You knew my mom?" It came out as an accusation. Why hadn't Clarissa told her this before?

"Barely," Clarissa said.

For Nina, even the tiniest glimmer about her mom felt like the clouds parting and the sun shining down.

"Where?"

"In Spokane."

"How?"

Clarissa struggled for a truth not too revealing . . . but still the truth.

"We met by accident, while we were both shopping at a mall. It was a crowded day and we ended up sharing a table in a restaurant. You were just six months old and weren't with her at the time. It was small talk mostly, about things like the weather and what was on sale. She told me how proud and lucky she was to have you, her first child. Shortly after that, she and your father were in the accident. When I learned you had been with a babysitter, and not in the car, I decided to try to find you when you were older."

Clarissa waited to see if her story would be accepted; or would Nina Bea challenge why someone (who had spent only a few minutes with her mother at a mall) would search her out so many years later?

Nina sensed Clarissa had mostly spoken the truth. But there was something which hadn't been said. Wasn't there? Momentarily overwhelmed and confused, she clung defensively to silence.

The fractured moment lasted far too long. Clarissa finally broke it by asking, "Is there anything else you want to ask me?"

Too many thoughts were colliding in her head. "No," Nina said in a quiet voice. Something was very out of place, and she needed to figure out what it was. For now, she had permission to proceed with the bunny project.

I can always come back tomorrow and ask her about my mom.

For Clarissa, there was still one thing too important not to mention.

"Nina Bea, there is something you must know about your bunny."

"What?"

"It has a lump in its chest. Have you felt it?"

"Yes."

"It's something very precious. I've always called it the bunny's heart. But it's actually a black pearl. If you take the bunny apart to make copies, be sure to safeguard that pearl."

"A pearl?"

"Yes. It was a gift my father gave to someone he loved. It came back to him, and he put it inside the bunny when he had it made for me."

"Okay. I'll be careful," Nina said. But this too would need explaining!

After Nina left, Clarissa considered her next step, and the unavoidable risks it would bring. She would have to trust Charlie to protect Nina, while she returned to San Jose. Valerie had to be told who and what she was. She had to be asked which side she would choose. And . . . if she would be willing to help.

CHAPTER THIRTY-ONE

Images from the new dream didn't vanish when Nina woke up. She remembered her mother and Clarissa sitting in a mall restaurant, talking about her future.

From the moment she awoke, she was unable to concentrate on anything but the dream. It was the hardest thing in the world to walk to the bus stop and wait with the other kids, rather than just skip school and run over to the Bosecker.

When the bus arrived, there was Chantha, looking out the window and waving hello. Reluctantly, Nina climbed aboard.

She came close to leaving in the middle of her second period class; just standing up and running to catch the transit bus to Portage. Aching to ask Clarissa everything she knew about her mother. From how her mom had been dressed, to what her voice sounded like, to how her hair was cut. And had she said anything about Nina's father?

So when the school bus dropped her off that afternoon, Nina dashed straight to the Bosecker without even considering whether Evelyn might be waiting for her at home.

When she bounded up the steps of the old mansion and pushed through the door, only to have Iris tell her, "She's gone out of town for a few days," Nina was beyond upset. She pleaded with Iris to let her use a phone. Iris came from behind the desk, took her into the dayroom, and said as long as it wasn't long distance she could use the one provided for guests. Nina assured her it was a local call, and Iris drifted back to the front desk.

"Chantha," Nina cried, tears streaming down her flushed cheeks. "She's not here! She's gone! What am I going to do?"

Earlier at school, Nina had told Chantha about Clarissa having known her mom. She promised to report everything from her next meeting. Now, there was nothing but desperation.

"She'll be back soon, won't she?" Chantha asked, hopefully.

"But I can't wait!"

"What about that Charlie guy?"

Nina had also told Chantha what little she knew about Charlie Dozen, describing how strange she felt around him.

"He doesn't know anything about my mom!"

"Not about your mom. I meant about Clarissa. Wouldn't he know where she's gone and how long she'll be gone for?"

Why didn't I think of that? But the answer was easy. *Because I'm upset and not thinking straight.*

"Okay," Nina said, wiping tears away with the back of her hand. "I'll ask."

She hung up and went to ask Iris if Charlie was around. Iris just shrugged and said, "I think he's off riding his new hog. I don't have any idea where he is right now. But he should be back for dinner around six."

"Hog?"

"Oh, sorry. I meant motorcycle. He bought a Harley Davidson." Iris got a dreamy look. "It's blue with white trim, and a high hammock seat for a passenger in back. It's like . . . wow!"

Nina figured Iris was at that moment picturing herself on the back of the "hog" with her hands wrapped around Charlie's waist and the wind blowing back her hair. Nina thanked her for the use of the phone, but as she walked out of the Bosecker, it was clear Iris was still in dreamland, seeing herself riding off into some delusional sunset with Dreamboat Charlie.

Pfffffffff!

By the time Nina reached home she was practically exploding. No way was she going to be able to last through dinner, with Dan giving her the skunk-eye while Evelyn sat like a nervous chipmunk. That's what it had come to since she'd hidden the bunny. Dan in a permanent sulk. Evelyn afraid of her own shadow.

Nina wanted out. At least for the evening.

When she came inside and saw Evelyn walking out from the kitchen, the words that involuntarily leapt from her mouth were, "Evelyn, may I go over to Chantha's for dinner tonight?"

Evelyn got a peculiar look, and in that instant Nina realized she had called her by her first name rather than calling her "Mom."

Big mistake.

Evelyn's face seemed to wilt. She hesitantly said, "Well, if it's okay with the Millers, I suppose so. I can drive you over to Dartmouth if you want."

"That's okay," Nina said. "There's a bus in a few minutes. I'm sure Mr. Miller will drive me back."

Evelyn looked even more disappointed. "Okay, sweetheart. But all you need to do is call me for a ride home. I don't want you on the bus after it gets dark. You never know who might be riding at night."

"Okay, Mom. I promise I'll call if I need a ride." Nina hoped using "Mom" would ease things. But it just made it even more obvious that her predilection was for "Evelyn" and not "Mom."

Evelyn politely retreated to the kitchen. Nina was left with no choice but to immediately turn and walk out the front door.

By the time she finally reached the Miller's house she was again in tears. Both Frank and Anna were still at work, so it was safe for Nina to totally break down.

She ended up sitting on the couch in the front room, crying her heart out. Chantha brought her a glass of water, and now sat beside her, patiently trying to calm her down.

"I can't believe she left without telling me! How could she do that? How could she tell me she knew my mom, and then just disappear?"

It really did seem crummy to tell a thirteen-year-old orphan you met her mom, and then vanish. But one of Chantha's best traits was forgiveness, and she now tried to find a reason for the sudden exit.

"Maybe there was an emergency?"

"Why didn't she at least leave me a note?"

"I don't know, Nina." It sounded entirely reasonable. Just a simple note: *Dear Nina, I've been called away for something urgent. I'll be back in three days. I'll share more with you about your mom when I return.*

Nina's sadness now began to morph into distrust. If this was the way Clarissa was going to treat her, who cared if she charmed squirrels? A new thought occurred. Clarissa had only known her mom for, like, a few minutes, right? So what could she really report from that tiny amount of time they had spent together?

"Maybe I don't ever want to see her again," Nina said, a fierce look coming to her face.

Chantha recognized that look. It wasn't often Nina got into a mood like this. But once she made up her mind about something—good or bad—it was difficult to get her turned around. The fact that she was almost always right made this even more of a challenge. Still, Chantha tried.

"Are you sure?"

Nina felt the urge to cry again, pushed it away into some dark corner of her mind, and said, "I don't know what I should do. I'm just tired of being confused. And it's not just Clarissa. It's Dan too. He's such a loser." Nina looked up at Chantha, her stubbornness resolving to a hard edge. "We are going to find a way to make bunnies and then we are going to sell them to all those people on Selena's list. And when we've got all that money, I'm going to find some better place to live."

It was Chantha's turn to worry. "You aren't going to leave the valley, are you?"

Nina realized what she'd said, and now reached out and took Chantha's hand.

What do I really want?

The answer was simple. She wanted to be loved. And not just because she filled a space in Evelyn's empty basket of needs.

"I don't want to go away," she said. "I can't imagine losing you and Selena." But it was really Chantha that she most feared losing. The tears again came freely, and Chantha held her for a long time before Nina stopped crying.

CHAPTER THIRTY-TWO

Charlie went for a long ride on his new bike, and was sweaty as he breezed past Iris at the reception desk, intent upon a shower before dinner. Her words caught him just as he was stepping into the dayroom.

"That girl was here earlier."

He stopped, turned. "Girl?"

"The one who came to visit Ms. Cumberland."

"Nina?"

Iris held onto the moment before answering, enjoying Charlie's full attention.

"Yes," she finally said. "She was here around three-forty."

Charlie walked back to the desk and stood face to face with Iris, who was suddenly sorry she'd been so flippant. For the first time he didn't seem at all attractive. More like . . . scary.

"What did she want?" Charlie's intensity was ramped up in a way Iris had never seen, and would likely never see again. She didn't hesitate to reply, and her words tumbled out in a hurry.

"She wanted to see Ms. Cumberland, and I told her she had gone away for a few days. She asked to use the phone. I let her use the guest phone in the dayroom." Iris felt a cold shiver run down her spine as Charlie's eyes flared a little wider.

"Who did she call?"

"I didn't listen. I'm sorry. I don't know who she called." Iris's upper lip began to twitch. It was a tic she got when she was really nervous. She bit hard at the edge, but that just made it worse. Charlie noticed—a warrior always notices—but he continued to focus upon Iris's eyes. "*The windows to your soul*," Shakespeare had called the eyes.

"And?" he prompted.

"She came back from the dayroom after using the phone and asked for you."

The first decent chance I get to establish some kind of bond with the girl, and I'm off riding!

"Look, I'm sorry," Iris said, beginning to shiver even though it was warm in the lobby. "I told her you would probably be back around six for dinner." Her eyes were becoming flashbulb glassy.

Charlie took all of this in, realized he was a fraction away from frightening poor Iris to the point of a brain hemorrhage, and eased back a notch. Punishing her would accomplish nothing.

"Is that all?" he continued in an almost forgiving voice. Iris's heartbeat slowed from something like one hundred seventy per minute, to around one thirty.

"Yes, I think so." She struggled to remember if there was anything else the girl had said, but it was nearly impossible to think with him staring at her. "She just left after that," she blurted out, then hurried to add, "She seemed kind of upset, I guess."

Charlie's eyes turned up towards the ceiling, breaking the lock with Iris's eyes. What a relief to be unchained from that!

"Thank you, Iris," Charlie said, turning abruptly towards the dayroom. As he walked away, he said over his shoulder, "Please tell me immediately if the girl—if *Nina*—comes back."

"Yes, of course Mr. Dozen."

Iris would never again think of him as *Charlie the cool Indian dude with the hot motorcycle.* Not after ninety seconds of feeling like she had been spun around inside a tornado.

Charlie stood under a cold shower and imagined how Nina must have felt. Before leaving, Clarissa had told him about her last meeting with Nina, and in particular about confessing to have met her mother. Now, Nina had come seeking precious information she'd never expected to have. When she discovered Clarissa was gone, it would have been massively upsetting. Charlie suspected the disappointment would settle not only upon Clarissa, but also upon himself.

In that emotionally fractured moment, Charlie found himself hating his new motorcycle.

CHAPTER THIRTY-THREE

Clarissa's meeting with Valerie began well, with Valerie obviously pleased to see her again so soon. But as they settled into chairs around the lacquered table, Valerie's first question was, "Please tell me more about this club you call the Order."

Clarissa made a brief prayer to ancient spirits, before opening with, "It's not so much of a club as it is a collection of people who naturally fit together."

"Meaning?" Valerie edged forward in her chair.

Clarissa took a deep breath, knowing she was stepping off a ledge from an unknown height.

"Each member of the Order is born with a special skill set that is beyond what most people have—even people who are gifted with great abilities. For instance, a member might be able to communicate with animals, but not like a circus trainer communicates with a show horse, or a zookeeper with a favorite monkey. These members can actually exchange information with animals. Because of this, even a wild animal's natural reactions can be overcome. Imagine someone who can walk up and pet a tiger as easily as ordinary people pet a dog."

Valerie settled back in her chair, shifting uncomfortably. "Is that all there is? Communicating with animals?"

Clarissa remembered how it had been with Charlie back in Berlin, over a hundred years ago. *Upset* didn't begin to describe what he'd been like on discovering who he was and what his future would be like.

"No. There's more. As I said, each member usually has only one skill, although we are all very good at sensing danger, and most of us are very sociable when we choose to be."

"What else?"

"Some are good at understanding the medicinal uses of plants. Others are exceptionally charming, to the point they can get normal people to do almost anything." Clarissa decided not to mention that a few members were warriors—equals to the greatest martial arts experts in the world. The situation was awkward enough.

"I still don't see the point. All you're saying is there are a few people who are exceptional at doing certain things."

Clarissa settled in for the big one. "It's much more, actually. Let me give you an example. Remember the last time I was here? You were given no advanced notice that your receptionist had set up a meeting with me."

"Yes."

"Tina didn't tell you I was going to be here."

"No, she didn't."

"And that was unusual for her not to tell you, wasn't it?"

"It certainly was." Valerie had spoken to Tina at length, explaining the necessity of knowing who would be waiting for her when she arrived at the office. Tina had nodded and agreed, and then in a way that was completely out of character, she had continued to insist that what she had done with Clarissa was okay.

As if work rules didn't apply in this one circumstance. Tina was a bright girl. She knew the rules perfectly well. Valerie had already begun to think of looking for someone more . . . disciplined.

"I ordered Tina not to contact you."

"You *what?*"

"I told her not to contact you by phone or email."

Valerie began to be upset. "Why?" she demanded.

"I think you'll understand why in a minute. But for now, understand that it was not something Tina would have ever done on her own. She was merely following my command."

It was here the meeting began to go sideways. Clarissa ordering her staff around crossed a line, and Valerie suddenly wanted this meeting to come to an end. Whether or not Clarissa had this power she claimed, Valerie would never let anyone close to her if they thought it okay to push her employees around in contradiction to her direct orders.

"Are you finished? Because I think I've heard about enough." Valerie was ready to send Clarissa away with directions never to come back.

Clarissa felt the resentment and resistance building. There might not come another chance. It was time to drive home the reality, whether or not Valerie found it pleasant.

"No, there's more," she said. And then she opened the can of worms with an analogy.

"Imagine an assembly line for cars. Nearly every car coming off the line has at least a few defects. Maybe the upholstery on one seat isn't sewn exactly straight. An engine part has a flaw, and in two years it will fail and leave the driver temporarily stranded until a tow truck arrives. It's like that with people. Some are born with bad teeth, poor eyesight, weak hearing. Others will develop diabetes or heart disease at an early age. And sometimes, really bad things happen, like cancer."

Valerie now looked totally confused. Clarissa took the plunge. "But every so often, one car rolls off the assembly line and it is perfect. No parts with defects. Every nut and bolt tightened just right. And for that rare, perfect car, you can expect to drive it for much longer than you would other cars from the same assembly line. Instead of two hundred thousand miles, you might be able to drive this "perfect" car for a million miles. If, of course, you don't get into an accident . . . and if you change the oil regularly." This last comment was meant to lighten the moment.

It didn't.

Valerie was still listening, but also beginning to look more angry than confused. "People aren't cars," she said flatly.

"No," Clarissa agreed. "But once in a while a person is born and their body is perfectly balanced. They never get sick. They age very slowly. They are like that perfect car coming off the assembly line."

Valerie was hunching up her shoulders and there was a defiant look on her face. "So what does this have to do with the group you belong to?"

And here it was. The moment of truth.

"People of the Order have perfectly balanced bodies. They can expect to remain healthy and live . . . for a very long time."

"How long?"

"Hundreds of years. *If* they don't get into an accident. We still die. Just not as soon as regular folks."

And now there was complete disbelief. Valerie wasn't dealing with someone special. She was dealing with a nutcase. *People who live forever? People who never get sick? People with special powers?*

"Well, I'm not interested in joining," she said abruptly. "Besides," and here she chuckled, "it sounds like you've got to be born into this society of yours. And since I wasn't born into your special group, that leaves me out." She was about to tell Clarissa that the meeting was at an end when Clarissa interrupted with,

"But you were."

"Were what?"

"You were born into the Order."

Now the woman was talking nonsense. And Valerie could prove it.

"How could you even know something like that? You haven't had me tested. And besides, I'm only thirty-four years old. So how could you possibly know that I'm going to live for hundreds of years?"

Now it was all wrong. This was exactly why the Order waited until someone was at least in their forties. Time was the best proof. You stare into the mirror and you look twenty-two, but your birth certificate says you are forty-eight, and you realize there is definitely something wrong. But the Order had never found a biological test to make things easy.

There was one way to tell, if you knew what you were looking for. It was a highly amplified version of what regular folks called *chemistry*—the feeling two people who meet for the first time have that says they are going to be friends. But how did one explain *resonance*?

Clarissa tried.

"Remember when you first saw me at the art museum?"

"Yes," Valerie said, now just playing along until this woman ran out of steam and could be shuttled out the door, by security if necessary.

"You immediately took a liking to me."

"Yes."

Unfortunately! How could I have been so dense?

"That instant liking is what we call 'resonance.' Members of the Order recognize each other by the way they *feel* when they come close. It's as if our body chemistries are totally in synch."

"So you're telling me that because I took a liking to you I should accept that I'm some kind of immortal. That I've got special powers, and this feeling I had of 'liking you' is proof? Wow! Do I also get a special membership card? A costume? A decoder ring. And isn't there supposed to be a secret handshake?" Valerie uttered a crazed, dismissive laugh.

Tilting towards disaster, Clarissa now saw just one way to prove she was telling the truth.

"I know it must sound remarkable—"

"Remarkable? No, it actually sounds totally absurd!"

Clarissa looked around the office and spotted a window with a handle. *Is there any other way?* But she couldn't think of one. Not without calling in Tina, or someone else from Valerie's staff, and making them do something crazy like stand on their head in a corner. A stunt like that lacked dignity. And in Valerie's state of mind she would find some way to explain it. Hypnosis, perhaps. But there was another way, a far more compelling proof. Clarissa pointed towards the window.

"Does that open?"

Valerie looked to where Clarissa's finger now pointed. It was the window she used when she wanted a bit of fresh air.

"Yes," she said, puzzled and thrown off balance by the sudden shift of focus.

Clarissa stood up and walked across the room. Valerie watched her until she realized Clarissa meant to open it. "Hey," she said. "What are you doing? Stop that!"

Clarissa said, "Come over here, please." It was purely a command.

Valerie hadn't intended to do anything this woman asked, but now found herself standing up, quite involuntarily, and walking over to the window that Clarissa had by now swung wide open. She was staring down into the green space, four stories below, at a large Bay tree.

"Do you see the three birds in that tree?" Clarissa asked.

Valerie nodded, and suddenly her stomach felt queasy. It seemed the room had filled with electricity.

"Please pick one."

"What?"

"Please pick one of those birds." It was said politely, but it was a command nevertheless.

Valerie looked down. There were three olive-and-yellow goldfinches on a high branch.

"Those?" She pointed to the branch.

"Yes. Just pick one," Clarissa insisted.

"Alright. The one highest up, near the end."

Clarissa stared down and focused her attention upon that one finch. Suddenly, it hopped up and down, spread its wings, and launched. With wings beating hard, it flew up in nearly a straight line directly towards the open window. When it reached the glass it hovered briefly and then landed on the metal frame; hopped onto the glass; slid down inside; the wings beat twice and it landed on the open palm Clarissa extended.

At that point Valerie fainted.

She was out for just a minute. When she came to she was breathing heavy, her face flushed. Her entire body tingled, as if lava were shooting through her veins.

Clarissa had caught her as she collapsed, and now cradled her head in her lap, kneeled on the carpet. "I'm sorry," she said. "But I needed you to know."

Valerie looked around, realized she was on her back, sat up like spring steel. She stared at Clarissa for a second, put out her hands to push her away, stood up and backed away in terror. All Clarissa could do now was to watch and hope. If she reached out with her powers, it would only do more damage.

"Who are you?" Valerie said, frightened almost to the point of panic.

"The only name that truly matters is 'Clarissa.' But as I told the girl I am desperately trying to protect, at one time or another the names that have counted for me are: Clarissa Julia Antonia Alexandria Cumberland."

"No," Valerie said, wiping away tears with the back of her hand, carefully forming each word. "I mean WHO . . . ARE . . . YOU?"

There was no way to cushion the blow. *Gods of my father please help me now . . .*

"I was born over two thousand years ago during the time of the Roman Republic. My family was wealthy, but ultimately unable to protect me because I did not age. I was forced to give up my patrician way of life and flee Rome, going into hiding near the end of the reign of the emperor Augustus. I was moved from Rome by a group who called themselves the *Osservatore*, which means 'Watchers' in English, and sheltered in Tuscany before fleeing to what is today known as the Black Forest in southern Germany. I was delivered to a woman from the Germanic branch of the Order, who called themselves the *Beobachter*, which in German also means 'Watchers.' They sheltered and educated me in what is today Zurich, Switzerland, where the Order has been based since the beginning of the third century B.C. I eventually became the leader of the Order because of my somewhat unique skills and abilities. Now I'm considered a renegade. And I'm desperately in need of help."

Valerie was staring as if it had been Clarissa who had launched from the tree and flown up to her window.

Clarissa barreled on, knowing this was her best—and perhaps her only—chance to tell Valerie everything she needed to know. But at the same time sensing it wasn't going to work out like she'd hoped. In fact, just the opposite. It was turning into a disaster.

"There is change coming to the Order, whether they like it or not. The information age—the age you specialize in, Valerie—is eventually going to reveal our existence. And if we don't act to control the release of that information, it will destroy the Order. Billionaires and governments will begin picking us off, one by one, hoping to unravel our genetic code to discover the secret of eternal life."

Valerie didn't want to accept what she was hearing. But the bird . . .

"Is that what . . . *we* . . . are? The genetic equivalent of a live-forever pill? And if it's that, why not just give them some DNA and have it done with and over!"

"No. As I explained, we are like the car which rolls off the assembly line perfectly put together. It's all just an accident."

"How do you know?"

"Because members of the Order have children from time to time. Every child I've ever known that was born to a member of the Order, whether it was the father or the mother, or even if both were members, has lived a normal life span. We simply don't breed true."

But Nina Bea's mother had the gift. And so does she. And that can't possibly be a coincidence.

Clarissa had the math skills, along with all of the other talents, and it was easy to calculate the probabilities. The chance of Nina Bea being accidentally born a member, to a mother who was also a member, was roughly two billion times two billion. It made winning the lottery seem like a certainty by comparison.

And this is the one thing I can never let become general knowledge. Because if the Order learns she might breed true, the distance between heaven and hell will seem like a daytrip in comparison to how far they will go to find and control her. To say nothing of what regular people would do for the chance to breed immortality into their families!

Valerie backed away another step.

"I don't want this."

"You have no choice."

"I certainly do. I can choose to live my life in any way I please. I refuse to believe you. I refuse to believe that I'll have to watch my parents die, and my friends, their children, their children's children. It's a nightmare. Now get out of my office!"

"Valerie—"

"Get out, or I'll call the police and have you arrested for trespassing!"

Clarissa turned for the door.

As she passed through the reception area she stopped at the counter, where Tina was studiously focusing on the surface of her desk, having overheard Valerie screaming even down the hallway and through the closed door.

"Tina?"

The head with colorful spiky hair obediently came up.

"Yes?"

Clarissa picked a business card from the holder on the marble counter.

"May I have a pen?"

Tina handed Clarissa a ballpoint. Clarissa wrote a phone number and *Bosecker Inn* on the back of the card and laid it on the counter.

"If Valerie needs to get in touch with me, this is where I can be found." She laid the pen beside the card and smiled the smile of someone saying a final goodbye.

CHAPTER THIRTY-FOUR

To ensure there would be no accidental encounters with Clarissa, or any member she had recruited to her cause, Trisha booked a hotel room in a nearby resort town, half an hour's drive downriver from Langston.

Before leaving New York, she promised Liesel to report when she arrived. So on her first morning in central Washington, she picked up the phone in her hotel room and punched Liesel's number. There was a click on the other end of the line.

"Ja?"

"Liesel?"

"Oh, Trisha. How was your trip?"

"Uneventful. No accidents along the way." Meaning she hadn't felt the resonance of any Order member.

"Are you still planning on one week?"

"A bit longer, I think."

"Two weeks?"

"More like three."

"Oh . . ."

Trisha heard Liesel sigh, and wished she could share details. If only she could describe her brilliant plan! But then she'd likely be telling the NSA and whoever else had the technology to listen in on their call.

"Liesel?"

"Yes."

"I wish you were here to enjoy the weather. It's perfect. Sunny and perfect." Meaning everything was proceeding smoothly. Liesel could expect a call for the jet as soon as Trisha had the girl in hand.

"Alright," Liesel replied, "Just be sure to wear enough sunscreen!" That last comment wasn't a part of their code. But Trisha didn't have any difficulty guessing what Liesel meant.

Yes, I will be watching my backside.

She hung up and sat in the chair beside the bed, eyes closed, imagining what must now be taking place in Zurich. Liesel would call Pieter, then Sandro. The Italian would take the delay in stride. That sunny Mediterranean disposition! But the Austrian? Pieter Hans Silberhof was a warrior, and used to having his own way.

Trisha was glad to be over five thousand miles away from the inevitable eruption.

CHAPTER THIRTY-FIVE

The last Saturday in May was sunny and held the promise of an early and hot summer. With only Monday and Tuesday classes standing between the girls and summer vacation, they met mid-afternoon on the Millers' back deck to make plans for the Money Bunny project.

Chantha had earlier dug up the jar and freed the bunny. It now sat in the middle of the table, none the worse for its time under the swing except for a little dust, its eyes seeming to beg for love and attention.

Nina took charge. "Did you bring the list of names, Selena?"

"Yes." She reached into the brown paper grocery bag she had brought and flopped a half-inch stack of copy paper on the table. From her jeans pocket she pulled out a thumb drive and set it atop the stack.

"Wow!" Chantha said. "How many?"

"Three thousand four hundred and eleven," Selena said proudly. "And more coming in every day." They stared at the names list, and each had the same thought: *It's going to take a lot of sewing to make that many bunnies.*

Nina turned to Chantha.

"Is your dad willing to meet with me again?"

"Yes. This coming Wednesday at his office."

"Can't he see me here?"

"No, he said it was best if you met him at work."

Nina would have preferred meeting in the Millers' home. If someone saw her entering a law office, and word got back to Dan, there would be trouble. But if an office meeting was what Frank Miller wanted, well, "Alright," she said. "I don't think Dan and Evelyn have anything planned for Wednesday. I'll tell them I'm going to see Selena."

The truth was, Dan, Evelyn and Nina no longer did anything together, except dinner. If they unexpectedly came up with family plans for next Wednesday, Nina would find a way out.

Chantha was puzzled. "Why do you still need a legal paper from my dad? I thought the woman already gave you permission to copy the bunny."

"We still need to have it in writing to make it legal," Nina said. "If it's not in writing, we can't show it to people like manufacturers. They won't just take my word."

But getting Clarissa's signature was not something she looked forward to. She still struggled to get past her anger and disappointment at Clarissa's unexpected trip out of town, and was having little success. Even the hope that Clarissa might share her memories of the few minutes she had spent with Nina's mom was fading. Nina had nearly convinced herself that Clarissa's recollections—from thirteen years ago—would be practically worthless. Getting signed permission to copy the bunny was now the only real reason she had for going back to the Bosecker. She hadn't even called to find out if Clarissa had returned.

Selena finally voiced the more immediate and pressing question. "What about making the bunnies? How do we make that many?"

Nina agreed this was the biggest hurdle they faced. If they made bunnies in the valley, it meant finding lots of women who could sew. They might wind up with fifty women, making fifty different-looking bunnies. Now that she sat looking at a list of over three thousand potential customers, it confirmed her earlier thought on what might be necessary.

"We need to find a company to do the work," Nina said.

"How do we do that?" Chantha asked.

Selena volunteered, "When I was looking on the Internet, I found tons of companies who do that kind of thing. I could put together a list of names and email it to you."

Nina's grin told all. "Thank you, Selena. That would be wonderful."

Selena beamed.

"We're also going to need a business plan," Nina continued.

"Right," Chantha said. "And that's where the business course comes in."

Selena looked surprised. "Business course?"

Nina and Chantha gave quick, apologetic looks. Chantha said, "The school summer program has a business class. It starts a week from Monday."

Selena felt a little hurt. This was supposed to be a three-girl project, wasn't it? Why hadn't they told her? So instead of instantly agreeing, she said, "That won't leave much room for summer stuff." Working to look more than a little put out.

Chantha wasn't having any of that. "Selena! The course only lasts for three weeks, and it's just three hours on Mondays and Wednesdays. You'll survive!"

"Okay, okay." Selena said. Now wanting to remind them that it was she who had put the bunny up on the Internet and gotten the whole thing started. *They should give me more credit!* But then she remembered how much she had upset Nina by posting the bunny in the first place, and decided that keeping quiet was probably best.

Nina turned to Chantha. "Do you know who the teacher is?" She hoped it wasn't Mr. Chessman, who taught accounting at the high school. He was young, and as far as Nina knew he had never been involved in a real business.

"The school posted it on line. It's a guy named Irv Goodwin. He used to be the vice president for a company in Seattle. He retired and moved to Langston three years ago. My dad's in the Rotary club with him and he thinks he'll be good."

"Great."

"So what do we do with the bunny until then?"

Nina said, "I still don't trust Dan." She gave Chantha a look that said *I guess we need to tell her.*

"I don't see any other way except to put him back in the jar and bury it under the swing again."

Selena rocked back in her chair. "It was buried under the swing? What a horrible place! Does he really have to get buried? Couldn't he stay in Chantha's bedroom?"

Nina was remembering the bunny's heart. If the bunny went missing it would be impossible to replace the pearl. She said, "I think we need to put him back under the swing. But wait again until after dark to bury him. I wouldn't want anyone finding out where he is."

"Okay."

Nina turned to Selena. "If you leak one word about where the bunny is, you're out of the project. Understood?"

"Completely," Selena said.

And this time she really meant it!

CHAPTER THIRTY-SIX

W hen Clarissa returned to Washington after her disas-
trous meeting with Valerie, she learned that Nina Bea
had come looking for her.

She and Charlie sat down to discuss strategy, coincidentally on
the same day the three girls were attending their last day of school.

"It's not looking very good, is it?" Charlie conceded. "We'd
have to get lucky to intercept a kidnapper. And even if we catch
the first one, others will follow. They have limitless resources,
and we have . . ." Charlie took a long time to admit the obvious.
"We don't have much to work with." And then he got a thoughtful look. "Maybe we're looking at this all wrong."

"What do you mean?" Clarissa said, wondering what she could
have possibly overlooked.

"We want to protect her, right?"

"Yes."

"And the Watchers are only concerned because they believe
you intend to use her to disclose the Order to the rest of the
world."

"More or less, that's correct."

"If we could convince them you were no longer pursuing Nina Bea for that purpose, might they be willing to back off?"

But Clarissa wasn't willing to abandon her plans. And even if she were, she was certain there was no chance of persuading the Order to let the girl mature on her own. She represented too much potential power. The only thing they might accept would be for Clarissa to die, and she wasn't ready for that, either.

"That's not going to happen," Clarissa said. "They wouldn't believe me. But even if they did, Nina Bea would still potentially be exposed to governments, the rich, even religious fanatics who will see her as a threat to their beliefs."

And if Nina Bea's genetics are as different as I hope they are? If she is capable of passing on the gift to her children? I will not have just done her a disservice. I will have spelled her doom. And maybe lost an opportunity for the human race that might not come again for a thousand years. Or ever.

"If only we had more people on our side," Charlie said wistfully.

It was Clarissa's turn to be inspired. Suddenly excited, she said, "You were right. We are looking at this wrong. There is someone we can enlist."

"You know someone else from the Order who might take our side?"

"No," Clarissa said. "But there are others."

Charlie's face was suddenly skeptical.

"You mean regular people?"

"Yes. And I have someone specific in mind."

"Who?"

"This girl who is Nina's friend . . . the Asian girl. What's her name?"

"Chantha? You can't possibly be thinking of telling a thirteen-year-old about the Order."

"No, of course not. But she has a father who is a lawyer. Someone who will be close to the girls all summer. Someone who could keep an eye out for trouble."

Charlie didn't like it. "Even if he's a lawyer and used to keeping secrets, how could anyone from the regular world be trusted to keep the secret of the Order to himself?"

"I can place a block. He'll know everything he needs to know, but will be unable to talk about it with anyone but me."

"You can do that with complete certainty?"

"Yes," Clarissa said. "I can make it stick no matter what."

"But you tried that with Nina Bea and it doesn't seem to be working very well."

"Charlie," Clarissa said, "I thought you understood that Nina Bea is a special case. Very soon, no one will be able to any exert control over her. Not even me."

"Okay," Charlie said. But it still made him nervous. And not just because the secret of the Order would be shared with a non-member.

A warrior wouldn't hesitate to kill Mr. Miller if he gets in the way.

CHAPTER THIRTY-SEVEN

A week after school let out for summer, the girls spent Sunday afternoon at the Millers' home readying for the business course that would start the next morning. They dug up the bunny from beneath the swing and carefully brushed his fur with a damp cloth, wiping the blue-rimmed eyes clean. He now lay on the couch in the family room while his fur dried. Nina sat down on the couch and picked up the bunny and stroked its damp ears, straightening the fur.

"Do you really think this will work?" Selena said, sitting down beside her.

"Why wouldn't it work?" Nina asked.

"Yeah, why not?" Chantha challenged, taking a seat on the other side of Nina.

"It's so enormous," Selena said. The list of potential buyers now numbered over six thousand. "Just boxing up that many bunnies and mailing them would take us weeks. And we don't really even know how to approach a company to get them made."

"That's what the course is for," Chantha said. "It's one step at a time."

"Right," Nina agreed. "And if some part of it won't work, I'm sure this businessman will tell us why. And he'll also tell us how to fix it. You just need to be patient, Selena."

But Selena still worried. She was also concerned about Nina, who had finally shared that she hoped money from the bunny would somehow let her escape from the Torgersons. She hadn't said where she might go, and that worried Selena the most. She didn't want to lose one of her very best friends ever.

When they were done with their planning, Frank drove Nina and Selena home and promised to pick them up early the next morning.

Dan hadn't said anything more about the bunny, but she didn't believe he'd given up. So Nina left the bunny with Chantha.

When she arrived home, Evelyn was in the kitchen. When Nina closed the front door, Evelyn didn't call out as she usually did. Nina went to her room, lay down on her bed, and stared up at the ceiling, hoping the retired businessman would have all of the answers.

She dozed off and began to dream. And found herself in a place that was by now familiar. She stood in a field overlooking a large lake, with enormous snowcapped mountains crowning the horizon. Her hands brushed the tips of long grass and tall white daisies.

Tents, striped in reds, yellows and blues and topped with colorful pennants, occupied the middle of the field. Dozens of young adults were laughing and talking as they moved between the tents.

Clarissa was standing beside her, wearing a long yellow summer dress. On the left lapel of the dress was stitched the same crest as the bunny's.

"We gather here each year," Clarissa said, "although not everyone is always able to come. It helps to be with others like ourselves. That way the loneliness isn't so bad." Clarissa sounded sad. "I've not been able to come for many years," she confessed.

"Why do these people get lonely?"

"Because they eventually lose everyone who comes into their lives, except for other members. After a while it seems pointless to make friendships with people outside the Order. There are only around three hundred of us, and we live so far apart. It would draw too much attention for us to live together."

Nina watched the people mingling amongst the tents, so happy, so joyous to be with each other. She wanted to share in that joy, to feel the special bonds between these people who only got to see each other once a year.

Nina was startled awake as she heard Evelyn calling from the living room.

"Nina? It's dinnertime."

She wiped the sleepers from the corners of her eyes, and for a moment she could still picture the field above the lake and the beautiful tents and the daisies. Then the image faded, the memory of it drifting away like smoke on a summer breeze.

CHAPTER THIRTY-EIGHT

The next morning Frank and Chantha went to pick up Nina and Selena. Frank had blocked out the first hour of his workday to make sure the girls arrived on time. He pulled up in front of the big brick schoolhouse at 8:45. As Nina and Selena climbed out, he reminded Chantha, "Come to my office after you're through and we'll all go out to lunch."

"Thanks, Dad," Chantha said, as she pushed the car door shut.

Frank waited until they reached the front doors of the school, just to make sure they weren't locked. He sped away as soon as the girls went inside, anxiously glancing at his wristwatch, hoping he wouldn't get a ticket for racing through the downtown streets.

By the time he reached the parking lot, he had only three minutes to spare. He'd hoped to beat his new client to the office, but when he entered, she was already seated in the reception area.

Frank's first impression was of a conservative woman of around 45, dressed in dark blue slacks and a light yellow blouse.

Her brown hair was pulled back and tied with a silver ribbon. On the chair beside her was a gray felt hat with a narrow silver band around the crown. Frank wondered if she might be a foreigner, perhaps from Europe. An American wearing a hat these days was a rarity. He extended his hand as Clarissa stood.

"You must be Ms. Cumberland."

"And you must be attorney Frank Miller," she replied. As Frank shook Clarissa's hand he would have sworn he felt a soft pulse of electricity pass between them.

Irv Goodwin stood at the head of the classroom and sized up the three students who had enrolled for his course. The low turnout was a disappointment, but Irv reminded himself it was summer break and maybe he was lucky to have even three kids interested in sitting indoors while others their age were outside playing. The real surprise was that his class consisted only of girls entering the eighth grade. Frank had hoped for at least a couple boys, and for older kids.

"Welcome," he said, a nervous smile betraying his unease. He looked at the brown haired girl with a stuffed bunny sitting on her desk. At first it made her seem younger than the other two—a child who was still so attached to a toy that she felt compelled to bring it with her. But when Irv saw the focused look of determination in her eyes, he realized the bunny wasn't there for security.

"Is the rabbit connected to your business idea?" he asked Nina.

"Yes," she replied.

Irv smiled. It really did seem like a nice stuffed animal. He'd never seen one quite like it, especially with the little round crest on its chest. "May I?" he asked, nodding towards the bunny.

Nina rose from her desk and reluctantly handed the bunny to Irv. He studied it for a moment before handing it back. "Lovely," he said. The girl hadn't so much as blinked until she had the bunny back in her hands.

"And your name is?"

"Nina."

Irv looked at the other girls, and they volunteered their names.

"Selena."

"Chantha."

"Frank Miller's daughter," Irv said pleasantly, hoping she would mention to her father he had remembered.

"Yes," Chantha said, realizing this man, who was practically ancient, was sucking up. It made her proud to think her dad was that important.

"Well, young ladies, there's a surprise this morning. I had planned to teach this course alone over the next three weeks. But your vice principal, Mr. Nedrickson was able to find someone else to help. And I think you will be thrilled with who he found."

Boyd Nedrickson had called Irv to ask if he might consider letting someone else present a few pointers to the class. Irv was already a little antsy about trying to fill up six morning sessions with enough material to hold the attention of kids this age. When Boyd described the credentials of the person who had volunteered, Irv thought even he might get a refresher on what the business world was doing in the digital age.

He proudly said, "This young woman comes to us all the way from New York City, where she is a top financial advisor with an investment firm." Irv turned to the classroom doorway, and through it stepped Trisha Peterson—with an entirely charming smile and a twinkle in her eyes.

CHAPTER THIRTY-NINE

I t began simply enough.

"I need your help," Clarissa said.

From where Frank sat—across a desk now cleared of paper—it was a plea he'd heard hundreds of times. He was ready to assure her it was his business to help people, but she continued before he could speak.

"This will be unlike any matter you have handled before. And it may have a lasting impact upon your law practice and on your family."

My family? That was something Frank had never heard in all his years of practice. And it was most certainly a red flag. He held his silence, now anticipating this might not be a case he would take.

"I believe you know a thirteen-year-old girl named Nina?"

The likelihood of Frank continuing to be interested in taking on this new client skyrocketed. "Nina Haas?" he said, freshly concerned.

"Yes."

"Of course. She is best friends with my daughter, Chantha. How does this concern her?"

He sounded protective—a good sign. Clarissa continued in a slightly milder tone, but still serious. "I must first ask you a question."

"Okay." Frank had already seen one red flag. This was another—when a client tried to seize control. For a moment he again considered telling her he would pass on being her lawyer. The thing holding him back was his concern for Nina. Frank nodded cautiously for her to continue.

A caution that was instantly recognized by Clarissa. She might have taken control right then and there. But she had already decided not to use her powers at the start. Frank's consent had to be solely his own. If it wasn't genuine—if there wasn't a true and heartfelt desire to protect Nina Bea—Clarissa had to know.

I will be fair to him this one time.

"How do you feel about Nina?"

Frank remembered the meeting with Nina, her worries about her foster parents, and her secretiveness about where the bunny had come from. He also recalled Nina being distracted while playing with his daughter and Selena at the sleepover. He looked across the desk at a woman who appeared to also be very concerned about Nina's well being, and he reached a decision. If she wanted to help Nina, he was willing to become involved, even if it meant—as she implied—a sacrifice beyond the usual requirements of a case. Increasingly curious about what the connection was between Ms. Cumberland and Nina, he took the plunge.

"Nina is a very special girl. She has a high sensitivity for others that few kids her age possess. She is a best friend to my daughter, Chantha. If the reason you are here is to help Nina, then I'm interested in at least listening to what you have to say."

A weight lifted for Clarissa.

"Good. There are things I'll tell you that must remain a secret."

"You needn't worry," Frank assured her. "The attorney client privilege prevents me from disclosing anything without you first giving permission, and I take that obligation quite seriously."

Clarissa's demeanor now took on a rueful edge that echoed down the centuries. The time for fairness was over. She said in a voice that was suddenly stronger, "A breach of the attorney client privilege is the least of my worries."

"I'm not sure I understand."

"Then let me explain."

And after that, nothing was simple. Nothing at all.

Clarissa was long gone by the time the girls arrived at Frank's office for lunch.

When he came out to the reception area the girls were chattering away, with Selena—as usual—doing most of the talking. She turned when he entered.

"Hi, Mr. Miller!"

"Hello, Selena." Frank turned to his daughter, "Chantha, how did things go this morning?" The evenness of his voice surprised Frank. He'd half expected to break down in tears; or to at least to show some emotion. But whatever Clarissa had done to him had been done to perfection; he sounded normal even to himself, despite the turmoil inside.

"It was great, Dad."

Frank turned to Nina, and wondered why he had never before noticed how her presence seemed to fill the room. "Nina, how about you? Did you like the instructor?"

"It was okay, I guess."

"Nina!" Selena chided, shaking her head in disbelief. "It was incredible!"

Nina looked at Selena and seemed to warm up a bit. "Yeah. I guess it was."

Selena turned to Frank. "It's all going to work!" She said this with absolute conviction, but didn't elaborate. The girls had been cautioned by Trisha not to give away secrets; to only share their ideas about the project with each other or with her or Mr. Goodwin. And after Irv had left the room, she hinted that sharing things with Irv was "iffy."

Frank smiled. "Let's go get some lunch." He said this as if food were the only thing on his mind.

But inside, Frank's world was forever changed. Clarissa had spared him nothing. The revelations, she assured him, were so he would recognize the signs as Nina's powers emerged. She had also warned Frank he would be unable to tell Nina, or any other person, about the Order or about Nina's potential. Not even so much as a lifted eyebrow, a frown, a nod.

Frank had already tried to break that restriction. Immediately after Clarissa left, he picked up a pen and tried to write down what he had just learned, the same as he would with any client, simple notes to the file. But his hand refused to move.

Concerned he might have entirely lost the ability to write, he tried writing his own name, and the pen moved and there was his name on the page in blue ink. He wrote the date, and then tried to write "the Order," and again, the pen refused to move. It was as if his hand had not received the signal from his brain. Next, he tried to write Nina's name, and he got "Nina" written just fine, but when he tried to add "Bea" the pen again failed to move.

"Damn it all!"

Frank shifted gears. He picked up the recorder he used to dictate work for his secretary, pushed the start button.

"Today I met a woman who belongs to the—" but his mouth refused to say "Order." Just simply refused! "She told me about—" and the next word did not reach his lips.

Frank tried a different angle, hoping to get a running start and then sneak something in. He again spoke into the recorder, "The girls will be arriving shortly from their summer business course, and I am taking them out to lunch. I'll give Nina the consent form she asked me to prepare, so that she can obtain full legal rights to reproduce the bunny. She will need to get this signed by Clarissa Cumberland." *There! I said her name.* He continued quickly, trying to sneak in a little more information, "who is—" and Frank wanted to say *a member of a most unusual group of people, whom Nina belongs to even though she doesn't know it,* but those words would not come out of his mouth, so instead he said, "Clarissa is the person who owns the rights to the bunny." And that came out just fine!

And of course that would be permitted. After all, the form might go to a manufacturer's agent, or even another lawyer, and they will expect to see a real person's name. I must be allowed to reveal that much about her.

Frank made several more attempts to record even just one of the remarkable things he had learned that morning, and failed entirely. At one point he even called in his receptionist and had her stand before his desk, and said, "Penny, I need to tell you something about my last client."

Penny stood attentively. "Okay," she said.

Frank began, "Ms. Cumberland is—" and that was as far as he got. After three tries without getting past the word "is," Frank gave up and sent her back out to the reception desk, shaking her head; hoping something serious like a stroke wasn't affecting her boss's brain.

Penny checked on him a few minutes later, bringing a document he'd asked for. Frank mumbled "Thanks" as he reached to take the paper she handed across his desk, and seemed to again be in full possession of his senses.

Now, as he sat with the girls at Brannagan's Grill, watching them devour burgers and fries, he wondered if he had any sensibility left. People who lived for hundreds of years? People with special powers? It was comic book fantasy stuff.

Clarissa had made one reassuring promise. "Nina may be at risk, but the Order will have no interest in interfering with you or your wife or your daughter. They are driven by a desire to remain hidden. Assaulting ordinary people simply isn't in their best interests."

Frank felt a little put out at being called "ordinary." And he wasn't entirely sure if he believed that his family was completely safe. But her promise was at least comforting.

There was a positive, even exciting side to the revelations. Clarissa said Nina would gradually become stronger, and more capable of doing remarkable things.

"Like what?"

"Communicating with animals. Persuading others to do things. She'll learn math as far as she wants to go with it. New languages will come easily. Many other things."

"And where does all of this lead?" It was near the end of their meeting and Frank felt exhausted.

"Hopefully," Clarissa said, "she will be accepted as a leader of the Order. If we do not have someone like Nina Bea to guide us into the twenty-first century, it may not go well."

"What do you mean?" Frank was fearful of what she might say. But by now, he was far too curious not to ask. His fears proved to be warranted.

"There are people in the Order who, if provoked, could do massive damage. For instance, a member who is capable of directing ordinary people to do things against their will could command a person in charge of nuclear weapons, or biological toxins, to use them."

"But why would any of you do that?"

Clarissa sounded matter-of-fact as she answered, and this scared Frank. It scared him because he saw it was the plain truth.

"Why does anyone commit an act of terror? Usually, because they themselves have been terrorized. Family members were killed. The village where they live was bombed. Their place of worship was burned to the ground. A person reaches a point where they see no future, and it opens up options they wouldn't consider if their lives were going well." Clarissa paused before continuing, with a look that said these thoughts brought her pain.

"Understand this, Mr. Miller. The Order's members have known each other for centuries. We love and care deeply about our people. If any of us were captured and examined *biologically,* it would cause a rage in the membership that could easily threaten society on a global scale."

Her voice now gained an edge of disgust.

"Nearly all of us had to endure the first and second world wars. Many of us lived through the Napoleonic wars, the revolutions in America and France, the Inquisition, and so much more horror and death. We are continually saddened by what humanity does to itself. We are peace loving. We don't kill each other. But if our independence was taken away? If we became frightened? If we were persecuted?" There was a long pause to emphasize the point. And when Clarissa continued it was in a stony voice that left no doubt about the seriousness of what she was saying.

"There is no limit to what the consequences might be." Clarissa paused to let this fully sink in.

"You are a lawyer, Mr. Miller. You have seen firsthand how human institutions—marriages, partnerships, neighborhoods—can easily and quickly disintegrate into conflict. Imagine the consequences of a marriage that has lasted for, say, four hundred years, coming to a bitter end because of outside interference. How might two people who are possessed of great powers react? If you picture what that might be like, you will begin to appreciate what might result from an uncontrolled outing of the Order."

Now, as he sat watching a thirteen-year-old girl slurp a vanilla milkshake through a red plastic straw, he wondered if someday she could possibly become strong enough to save the human race *from itself.*

CHAPTER FORTY

The first day of class did not go as well as Trisha had hoped. Sandro's story of his earlier experience had prepared her to expect something. But even so, Trisha thought he must have exaggerated. He had not. When she stepped into the room, the wave of power emanating from Nina nearly overwhelmed her. Irv made things worse by immediately heading for a seat at the back, leaving her to facing the three girls on her own.

To cover her shock, Trisha turned to Selena, whom she sensed was the easiest to influence, and asked, "What kind of project do you have in mind?"

Selena temporarily rescued Trisha by talking nonstop for the next five minutes about the bunny and how she had posted its picture on the Internet, and the resulting surge of interest from girls across the country.

It was a private joke with Chantha and Nina, hearing Selena talk on and on like this. They even had a name for it: *Going Selena*. But on this particular morning it proved useful. Both girls studied the woman who was their new teacher. Chantha was enthralled. Nina wasn't sure what to think.

When Selena finally stopped, Trisha looked to Chantha and said, "Well . . . it certainly seems like a doable project. Don't you think?"

"Yes," Chantha said, with a brief glance to Nina, who barely nodded.

Trisha saw she wasn't on solid ground with the one girl who was important. Not in the least. For a woman who routinely marketed sophisticated and often illegal financial instruments to millionaires and billionaires, the ability to change directions when a situation got sticky was second nature. So she launched into what seemed like the safety of a lecture about starting a business, hoping to regain her balance.

"Just because there's a strong interest in the bunny doesn't mean that manufacturing and sales will easily follow. There are plenty of hurdles to clear. For instance, there are import regulations for bunnies manufactured overseas. Safety concerns such as securing the eyes so a toddler can't pull them off and swallow them. You'll need to find retail outlets, and consider what kind of advertising will work best." She went on for several minutes, now wanting just to get through the morning.

Blah, blah, blah, thought Nina, as the woman droned on. *Why are you so scared?* But she said nothing, just crossed her arms and sat at her desk and stared at this woman, who for some reason got her all stirred up inside.

Trisha sensed Nina's rejection continue to strengthen, and it eventually started to throw her off balance. This led her to say something uncharacteristically stupid for a member of the Order whose skill was charm.

"One problem you face is that you are not yet adults. Money generated from sales will need to be administered in some kind of trust."

Nina's attitude hardened immediately. To Trisha it felt like a grenade had gone off. Now totally off balance, she blurted out, "You will need to form a trust with an adult in control."

Nina finally ended her silence. "Why?" she demanded, with a determined anger.

Trisha attempted to defend what she'd said, addressing Nina directly for the first time.

"That's the way the world works, Nina. A bank won't let you open an account if you are under the age of eighteen. It has to be in the name of an adult. Large sums of money just aren't turned over to a girl." Trisha immediately regretted using *that* word.

Nina's face took on the glazed look of an executioner.

I've lost her.

"Don't worry," Trisha continued quickly, desperately trying to reassure the only person in the room who mattered. "I'm sure we can find someone to handle the money end of things. Maybe your father?"

Selena cut in. "Her real father is dead, and her foster dad is a creep."

Nina shot a hard look at Selena.

"Well it's true," Selena defended.

"Yeah," Chantha agreed. "Dan Torgerson is not the guy we want to be in charge of *anything*."

Nina seemed to settle down a little. The girls had her back. She gave Trisha a glance that said she wasn't going to ever like her for any of this.

"Okay," Trisha agreed. "Nina's foster dad is out of the picture. Is there someone else you would trust?"

Nina said carefully, "Chantha's father is a lawyer. I'd trust him." This brought a smile from Chantha.

Selena said, "He's perfect."

"Alright," Trisha said. "I could certainly talk to Chantha's father about making appropriate arrangements."

But that's one conversation I'll never need to have.

Nina gave her a look that said she knew she was lying.

Trisha now felt desperate, and shifted gears, pulling Irv Goodwin from his nearly catatonic listening trance at the back of the room, hoping he might rescue her from the pit she'd fallen into.

"Mr. Goodwin?"

Irv almost didn't recognize his own name. He blinked rapidly when he realized Trisha was speaking to him. "Yes?" he said from his chair, squarely backed up against the wall.

"Why don't you come up and tell the girls a bit more about forming a limited liability corporation in the State of Washington."

Irv stood, feeling honored. "Of course. Glad to." When he reached the front of the classroom, Trisha gracefully stepped aside and headed for the seat Irv had just vacated.

But as she walked past the girls, she felt Nina's mind probing, questioning. *Who is this person? Why am I reacting so strongly towards her?*

Nothing was going to be simple. And for the first time, Trisha wondered if her brilliant plan might not work at all.

CHAPTER FORTY-ONE

After lunch, Frank Miller drove Selena home, and then took Chantha and Nina to his house before returning to work.

They retreated to the deck, where Nina laid the bunny on his back on the table. She sat down, looking confused.

Chantha asked, "Nina, what's wrong?"

It was the same question Nina kept asking herself. *What is wrong?* And the answer that kept popping up? *I'm going crazy.* A weirdness seemed to be unraveling her life. Class this morning seemed like just one more step towards complete confusion.

"Our new teacher is strange," Nina finally said.

"Miss Peterson?"

"Yes."

"How do you mean?"

"It's hard to explain," Nina said, struggling to understand what she felt. "It's as if some of the people I meet these days, like Trisha Peterson, are connected to me by some invisible force."

Experience had taught Chantha to trust Nina's observations about people. Like the time, a few months back, when Nina pointed out a boy who'd grown more and more quiet in class, and then began to sit apart from other kids at lunchtime. As they sat in the cafeteria, watching the boy eat, Nina said, "He's got some kind of disease. I think he may be about to die." And sure enough, a month later the boy was gone from school, and word came he had terminal cancer. It was eerie, Nina sensing the boy's death before it happened.

That wasn't her only ability. She also knew when someone was lying. Her willingness to confront people and tell them exactly what they had lied about hadn't made her any new friends. But it was useful. Chantha had come to depend upon Nina's ability to *see* things other kids missed.

So this statement about Trisha had to be taken seriously. Especially since Chantha thought Trisha Peterson was perfectly wonderful.

Chantha tried to not sound disbelieving as she asked, "Who is strange? Like . . . most people you meet?"

"No," Nina said. "I didn't mean it that way. What I meant is that every person who seems important that I've met over the past few weeks is somehow different from everyone else I've ever met."

"Like?"

"Like Clarissa, who I ran into in the forest, and who gave me a stuffed rabbit."

Both girls looked at the bunny. Nina reached out and stroked its stomach once, softly, before continuing.

"And her friend Charlie, who Clarissa says will help me if I need it. The guy she describes as a warrior."

Chantha hadn't heard that before! *A warrior?* But Nina needed a listener, not a questioner. Chantha held her silence.

"Why does Clarissa think I might need help from some Indian in his twenties who rides a Harley?"

Chantha shrugged, trying to picture an Indian warrior on a motorcycle.

Nina hurried on, hoping she was making sense. "And now there's our 'surprise' teacher Trisha Peterson. She comes all the way from New York to teach three weeks of summer school. Doesn't that sound strange to you?"

"I thought she was pretty awesome," Chantha countered, wanting Nina to be wrong. There were few people whom Chantha had met who seemed as special as Trisha Peterson.

"Yeah, well I think Selena thought so too. And everything she said sounded great . . . on the surface. But while I was listening to her, it was like there was something else she was thinking that was really important, and no one could know it but me."

"Like what?"

"I'm not exactly sure. But it felt like I was the only person in the room that she was really talking to. Like she was trying to gain my trust, but it wasn't working, and she was frustrated about it not going well."

"Weird."

"Yeah. Totally."

Chantha thought Nina must be wrong. Trisha Peterson was perfect for helping them with the bunny project. And there was something else, wasn't there? Trisha Peterson was . . . *charming*. The kind of person you would want for a big sister. But Nina was her best friend, and if it came to a choice between Trisha Peterson and Nina, there was no question who Chantha would pick. Still, it seemed like Nina was dreaming up demons where none existed.

"That's only three people, Nina."

Nina's face changed, as if she was replaying something in her mind. "There was someone else . . ."

Chantha remembered seeing this same puzzled look, near the end of school. She volunteered, "Do you mean that guy with Mr. Nedrickson? The one with the straw hat?"

"Exactly!" Nina said, triumphant. "How did you know?"

"Cause you have the same look on your face you had then."

"Really?"

"Yes. Really. When you told me about that guy standing next to Nedrickson you said you felt like you knew him. Is that the same way you feel about the other three?"

Nina thought about it, and realized there was one difference. "That guy was really scared of me."

"What?"

"He was scared. He wanted to run away. But with Clarissa and Charlie, and even with Trisha Peterson, it's like they have a special interest in being around me."

"What's wrong with that?"

Nina smiled, realizing she hadn't persuaded Chantha. "Nothing, I guess." But the tone in her voice didn't say it was nothing. Just the opposite. Everything was wrong.

Chantha stared at the bunny, then at Nina, then back at the bunny.

"Do you still want to do the project?"

Nina had struggled with that question since lunch. The only other way she could think of to raise enough cash to get away from the Torgersons was to take the black pearl from the bunny's chest and sell it. *If there really is a black pearl. But even if there is a pearl, who would buy a pearl from a thirteen year old girl?* Trisha Peterson might have seemed strange, but what she said about kids Nina's age needing adult agents to conduct business in the real world had struck home. There was no way a jeweler would take a kid's word that she had the right to sell a monster sized pearl.

Nina finally said, "I don't see any other option." And then she brightened a little. "Besides, I want to do this with you and Selena. We're already started, and maybe I am just imagining things. What could make these four people so different? And why should I worry about it even if they are? I'm just a thirteen-year-old girl, right? Why would they have any special interest in me? And what could they really do?"

"Right," Chantha said, relieved. "It's not like you're related to them. Or that you have anything valuable they would want to take away from you."

"Okay," Nina said. "I'll get past this, I promise."

Selena looked at the bunny. "Would you mind if I kept him in my bedroom from now on? It's a real pain to dig him up. And I'm afraid that someone might eventually see where I'm putting him."

"Okay," Nina agreed. Maybe the bunny would be safe inside the house. Sooner or later someone was bound to see Chantha digging it up. And it also didn't seem fair to make her do all of that work.

The girls stood, hugged, and Chantha whispered, "Mom baked an apple pie and stashed it in the fridge."

"Whipped cream?"

"Doubtless," Chantha said. The girls scrambled off the deck and raced for the kitchen.

But even as Chantha was cutting huge slices and squirting squiggles of whipped cream across the golden crust, Nina remained troubled.

I thought she would understand. But I was wrong. I'll have to figure this out on my own. Because no one else could possibly believe me if Chantha can't see what's happening.

In that instant she remembered the dream—the field filled with colorful tents; a happy gathering of young adults.

They would understand!

But as quickly as the dream memory had come, it disappeared, almost as if a force had surfaced from some secret corner of her mind to push it away.

CHAPTER FORTY-TWO

For two weeks, Valerie Chun Li thought of little else but the meeting with Clarissa. She finally gave in and called her former math advisor at Stanford.

"I'm in trouble, Mitch. I need to talk."

Mitchell Young, PhD., dean of mathematics at Stanford University, considered Valerie Chun Li to be his brightest ever graduate student. Since receiving her PhD in 2002, at the age of 22, they had remained friends. Mitch often filled the role of sounding board for mathematical problems Valerie was wrestling with. And sometimes he weighed in on personal problems as well. He perpetually hoped Valerie would find a man who was somewhere near her intellectual equal; someone whom she could both fall in love with and respect. It hadn't yet happened. He was hopeful this might be that breakthrough.

"Is it about a guy, maybe?"

"No," Valerie said abruptly. "Nothing like that."

There was an awkward silence on the line, and Mitch hoped he hadn't offended her. This was the one topic they never managed to find some way to agreed on. She usually told him it none of his business. But Mitch had seen the loneliness welling up in her eyes when she didn't know he was looking.

"Valerie?"

Her response was rapid, forced.

"It's something I learned a few days ago. Or . . . I think I learned. Could you please come see me in person? I don't want to talk about this over the phone."

She'd always been a little paranoid about spying, telling him that if he knew how easy it was for anyone with even "modest skills" to tap into virtually any electronic transmission, he'd be more careful about what he said on the phone. Mitch suspected that what Valerie thought of as "modest skills" and what other people thought those might be were several quantum leaps apart.

So . . . if it wasn't a man, was it her health? Mitch had a premonition it might be something serious, like cancer.

"Where do you want to meet?"

"Could you come to my office in San Jose?"

"Certainly."

"Now?"

It was Mitch's turn to fall silent. As the department chair, he had considerable leeway for leaving the campus. His one class for the day was already finished. But he'd planned on taking his eight-year-old grandson Tommy to the aquarium in San Francisco that afternoon. Palo Alto to San Jose was twenty miles south on the I-101 and not usually a problem at 11am. But after a meeting with Valerie, Mitch would need to backtrack in rush hour traffic on the Interstate to Palo Alto and then 30 miles further north to his son's house near Golden Gate Park. He weighed how disappointed his grandson might be against the concern he'd heard in Valerie's voice and came to a quick decision.

"I can be there within an hour."

"Thank you!"

The relief in her voice confirmed his decision. She was in some kind of trouble for sure. Mitch hung up and placed a call to his son, explaining something urgent had come up, and asking him to tell Tommy that grandpa couldn't make it this afternoon. And then Mitch went straight to the underground garage and climbed into his Prius.

By the time he reached Valerie's building he was certain she had some serious disease. So when Tina ushered him back to Valerie's office, and he saw Valerie take quick and determined steps to greet him, with the same vibrancy in her eyes that had so pleased him when she was his student at Stanford, he took a deep breath and felt relieved.

He reached out and Valerie took his hands in hers and squeezed hard. "Would you mind sitting down?" she said, closing her office door before choosing one of the leather chairs for herself. Mitch sat across the corner of the Ming table, close enough to reach out if she became teary.

"So," Mitch began. "What's all this about?"

Valerie looked momentarily confused. It was a new look for her. Mitch had seen *puzzled* on that sweet face. Even *concerned*. And once he had seen *bewildered*, over a disagreement between her and another graduate student. But he had never seen confused.

"Do you ever remember me being sick?"

Mitch's fear about her having an illness returned. "Are you now?"

"No. I'm perfectly fit. In fact, I've always been perfectly fit. I was trying to remember this morning if I've ever been sick in my whole life. I couldn't remember a single time. Do you ever remember me being ill? Like with a cold, or the flu?"

He thought about her question for a moment, shook his head in the negative. "I've seen you tired, like when you went two days without sleep working on your final thesis draft. But I don't remember you ever catching anything, or even missing a day of class. Why?"

"I don't ever remember getting sick either. I never caught a cold when I was a kid. I never had inflamed tonsils or earaches or even something as simple as a rash. I've always been healthy."

"So?"

"That's the point, Mitch. Have you ever known anyone who never gets sick? Not even once?"

Mitch was still in the dark. "I don't suppose so. To tell the truth, I've never given it much thought. Is there something wrong with always being well? It seems like a good thing to me. Means you've got a great immune system. You take care of yourself. So what's the problem?"

"It's not just that. Do you remember when I became your student, when I was sixteen?"

Mitch thought back to that magic moment when a girl everyone said was a genius had first entered his office. They had talked about Riemannian manifolds, a challenging subject even for graduate students, and this girl understood the math perfectly, even though she'd just graduated from high school. "You were a beautiful young lady, and brilliant beyond my grandest expectations," Mitch said.

Valerie was momentarily embarrassed. She almost blushed. But it passed. "Sure. Yeah. But when I got my PhD at twenty-one, did I look much older?"

"A little, I suppose."

"What about today? Twelve years later, how much older do I look from when I graduated?"

Mitch hadn't thought about how Valerie looked. But now that she mentioned it, even under whatever stress she was going through, she looked terrific. He made a stab at trying to reassure her, still uncertain what might be wrong.

"You look great. Not much different from when you graduated. Is that a bad thing?"

Valerie reached and picked up a photograph that was lying face down on the table. She handed it to Mitch. "Look at it. Then look at me."

Mitch looked at the photo. It was of Valerie in her PhD graduation gown, black with long red sleeves and wide golden cuffs, a soft hexagonal hat with a golden tassel at a slight angle atop her head, a satisfied smile on her face. *She looked like an angel.* He glanced up at Valerie. Back to the photo. Again, to Valerie. His lower lip pressed hard into his upper lip, and a first inkling of what she was getting at took hold. *She still looks angelic.* "You've held your age well," he said.

"Not 'well'," Valerie said stubbornly. "Perfectly."

"Meaning?"

"I have friends my age, and to remind you I am now thirty-four, who have grey hairs. Many of them have a few first wrinkles around their eyes. Some have had sports injuries, even arthritis, that bring pain. One guy I know almost lives on aspirin and ibuprofen because of the pounding he took in college football. Most of them need glasses, or have had Lasik surgery. Mitch . . . I've had none of that. My hair is still the same jet black, no grey hairs, not a single one. I still spring out of bed every morning!"

Mitch groaned at this last observation. "I wish I could say the same. When I woke up this morning, my left arm had fallen asleep and my shoulder was killing me. I had to take a couple of those wonderful ibuprofen capsules." He looked steadily at Valerie, looked hard at her face, her hair. And she was right. She hadn't seemed to age over the past twelve years. And this brought a question.

"So where did all of this come from?"

Valerie told him about Clarissa, about the bird flying up to the window, everything.

After she finished, Mitch sat in silence, stunned, wondering if it could possibly be true. He was entirely lost in thought when Valerie broke his concentration.

"What do I do, Mitch? What if this is real?"

That same question had come to him. And the answer he arrived at seemed simple, really.

"If it is true, then I'd say you are one of the luckiest people on the planet. Imagine being able to think clearly about math without losing brain cells to aging, without having to deal with health issues that pull other people down—arthritis, decreasing energy, gout, even worse things like dementia. What a blessing to remain young."

"And what about seeing everyone around me get old and eventually die? What about people thinking I'm a freak? What about the day when someone arrives at my door and asks if I wouldn't mind giving them a tissue sample, some blood. They want to study me, find out why I'm still looking twenty when I'm fifty . . . or seventy. Mitch . . . it's a nightmare!"

"No," Mitch said slowly. "This is definitely not a nightmare. A nightmare is when someone tells you you've got cancer or HIV. This 'living a long time in perfect health' is a thing you can deal with. But before you worry any more, there's something you must do."

"What?"

"This woman Clarissa. If what she told you is true, you need to talk more with her about it. Unless you think she is a danger—"

Her reply bolted out. "No. She's no danger." *But can I really be certain?* Clarissa had said she needed help. And that implied confrontation. And that further implied risk.

But Mitch was right. She couldn't afford to put her head down and try to ignore it. If it was all hogwash, the uncertainty of wondering whether or not it was true would drive her crazy, at least until that first gray hair appeared. And if it was true? If the gray hairs never showed up? How long could she hope to avoid the consequences of not making alternate plans for the future? She looked at her mentor and friend, someone she trusted.

"Do you really think I should?"

"Yes," Mitch said firmly. "After you know more, come back and we'll talk and sort out whatever needs to be sorted out. I promise."

Valerie stood up, bent over and put her forehead on his shoulder. He put an arm around her shoulders, and she cried a little before standing up straight again.

"Okay," she said, brushing away the tears, cinching up her courage. "I'll go and talk to her. May I call you if I get in over my head?"

Mitch reached out and took her hand. "You know you can. I'll keep the cell phone near at all times. You can call me day or night."

After Mitch left, Valerie buzzed Tina.

"Yes?"

"I need you to book me a hotel room in Washington State near a town called Langston. But don't make it too close. At least half an hour's drive away."

She would approach Clarissa with caution. If she kept her distance, at least at the start, then the "resonance" thing Clarissa had described shouldn't be a problem. And maybe she would try to locate this Nina and check her out, to see if there was something special she could spot.

Tina got to work finding a room as the boss ordered. She located Langston on MapQuest, pulled back and spotted a nearby resort town. The hotel directory on the chamber of commerce website listed one resort as the largest in town—first class, just like Valerie would expect. She dialed the number and made the reservation.

Fate can at times be extraordinarily strange. The room Tina booked was just two doors down the hall from the one that Trisha Peterson presently occupied.

CHAPTER FORTY-THREE

"Three more weeks is not acceptable!" Pieter Silberhof pounded his fist against the window casement before he turned to face her.

Liesel sat at the conference table, struggling to remain calm. She had finally shared what she learned from her phone call with Trisha two days ago, and now regretted passing that knowledge on to Pieter. Better to have kept him in the dark.

Outside, a thunderstorm lashed rain against the leaded windowpanes. Water ran in wide rivulets down the glass and streamed off onto the cobblestones below. A bolt of lightning flashed across the clouds and thunder vibrated the glass.

"What would you have us do, then?" Liesel's eyes focused on Pieter's face. Was he willing to push for another full meeting of the Council? Or worse, take action on his own? She knew he'd already taken steps in that direction, but doubted he was ready to confess a willingness to go it alone.

For a moment she saw indecision. It quickly hardened. Pieter had made up his mind. His reply came with absolute conviction.

"We must get word to Trisha Peterson that her time has run out. No more delays."

"And how would we accomplish that?"

"Someone should go and see her in person."

"And that someone would be you?"

Pieter wasn't stupid enough to insist on that. She could always call an emergency session of the Council to prevent him from going. "Perhaps," he relented, "it should be you. I believe you and she have formed something of a bond. Am I correct?" It was said sarcastically.

Liesel chose her next words carefully, knowing they might someday be used against her. "I don't advise sending anyone at all," she said firmly. "I trust Trisha is doing what is necessary to produce a successful result. How would sending me possibly quicken the retrieval of the girl?"

"What if we sent someone capable of helping her to finish the job?"

"Did you have anyone specific in mind?" And now she was the one who sounded sarcastic. Both knew who Pieter wanted.

It was now Pieter who spoke with care. His facade of leaning towards the desperate needed to last for another minute or two. "We could send Sandro. He's already been there. He knows the turf."

"And he might be recognized by the girl before he has an opportunity to take her. Sandro wouldn't be smart."

"Is there no one else you would find acceptable?"

Liesel had endured enough of the charade. "Such as Gunther?" She waited for his response, certain his temper would again flair. Or would he try to deny the obvious?

Pieter's response came as a surprise. He walked to the table and sank tiredly into a chair opposite Liesel.

"I know you object to the beast. And quite honestly, I find him to be lacking in certain qualities. But I know of no one else who is available, and capable of doing what may need to be done. I suppose I should tell you that I took a train north after our last meeting and spoke with him in Wilhelmshaven."

An amazing concession!

Liesel fought to hold her emotions in check. "How did it go?"

"As one might expect. He was eager for the adventure, even for contesting possession of the girl directly with Clarissa."

"Could he ever be trusted?"

"As much as one can trust a fool."

"Not so much, then?"

"No," Pieter conceded, with a brief chuckle that finally broke the tension in the room. He even smiled as he confirmed, "Not so much." A pleading look animated his face. "But who else do we have?"

"You mean if we don't leave it to Trisha?"

"Yes."

"No one, Pieter. Which is why I want you to consider letting Trisha finish the task she was assigned. Let her complete her plan, whatever it is."

"And if I do this, will you let me take Gunther on the plane when we go to pick up the girl? Just in case?"

She didn't like it. But if Pieter was willing to make a deal to let Trisha do her work unimpeded? How could she pass up the opportunity? Liesel thought about it for several heartbeats before she gave her answer. And even then, it was said with some reluctance.

"You'll promise to let Trisha finish?"

"Yes. I promise. If you will let me involve Gunther."

"Alright," Liesel agreed. "But I want to be on that plane."

"Agreed," he said, reaching out to shake her hand. "We'll be one happy little family on the Gulfstream, won't we!"

Liesel smiled, and Pieter knew he had succeeded.

I don't believe she even suspects that I got precisely what I wanted when this conversation began.

CHAPTER FORTY-FOUR

Nina waited for several days before calling the Bosecker Inn. She decided not to ask Clarissa about her mother. That would come later. But there was something she needed, and it couldn't wait.

The phone rang twice before a woman's voice said, "Bosecker Inn."

"Is Mrs. Cumberland back yet?" Nina asked.

"Yes," Iris said. "Would you like me to go and get her?"

"No," Nina said. "But would you please tell her that Nina Haas is coming by at five-thirty with something for her to look at?"

"Of course," Iris said.

Immediately after the call ended, Iris first reported to Charlie, then to Clarissa.

"I'll meet with her alone," Clarissa told Charlie.

"Should I leave so she won't sense me being here?"

"That shouldn't be necessary. If she were one of the experienced members of the Order she might detect there were two of us, but there's no way she'll be able to do that now."

When Nina arrived, she looked for Charlie's motorcycle and was relieved to find it gone. She couldn't have known he'd sold it. He now drove a used white Nissan Sentra, currently parked in the graveled lot behind the Inn.

Nina climbed the front steps, clutching a brown Manila envelope.

When she entered the lobby, the air felt electric. There was no one at the reception desk so Nina walked into the dayroom and caught Clarissa just entering through a door at the back. Clarissa carefully closed the door behind her, and said, "Nina Bea!" with a bright smile.

"Hi," Nina said.

"You've brought me something?" Clarissa nodded towards the Manila envelope. She knew exactly what was inside. Frank had faithfully reported what he'd drafted, and Clarissa had already read the document.

Nina held it out and Clarissa took it from her, pinched the metal clasp, lifted the flap, and pulled out two sheets stapled at the corner.

"What have we here?"

"It's a consent form from Mr. Miller. He's the attorney who is helping us with the bunny project. He says it's necessary for you to sign it if we want to work with a manufacturer." She fell silent. If Clarissa refused, she was prepared to leave.

Clarissa took a minute to pretend she was carefully studying the front page. The attachment was a photo of the bunny. She then walked to a small table at the side of the room where stationary and pens were kept for guests. She selected a pen from the pewter jar, and with a flourish signed her name at the bottom of the page. She slid the form back into the Manila envelope and handed it to Nina with a *done deal* smile.

"So," Clarissa said, "how are things with your two friends . . . what were their names?"

"Selena and Chantha. We started a summer class today up at the school. Our teacher is going to help us put together a business plan for the bunny."

"A summer business class? That sounds wonderful. Is this being taught by one of your regular teachers at school?"

Nina had gotten what she came for, and now she wanted to leave. But it seemed impolite not to answer the question. "He's a retired businessman who lives in Langston." She almost added that there was another teacher, but it seemed important not to say anything about Trisha Peterson.

Clarissa saw the hesitation. *She's holding back something.* And there was really no way to force it out without losing points. Big points. So with the conversation threatening to become a duel—one that Clarissa could only lose—she decided to cut it short.

"They'll probably be expecting you at home for dinner. Maybe you'd better head back so you won't be late."

"Okay," Nina readily agreed, standing up quickly.

And suddenly, Clarissa wished she hadn't moved to end it. "You're always welcome, Nina Bea," she said, trying to sound encouraging. "I enjoy talking with you very much."

"Thank you . . . Clarissa." She'd almost said "Mrs. Cumberland." "Maybe I'll come by on the weekend."

"Please do. I'd love to hear more about your bunny project. I might even have a suggestion or two. I'd love to help . . . but only if you want it."

How could she say no? "Okay. Thanks again for signing the form." And with relief, Nina walked out of the room, past the reception desk, down the front steps, and briskly up the sidewalk.

When Nina's resonance had faded away, Charlie came out from his room and settled into the chair Nina had just left.

"Did you hear?" Clarissa asked.

"Most of it. She doesn't trust you."

"Yes. If it weren't for Frank Miller, we'd be in serious trouble."

"So what's next?"

"Getting anxious?"

"A little, yes."

"Well, there is something you can do."

"What?"

"I'd like to know more about this class she's taking. There was something she wasn't telling me when she mentioned her instructor. It might be important." Clarissa paused, unsettled. "It's become impossible for me to probe beyond the surface of what she says. Her mind is now entirely closed off."

"She's come that far?"

"She has. But there's an upside to it. When we eventually come up against the Order, she'll have a real chance of standing up to them and making her own decisions."

"When do you think she'll be ready?"

"Maybe in a year, if we're lucky."

"And until then?"

"We protect her as best we can."

"Any suggestions on how I should handle the school?"

"Keep your distance. Try to spot this man she says is her teacher. Find out his name. I can then ask Frank Miller if he knows anything about him."

"Okay. Consider it done."

CHAPTER FORTY-FIVE

Charlie was driving the lake road, headed towards Langston and the school, when he saw blue lights flashing in his rear view mirror. He glanced at his speedometer, which read a couple miles under the limit. He slowed and pulled onto the shoulder to let the cop pass. Instead, the dark blue cruiser settled in behind and there was a brief *whoop!* of a siren.

Charlie braked to a stop, pushed the button to lower his driver's side window, took the keys from the ignition and placed them on the dashboard, planted his hands in the *ten and two o'clock* position on the steering wheel, and waited.

The cop didn't immediately leave his patrol car, and Charlie figured he was running the Sentra's plate. After a couple minutes the driver's door swung open and the cop stepped out, holding a small clipboard, a dark blue skimmer firmly on his head, natty light blue uniform with dark blue trim looking like it had just come from the drycleaners. A bit of muffin top crested his beltline.

Charlie stared straight out the driver's side window, hands still firmly planted on the steering wheel, and smiled politely as the cop walked up.

"Good morning, officer."

"May I see your license?"

Officer Troy Johnson loved this first part of a stop. He even practiced it in front of a mirror, and sometimes recorded himself on video. Gruff. No nonsense. Almost military, although he'd never served in the armed forces. *Take charge and make sure they know who the boss is!*

Charlie cautiously lifted his right hand off the wheel, reached to the back pocket of his jeans, and withdrew his wallet. Only then did he take his left hand from the wheel to open the wallet and pull out his license. He handed it out the window. The cop stepped back so he could both watch Charlie and examine the license. After close scrutiny Troy handed the license back.

"Do you have the registration for this vehicle?"

"It's in the glove compartment, sir," Charlie said. He calmly leaned to his right and thumbed open the latch and reached for the registration, aware that the cop's hand had dropped down to waist level, just inches from his holster. Charlie withdrew the registration certificate, slowly sat up straight, both hands in full view at all times, and handed it over. And finally, he asked the question.

"Is there a problem, officer?"

Troy ignored him, instead studying the registration.

"Did you purchase this vehicle recently?"

Charlie now wondered if it might be stolen. The place where he'd bought it appeared to have been in business for quite some time, so it seemed unlikely the car was hot. But not impossible.

What kind of bad luck would that be?

"Yes, sir. Just a couple days ago from the Nissan dealership in Langston. Is there a problem with the registration?"

Again, Troy ignored his question, instead asking another of his own. "I thought I saw you a couple days ago riding a cycle."

Is that what this is about?

Charlie considered telling the cop it was none of his business what he had been riding a few days ago. He'd been hassled by police before just because he was an Indian. But a protest would only get him down to the stationhouse in a hurry. Then, there would be fingerprints, overnight in a cell for "resisting arrest" or some other bogus charge. Fingerprints were of far more concern than a ticket or a night behind bars.

"Yes, sir. I owned a Harley for a few days, but it turned out to be something I really couldn't afford. I traded it in at the dealership when I bought the car."

The cop appeared to soften up a bit. "That's a shame," he conceded. "It looked like a nice ride."

"Yeah," Charlie agreed, sounding wistful. It didn't take much effort. He now regretted letting go of the Harley.

Which left Troy hanging. He'd made a stop to check out a young Indian he'd seen tooling around town on a fancy motorcycle that he shouldn't really be able to afford. But now the Indian turned out to be someone who seemed like a fairly decent fellow. He'd even admitted the bike was beyond his means. As Troy handed back the registration, he offered the excuse he'd given many times during his career, after stopping someone without probable cause.

"We've been looking for someone on an out-of-state warrant. No offense, but you came close to fitting the description. Sorry to have bothered you, Mr. Dozen. Have a nice day."

"Thanks, officer. Glad you're here to keep the public safe." Charlie smiled. The cop finally begrudged him a nod of approval, and then strutted back to his car, turned off the rack of lights, and waited for two cars to pass before pulling a u-turn and speeding off in the opposite direction.

"Jeez!" Charlie said, as he pulled back onto the road.

Five minutes later he arrived at the city library.

When Clarissa had asked him to find the instructor's name, he hoped the school might have the course posted on its website.

He now used one of the library's computers to access the Internet, and sure enough, a course description yielded Irv Goodwin's name plus a bio and a photo. He saw the times for the course, realized the business class was just letting out, sprinted back to his car and drove to the school. But by the time he arrived, no one was there.

If Charlie had arrived just a few minutes earlier he would have seen Irv talking to Trisha out on the front lawn. If he'd come close enough, he would have sensed that Trisha was of the Order. The reverse was also true: Trisha would have sensed his resonance. No such luck for either of them on that particular day.

Charlie decided not to attempt tracking down Goodwin in person. The school's website hadn't listed a home address. But the name was enough for Clarissa to ask Frank Miller.

He headed back to Portage.

The girls were several blocks from the school, walking to Frank's office, when Nina caught that strange feeling of *someone* being near. She paused on the sidewalk, eyes unfocused as her mind traveled, searching.

Chantha recognized *that look* and stopped. "Are you okay?" she asked Nina. There was no response—just as if Nina hadn't heard.

Nina had no way of knowing that Charlie's car was a full block away, on the other side of a row of buildings, headed away from her. And no way of knowing that her sensitivity to resonance was growing by leaps and bounds on practically a daily basis. In a few seconds the weirdness was gone. Nina's eyes refocused upon Selena and Chantha.

"I feel like I just tripped on my shadow," she said, struggling to overcome the dizzy feeling in her head. "It's like a ghost just passed overhead."

"That's creepy," Selena said, nervously glancing up. And feeling relieved when all she saw were a couple of fluffy clouds.

Chantha took Nina's hand and it felt cold. She rubbed it briefly, and said, "Let's get over to Dad's office."

Nina let herself be led along, trying to reach out with her mind and capture what had been there, and drawing a total blank. After two blocks of *nothing* she finally gave up.

When they reached Frank's office, he came out to greet the girls. And then he asked to spend a few minutes alone with Nina before he drove them all home. Chantha gave her dad a look that said she didn't understand. He offered a lame shrug for an excuse as he led Nina to his office.

Once they were behind the closed door, Frank said, "Three weeks ago you told me you were an accommodation to mollify Evelyn. Do you still feel that way?"

Nina didn't remember using the word "mollify" but it was an accurate way to put it. She was pleased he felt comfortable using a "big" word with her. "I do," she said.

"What if you had another option for a place to live? Would you be interested?"

"Maybe," Nina said. "But the state usually moves kids far enough so there won't be any conflict with previous foster parents. I'm afraid they'd move me away from the valley if I asked for a change. I'd like to stay here because of Chantha and Selena."

"What if you were to come and live with our family?"

Nina was stunned. Her voice trembled as she said, "Is that possible?"

"Yes. It's possible. Anna and I were once licensed for foster care. I'm certain we could put it together." He reached for a thick manila folder that lay at the end of his desk. "I've even drafted a few documents for the legal proceedings."

In fact, since the meeting with Clarissa he'd done little else. He now had every form prepared, including a temporary restraining order removing Nina from the Torgerson home if things got out of hand.

"Before we go to court, you'll have to meet with a state worker and convince her there's an urgent need for a change of residence. Do you think you could do that?"

Nina remembered the confrontation with Dan over the bunny. Evelyn sitting passively while he grilled her. And before that, Dan's sudden exit for the weekend to "think things over."

"You bet!" She understood how the system worked. She'd just never had a chance to choose where she'd go next.

"Okay," Frank said, relived. And getting a little excited. "I'll contact protective services and get the ball rolling." He stood, and then paused. "Nina, you shouldn't tell any of this to Chantha or Selena. In fact, you shouldn't tell anyone. It will take a few days to schedule a hearing, and if word got back to the Torgersons, it might get very awkward."

"Of course," Nina said, wishing she could at least share the news with Chantha. How wonderful to be living in the same house with her best friend!

But when she entered the reception room her face was calm. Frank was right. Especially about Selena. It had to remain a secret for now.

"What did Dad want?" Chantha asked, as they stood in the parking lot, waiting for Frank to bring the car around.

"He had a question about how I got the signature from Clarissa," Nina said in a steady voice, with no hint of something more important.

"That's all?"

"Yes," Nina insisted.

Chantha gave her a suspicious look, shrugged, and decided it wasn't important enough to press for more of an answer.

CHAPTER FORTY-SIX

Following Wednesday's class, Trisha left the school exhausted, but with a growing sense of hope that all had not been lost on Monday.

The morning started with Nina still withdrawn, practically silent. Chantha seemed prepared to defend her, so Trisha had again focused on the third girl.

"Selena, please tell me more about the response you got on Facebook."

Once again in the spotlight, Selena became a nonstop fount of enthusiasm. Thousands of girls were interested in the Money Bunny. One of these had even formed a fan club, asking Selena to be its president. Selena declined, telling the girl that decisions about the bunny had to come equally with her partners. She looked at Nina and Chantha. "Is it okay if I tell them your names?"

"Sure, why not?" Chantha said.

Nina hesitated, looked at Chantha, who nodded her approval. "I guess so," she reluctantly agreed.

"Great!" Selena said, motoring on to describe a problem she now faced. "It would be so much easier to keep track of everyone if I didn't have to share the family computer with my brother."

Trisha nodded sympathetically. "Tell us more."

Selena's parents insisted that no matter how important she thought the bunny project was, her brother Benny was equally entitled to computer time. And Benny capitalized on this by insisting upon using up every second of his allotment before turning the computer over to Selena. "He's a pain!" she anguished, throwing up her arms to emphasize just how much of a brat her brother was being.

As Trisha listened, she gave an occasional glance at Nina and Chantha. When it seemed clear they sympathized with Selena's plight, Trisha offered a solution designed to place Selena completely under her control.

"I think this project has good prospects," she began, "and clear lines of communication will be a vital key to long term success. Since Selena is the one keeping track of thousands of potential customers, wouldn't it be a good idea to give her the proper tools to work with?"

"What do you mean?" Chantha felt a twinge of envy, guessing what Trisha was about to propose. She might not be as pretty as Selena, or as smart as Nina, but she currently held the advantage of having the best resources for accessing the Internet. That now seemed about to change.

"Well, at least a tablet with some advanced capacity for spreadsheets. A laptop might also be something to consider."

Selena's eyes grew wide.

When Trisha finished describing the list of hardware and software that she thought could get the job done, Selena said with a heavy sigh, "We don't have money for that kind of stuff."

"I wasn't thinking about you three, or even your parents," Trisha said carefully. "I was thinking of personally advancing the funds. Of course—" she said quickly "—I would expect to be re-paid after you begin making sales."

Selena looked like she might float right off the ground. "You'd do that?"

"Of course," Trisha said.

She now addressed all three, careful to share eye contact even with Nina. "I'm completely on board with this project, ladies. It's a terrific idea. You already have the two most important keys to success: You've got the cutest bunny, plus a huge base of customers lining up to buy one. With the right financial support, this business could really take off. A few hundred dollars for a good laptop, plus some software . . . those would be easy investments for me to make. And please don't think of these as big-ticket items. I make a lot of money in New York. Which is not to say I'd throw it away on something I didn't believe in. But I do very much believe in you and your project. Truly, I do." Trisha pushed with every ounce of her charm. And for Selena—and now even Chantha—it worked. With Nina, it seemed to just barely edge her up towards the crest of the hill. Still . . . with this unique girl, "just barely" felt like a huge victory.

From there on the morning improved. Trisha explained the basics of spreadsheets and mass mailing software, and got Selena to promise to watch a series of basic business videos on YouTube during the next five days. When they met next Monday, she wanted Selena ready to actually start drafting documents on the equipment Trisha promised she would buy. She was also careful to insist that Selena closely coordinate with Chantha and Nina so they could help in the start-up work. This seemed to draw Nina in just a little more.

The payoff finally came. By the end of two hours, Nina was showing interest, seeming to want more input, even a bit of control.

The humorous part for Trisha was Irv Goodwin. He only lasted half an hour at the back of the room. He finally spoke up from his chair. His back had grown stiff, his patience was gone.

"I think you girls can handle it from here on out."

Heads turned, having forgotten he was even there.

"I'm going for coffee. Ms. Peterson has my cell number if you need me."

They all thanked him, and after the classroom door closed, Trisha didn't bother to hide her smile.

Now back at the hotel parking lot, she decided to go for a swim. It was nearly a hundred degrees, and the thought of a long dip in the lake made for quick steps up the stairs and down the hallway to her room.

As she inserted the key card, there came a moment when it seemed someone was standing behind her. *Resonance?* But no one was in the hallway. *Could this be a leftover from being around Nina this morning?* It seemed plausible, as there was no other ready explanation.

As she grabbed a swimsuit from her suitcase and stepped out of her slacks, she shrugged off the feeling. By the time she reached the beach she was certain it had only been her imagination.

CHAPTER FORTY-SEVEN

V alerie made the all night drive from San Jose to central
Washington in her red Maserati GranTurismo.

To keep her mind busy on long drives, she had invented
a game that tested her mathematical skills. After talking to a
traffic cop about where police drew the line with speeders, she
created an algorithm that incorporated things like how rural
was the road, whether the drive was on a weekend, the time
of day, how many small towns she would pass through, were
the police more likely to be local cops, sheriff deputies or state
patrol, and the type of radar or laser equipment they might
have. And finally, she applied a special constant—what Valerie
called the "red sports car factor." The Maserati always drew
more attention.

On the day before a long drive, she scanned the route on
MapQuest, memorizing distances, town sizes, and calculating
where there might be rush hour traffic.

It had turned speeding into a fine science. In all, there were
thirty-one factors she ran in her head. In the five years since

she'd invented the math, she'd been stopped twice and given warnings . . . but no tickets.

She considered selling her invention as an app for cell phones, but decided most people wouldn't take the time, or have the smarts, to collect and input the data. And besides, it was her private joy. There were times when the algorithm said it was safe to push the car up over a hundred miles an hour, usually on un-populated stretches of country road late at night. And why would you want to share that kind of temptation with teenaged drivers and drunks?

Risk wasn't completely eliminated by her nifty algorithm. There remained the possibility of deer, fallen rocks, and small animals like porcupines, foxes, and even birds. If you hit some-thing at high speed there would be damage, possibly a blown windshield if something came over the hood. On most trips, Valerie obeyed the speed limit. But there were times . . .

She arrived early on Wednesday morning, checked into her room, and promptly fell into a deep sleep from which she did not awaken until 2pm.

There was a moment when something nearly woke her up—a dream about a woman wordlessly beckoning to her. But it quickly faded, and Valerie coasted back into soothing blackness.

When she finally awoke her first thought was of food. It was twenty hours since she'd last eaten. A call to the front desk con-firmed there was a pub in the hotel complex. Valerie took a show-er, pulled on jeans and a blouse, slipped on open-toed Trotters, and headed off in search of a late lunch.

As Valerie was digging into a chicken Caesar salad, Trisha returned to her room from the swim. After a short shower she, too, felt hungry. She padded downstairs and crossed the drive-way and started up the flight of metal stairs leading to the sec-ond floor pub. Halfway up the steps, the feeling of someone nearby—someone with resonance—pressed into her like a wave.

Clarissa?

But as she took one hesitant step, then another, the sensation remained steady, far below what she'd experienced with Nina, or with Clarissa at the annual gatherings many years ago.

Accidentally coming across someone who *belonged* was a needle in a haystack proposition. So . . .

Have they already flown someone in from Zurich? Or is it someone aligned with Clarissa!

Whoever it was, they would have already sensed her presence. Trisha resumed her climb, hoping the member she was about to confront was not a warrior working for the other side.

When she reached the veranda, she peeked in through a bank of windows and there was just one customer inside—a Chinese woman who sat alone, eating a salad. The woman's concentration remained upon her food.

Is she purposefully ignoring me? Why would she do that? Another thought occurred. *Is this who I sensed when I got back from Langston?*

Trisha walked around the corner of the veranda to the door. As she pushed it open, the woman finally did look up, first towards the bar, and then to her left and right, as if she might have heard a noise. She reached for a glass of water and took a long drink.

She doesn't know!

This realization brought a thrill. There were at present just 321 identified members who belonged to the Order. Even with Watchers around the globe on the lookout, it was a remarkable year in which they discovered two or more new members. To have stumbled upon this woman by accident was remarkable. So remarkable, in fact, that Trisha reassessed her conclusion that this woman apparently didn't know what she was.

Maybe she's just a very good actress.

Valerie entered the room and angled for the bar, passing close enough to reach out and touch the stranger if she had wanted to. When she reached the long counter, she asked the bartender, "Do you have lemonade?"

"Certainly," he said, turning around and pulling open a mini-fridge. He fished ice cubes from an insulated bucket, poured lemonade from a silver pitcher, set the pitcher back in the fridge, and shoved a lemon wedge onto the rim before sliding the glass towards Trisha. "Is that all?"

"Yes." Trisha showed him her room keycard and signed the receipt.

Picking up her glass, she turned around just in time to see the woman headed out the door. She was tempted to follow, but instead turned back to the bar, set her glass of lemonade on the polished wood, and said to the bartender, "I've changed my mind about food. May I please have a menu?"

The woman had given her something new and entirely unexpected to think about.

CHAPTER FORTY-EIGHT

Dan Torgerson finally reached the limit of his patience on Wednesday evening.

When Frank Miller dropped Nina off just before dinner on Sunday, she seemed like a different person from the girl who'd gone for a weekend sleepover. She barely spoke during the meal, and went straight to her room as soon as she finished eating. This pattern of behavior had persisted into the week. Dan didn't really care whether or not she spoke to him. But Evelyn was a different matter. The woman he loved had been moping around the house for days. It was the kid's fault for sure.

Even more frustrating, there was still no sign of the bunny. He'd searched Nina's room when she left the house, searched the garage, with no luck.

It was time for action.

Dan headed for the den. As a Rotary member, he figured this entitled him to contact any officer at home. The club secretary, Irv Goodwin, who was listed on the school's website as the summer class instructor, wasn't in the phone book. Dan found the number for Rotary president Ricky Erickson. He stabbed at the keys on the handset and waited.

"Ricky here," said a voice on the other end of the line.

"Hey, Ricky. It's Dan Torgerson. I need to get in touch with Irv. You got his home number?"

"Why 'd ya need to bother him at home?"

Dan nearly told Ricky it was none of his business. But he and Ricky weren't like, well, what you'd call "good buddies" so Dan played it nice.

"My kid's in a summer class he's teaching and I need to ask a question is all."

Ricky's opinion of Dan was roughly equal to pond scum. Compounded by the fact that Dan hadn't attended a Rotary meeting in three months. But what could you do? Kick him out? Sure. But where was the gain in that? You just lost his dues.

"That's your foster girl, right?"

Nice call, Ricky. Guess you're not quite ready for the nursing home yet.

"Our lovely Nina," Dan gushed, even though it made his stomach turn to sound that pleasant about the kid. "She's learning about running a business in a summer class Irv is teaching. I've got a quick question about what they're doing."

"Oh. Well, I guess I can give out his home number for something like that." There was a long pause. "You ready with pencil and paper?"

"You bet."

Ricky rattled off the number.

Before Dan could hang up, Ricky asked, "Are you planning on making it to the meeting tomorrow? We've got a great program on the Columbia River salmon restoration project."

"Sure thing, Ricky. Sorry I've been missing so many meetings. Things have been chock-a-block busy with my business."

And what a lie that was. Everyone in town seemed to know he was going broke.

"Okay, then. Hope to see you tomorrow. Hey . . . Irv's going to be at the meeting. Why don't you just come and ask him your question in person?" There was a fast click on the other end of the line.

Dan was about to utter an obscenity into the now-dead line, when he realized he'd just been handed the perfect way to chat up Goodwin, maybe even get a little extra info he wouldn't expect from a phone call. So instead of rousting Irv from the couch, where he was probably watching some stupid sitcom, Dan decided to attend the Rotary lunch, catch Irv before things got started, and have a few words to sort out what was happening with the bunny. If he was lucky, he might even escape before the guest speaker took to the podium. Salmon recovery? No thanks.

CHAPTER FORTY-NINE

O n Thursday morning, Trisha moved into a new room a hundred yards away from the Asian woman's room. Then she slipped into a light blue cotton dress and pulled on a pair of low-heeled pumps, intent upon putting the stranger to the test.

First she tried the pub, but the woman wasn't there.

Next came the beach bar and the rows of deck chairs and recliners. There were plenty of tourists catching an early tan, but none were her target.

She set off up the main street, walking the hot concrete, searching for the telltale sign of resonance. As she passed a real estate office and came to a coffee house, she finally caught the familiar tingle. Looking in through the glass she saw the woman seated alone. Trisha pushed the door into a wash of cool air.

She placed an order at the espresso bar, and when her drink was ready, she turned. Their eyes made brief contact, and the woman smiled, looking momentarily confused.

Valerie returned a smile and took an encouraging step. "Didn't I see you in the restaurant yesterday?"

The woman nodded. "Yes. Have we met before?" Again, confusion.

"I don't think so. May I join you?"

"Sure. My name's Valerie."

"Trisha," she said, sitting down across the table. "I'm here for a break from work. How about you?"

"Just arrived yesterday," Valerie said. "I drove up from San Jose, and frankly I'm still a little beat from pulling that much time behind the wheel."

San Jose?

"Are you part of that Silicon Valley crowd?"

Valerie said, "If you mean 'IT' then yes, I'm a part of that 'Silicon Valley crowd.' I own an information services company. And you?"

"I work in finance. Mostly offshore banking. Let's just say I have some interesting clients who'd rather remain anonymous." Trisha gave a wink that said, *Might have to kill you if you knew too much. Hah! Hah!* But it wasn't that funny, really. Some of her customers actually thought that way. "So, you're here for fun?" Trisha continued, casually taking a sip of her cappuccino.

"More like business," Valerie said. "I'm supposed to meet someone."

Uh Oh!

"And in the mean time?"

"I hadn't really thought much about it," Valerie said.

She's lying. But I can't ask her that *question, can I? I can't say Clarissa's name. But I need to know more.*

"I came up the street to shop for a new swimsuit. Care to join me?"

"No," Valerie said. "I need to catch up on my sleep."

"Okay." Trisha cradled her cappuccino in both hands, pushed back her chair and stood up. "Maybe we'll run into each other later." She walked out onto the sidewalk and turned for the hotel, now intent upon another meeting where she expected nothing but success.

And leaving Valerie completely confused.

I've just met the most incredible woman, and I drove her off! What is wrong with me? But the answer was simple. Worrying about a meeting with Clarissa had frayed her confidence to the bone.

A few minutes later Valerie left the coffee shop. When she reached her room she pulled the blinds and collapsed onto the queen-sized bed, and then screamed into the big fluffy pillow in total frustration.

CHAPTER FIFTY

When the doorbell rang shortly before noon on Thursday, Maria Hernandez went to find out who was there and discovered a willowy young blonde standing on the front porch. Her fashionable black jacket, knee-length skirt, and white blouse shouted *selling cosmetics,* or *soliciting for charity.* Maria had little patience for door-to-door solicitors, no matter how well dressed, or how honeyed their words.

"Good morning," Maria said, polite but crisp. "May I help you?"

The blonde returned a glorious smile. Maria suddenly felt as if the sun had risen that morning for the sole purpose of brightening her day.

"We haven't met yet," the woman said, almost apologetically, with a slight inflection suggesting the East coast. "I'm teaching a summer business course up at the high school, and I have the pleasure of having your daughter Selena in my class."

Maria's heart beat a little faster.

"My name is Trisha Peterson."

Maria pushed the screen door wide, and said, "Please come in, Miss Peterson. Selena has told us how much she loves your class." As Valerie took a step over the threshold, Maria confessed, "Sometimes Selena isn't too excited about sitting in a classroom. We sometimes even worry about her completing high school. But if all teachers were like you, I think she would already be planning for college."

"You're much too gracious," Trisha said, taking the hand Maria extended, squeezing gently, perfectly.

"No. You deserve full credit for what you are doing. You should have been a teacher."

"Well, thank you. I find the volunteer work to be more than enough of a reward."

There came an awkward pause as Maria remembered she had no idea why Miss Peterson had shown up at her front door. Trisha recovered the moment perfectly.

"Has your daughter mentioned my offer to purchase the girls some equipment for the project they're working on?"

Selena had most certainly told her mom about this wonder of wonders. In fact, she hadn't talked about much else since Frank Miller dropped her off yesterday afternoon. The way she described it, Miss Peterson was ready to fill a room with computers loaded with every imaginable kind of software. Maria had assured her daughter that someone teaching in Langston for only three weeks would never follow through on such a promise. But with Trisha Peterson now standing in her living room, she wondered if she might have been wrong.

Embarrassed by her earlier judgment of someone she hadn't even met, Maria was about to ask what Trisha actually intended, when Selena—who had been in the family room watching TV—came to investigate who her mom was talking to. When she saw who it was, her response was spontaneous and unstoppable.

"Trisha!" Selena shouted, rushing to give Trisha a hug.

Trisha appeared unprepared. She reluctantly accepted the enveloping arms, looking past Selena's head, at Maria, with a lift of eyebrows and upwards roll of her eyes to confirm her surprise. Maria smiled and gave a shrug to acknowledge the wonder of it all.

When Selena finally let go, Maria stepped forward and said, "Selena, please!" Selena looked sheepish for a moment. Maria turned to Trisha and said, "Would you like a cup of coffee, Miss Peterson?"

"Thank you, Mrs. Hernandez—"

"Please call me 'Maria'."

"Well, okay, Maria. And please, call me 'Trisha.' Thank you for the offer, but there's a lot I need to accomplish today. So I'd like to get straight to the reason I came."

Maria again felt uncomfortable. "Selena told us something about a computer. We have a computer here at home for her to use. You really don't need to buy her anything." Maria and Ernesto had worked hard and made sacrifices so their children would have a better life than their own early years of struggle after crossing from Mexico, learning English, becoming citizens. Family pride was at stake.

Selena opened her mouth to speak, but Trisha raised one hand and Selena settled. Maria stood amazed. Trisha's hand dropped as she returned her attention to Maria.

"I'm sure your computer is excellent, but there are some advanced graphics the girls will need, plus business software to organize a large data base. This will require lots of very fast memory. So rather than add new cards to your computer, and possibly mess up other programs you are already running, it's just simpler to start with new equipment. That is . . . if it's okay with you and your husband?"

What could Maria possibly say? "Well, if you think it's necessary."

"Oh, Mom . . ." Selena pleaded. Maria's face promised a reprimand, and Selena responded with a rebellious look.

Trisha picked up as if nothing had passed between mother and daughter.

"What I'd like to do is take you and Selena down to the store so we can pick out what the girls need."

"Right now?"

Selena was ready to jump straight up in the air, but somehow managed to stand still, eyes bright with hope, looking back and forth between her mom and Trisha.

Maria's uneasiness surged a little. This had all happened so fast. She wished Ernesto were home so they could talk. "I was doing some housework—"

"I could come back tomorrow if that works better." Accompanied by a gentle nudge: *We really should do this right now. Can't you find some excuse to just go with it!*

Maria saw her daughter was practically ready to scream, and now remembered something her own mother had told her years ago.

If someone offers to give you something, you go and get it.

"Okay," Maria relented. Selena abruptly gave her mom a big hug, and then gave Trisha yet another hug.

Maria said, "I'll go and get my purse. We can meet you there."

"Let's take my car," Trisha offered. "It's got a big trunk."

Selena's improbably wide smile grew even wider.

When Maria stepped out the front door and saw the blue Mercedes parked in their driveway, her last urge to resist faded away completely.

As Trisha was pulling up in front of *Ken's Computers* in downtown Langston, Dan Torgerson was nervously shifting from foot to foot in the hallway outside the Holiday Inn's conference room.

The Rotary meeting was about to begin, and Irv Goodwin was still missing. Dan thought he might have to make that phone call after all. And then, just as chapter president Ricky Erickson walked out to tell straggling members to come inside for the flag salute, in walked Irv.

Dan stepped in front of him.

Irv was puzzled by "No-show Torgerson" blocking his path, and tried to step around Dan.

"Got a minute, Irv?" Dan said, moving to stay between Irv and the doorway.

Irv wanted to say "No." But Dan held his ground. Irv sighed.

"What's up, Dan?"

"You know that class you're teaching up at the high school? My kid's one of your students."

Irv remembered Nina as the quiet one. "She's in there with two other girls. Why?"

"The bunny project. How's it going?"

"Fine," Irv said.

Inside the meeting room, Ricky was leading the flag salute. Dan leaned in close, his voice now a whisper. "Is it going to be a money maker?"

Irv's already low opinion of Dan plummeted. He stepped past Dan, and said over his shoulder, "Let's talk about it after the meeting's done." Leaving Dan standing alone in the breezeway, fuming. He was going to have to listen to all that crap about salmon recovery after all.

⊶ ⊷

Three blocks away, Trisha, Maria and Selena entered *Ken's* and met "Robert," a gangly kid with a red mop-top that looked like it might never have seen a barber's shears.

After a brief look at several box computers, Robert suggested a laptop. "It has a smaller screen, but the resolution's better."

"It's more expensive," Maria objected, feeling guilty about taking advantage of Trisha.

"That's not important," Trisha countered firmly.

Selena stood beaming, certain that Trisha was the most special person in the entire world.

Robert unconsciously brushed back a greasy lock from his forehead. "Kids love laptops," he continued smoothly, with a quick glance at Selena to be certain she was on board. No problem there! Robert turned it up a notch.

"Lots of memory, very fast—I mean VERY FAST—and easy to move. Is sharing the computer going to be important?"

Selena's joy dimmed. She hadn't thought about sharing. But certainly, Chantha and Nina would need to see her work. She tried to sound upbeat as she volunteered, "I guess it would be nice to be able to bring the computer to class."

Trisha nodded in approval. Maria shrugged. Robert grinned—selling a laptop meant a bigger commission.

Trisha asked Maria, "What kind of Internet connection do you have?"

"Fiber," Maria said. "Ernesto and I don't know much about the Internet, but the kids, they deserve the best, so we got something fast."

"It's a hundred meg download rate," Selena said proudly. The service provider had offered several plans. Selena and her brother had pleaded for the faster connection, even though it cost nearly fifty bucks a month. Maria and Ernesto decided it was a good investment. Computers were the gateway to the future.

Trisha added, "I think a cell phone would also be helpful."

Selena couldn't believe what she was hearing.

Maria felt she had to draw a line somewhere. "Cell phones are too expensive," she said. "We bought a plan for Ernesto's yard service and it's over eighty dollars a month. We really can't afford another phone."

Trisha turned to the clerk. "Robert. Do you have short-term prepaid plans for a smart phone?"

"Sure," Robert said, again calculating what his commission might be. "You can buy service one month at a time if you want. Of course, it's more expensive. And it's not like the two year plan, where you get a phone for free. Depending on the model, it'll cost between five hundred and eight hundred bucks to buy the phone. Over time, a longer plan is the cheapest way to go. But whatever you want, we can put it together."

They settled on a mid-level droid-based smart phone, with Trisha prepaying the first three months of service. Beyond that, it was up to Selena and her parents to decided if they wanted to keep the plan active. If not, Trisha said they could mail her the phone and she'd sell it for whatever she could get.

The shopping spree continued with a color printer, cables, and software. The final tally ran to just over four grand.

Maria felt trapped, and was about to protest when Trisha turned to her and said, "Am I right that Selena currently shares the family's computer with her brother Benny?"

"Yes." And that was another problem for Maria. Benny would no longer have to share the family computer with his sister— something he would have been overjoyed with before now. But his sister was going have a computer much more powerful than the older model, and Benny wasn't going to like that one bit. She knew her son well enough to know that he would test the limits by sneaking time on the new computer when Selena wasn't around.

It was as if Trisha had read her mind.

"It might be a good idea for this equipment to be kept in Selena's room. The girls will need to keep what they are doing under wraps until they are ready to launch their product. Do you agree?"

"You're probably right," Maria said, wondering how she had lost the ability to say "No."

"Absolutely," Selena said, with a vigorous nod. Both Maria and Trisha gave Selena a look, but her enthusiasm was undeterred.

Robert saw yet another commission chance, and said, "We've got a few computer tables on clearance right now."

Maria gave him a look that said he'd taken one step too far.

"I was just sayin'," he defended, sheepishly.

Trisha decided to have a little fun.

"After all we've bought today, why don't you throw one in for free?" Robert's face got sober real quick. "It doesn't have to be your most expensive one, just something reasonable," Trisha continued easily, not allowing Robert a chance to object, enjoying a moment of the arm-twisting power her charm was capable of.

"Well . . . okay," Robert said. "I think we can make that happen." But he was not happy.

Trisha decided to improve his mood.

"Do you do installation work, Robert?"

He hated installations. But what the heck. He was going to catch a load of grief from the boss for having just given away seventy-five bucks worth of cheap pressed-board computer table. Maybe he could cut his losses. "Sure," he said.

"If you do the installation at Maria's house, it would be worth a couple hundred bucks. How's that sound?"

It sounded terrific. "What's the address?" he said, reaching to his pocket protector for a pen.

Maria gave him the address, along with a look of hopeless wonder. They talked about miracles in church. Maria had just never expected one to come along in the person of a tall blonde from New York!

⋯⊰⊱⋯

As things wrapped up at *Ken's Computers*, the Rotary meeting was breaking, and Dan finally cornered Irv in the hallway.

"So how's it look?"

Irv was disgusted. His reply was both dismissive and condescending. "They're kids, Dan. I have no idea whether or not it'll make money. You'd have to talk to Trisha about that."

"Trisha?" Dan was puzzled. "Who's that?"

Irv felt sick. If the girl hadn't told her stepfather, well, didn't that speak volumes? But Dan was still Nina's foster parent, and legally he had the right to pry. Irv saw no alternative but to explain.

"She's a gal from NYC who volunteered to teach this summer. She works in a high powered investment firm." Irv now found it hard to suppress the same excitement he felt every time he thought about the most remarkable woman he'd ever met. "I'll tell you this . . . she can't be more than in her mid-twenties, but this woman really knows her stuff. If anyone can help the girls make this bunny project happen, it's Trisha."

"Does she have a last name?" Dan asked.

"Peterson," Irv said. "It's Trisha Peterson."

"And where exactly does she work?"

"Like I already said, she's from New York City."

"Name of the firm?"

Irv didn't have a clue. Boyd Nedrickson would have checked her credentials before he brought her onboard. And it wasn't like Irv was worried. He'd heard her talk, seen her work with the girls. Trisha Peterson was the genuine article. Still, confessing a lack of knowledge about someone entrusted to teach kids probably wasn't the brightest move, so Irv's cynical reply was, "That's something we don't disclose. Someone who volunteers, the school always checks them out, but these people deserve their privacy. We can't have parents calling up and pestering them. If we let that happen, we'd never get anyone to volunteer. I'm sure you understand."

The only thing Dan "understood" was that Irv was being a turd. But if she was as high flying as Irv had painted out, Dan could find her on the Internet. There couldn't be that many "Trisha Petersons" working for investment firms in New York.

"Thanks, Irv. You've been a real help," Dan said, thinly holding onto the sarcasm.

"You're welcome," Irv said, in a tone that stung back just as hard.

⊷⊷ ⊷⊷

As Dan and Irv walked away from each other, Trisha was driving south along the Columbia River. Having brought Selena's mother into the fold, she was now preoccupied with a far less certain hurdle.

Valerie.

CHAPTER FIFTY-ONE

Nina boarded the bus to Langston on Friday morning for her meeting with Frank. As she walked up the aisle, she half expected another episode of feeling someone *different* and *special* being *here*. But the dozen-or-so passengers seemed entirely normal. No shadows. No ghosts.

Maybe I am going crazy.

She settled into a seat near the middle, beside a woman who was talking on a cell phone. The woman ignored her, and that was fine. There was a lot to think about and Nina wasn't in a chatting mood.

She had again dreamed about the field filled with tents. The memory of the tents was still there, and she also remembered a jagged line of snowcapped mountains. She knew in time she would remember everything, and that she would eventually understand why she was having these peculiar dreams.

On this particular morning there were two other things on her mind.

She would finally learn from Frank when her appointment with the state caseworker would take place. She could then look forward to a more definite date for the move.

And then there was last night's call from Selena.

Dan had come to her room, and said, "Your Hispanic girl-friend says she needs to talk to you. Please use the phone in the den." He sounded put out, and Nina realized he was baiting her by calling Selena "Hispanic." She refused to give him the satisfaction of a reaction. Soon she'd be gone, and Dan could dry up and blow away in the wind for all she cared.

She walked to the den and picked up the phone.

"What's up, Selena?"

"You won't believe it!" Followed by silence. Selena being a drama queen.

"So?" Nina finally insisted.

The words poured out. "Trisha Peterson showed up at our front door yesterday and took mom and me down to the computer store and bought everything we need for our project!"

A little voice in the back of Nina's head said this was maybe cause for concern.

"What does 'everything' mean?"

"Laptop, software, cell phone—"

"Cell phone?" Nina hadn't imagined Trisha would go that far.

"In case I need to get on the Internet if I can't connect to fiber." There was a pause, then, "I'll bet she would get you a cell phone too, if you asked."

Nina didn't want to ask Trisha for anything. But she was curious what else Selena had shaken her down for.

"I'm coming into Langston tomorrow morning. I could come over to your place after my appointment."

"Appointment?"

Why'd I say appointment? If Selena learned about her meeting with Frank, there would be a string of questions. She didn't want to lie, but . . . "It's for a routine medical check-up. The state requires it every year for foster kids."

"Oh . . . okay," Selena said. "When do you think you'll get here?"

"Around ten." She was set to meet Frank at 9:30. The Hernandez house was six blocks from his office. It wouldn't take long for Frank to tell her about the caseworker and the interview.

"Great! Wait till you see all this stuff. My little brother nearly exploded!"

Benny was an okay kid—for a ten-year-old—but when he was around his sister, the rivalry could get pretty fierce. A jealous Benny would have surely pumped up Selena's ego. Nina decided not to stoke the fire, and simply said, "I'll see you at ten," before hanging up.

As she passed through the living room, Dan and Evelyn were sitting on the couch talking. Dan ignored her. Evelyn looked up.

"Honey, what did Selena want?"

Nina hadn't yet asked if she could go into Langston the next morning, and saw an opportunity.

"Selena's got a new computer she wants to show me. Would it be okay if I went into town tomorrow morning on the nine o'clock bus?"

"Of course. Just be sure to call when you arrive so I'll know where you are."

"Of course—" She almost said "Mom." But it seemed no use to pretend anymore. Before she reached her bedroom, she heard Dan and Evelyn resume their conversation in low voices.

CHAPTER FIFTY-TWO

The next morning Charlie followed the bus from Portage, keeping it barely in sight out of concern for the range of Nina's resonance. There was no danger of losing her. He knew exactly where she was headed. Frank Miller had called to tell Clarissa.

When she stepped off the bus in downtown Langston, Charlie found a spot to park. He had plenty to think about.

With Frank's recruitment, Clarissa's mood had brightened. But Charlie didn't share Clarissa's enthusiasm for what she called *the progress we're making.* They had recruited a lawyer. Really, it was no big deal when compared to the Order's infinite resources. For Clarissa to be thinking this might make a difference seemed to Charlie like grasping at straws.

And then there was the government. Clarissa thought they had at least four or five years before the "regulars" closed in. Charlie figured it was less. Maybe a *lot* less. The NSA was actively gleaning information in its search to identify terrorists. Sooner or later, one of those "misfits" who turned up in a search would be a member of the Order.

When the agents came, there would be no telltale resonance for a warning. There would simply be a black van pull up and guys in dark suits would jump out and it really didn't matter who they came after—no skill a member possessed would defeat a coordinated attack by armed agents. Well . . . maybe if the member was a warrior there would be a chance. But even if a warrior won the first round, it would only be a matter of time before they came again, and in such strength that the outcome would be certain.

Charlie hoped it wasn't him they came for. But if it was, he had already made a solemn vow to the spirits of the Wind River that it wouldn't be pretty.

CHAPTER FIFTY-THREE

Nina wasn't in the best of spirits when she reached Selena's front door. Frank had reported that no caseworker was available for an interview until next Thursday. He'd asked for an earlier time, but the supervisor wouldn't budge.

"They asked if there was some kind of emergency. Were you being abused? Were you in danger? I couldn't lie and say that you were."

In truth, Frank had wanted to say that a group called "the Order" was coming to kidnap Nina, that her current foster parents were clueless, and that she'd be far safer in his home. But Clarissa's block stopped the words cold in his throat. After that failure, he gave up and agreed that next Thursday would work just fine.

Now, standing on the front porch of the Hernandez home, Nina tried to force a smile as the door flew open. Selena's joy faded when she saw Nina's face. "What's wrong," she asked, her smile gone in an instant, hoping the medical exam hadn't turned up something bad.

"I'm okay," Nina insisted. "I've just been thinking about how big this whole thing is."

Selena reached out and took Nina's hand, remembering her own earlier complaint about not being able to plan much else for the summer. But that was eons ago; long before she had a desk full of new computer gear.

"You have Chantha and me to help, and wait till you see what Trisha has bought us."

Nina let herself be led through the house, and there, covering Selena's new computer desk, were a laptop, color printer, and a smart phone. Across the computer screen floated an image of the bunny.

Selena sat down and grabbed the mouse; the screen resolved into dozens of icons. "Check this out," she said, moving the pointer to an icon and clicking. A screen opened, and Selena clicked on a file, and now, centered against a grid, was an image of the bunny. Selena set the pointer on one corner of the image and dragged it, and the bunny rotated through three dimensions. The sides and back were not golden fur, just a grid image. "If you bring the bunny over I can take more pictures and build up a total three dimensional picture."

This finally brought a smile to Nina's face. They might not have to take the bunny apart after all. The bunny's black pearl heart suddenly seemed safer.

"I thought you'd like it," Selena said, interpreting Nina's smile as approval. "I'm just starting to learn, and it will take time to figure it all out, but Trisha promised she could help me, even after she's gone back to New York."

Selena had been so excited she'd stayed up late to watch tutorials. When her mom headed for the bathroom around midnight, and saw light leaking under her daughter's bedroom door, she knocked. Only to discover Selena was studying a software video. Selena staying up late to learn? When Maria returned to her bedroom she briefly got down on her knees, fingered her rosary beads, and asked the Lord to bless Trisha Peterson.

Nina figured there was no stopping Selena's enthusiasm, or even slowing it down. But it still bothered her that Trisha Peterson would spend so much money on them. It just didn't make sense.

She now remembered Evelyn's request to keep in touch. There was no use in aggravating the situation at home, so she asked Selena, "Can I use your new cell phone to call Evelyn?"

Evelyn answered on the second ring.

"Hello?"

"It's me," Nina said. "I'm at Selena's."

"Okay, sweetheart. When should I expect you home?"

"Would it be okay if I go over to Chantha's house and have dinner with the Miller's tonight?"

There was a delay before Evelyn answered. "Of course, sweetheart. Are you headed there now?"

"I want to spend some more time here at Selena's before I go."

"Okay," Evelyn said. "Do you need a ride? I can come into town and take you." She sounded hopeful.

"The bus runs every hour," Nina said. "There's a stop just two blocks from Selena's."

"Well . . . please call me when you get to the Miller's." The disappointment was so clear it made Nina wince.

"Okay, Mom." The word "mom" slipped out naturally.

"Have a good time with your friends," Evelyn said, a little more upbeat. "Before you know it, summer will be over and school will be starting up again." There was a quick click—as if Evelyn didn't want to risk a rare positive moment turning sour.

Nina handed the phone back to Selena, and said, "Can you show me more of what you've learned on the computer?"

Selena's eyes were eager as she laid the cell phone on the back of the desk. "Of course," she said, grabbing the mouse. "Let me show you the spreadsheet I've put together."

As Selena opened an Excel worksheet, Nina began to wonder why Trisha might have singled her out for special treatment.

Did I mess up by staying quiet in class?

And for the first time, she began to feel just a little jealous.

⚒ ⚒

As Selena was showing off her new spreadsheet skills, Charlie was checking in with Clarissa on *his* new cell phone.

It had taken a lot of convincing to move Clarissa this one small step into the twenty-first century. "We need to be able to communicate," he had argued. "I know you're concerned about being monitored, but if we keep the conversations simple, there's hardly any risk. And the benefit of being able to communicate more-or-less instantly outweighs any downside."

"I suppose you're right," Clarissa eventually conceded, after a lot of hemming and hawing. "I've been so careful for so long, and it's hard to change."

Charlie immediately went to buy prepaid cell phones at *Ken's Computers*. He missed Trisha, and the starry-eyed Selena and her mother, by half an hour.

When Clarissa answered his call, Charlie reported, "She's at Selena's house."

"Good. Frank says after she's done visiting with Selena she'll return to his office and his secretary will drive her to his house in Dartmouth Village."

Charlie slid the phone back into his shirt pocket, reclined the seat two notches, and tried to ignore the little voice in his head that insisted something was about to go wrong.

CHAPTER FIFTY-FOUR

Valerie waited until Friday morning to drive to Langston. Twenty minutes after leaving the hotel, she turned the Maserati off Highway 97 and began the climb to Turner's Notch. As the road crested into the valley, she saw the beauty of Lake Cascade for the first time: a shimmering iridescent blue that stretched for nine miles until it reached the foothills of the snow-capped Cascades.

She pulled over once she reached the city limits and consulted the GPS, then drove through the downtown district until she found the East Lake Road.

Shortly after she turned onto the two-lane strip of asphalt that wound along the eastern shore of the lake, she lost her nerve. She pulled over, intending to call Mitch at Stanford, reached for her cell phone, and realized she had nothing to report except cold feet. Instead of placing the call, she made an abrupt u-turn and drove back through Langston, angry at herself.

Why can't I face this thing?

When she hit Highway 97 along the Columbia she gunned the eight-cylinder engine. As the speedometer broke past 100, Valerie had just one thought: *Coward . . . Coward . . . Coward!* It took all of her willpower to reduce the speed of the Maserati back to the sixty-mile-an-hour limit.

When she reached the hotel parking lot, she turned the key off and slumped forward against the leather-covered steering wheel, wishing she were still in San Jose.

She eventually pushed open the door, climbed out, and trudged up the steps to her room and flopped onto the bed. She again thought of calling Mitch, but knew what he would say: "You need to go talk to Clarissa."

But I'm not ready.

Unable to gain the solace of sleep while wearing a dress that felt sticky from the day's heat, she eventually rolled off the bed, wishing she had packed a swimsuit. After a quick shower to wash away the sweat, she pulled on a light yellow shift and slipped on sandals and went downstairs and found the concrete steps that led to the beach. Finally beginning to relax as she lay on a re-cliner, shaded by a sun umbrella, she was near to falling asleep when a voice surprised her.

"Hi," it said.

Valerie opened her eyes and looked up and there was the woman she knew only as "Trisha," wearing a black two-piece, dripping wet. "The lake's wonderful," Trisha said. "You should go for a dip."

Valerie rolled onto her stomach so she was no longer looking at Trisha upside down. "I didn't bring a suit," she confessed. "And I'm not really in the mood."

Trisha's mouth formed a little moue of sympathy. "Then how about a martini from the beach bar?"

"I'm not a drinker," Valerie said. And then she realized how grumpy she now sounded. Not wanting to again run off this in-triguing stranger, she quickly added, "How about an iced tea?"

Trisha didn't hesitate. "Sounds perfect. I'll be right back."

She came sauntering back across the lawn, carefully carrying two large glass tumblers with thin bands of sugar around their rims and lemon wedges floating amongst ice cubes.

"Here's to your health," Trisha said, handing Valerie a tumbler.

"Cheers," Valerie said, taking a sip, and pointing to an empty recliner. "Pull up and join me."

"Gladly." Trisha dragged the recliner over and stretched out on it, damp hair clinging to her head, swimsuit drying rapidly in the heat. "So," she began, "why so glum?"

Valerie begin to invent a story, knowing she needed to talk. Also knowing she couldn't risk telling anything close to the truth.

"I drove up here to talk to my aunt."

"That doesn't sound so bad. Is she sick or something?"

"I wish it were that simple. Actually, until a few weeks ago, I didn't even know I had an aunt."

"That must have come as a surprise." Valerie meditatively cradled her drink with both hands. "So you've got a new aunt. What's the problem?"

"It's not just my aunt. I also learned that I've got a second cousin—a girl who is thirteen years old. She's an orphan, and my aunt thinks she should have more contact with family. I'm afraid she's going to ask me to go for custody. I don't want to become someone's mother. But I also don't want to make the girl feel like I'm rejecting her. So I'm stuck between a rock and a hard spot."

Trisha was working not to betray her surprise. *She has met Clarissa and they've spoken about the girl.* She began to tap the sugar-frosted rim of her glass with one finger, as if contemplating what action to suggest. Finally, she said, "Do you still want to meet up with your aunt?"

"I have to," Valerie said, with a resigned sigh.

"Does she live here in town?"

"No, she's up in Portage. Do you know where that is?"

"It's on Lake Cascade, isn't it?"

"Yeah."

Trisha had just one thought. *I need to know more.* She stretched, looked at Valerie, who appeared lost in a moment of deep thought. "I'm going up to my room and get out of this suit. Do you have any dinner plans?"

"No," Valerie said. "Do you?"

"No. How about we meet up in the pub at seven? We can talk more about your problem over some good food."

"Sounds great."

Trisha stood with tumbler in hand. "See you later," she said, heading for the steps to the lodge.

"See you at seven!" Valerie called back.

She picked up her tumbler, put the rim to her lips, and licked along the ridge of sweet sugar granules, thinking how nice it would be to spend the evening with a new friend. So much better than staring at the wall in her room and wondering what her life would be like in, say, five hundred years.

CHAPTER FIFTY-FIVE

Gunther had grown weary of Wilhelmshaven long before Pieter Silberhof knocked for the first time on his apartment door. He'd lived in the port city for nine years, and for him that was practically the record.

It wasn't uncommon for a member of the Order to live for as much as ten years in one location before feeling the pressure to move on. One could always "dress older" to camouflage perpetual youth. But that took a bit of effort. Gunther was disinclined to do anything to disguise his early thirties appearance. He wasn't particularly lazy. Just stubborn.

There was another problem he perpetually created for himself. It wasn't long after he'd moved to a new place before every local policeman, bar bouncer, and tough guy—from both organized and unorganized crime—heard about the new player; the guy who always looked for a fight and usually came out on top. Gunther had already spent time in Wilhelmshaven's local jail. So far it was just a day or two and with small fines. But on his last visit the magistrate had warned that if this kept up, he would soon graduate to a longer prison stay.

He was waiting for a letter or a phone call about where and when to join the others on what he now thought of as *the expedition,* so Pieter's second appearance at his door came completely unexpected.

"I thought you were going to call," Gunther said, as the old wooden door creaked open. Pieter was dressed impeccably, as always, this time in brown wool slacks and a herringbone jacket. He carried a thin briefcase. "Have things changed?" Gunther asked, nervously. "Have I somehow caused trouble that has reached all the way back to Zurich?"

Pieter stepped inside and firmly closed the door before he replied. "No, we've heard nothing new. Why? Is there some reason we should have special news of your troublemaking?"

Gunther just grinned.

Pieter looked around the room to make sure the answer wasn't right before his eyes. And was relieved.

At least there's no body.

It seemed almost comical for a moment. But then Pieter remembered the time when there *had* been a body—a Gestapo officer during WWII. The Order had spirited Gunther out of the small Austrian town where he was living, first to Switzerland, then as far away as possible—to South Africa—where he fit in quite nicely with the ruling whites.

Gunther found work as a gang boss in the diamond mines, and production on his shifts immediately soared. Not that Gunther was particularly a bully towards blacks. He simply laid into his crew with the same aggression he visited upon everyone. The muscular workers, in grimy clothes and with moon eyes set deep in coal-black faces, responded to Gunther's relentless prodding far more readily than they ever had to the Dutch Afrikaners.

Pieter's nervous glance around the room wasn't lost on Gunther. He extended his own pleasure at Pieter's discomfort by walking to the sink in the kitchenette to run a glass of water from the tap. "Why have you come?" he asked, returning to stand before Pieter.

Pieter now delivered his surprise, with a grim satisfaction.

"There's been a change in plans. You'll no longer be going with us on the Gulfstream."

Gunther's eyes narrowed.

"Instead," Pieter continued, before Gunther could voice a protest, "you will go ahead and be ready to act in case something goes wrong. Or, in case someone gets cold feet."

Joy returned to Gunther's face. "Aha! You think the Council will back off from challenging the mighty Clarissa!" With a nasty grin he added, "It's such a shame we have the rule about respecting each other. About not *killing* each other."

Pieter's face hardened. "You will follow my directions, or I will have you removed to some place where you will no longer be of concern."

"You'd better bring some special talent for that," Gunther countered. And then he realized he'd gone too far, as usual. Angering Pieter was counterproductive. "Alright," he conceded. "You are the boss. I will follow your directions. 'To the letter' as some idiots like to say."

Pieter would remember that moment; the very instant when he could have dismissed Gunther. And he would regret that instead of telling Gunther he wouldn't be needed, he instead said, "I have purchased a first class air ticket for you out of Frankfurt tomorrow morning. You will need to close out your affairs here and be on the last train south this evening." He opened the briefcase and withdrew tickets and a new passport and handed them to Gunther.

Gunther fixed Pieter with a hard stare.

"Why am I not going on one of the Order's jets? You know the risk of flying with *others*." He fingered the German passport.

"Even with this, there is no guarantee it will get me past the American immigration."

"Yes, I know all of that. But there is no other way. You must take a commercial flight."

Gunther gave a short bark of laughter as realization dawned. "Because no one else in the Order knows that I'm going on ahead, correct? That is why you cannot call up one of the private jets."

Pieter's grim look came with, "You are correct. No one knows. And I am taking a great risk in doing this. I hope you appreciate that."

Gunther felt like demonstrating what he thought of this new plan. Maybe by spitting in Pieter's face. Instead, he let loose with a venomous, "Imagine that! You taking a risk for me. But the truth is that I am taking all of the risk." For a moment he pictured the girl, and felt a rare moment of pity for her. *Will they treat her as shabbily as they treat me?*

Pieter stood waiting, left hand now slipped into the pocket of his jacket, right hand holding the briefcase.

"Alright, I'll do it your way," Gunther said. When he saw satisfaction cross Pieter's face he disliked the man even more.

"Good. There are a few things we need to go over." Pieter walked to a small table in the corner and pulled a rough wooden chair to sit. Gunther followed, placing his half-drunk glass of water on the table, reaching for the other chair. It had recently been thrown against a wall, and it shifted and creaked as he sat. He glared at the Austrian.

Pieter ignored the childish attitude. He pulled out a map and several documents from the briefcase, and said, "Let's begin with where she lives."

CHAPTER FIFTY-SIX

Nina was totally wound up as she sat on the Millers' back deck, describing to Chantha what she'd seen at Selena's house. "This woman from New York spends just two mornings with us, and then she goes and buys four grand worth of computer and software, plus a cell phone, and then pays someone to set it up. Doesn't that seem completely weird to you?"

Chantha just laughed. "Selena must be in heaven."

Nina drew in a sharp breath. "Oh, yeah. She's way up in the clouds. And the way her mom spoke about Trisha at lunch, it was like an angel had visited their house."

"Really?"

"Yes, really."

"Wow." Chantha's face turned serious. "Are you sure you're not just a teensy bit jealous?"

Nina stubbornly shook her head. "It's great that Selena is working hard to learn. And I suppose it's neat that she got all that stuff. But that's not my point. There's no way a woman who is nearly a total stranger should be willing to spend a small fortune to get us started."

Chantha wasn't buying it. She stubbornly crossed her arms. "Maybe she just believes in us. What if she simply thinks we're worth it? What if she thinks our idea about selling bunnies is a winner? And isn't she supposed to get paid back for all the computer stuff after we start making money?"

Nina's look of disbelief only served to encourage Chantha, who motored on, convinced she was right.

"It's not like it's a big deal for Trisha. She probably makes ten times more money than my mom and dad combined. So for her, four grand is practically nothing. And if she's getting paid back later, it's not even going to cost her a penny."

Nina appeared to soften, but only just a little.

Chantha was on a roll. She was finally making Nina think twice. Trisha was like gold, and entirely worth fighting for. Even if it meant contradicting her best friend, someone she trusted to be right about everything else. But not this time. This was too good to let Nina derail it.

"There are rich people who do good things without expecting to be repaid. People give college scholarships to poor kids. Mentors invite teenagers to come to their businesses and learn about what they do. My dad volunteers his time if someone at school wants to talk about becoming a lawyer. And there are people who give millions for things like fighting disease in Africa. They don't expect to make a profit from it."

Nina began to nod ever so slightly, as Chantha launched a final salvo.

"So Trisha Peterson thinks we've got a good idea and maybe it will make a lot of money and she wants to see us succeed. It's something she can feel good about. She can look back when she's older and say to herself, 'Gee, I really did something great for those kids.' And I think that's all she's interested in, Nina . . . doing something good. And besides, as long as Trisha Peterson doesn't want to take over our business, which I'm sure she doesn't because she's got a high paying job in New York, what bad reason could she possibly have for making this loan? A loan she's already told us we will have to repay if—when—we make money." Chantha crossed her arms, unwilling to back down a single inch.

Nina searched for a reason to counter Chantha's logic but couldn't find one. It didn't cure the feeling that something else was happening. Still . . . this was her best friend talking, and with a level of conviction she had never seen in her before. And so, for the moment, she decided to push that funny feeling aside.

"Okay," she said, reluctantly. "I guess you're right."

"Of course I'm right." Chantha couldn't resist driving home one last point. What she thought was the real reason behind Nina's concern.

"I know it seems strange what she's done for Selena. But I think you've overreacted because you aren't used to adults being nice, especially with money." From the look Nina returned it was clear she had gotten the message.

"So," Chantha said quickly, realizing from the fleeting look of pain on Nina's face that it had actually hurt, "shouldn't we take the bunny over to Selena's so she can take more pictures for her computer model?"

Nina finally uncrossed her arms. "I suppose so," she said.

"So what's stopping us?"

"There's something I haven't told you about the bunny."

"What?"

"He has a pearl for a heart."

"A pearl?"

"Remember that lump in his chest?"

"Yes."

"Clarissa told me it was a black pearl."

"That's one gigantamongous pearl, if that's what it is."

"I know. And I think it's worth a lot of money."

Chantha remembered the strand of pearls her dad had given her mom as a birthday present. It had cost two grand, and those pearls were the size of chickpeas. The lump inside the bunny . . . it was more like a small egg.

"I'll bet it's a fake," Chantha said. "It's probably just plastic."

"I don't think so," Nina said. "Clarissa had no reason to lie to me. I think we should take it out."

"Why?"

"I'm worried about losing it."

"How would you lose it if it's sewed up inside the bunny?"

"I don't know. I'm just worried."

Chantha was now curious to see if there actually was a real pearl in the bunny. "Okay," she said. "Let's take it out."

The bunny lay on the table between them. Nina picked it up and worked a finger into the fur and found a line of stitches. "I think all we need to do is to cut a few of these," she said.

"Okay," Chantha said. "I'll get some scissors." She went inside and came back with a pair of toenail shears. She handed them to Nina, who carefully began to clip thread in the bunny's chest.

When the opening was two inches wide, Nina laid down the scissors and reached in and carefully pulled out a small black silk pouch. There was a knotted drawstring. Nina picked at the knot until it was loose, and then she reached in with two fingers and grabbed the lump.

Out came a black pearl the size of a walnut. It wasn't perfectly round; more lumpy and irregular. And if you looked at it from a certain angle you could see that it was nearly heart-shaped.

"Wow," Chantha said softly. "I didn't think they got this big. Do you think it's real?"

"Yes," Nina said.

"What do you think it's worth?"

"Let's go look on the Internet."

Nina carefully slid the pearl back into the pouch and drew the strings tight and pushed the pouch into her jeans pocket.

A minute later they sat in front of the computer screen, staring at each other.

"Maybe a million dollars," Chantha said, in awe. "But it can't be real, can it?"

"Why not?"

"Why would she give you something worth that much?"

Nina had no explanation for why Clarissa had given her a million dollar pearl. But as she thought about it, she began to reconsider being upset with Clarissa.

"What do we do with it?" Chantha asked.

"I'm going to keep it safe. I'm not sure where, but I'll find someplace."

"Selena's going to notice the lump is gone."

"Right," Nina agreed. "We need to put back something that's the same size. Does your dad have any big marbles?"

"I don't think so."

"Any ideas for what else we could use?"

Chantha thought for a moment. "Dad's got a can full of tumbled rocks out in the garage. Maybe one of them would work."

They found an old square can the size of a gallon milk carton, filled with tumbled agates. Nina pushed around until she found a caramel-colored carnelian the right size. They took it back into the house and wrapped it in a square of cloth and then placed it inside the bunny's chest.

Chantha went to her parents' bedroom to get a needle and thread from her mother's sewing kit, and then she stitched up the bunny. "There," she said, handing it to Nina, who tested the seam.

"Perfect," Nina said, sitting the bunny upright on the table.

She could feel the pearl in her pocket, and wondered where she could safely hide it.

CHAPTER FIFTY-SEVEN

The pub was crowded on Friday evening.

Trisha asked the hostess for a small table at the back corner of the veranda, far enough from the jostle and chitchat to allow for some privacy. When Valerie appeared at the top of the stairs, Trisha waived her over.

Valerie threaded her way between the tables before sinking tiredly into a chair. Trisha saw gloomy eyes, and with them perhaps an opportunity.

"Hi," Valerie said, as she picked up a menu and tried to relax.

"Hi, yourself," Trisha said, sending a gentle message across the table: *You should tell me what's wrong, because I want to help.*

Valerie pretended to read the menu, although she was too upset for the printed words to fully register. In a reckless moment earlier that day, she had phoned the Bosecker. The receptionist, who identified herself as "Iris," said the lady was out, but promised she would let Mrs. Cumberland know she had called. Valerie declined to leave a number, telling Iris she'd call back later. Only she got nervous again and didn't make that follow-up call.

She looked up from her menu, saw a concerned Trisha, and felt a sudden urge to share her troubles. A stumbling confession began to pour out.

"I tried to call her today."

"Your aunt?"

"Yes. She wasn't in, so I left a message saying I'd call later."

"Did you?"

"No. And I feel like a real loser for not having the courage."

Trisha gave a shrug. "Just remember that you have control over your own life, and you can make whatever decision seems best. I know you don't want to signal rejection to this niece. But she's only meeting you for the first time, and she might not be at all interested in you stepping into a mommy role."

At that moment a perky young waitress with mousy hair and a *we're busy tonight* look arrived, and said, "The specials are a blackened tuna salad or baby back ribs. Do you gals want to start with a drink? Wine coolers are half price this hour."

"No thanks," Valerie said, a little too sharply.

Trisha covered for Valerie's abruptness, smiling up at the waitress. "I'll have a club soda with a twist of lime, please."

Valerie sighed, and said, "Me too." It came with a forced smile that was mostly for Trisha. And then, with kinder eyes for the waitress, she added, "Please."

Trisha gave a quick smile to reward Valerie, before she asked the waitress, "Is the shrimp Caesar good?"

"The best," the waitress replied, wondering what had just passed between the two women. A man two tables away hollered for service. She determinedly ignored him.

"Do you want anchovies?"

"Yes. And please put the dressing on the side."

The waitress turned to Valerie.

"I'll have the same," she said. The waitress collected the menus, smiled her thanks for the quick decisions, and hustled off.

Valerie looked across the table and saw Trisha was watching her with concern. She felt a tinge of guilt for dragging a woman who was still practically a stranger into the drama of her life. A drama she had no idea how to explain in any way that would make it believable. Instead of even trying, she volunteered, "I'm sure it will all work out. I just don't want to hurt the girl. I'll figure out something, but I don't need to burden you with the details."

"Okay. So, let's change the topic."

"Agreed."

"What do you want to talk about?"

"Let's skip the weather," Valerie said. Both laughed a little, and the tension eased a bit.

Trisha said, "You mentioned an 'IT' company?"

"It's in San Jose. We do mathematical analyses, mostly for marketing, buying trends, that kind of stuff. I'm fluent in Mandarin, and many of my customers are from China."

"Do you travel much?"

"More than I want to. How about you? What's your world like?"

"Investment, if you want a label. I'm with a small firm that handles large sums of money for an elite clientele. Let's just say that my clients are very interested in saving as much as they can on their taxes."

"You mean 'off shore investments'."

"That's one way of putting it. We like to call it something less—"

"Illegal?"

Trisha just smiled. "Let's just say we offer 'creative' solutions for the rich."

Valerie now found sudden inspiration. A way to explore the topic she hadn't thought it possible to talk about.

"I've always wondered what the 'creative' investment world is like. Let's say I had a few million I wanted to invest. What would you recommend?"

Interesting . . . and I don't think she's asking because she wants to have me handle her money.

"It depends on your goals. Do you want safety? Quick growth? Long term growth?"

"Let's say long term growth."

Ah!

"How long?"

"Let's say I'm putting together a trust for this thirteen year old girl. I want her to have money for college, but not a big wad of cash until she's older."

"Okay. So, maybe you want a piece of an apartment complex in Japan that's issuing thirty-year bonds with bi-annual dividends?"

"And if I wanted to provide for her children? Or her grand-children or great-grandchildren?"

So . . . Clarissa has told her about the Order.

"Well, most people don't plan so far out. But if you wanted to look forward a hundred years, I'd suggest real estate in a stable country—the U.S., Sweden, Switzerland. Perhaps some quality art. Investors who bought Picasso in the nineteen twenties did very well for their grandkids."

"I never thought about it that way," Valerie said.

Au contraire mon ami! You have thought about the distant future a great deal. And if I'm not mistaken, only very recently!

Valerie now attempted to sound nonchalant, but for Trisha the message came across loud and clear.

"How could you possibly predict what might happen a hun-dred years into the future?"

It's easy, girl, if you've lived it.

"The partners in our firm have developed long term strategies based upon decades of experience. We try to give our clients good options, but in the end they have to make their own choices. Each investment is to some extent always a roll of the dice."

"So if you knew you were going to be around a century from now, what would you personally invest in?"

We're getting close.

"Well, since I'd look like a mummy that just escaped from a mausoleum, I guess—"

"No. Imagine you would look just as you do today. If you could step into the shoes of your great-granddaughter, is what I'm getting at. What would you buy for yourself—I mean for *her.*"

Now we're getting down to it.

"Okay. So I'm going to pretend that I'll not age for the next hundred years, and I want to wind up with something which yields an income and where my principal increases in value to keep pace with inflation. Correct?"

"Yes."

Trisha closed her eyes for a moment, as if reviewing the various investments she might select. When she reopened her eyes, she ticked off the choices on her fingers.

"First, I'd hold cash-based assets only in currencies you could trust to remain stable. I'd never go with the Euro because the jury's out on whether or not it will survive in the long term. I'd prefer the British Pound or the Swiss Franc."

"Why not the American dollar?"

"It could lose safe haven status and quickly devalue if the U.S. falls out of favor with other large economies. Compared to Europe and Asia, the U.S. has only been around for a relatively short period of time. We can't predict with any degree of certainty whether the 'Great American Experiment' is going to eventually succeed."

"Wow. Okay. Next?"

"I'd diversify my portfolio. Precious metals. Quality gems. Art work. Real estate. Mineral deposits like coal, iron ore, copper. Never look for a killing, always look for durable value and the potential for steady growth. By the way, any real estate needs to be away from the coastlines."

"Why?"

"Remember global warming? In a hundred years there probably won't be much left of Florida, the Gulf Coast, Holland. And Venice is going to be completely under water. Get the picture?"

"Yeah." Valerie hadn't thought of that. Parts of San Jose, where she worked and lived, were near sea level. The hills of the city might become a series of islands.

Trisha saw she had Valerie hooked, and ticked off another finger.

"Third, I'd factor in political stability, holding assets only in countries with a proven history of long term stability. Switzerland, again, is a good choice.

"Fourth, to manage my assets I'd choose a company that's been around for a while; one that holds a long term view of the future."

"Like?"

"The bank of Lichtenstein. Private banks in Switzerland. There are others. "

"You wouldn't want to name a few, would you?"

"A girl's got to have her secrets!"

Both laughed, and the tension was nearly gone.

Valerie figured it was time for *the* question. She took a long, deep, slow breath, as if thinking of something fantastical, imaginary, and hopeful.

"I wonder what it would be like."

"What?"

"To live for a hundred years and not age."

Bingo!

Trisha's face gained a playful, curious smile. She teased the white tablecloth with the tip of her index finger, drawing little imaginary circles. Looking up at Valerie, she knew this was the payoff.

She wants someone to tell her it's okay to live practically forever. And she's desperate for a little sympathy. But she couldn't ask for it outright. She had to couch it in investment metaphors. Clever girl!

"It would be difficult at first, I suppose. You would lose family and friends. But after a while I'm certain you would get used to it." She laughed. "I think at one time or another everybody fantasizes about remaining young. But it never happens in real life, does it?" Trisha's face turned wistful. "It sure is a great fantasy though, isn't it?"

"Yeah, I suppose."

Trisha now had a question of her own that she dared not ask. Not yet.

If Valerie was approached in the right way, would she be interested in joining our side?

CHAPTER FIFTY-EIGHT

Gunther hadn't set foot in a commercial airport terminal in over thirty years. As he paced along the polished walkway towards the Z gates, he tried not to stare at the security cameras regularly spaced, no doubt recording his image. *And no doubt comparing my face to their terrorist database. They won't find me. But my image will now exist somewhere in their system. It will be shared with Interpol, the CIA, the NSA, possibly even the Russians and Chinese. And this is* entirely *Pieter's fault.*

Of course, his recorded image would be paired with a non-existent "Wolfgang Arthur Spindler"—the name on his new passport. But a face was a face. Names could be changed. The face of someone in the Order could not.

Fifty years ago, a member had tried to change his looks with plastic surgery, purely for vanity reasons. After two hundred years, he was tired of looking in the mirror and seeing a large Roman nose, droopy eyelids, and thin eyebrows.

Almost immediately, his face began to revert back to the one he was born with. In three months, he looked exactly the same as before surgery.

The spontaneous reversion had been a popular subject at that year's gathering—an event the man chose not to attend for obvious reasons. Amongst the colorful tents set out in the grassy field far up in the Alps, the members took note of the lesson: you were who you were, and if you became known to the outside world, there was no possibility of surgically changing your appearance.

There was already a crowd in the waiting area when Gunther reached the gate. He presented his first class ticket and was directed to a cordoned-off spot from which the fortunate few would be ushered aboard, before the masses were herded into economy.

Pieter had urged him to buy something classier than his usual dungarees and work shirts. "Try not to stand out," Pieter had scolded, as though talking to a child. It was wise advice, just poorly delivered.

Gunther now sat amongst travelers who wore Gautier and Prada, and was glad to be wearing an Italian leather jacket, Salvatore Ferragamo loafers, and black wool slacks.

A humorous thought occurred.

I look like Mafia.

Even this failed to improve his mood. Warriors were often given second-class treatment by non-warrior members. To now be treated so by Pieter, who was also a warrior, seemed the ultimate insult.

When he was finally on the plane, one vengeful idea occurred as the jet taxied for takeoff. Pieter had told him the Council was planning to keep the girl in the dark until plans could be worked out to manage her development. "She will be allowed the comforts of life, but in seclusion, hidden away at our alpine retreat."

Gunther saw an opportunity. *If I were the first to tell her she is a member, and that she will rise to greatness, perhaps she would look kindly upon me later on.*

"How long do you plan to keep her isolated?" he had asked.

"At least until the threat of Clarissa is neutralized," came Pieter's coldly practical reply.

"You intend to *neutralize* Clarissa?" *What an intriguing idea!* "Do you want me to kill her if she gets in the way?"

"No, of course not," Pieter said, dismissively. As one might order a servant.

"Such a shame." Gunther's sarcasm bit deep for the nervous Austrian. Gunther drove the stake in a little further. "I might enjoy taking down the great Clarissa. Of course, it would violate the pledge, wouldn't it? I'd be a marked man." Gunther laughed, enjoying the deer-in-the-headlights look it brought to Pieter's face.

Pieter slammed shut his briefcase, stood up and glared at the still seated Gunther, as if staring down a flaring cobra. "It would be wise for you not to mention to anyone what we've spoken about today."

"Oh, for certain," Gunther agreed. "Not a single word."

But now, as he settled into a comfortable seat at the front of the plane, Gunther didn't think he wanted to remain quiet. As the jet lifted off, Gunther knew that Pieter had inadvertently handed him a unique opportunity.

The only question was: How to play it out?

CHAPTER FIFTY-NINE

On Saturday morning, Nina planned to go to the kitchen and fix herself a bowl of cereal with banana slices. But as her bedroom door swung open she caught the smell of eggs and bacon.

When she reached the living room, she found the table set with Evelyn's sterling silver and "for nice" English bone china— off white, with garlands of yellow and red roses. Glasses of fresh orange juice, a basket of blueberry muffins, a white linen table-cloth. Nina stared at the unprecedented finery, not sure what to think.

Dan was already sitting at the table, hair jelled and combed, dressed in slacks and his favorite golfing shirt.

"Good morning, Nina," he said, in a strangely pleasant voice. "Did you sleep well?"

"Yes," Nina said, cautiously glancing around for some clue as to why this was happening. Evelyn came from the kitchen at that moment, carrying a platter of scrambled eggs, crispy bacon, and a stack of cinnamon toast.

"I've got hot cocoa coming right up," Evelyn said, in a voice that was way too cheery. "I'll be right back."

"Why don't you have a seat, Nina?" Dan asked in that too-pleasant voice, and with a grin that reminded her of the time he'd bought a vintage shotgun off an eighty-year-old man for fifty bucks and later bragged about how he'd taken the old fart to the cleaners.

Nina warily pulled a chair and sat down, too nervous to look across the table at Dan. She instead stared at her glass of orange juice.

Dan reached across the table and took her plate. "What would you like?" He waited politely—again so uncharacteristic—and Nina wasn't even sure she was now hungry. But there was Dan, holding her plate, grinning, and waiting.

"Some eggs and toast, please," Nina said.

Evelyn was humming a little tune out in the kitchen. In a way, Evelyn's humming was scarier than Dan's plastic grin. Dan scooped eggs and put two pieces of toast on her plate and then reached across and set it down in front of her.

Evelyn returned from the kitchen carrying a china teapot with glazed lavender blossoms adorning the side. It was something she had inherited when her mother died and was as precious an object as Evelyn possessed. In her other hand she carried a matching porcelain cup, which she sat beside Nina's plate and poured steaming cocoa into it from the teapot.

"There," Evelyn said with satisfaction, setting the teapot in front of Nina. "Help yourself if you want more." She sat down in a chair at the end of the table nearest to the kitchen.

Nina stared at the steaming cocoa. *Please let it be they have won the lottery. Let it be that Dan has made a huge wine sale. Let it be that Evelyn has miraculously gotten pregnant.*

"Honey," Evelyn said, with growing excitement. "We have some news to share with you."

Nina's stomach bottomed out.

"Yes," Dan agreed. He nodded to Evelyn, giving her the pleasure of the moment she had hoped and prayed for.

"Dan filed for your adoption this week," Evelyn said, eyes glistening with joyful tears.

Nina felt her gut tighten. Her stomach gurgled. She swallowed hard, forcing the acid surge back down.

Dan continued quickly, "Of course, it's going to take a while for it to get through the courts. And you will absolutely have a say in all of this. There will be plenty of time to adjust and get used to a new life—"

"—Daniel," Evelyn cut in—an interruption that usually would have drawn a sharp word, but he pretended not to mind at all. "Please share with Nina what we talked about."

Dan's grin suddenly changed from *plastic* to *goofy*. What Nina thought of as his *salesman's smile*.

"I know there have been a few times when it seemed like I wasn't set on making this a long term thing. But I've come to realize what a special young lady you are. I'm going to do my very best to make this work. We may even hire a family counselor. Anything is possible." He glanced at Evelyn with an extra-effort *I'm truly serious* look, one eyebrow lifted. She beamed back.

Nina somehow managed to not bolt from the room screaming "No!" at the top of her lungs. But just barely.

Evelyn nodded for Dan to continue.

"I plan to be a lot more involved in your life, sweetheart."

Dan had never before called her *sweetheart*. Nina felt sick.

"I thought maybe you and I could go for a walk after breakfast, maybe down to the docks, so we could talk about things—" Dan checked himself, wondering if what he'd just said sounded like so much crap to Nina. It certainly sounded like crap to Dan. He quickly covered with, "What I mean is talking about things you might want." Dan struggled with the thought of being generous, and it showed. Evelyn enthusiastically nodded encouragement, oblivious to Dan's internal struggle. Dan gamely plunged on.

"We want you to know that you are important and that your goals will become our goals. After all, if you're going to be our legal daughter, you should have a full say in everything that happens here in the Torgerson home."

Dan finally ran out of lies to peddle. Evelyn remained googly-eyed with joy.

They both looked at her, waiting for some response.

What Nina wanted to say was that Frank Miller was going to file for custody, and Dan and Evelyn could expect her to be moving out real soon. But Evelyn would then descend into tears, and Dan's famous temper would erupt. Things would turn ugly.

Nina realized that wasn't necessary. Not yet.

She finally said, "I didn't realize you were interested in adopting me." Her genuine look of confusion finally erased Evelyn's smile. It was replaced by a look of bewildered concern.

Dan now backpedaled.

"Of course you didn't. And we should have talked to you about it—"

"It was a surprise for me, also," Evelyn cut in, defensively. "Dan met with the lawyer and had the papers drawn up and I didn't even see them until a couple nights ago when he brought them home for me to sign."

Dan flicked a look at his wife, finally grown tired of being cut off. But he bit his tongue and forced a smile just the same.

Nina kept telling herself there had to be a way out of this. *I need to talk to Frank.* And somehow, she kept her cool.

Evelyn saw Nina's calm as a hopeful sign. "Do you want to go for a walk with your—" Evelyn wanted in the worst way to say "father," but settled for "With Dan?" She saw Nina's eyes grow wide, and quickly offered, "Maybe we should wait. I know this has been quite a surprise for you." She turned to Dan. "What do you think, honey?"

"Whatever Nina wants," Dan said.

Nina needed time. "It's all so sudden," she said, hesitantly. As if there might be a real possibility—after she'd had a chance to think it over—of her agreeing to move forward with an adoption.

"Then let's give you more time," Dan said. And with a thoughtful look, he added, "But I really do want to start being involved more in your life. Like this business class at the high school. I think that's just about the greatest thing I've ever heard of a kid wanting to do, taking on extra studies during the summer." Dan paused, as if he had just had a new thought. "In fact, I'd love to meet your teacher. It's a woman, isn't it, who's teaching you now?"

Nina wondered how Dan had gotten that information. Certainly not from the Millers or Chantha or Selena. Maybe Selena's mom? She knew Maria and Evelyn talked on the phone.

Dan plunged on, more in character, taking control. "In fact, why don't I drive you over to school on Monday? That way I can say a quick 'Hi' to this gal, just to touch bases and get introduced."

She was trapped and she knew it. "Okay," she mumbled.

"Great," Dan said. He and Evelyn exchanged smiles. "Let's chow down before the food get cold." Dan reached for a large spoon, as if everything had returned to normal. He asked Evelyn, "Darling, may I dish you up?" Evelyn handed across her plate.

Dan and Evelyn talked about the weather, a trip to Spokane he had to make later next week, a quilting project at Evelyn's church. Nothing more was said about adoption.

Nina barely managed to eat three bites of egg and one slice of toast. When she was finished, she looked at Evelyn and asked, "Is it alright if I go over to Chantha's this morning?"

"Of course, sweetheart," Evelyn practically purred.

"I'll take you," Dan volunteered. Evelyn gave him a loving glance, looked back to Nina, and smiled.

When Dan loaded Nina into his big black pickup he actually held the door for her. She sat quietly staring out the front window, afraid to look at him.

Dan said nothing until he turned onto the street where the Millers lived. As he slowly drove towards the end of the cul-de-sac, and while staring straight ahead, he said, "This is really important to Evelyn, Nina. I'm sure you know that." He waited. Nina knew she had to say something, or else Dan might pull to a stop and then they would face off.

"I know," Nina said in a resigned voice.

Dan nodded slightly, ran his tongue along the inside of his bottom lip. As he pulled up in front of the Millers, he said, "So let's you and me be friends and try to make this work, okay?"

Nina wanted to say anything other than what she said next, which was, "Okay."

"Okay," Dan said cheerfully. "Do you want me to come and pick you up when you're done?" It wasn't so much a question as a challenge.

"If Mr. Miller can't bring me, I'll give you a call," she replied. And before Dan could say anything else, Nina pulled the door handle, stepped onto the running board and down onto the ground, and practically slammed the pickup's door behind her.

Dan pulled a u-turn and actually waived as he drove away.

CHAPTER SIXTY

As Nina sat through the uncomfortable breakfast with Dan and Evelyn, Trisha was punching out a number on her cell phone. The ring tone sounded just once.

"Ja?"

"It's me."

"Good morning, Trisha. How's the weather in Washington?" Liesel sounded relieved.

"It's getting hotter," Trisha replied. "I met a new friend yesterday. A woman who's up here from California."

"Really? What's she like?" Liesel hadn't expected Trisha to make contact with anyone from the Order. *Has our mission been compromised?*

"It's her first time here."

"Really?" *Someone new to the Order?*

"Absolutely."

"What's she like?"

"She owns an information services company in California. They're good at math, stuff like that."

"Interesting." For Liesel, sitting alone in one of the three apartments the Order maintained in Zurich, this wasn't the worst possible news. It could have been a warrior. But it wasn't good news, either. Especially if . . .

"Do you have mutual friends?" Liesel didn't want to hear "Yes."

"At least one."

That would be Clarissa. But what does she mean by "at least?" Is the girl involved already?

"So . . . do you think the two of you will be doing anything fun together?"

"Possibly. But she's thinking of making a trip up to Portage, to check things out. She may be moving up there for some of her vacation."

There was one last key piece of information Liesel needed.

"How long do you think you'll be staying?"

Trisha had expected this. And she'd already come to the conclusion that it was time—as the saying went—to fish or cut bait. Trisha figured it was time to reel in the fish.

"I'll be out of here on Wednesday night."

"So soon? I thought you were staying another couple of weeks."

"No. I've had enough sun. I think there's a flight around eleven in the evening."

"Okay. Have fun until then."

"Thanks. Hope to see you soon."

"Me, too."

Trisha punched out and stared at her cell phone, knowing the Gulfstream would be on the tarmac waiting for her and the girl on Wednesday. *So I've got four days to figure out how to get her down to East Wenatchee in a condition that won't cause problems at the airport.*

As Trisha considered her options for the kidnapping, Liesel was placing a call on the secure landline, nevertheless feeling a twinge of regret at finally setting things in motion.

"Yes?"

"Next Wednesday, departing eleven in the evening Pacific Standard Time. Please have everything ready." Liesel wanted to tell Pieter to drop Gunther from the passenger list, but she'd made the deal and there was no point in arguing when she knew he wouldn't yield.

"Excellent. So do we fly out that morning?"

Liesel thought for a moment. They couldn't afford to miss the connection. Better to be there early. "No," she said. "I think it would be wise to go the day before. We can rent rooms at our port of entry. It's a city called Spokane, a couple hundred miles to the East."

"Alright."

Liesel waited, and when nothing more came, she said, "I'll be in touch," and hung up the phone.

Pieter picked up his secure satellite phone.

"Yes," came a disgruntled voice on the other end.

"Are you there?"

"I'm in Seattle."

"And?"

"I rented a hotel room as you asked. Do we have a time schedule?"

"Yes. Next Wednesday. Move into position on Tuesday and wait for further instructions."

"Good."

As the call ended, Gunther looked out the window, across the city to the distant white peaks of the Cascades, knowing the girl was somewhere on the other side of those mountains, waiting for her destiny, waiting for him to come for her. He felt a growing excitement and knew it would be hard to fall asleep with so much pent up energy screaming for release.

Soon, I shall have an opportunity for greatness!

CHAPTER SIXTY-ONE

Anna Miller opened the front door and saw a panicked Nina. "I need to talk to Frank," she said, anxiously looking past Anna.

"Come in," Anna said. Followed by a shout back into the house, "Frank, Nina is here and she needs to see you!"

Frank took Nina into his study, closed the door, and listened to her explanation of what had happened at breakfast. When she finished, Frank took a moment to gather his thoughts, then said, "This is going to involve Anna and Chantha. Would you mind if we had a family meeting to talk about what comes next?"

"Of course not." Nina felt a surge of excitement about Chantha finally knowing she was going to come to live with her. *A family meeting!* The thought was wonderful.

When the four of them were gathered around the dining room table, Frank told his wife and daughter what he and Nina had discussed earlier in the week. He would have liked to add what Clarissa had told him about the Order. But the block was still in place.

Chantha was sitting next to Nina, and immediately reached to hold her hand under the table as Frank continued.

"The filing of an adoption complicates matters. I don't expect a judge to approve one over Nina's objections. But there will still need to be an interview by a guardian ad litem and a report by the adoption caseworker before we can move for a dismissal of the petition. There is no easy way around the fact that the Torgersons filing for adoption is going to delay things."

"How long?" Nina was angry—a focused anger whose burn point was Dan Torgerson.

"I could ask Dan to withdraw the petition, and if he agrees, it would just be a matter of days. Otherwise, it will be longer. Possibly three or four weeks, or even a couple of months."

Nina doubted Dan Torgerson was going to withdraw anything. She knew what his price would be for cooperation.

I'll run away before I let that slime ball touch so much as one hair on the bunny's head.

Frank saw Nina's determined face and realized he was the only one at the table who knew how much potential strength was behind it. What he had to say next would push buttons, but he saw no other option. Nina had to know how to play the game, and how to *win* that game.

"If I ask Dan to withdraw the petition, it will make your life uncomfortable. But if you can hold on for a bit, once the guardian ad litem and the caseworker interview you and learn you are not interested in an adoption, we could move quickly. I can file for a change of foster care as soon as the reports are delivered to the judge. In the meantime, I'll be ready to appear as your lawyer if things go sideways. One way or another, I will get you through this."

Nina didn't want to spend even one more night in the Torgerson house, but she was in no position to argue. Dan had made his move and momentarily held the advantage.

"Alright." she said. "If I have to wait, I will. I'll pretend to go along with the adoption until I talk to whoever it is I have to talk to. But if there's anything you can do to make it happen more quickly, please do it."

"I will," Frank promised, pleased by her strength.

With the family meeting dismissed, Nina and Chantha retreated to the back deck.

Chantha said, "I wish you could stay right now."

"Me too. But what your dad said makes sense. I just hope the interviews take place real soon."

"Do you want me to keep the bunny?"

"Definitely. That's what Dan is after."

"It's a good thing he doesn't know about the pearl. What have you done with it?"

In answer, Nina pressed down on the front of her shirt. In the middle of her chest a lump stood out against the fabric. She reached around her neck and fingered a thin nylon cord, lifting it over her head. On the end of the cord dangled the little black draw-bag. "It's here," she said. She looped the cord back over her head and pushed the bag safely down inside her shirt. "It's my insurance policy. I'm not taking it off until I'm out of there for good."

"Should we tell Selena about any of this?"

"Absolutely not! I love Selena, but for now we can't trust anyone outside of your family."

"Okay," Chantha said. Wondering what the fallout might be if Selena learned she'd been excluded.

CHAPTER SIXTY-TWO

Valerie was tempted to climb into the Maserati and drive back to California. For a moment she again considered calling Mitch. But he'd just encourage her to be brave, and tell her that she was putting off the inevitable. He'd say go and find Clarissa.

And he would be right.

So it wasn't Mitch she finally placed a call to. After she reached the restaurant and ordered breakfast, she pulled the cell phone from her handbag. It rang just twice before there was an answer.

"Bosecker Inn, Iris speaking. How may I help you?"

Have courage.

"I need to speak with someone who is staying with you. Her name is Clarissa."

"Aren't you the woman who called before?"

"Yes," Valerie said.

There was a sudden, surprising enthusiasm in Iris's voice. "I think she's in her room. Would you like me to ask her to come to the phone?"

Courage!

"Yes, please. Tell her Valerie is calling."

"Just a moment."

Valerie heard the handset being laid down in what sounded like a hurry. Shortly, Iris's voice came back on the line.

"I'm going to transfer you to the dayroom."

There was a click, and a new voice said, "Valerie?"

"Yes."

There was a nervous pause for both women. Clarissa eventually broke the silence.

"Where are you calling from?"

"I'm about half an hour's drive from Portage."

Clarissa cautiously said, "Were you thinking of coming for a visit?"

The blood roared in Valerie's ears, as if she were standing on the edge of a cliff.

So jump!

"Yes."

"Do you know where the Inn is located?"

"I can get it off MapQuest."

"Are you sure you're ready to take this step?"

"Yes, I'm sure." The words came too quickly, almost dismissively. "I'm sorry," she apologized, hoping she hadn't sounded rude. "I guess I'm nervous."

"Perfectly understandable. When should I expect to see you?"

"I should be there within an hour."

"Goodbye, until then."

"Until then." Valerie stared at the cell phone before sliding it back into her handbag.

When she reached the foyer she saw Trisha walking across the parking lot from direction of the far lodge. She considered ducking back into the restaurant. But Trisha had already seen her through the glass. She waived, and walked briskly towards the restaurant door.

"I've been looking for you," Trisha said as she pushed wide the door. "I thought I might see you again at the beach, but no luck. Where've you been?"

"Worrying about my aunt and my niece, mostly holed up in my room. And I still don't have a swimsuit, so what's the point of going down to the beach?"

"Let's go uptown and buy you one," Trisha said, with a cheeriness Valerie wished she herself felt. "There's a place called Blue Moon that has a nice selection."

Valerie sighed. "I really wish I could. But I've decided to go and visit with my aunt. I called a few minutes ago to set up a meeting. We're supposed to get together in Portage in less than an hour, so I'll have to take a rain check."

Trisha flinched a little, but Valerie didn't appear to notice. "Okay," she said. "Maybe I'll catch up with you later on today. I'll certainly want to hear how it went."

"It's a deal."

"Good luck!"

"Thanks!"

As Valerie drove out of the parking lot, instead of turning left and heading through the downtown, she mistakenly turned right. Ten minutes later, realizing she was headed in the wrong direction, she turned around and drove back through town. Once she reached Highway 97 along the Columbia she glanced at her watch and realized she was going to be late.

She was doing seventy when she came up behind a slow moving line of cars, headed by a battered old pickup. Traffic was heavy in the opposite direction, and it was five minutes before there was an opportunity to pass, along a straight stretch of road locals half-jokingly called the "drag strip."

Valerie waited for the first car behind the pickup to pull around. When it refused to go, the other cars stayed in line.

What's the sense in owning a Maserati if not for moments like this?

Valerie signaled, pulled out, and floored the gas pedal. The Maserati shot forward like the road missile it was built to be.

By the time she passed the pickup she was doing one hundred and sixty miles an hour. At least that's what registered in red digital numbers on officer Troy Johnson's radar.

She saw the blue lights begin to flash up ahead and knew she'd been caught. She pulled in behind the patrol car and shut off the engine, expecting a brief lecture and probably a hefty fine.

Officer Troy ordered her out of the car, took the license she handed him, and then cuffed her hands and guided her to the back door of his cruiser.

"But I was passing!" Valerie protested. "It's legal to exceed the speed limit to pass another car!"

"Not at a hundred and sixty miles an hour," Troy said sternly. "And not while you're passing a string of cars, any one of which might pull out at any moment. That's reckless driving. You need to learn to wait your turn." He would teach this chick in a red sports car with California plates a lesson she wouldn't soon forget. Her license said she was thirty-four, and she should know better at that age. Troy fingered the license, looked at the photo, then at Valerie, thinking she looked more like twenty-two.

So maybe it's a fake license? And is it really even her car?

"Can't you just write me a ticket or something?"

Troy frowned as he placed a hand atop her head so she wouldn't bump it as she ducked into the back seat. "Lady," he said stiffly. "You need a little time to calm down. I'm not sure what you mean when you say 'or something' but if I were you, I'd remain quiet until you've had a chance to talk to a lawyer."

Remembering he hadn't yet read the woman her rights, Troy now said she had the right to remain silent, the right to hire an attorney, and then he shut the back door and walked around to the driver's door, opened it, and climbed in as if he were John Wayne mounting a horse.

Valerie was livid. She shouted at the Plexiglas screen, "But I've got an appointment in Portage! Can't I at least make a call to let her know I'll be late?"

Not bothering to turn his head, Troy said, "You'll get to make a call after we reach the jail and you've had a chance to settle down. And it'll have to be to a lawyer." The engine started and Troy gently pulled onto the highway, grinning. It was Saturday, and he doubted any of the local defense counselors would be in the office on such a nice sunny day.

⭤ ⭤

Clarissa waited for two hours. When Iris finally buzzed to say she had a phone call, it wasn't the voice she expected to hear.

"Clarissa?" Frank sounded stressed. Clarissa's thoughts of Valerie vanished.

"What's wrong?"

"We've got a problem."

"Is Nina Bea safe?"

"Oh, yes. I'm sorry. I should have said it differently. It has nothing to do with those people from Europe you told me about. This has to do with her foster parents. They have filed a petition to adopt her."

Clarissa gave a quiet sigh of relief. This, she could deal with. "How did you learn about it?"

"Nina came over to our house practically in tears. It seems Dan filed his petition with the court earlier in the week and he only told her about it at breakfast this morning. I assured her if she didn't want it there is no way a judge will grant it. That calmed her down a little. Then I had to tell her this will delay our petition to become her new foster parents, and that got her upset again."

What had seemed like a minor bump suddenly got larger. Moving Nina to a safe home needed to happen as quickly as possible.

"What can we do?"

"I could talk to Dan. Try to get him to back off. But it would likely make life more difficult for Nina in the short term. I plan to wait until Nina meets with the adoption caseworker next week. She can tell the caseworker she's not interested in being adopted, and at the same time she'll say she'd like to move out of the Torgerson house and into our home. That way we get two birds with one stone. It's the best way to handle it."

Clarissa wanted to tell him it wasn't anywhere near the best way to "handle it." The best way to handle it would be she going to the Torgerson home and taking control. Talking about mind control wasn't something she wanted to do on the phone.

"Can we meet at your office in an hour?"

"Of course. Do you want me to bring Nina?"

"Is she still at your house?"

"No. She took the bus back to Portage. But I could call and go pick her up."

Clarissa imagined the damage a confrontation between the Torgersons and Frank might cause, and said, "No. Let's just you and I meet."

"Okay."

Clarissa hung up and went to find Charlie. He was sitting in a chair on the back lawn, reading a paperback novel. He looked up from his book.

"More complications," she said. "The Torgersons have filed to adopt Nina Bea."

Charlie folded a page and closed the book. "You're kidding?"

"No, I'm not. Frank Miller called to tell me. I'm driving over to meet him at his office. I was expecting to meet Valerie, but she's already over an hour late, and I'm afraid she won't show. If she does, I need you to stand in for me. Call me at the law office on the cell phone if she arrives."

"Right."

Clarissa paused, remembering that Valerie had never met Charlie. Maybe putting those two together at this point wasn't such a brilliant idea. "On second thought," she said, "I want you over near the Torgerson house. Not close enough that Nina Bea could sense your presence. Just close enough to follow her if she leaves."

"Right." Charlie stood up. "When should I expect you back?"

"It shouldn't take more than a couple of hours."

CHAPTER SIXTY-THREE

Officer Troy took his own sweet time at the stationhouse. Running the license (it turned out to be valid) the car title (clean, and in the same name as the driver's license) and administering a breath test (which read "0.") In the process he drew the attention of his duty sergeant.

Sgt. Paul Crenshaw had been with the sheriff's office for thirty-two years, and knew well enough to keep an eye on the deputy everyone called "Gung Ho." The well-dressed Asian gal he'd just seen sitting in the holding cell practically shouted heavy-handed police work. He ambled down the hallway, pulled the door shut as he entered the dayroom, and walked over to the desk where the deputy was writing up the paperwork on the new prisoner.

"Whatcha got, Troy?"

"Caught her in a red sports car doing one-sixty on the 'drag strip'."

"One-sixty?"

"Yup."

Crenshaw knew there had to be more to the story. He stared at Troy. "Out there on the straight she was doing one-sixty all by her lonesome?"

"She was passing a string of cars. Maybe seven or eight."

"How fast was the line of cars going?"

"About forty," Troy said. "There was some old codger in a pickup out front.

"And nobody else pulled out to pass, so she went around?"

"They never had a chance," Troy said, defensively. "She went around them *like a rocket*. I never saw anyone drive that crazy. That's why I brought her in."

"That must be a pretty hot car she's driving to go one-sixty." Crenshaw was having a hard time believing anyone could have been going that fast in *any* kind of car. "What's the make?"

Troy spelled it out for emphasis. "M-A-S-E-R-A-T-I."

Crenshaw had never actually seen a Maserati. He recalled the lines from Joe Walsh's song "Life's Been Good" that went "My Maserati does one-eighty-five. I lost my license, now I don't drive." He'd always thought that was made up. But maybe Troy wasn't exaggerating after all. "Where's it at?" he asked, curious to see one up close.

Troy said, "It's parked at that pull-off near the end of the strip."

Crenshaw's next thought was that a few of the shadier locals wouldn't think twice about lifting an expensive radio, maybe a gearshift knob, for a souvenir. And if this gal could afford a Maserati, she could certainly afford a lawyer to make trouble if her fancy Italian sports car was vandalized. Crenshaw doubted this thought had crossed *Gung Ho's* mind, and decided to clue him in.

"Cars like that are an easy target for thieves, Troy. Did you consider getting it towed for safe keeping?"

Troy now remembered being told that securing expensive cars might save the county from a lawsuit. "Yeah, sure," he readily agreed. "That's a good idea. I'll get it towed right away."

"I've got an even better idea. This gal you have in the cell . . . has she been drinking?" Crenshaw didn't think so. It was too early in the day. And someone who could afford a Maserati, and who'd successfully taken it to warp speed, wasn't likely to be under the influence.

"The breathalyzer said 'zero'," Troy reluctantly confessed.

"Did the license and title check out?"

"Yes." Troy felt resentment welling up in his chest. *I was only doing my job.*

"And she's got insurance?"

"Yeah . . ."

"It's the weekend," Crenshaw said sagely. "There won't be a judge around until Monday morning. Is there any real reason to keep her locked up until then?"

It was hard to spit it out, but Crenshaw was giving him *that look.* Troy surrendered to the inevitable. "I suppose not," he finally said.

"How about we have her post a five hundred dollar bail and give her a summons for Monday morning, okay?"

"Sure," Troy agreed.

"And maybe it would be a good idea to give her a ride back down to that Maserati so it doesn't get broken into."

Troy was about to protest that sheriff's deputies weren't hired to be cab drivers, but one look from Crenshaw was all it took. "I'll finish the paperwork and then run her back down," he said in resignation.

"Good." Crenshaw slapped Troy lightly on the shoulder. "No sense in doing unnecessary damage to someone just because they wanted to get by some old fool in a beater pickup." He walked away before Troy could say anything.

When Troy dropped Valerie at her Maserati an hour later, he even tipped his hat to acknowledge that he might have gone a bit over the top, hoping it might discourage her from filing a complaint. "Please be more careful in the future, ma'am," he said, before climbing back into his patrol car and speeding back towards Langston.

Valerie waited a full minute, fuming over the officer's condescending hat-tipping gesture, before she, too, pulled onto the highway and headed north.

When she finally reached the Bosecker she was more nervous than ever. So it was both a relief and a disappointment when Iris informed her that Clarissa was not there.

"I'm sorry, but she left quite a while ago. Do you want to leave her a message?"

Valerie decided she didn't want to write a detailed explanation of the police stop. She took the pen and pad Iris offered, and was short and to the point: *Was delayed by unforeseen event. Promise to be in touch. Valerie.*

As she drove back along the lakeshore road, Valerie wondered if she would have the guts to make good on her promise; thinking how nice it would be to simply forfeit her five hundred dollar bond, head back to California, and hope a warrant didn't arrive by mail.

By the time she reached the resort she needed to let off steam. There were only two people she could talk to. One was Mitch, who would certainly tell her to go back to the Bosecker Inn and wait. That was not what she wanted.

She instead went to the hotel's front desk. The young man behind the counter looked up as she approached.

"May I help you?"

"Yes. I'm looking for another guest. Her first name is Trisha. She's a slim blonde, about five foot eleven?"

"Yes, of course. That's Trisha Peterson you're looking for."

"Do you know if she's somewhere around the hotel?"

"I haven't seen her, but I could call her room if you like."

"Please, yes."

Valerie waited as he placed the call. After several seconds of holding the handset to his ear he put it down. "No answer," he said. "But she drives a light blue Mercedes. I don't think there's anything else like it in our parking lot."

Valerie found the Mercedes at the far end of the last building. A powder blue Mercedes SLS. *With New York plates?* Valerie realized Trisha had never told her where her high powered investment firm was. *Who would drive all the way from New York for a vacation?* She made a mental note to ask Trisha why she'd driven so far. And went looking.

She finally found her down at the beach, in the same spot where they had talked before. Laid out and wearing the black bikini.

"Hello, stranger," she said, as she came up behind the recliner.

Trisha had sensed Valerie's approaching resonance. Without turning she said, "Hello, yourself. How'd it go with your aunt?"

"It never happened," Valerie confessed. "I got stopped by a cop for speeding, taken to jail, held in a cell for two hours, and I am now officially released on bond. "

Trisha's head jerked around. "You got put in jail for speeding?"

"Well . . . I was doing a hundred and sixty."

Trisha laughed so hard she nearly fell off the recliner. When the laughter subsided, she said, "What kind of rocket are you driving?"

"A Maserati GranTurismo MC with a four hundred and fifty-four horsepower engine."

"That would do it." She chuckled, this time more soberly.

"And it's red."

"Okay. I get the picture. How'd the cop ever catch up to you?"

"Actually, I caught up to him. Or more precisely, I caught up to his radar. I just pulled over when he turned on the strobes. I could outrun any cop car, but radio is a little harder. And it's not like I'd blend in driving a red Maserati in these parts."

"I think you're right about that."

"How about an iced tea?" Valerie volunteered. "My treat today."

"Sure," Trisha agreed.

When Valerie returned, she handed over a tumbler and settled onto a recliner, took a sip from her own glass, and gazed out across the grass and the beach to the wide expanse of lake. "What a day," she sighed.

"Will you be going back to meet her?"

"I've been giving that a lot of thought. And I think I'll just forfeit the bond and head for California."

This drew a long and thoughtful look from Trisha. *I need to be sure.* "That seems like a waste, coming all this way, just to turn around and go back home."

"I know," Valerie agreed. But a little voice in the back of her head insisted she not waiver, even though she was uncertain what she would actually do. "It just seems like the right thing for now. What do you think?"

Trisha didn't hesitate. "Follow your gut. If it says head home, then head home." She took another sip of her drink, beginning to feel more relaxed. Something had finally gone right. "In the meantime, how about you and I go for a stroll up the main street and find you a swimsuit? It'd be a shame if you drove all the way from California and never went swimming in this lovely lake."

"Agreed," Valerie said.

And so two women, both of whom looked to be twenty-two, both with terrific figures, one of whom was 34, the other having been born in 1911, spent the next hour looking for the perfect swimsuit.

The one Valerie finally chose was candy apple red—nearly the same color as her Maserati.

In the excitement and pleasure of Trisha's company, Valerie forgot to ask about the New York plates. As she lay in bed that evening, she remembered.

I'll just ask her the next time I see her.

But that opportunity would never come.

CHAPTER SIXTY-FOUR

Nina's ride to class on Monday morning quickly became a contest, with Dan trying to pry information, and Nina giving up the bare minimum.

Dan fired his opening salvo as he shut the pickup door and keyed the diesel engine to a rumbling start. "So what's this teacher look like?"

"She blond and tall."

"Hmmm," Dan said, seeming to weigh this information as if it meant something. "Is she smart?" He backed onto Mellison and goosed the still-cold engine. Black smoke trailed onto the pavement. A pen lying on the dashboard fell to the floor, and both of them ignored it.

Nina could have replied that *of course* Trisha Peterson was smart. She worked in a New York investment firm. That meant she had to be bright, hard working, good with people, everything expected of someone who'd reached the top. But the question seemed so dumb, so insulting, that Nina chose not to answer, hoping Dan would take the hint.

No such luck.

Dan pulled onto the highway and drove down the East Lake Road in the direction of Langston, waiting for a reply. "So?" he finally urged, reinforcing it with a determined glance across the cab.

"She's smart," Nina said.

"Uh huh." Dan stared down the road, wondering what it would take to loosen up the information he wanted. He made another stab at starting a real conversation.

"What's she been teaching you girls?"

"Stuff about business."

Dan tried to sound playful, but it came out sounding more like he was mimicking what she'd said.

"What kind of stuff?"

Nina was beginning to fume. Why couldn't he just shut up? With what she hoped was a poker face, she said, "How to put together a business plan. Setting strategies. Finance. Stuff like that."

"Finance, huh." Dan's banter turned serious. "So does she think this is a money maker?" His eyes left the road for uncomfortably long seconds, as if to prove that compelling a better answer was more important than missing the next car.

"I don't know what she *thinks*," Nina said, her face turning glacial. "I'm not a mind reader."

That finally shut Dan up.

Nina focused straight ahead, counting the stripes in the middle of the highway, working to hold her anger in check.

After Dan parked in front of the high school and shut off the engine, he said, "Okay, let's go in and meet this high powered New York investment gal." He jumped out onto the asphalt, intent upon opening Nina's door—just in case the New Yorker was watching from inside the schoolhouse. Before he got around the front end of the pickup, Nina had already opened her door and climbed down. Dan gave her a *so that's the way it's going to be* look and slammed the door shut behind her. Together they walked up to the main entrance.

There was one unintended consequence of Dan's badgering. For the first time, Nina was ready to take Trisha's side.

Trisha, Selena and Chantha were already waiting in the classroom. Irv had earlier declared his presence to be unnecessary and left for the golf course.

Trisha hadn't expected a man to arrive with Nina, and realized from the veritable blast furnace of emotion radiating from the girl that this must be the foster father.

Dan was stunned from the first moment he laid eyes on Trisha. And not just because she looked great. Which she did, even in simple black slacks and a yellow blouse. There was something else he couldn't put a finger on. Dan would later comment to Evelyn that Trisha Peterson seemed to be more than alive; as if some vital energy flowed out from her in all directions.

"Hi," he said, with a firm nod, walking up, thrusting out his hand. Thinking he was acting like a real man, when in reality he felt about two feet tall. "I'm Nina's dad."

Nina wanted to scream that he wasn't her dad. He was her foster parent, and there was a huge difference. But there was no gain to be had in a fresh confrontation. She just wanted him to leave. Keeping quiet seemed the best way to ensure a quick exit.

Trisha shook Dan's hand. "Trisha Peterson."

"Yes . . . Miss Peterson. It's a pleasure to finally meet you." Dan was surprised by the strength of her grip. Uneasy, and not sure why, Dan pressed on with, "Nina's told me so many good things about you." A salesman's smile now played his face. "I've got a question or two, and then I'll get out of here and let you and Nina and her friends do your thing." Another fake smile, but increasingly uncertain.

"Sure," Trisha said brightly. "What would you like to know?"

Dan's smile was quickly replaced by a look that attempted *I'm-one-of-the-adult-gang* seriousness. "Do you think this bunny project the girls have come up with has legs?"

"Legs?"

"Yeah, you know, does it have a good chance of success? Does it have *legs*?"

Trisha saw a chance to make points with Nina. Her reply was smooth, and brutal.

"The girls certainly have hopes. But any new business has at best a one-in-five chance of just breaking even. The odds for coming up with a real hit—'legs' as you so succinctly put it—well, that's more like one in fifty."

Trisha's charm skill wasn't limited to making someone anxious to please. It could also depress and cause a person to lose confidence. At its worst, it could make you want to mix up some cement, dump it down your trousers, and go find a bridge. Trisha now pushed hard, and was rewarded when Dan's face fell into sober lines.

"But I thought with all of those girls on Facebook wanting bunnies of their own . . . this would be kind of a slam dunk." A last ditch, hopeful half-smile crossed his face. A smile that pleaded: *Haven't they already primed the pump? Can't we expect a business geyser to erupt without any heavy lifting required?*

His whiny plea was pathetic, and everyone but Dan saw it for what it really was: Greed being dashed on the rocks of reality.

"Well," Trisha said calmly, anti-charm now crushing Dan like fast-moving lava, "there's no such thing as a slam dunk in the business world, especially for this kind of venture. There are dozens of companies that make plush pets. And besides, I'm not here to guarantee success. I'm just here to teach the girls some basic business principals."

"Oh." Dan said, now completely discouraged. He began to take steps backwards, in the direction of the classroom door. "I guess I'd better take off and let you and the kids get down to it."

When Dan's footsteps ceased echoing in the hallway, Chantha said, "Gee, we went from being 'friends' to 'girls' to 'kids' in the space of less than two minutes."

Trisha began to laugh, and everyone except Nina joined in. Trisha saw Nina's discomfort, went over, put an arm around her shoulders. "Honey, with a foster dad like that I can only imagine how tough things are for you."

Nina seemed to brighten just a little; she looked at Trisha, appreciating how she'd leveled Dan. But she was newly worried about what Trisha had said.

"Do you really think we only have a one in fifty chance?"

"Of course not!" And now Trisha pumped charm as hard as she dared in Nina's direction. "Dan was absolutely right when he said this is a slam dunk."

"Really?"

There was so much hope behind that one word, and Trisha jumped on it. Knowing she might have stumbled upon a solution for getting Nina to the airport.

"Yes, Nina. I really do think you've got a winner." She was quick to qualify this with, "That's not to say there aren't challenges to overcome. For one thing, you're going to need to find a source of funds to manufacture the bunnies. Setting up production will cost far more than what I put up for the computer and software." She gave Selena a smile, and was rewarded by a grin. "But I may have a solution for that hurdle. However . . . that's getting way ahead of where we are today. We need to cover a few more basics before leaping into the actual nuts and bolts of getting you ladies up and running."

"Ladies," Chantha echoed. "That's more like it."

And with that simple statement, Trisha knew she'd conquered Chantha.

She'd also taken a big step in converting Nina with her mauling of Dan. But there was still work to be done.

Patience.

"So," Trisha said, her demeanor suddenly practical. "Let's talk about contracts."

CHAPTER SIXTY-FIVE

Valerie awoke on Monday determined to return to Langston and deal with the reckless driving ticket. And then to seek out Clarissa. A night of good sleep had cleared her head of any doubts about what she wanted to do on either count. Running away was not her style.

She had an early breakfast in the upstairs pub, hoping to see Trisha again and at least report her decision to attend court. The young blonde never appeared.

When she drove her Maserati past the last lodge unit to see if Trisha might still be in her room, there was no sign of the Mercedes.

Valerie headed north on Highway 97 at a cautious and very law abiding sixty miles per hour.

The written citation had an address for the courthouse. When she reached the outskirts of Langston, she keyed the street number into her GPS and a female voice from the dashboard speaker began giving directions that soon led her to an old-fashioned four-story brick building.

Once inside, she found the district court on the third floor. She pushed through the dark-stained oak door, and took a seat at the end of a long oak pew halfway up the center aisle.

The courtroom began to fill. As the top of the hour neared, there were over two dozen faces, ranging from hopeful to resigned, a few sitting beside their attorneys, all facing the high bench.

Wearing a light green cotton skirt, white blouse, and shiny black Jimmy Choo flats, Valerie felt like an alien, sitting amongst people who seemed to believe appropriate courtroom dress included sweatshirts, T-shirts, and jeans. Most looked like repeat customers. Several had multiple tattoos. Except for the handful of attorneys, and Valerie, the only other attendee who was nicely dressed was a middle-aged man in a navy blue suit with a yellow tie. A bulbous red nose and flushed cheeks betrayed a drinking problem.

A woman bailiff entered, and the room settled down quickly.

"All rise for the Honorable Cynthia Waldner." Everyone stood. A woman, gowned in a black robe, entered the courtroom and climbed the three steps. She plunked down in the tall-backed leather chair behind the bench, her eyes briefly scanning the courtroom to confirm that everyone had risen for her entry.

"Please be seated," the judge said, her voice seeming to say *Don't worry. I'm in a fairly good mood today.* Everyone settled back against the varnished oak, faces on high alert—even those with multiple tattoos.

The bailiff called out, "State versus Kelsey," which turned out to be the man in the blue suit.

He walked through the bat-wing oak gates in the railing and stood at the nearest of the two counsel tables, looking up at the judge. From her resigned expression it appeared this wasn't his first time. She looked progressively more disappointed as he told a tale that included how the police officer had not treated him kindly. She remained patient, but was obviously bored by the time he finished.

When he stopped, she said, "Is that all?"

"Yes, Your Honor."

"As you already know, this morning is just for arraignments and pleas, Mr. Kelsey. I take it you will be using your usual attorney and now wish to enter a 'not guilty' plea?"

"Yes, Your Honor." His head drooped a little.

"Bail is waived in lieu of your personal recognizance to appear before the court."

"Thank you, Your Honor." He stepped back from the table. With slumped shoulders, and head straightforward so as to avoid making eye contact with the lowlife, he walked stolidly to the door at the back.

The bailiff looked up expectantly at the judge, who now gazed out across her courtroom. "Are there any of you who wish to either plead guilty or offer forfeiture of bail this morning?"

Valerie raised her hand.

"And your name, miss?"

"Valerie Chun Li, Your Honor."

The judge motioned with her hand. Valerie stood and walked down the aisle and through the little gate, up to the table Mr. Kelsey had just left.

The bailiff pawed through her stack of files. She finally pulled out a thin folder and handed it up. The judge scanned the file's contents for a few seconds before her head came up again.

"It says here, Ms. Li, that you were doing one hundred and sixty miles an hour."

From the rows of pews came several "Whew's" and one man let out a low "Woooooooooh!"

This did not please the judge. She swung her gavel down in one sharp *Bang!*

"There will be quiet from those of you who are waiting your turn, unless you wish to be found in contempt and spend a few hours in our fine jail facility." The words "fine jail facility" caused the courtroom to immediately fall silent. The judge looked back to Valerie, nodding that she continue.

"Yes, Your Honor. I was stuck behind a line of cars with a pickup in the lead doing about forty miles an hour. There was plenty of room to pass, but for some reason the cars behind the pickup didn't want to go. I just floored it to get around. I didn't realize I was going that fast until the officer stopped me."

The judge glanced at the file. "And that would have been Officer Johnson?"

Someone at the back of the courtroom coughed. Another uttered a thinly disguised snort of laughter. The judge gave the gallery a disgusted glance, but said nothing. Her eyes refocused upon Valerie.

Who certainly remembered the redneck cop. "Yes, Your Honor."

"It says in the file that he arrested you. Is that correct?"

"Yes, Your Honor."

"Was there some special reason why he arrested you—I mean, other than for going that fast?"

"I don't think so, Your Honor. I think he just felt I was going so fast that he . . . oh, I really don't know, Judge. I guess he felt he was doing what the law required."

The judge actually smiled. "Officer Johnson . . ." She smiled again, and looked at Valerie with eyes that were both sympathetic and amused. "If you would be willing to forfeit your bail and enter a plea for speeding, I would be willing to drop the reckless charge."

"I'd like that very much, Your Honor."

"Done," the judge banged her gavel. And then, as an afterthought, "I know you were driving a Maserati, and I have no doubt it is capable of going even faster, but Ms. Li, I don't think it's a particularly good idea on our local roads. Would you agree?"

"Yes, Your Honor. It won't happen again, I promise."

"You may go out to the clerk's office and sign the paperwork." The judge looked back across her courtroom, at sweatshirts, tattoos, torn jeans. She took a deep breath that ended in a quiet *Hmphhh*. "Is anyone else prepared to plead guilty?"

Valerie heard no volunteers as she pushed through the batwing gates and hurried down the aisle.

CHAPTER SIXTY-SIX

Following Dan's departure, Trisha couldn't have hoped for better progress in the classroom.

Selena had spent practically every waking minute since the trip to Ken's Computers learning how to use the software on her new computer. She was already building spreadsheets, and had transformed the emails and Facebook posts into an alphabetized mailing list.

Chantha was in awe, not having thought Selena capable of such intense learning in so short a period of time.

Even Nina was beginning to shed a little of her uncomfortable jealousy. "Selena, you're totally awesome," she said. She turned to Trisha for confirmation. "Isn't she?"

"Absolutely," Trisha agreed. "In fact, all three of you are awesome in your own ways. And it's partly your differences that make you a terrific team." The girls were all smiles.

Near the end of the morning, Trisha knew it was time to make her move. If recruitment of Nina was ever going to work, it had to be now.

"I've been saving a bit of a surprise," Trisha said in a teasing voice.

"What?" Selena asked, practically ready to jump up out of her chair.

Valerie took her time, face serious, eyes intense. "This Wednesday, one of my international clients is flying into Seattle in his private jet. He happens to be a major manufacturer in Europe, and, coincidentally, he also happens to have a daughter who is thirteen."

The girls caught their breaths.

"I spoke with him by phone a couple days ago and told him about your project. He asked his daughter to find the bunny on Facebook, and she was quite excited by it, just like the other girls who have posted." Nina, Chantha and Selena leaned forward, and Trisha knew she had finally captured all three.

"Ladies . . . my client wants to provide the seed money to finance your new company."

All three girls shouted "Yes!" And then gave each other high-fives.

Trisha continued quickly, "Of course he will eventually want to meet each of you. It's even possible his daughter might be with him on the jet. He's willing to fly into East Wenatchee tomorrow for a quick stopover on his way home." And here it got tricky. Trisha wasn't interested in kidnapping three girls. And she was repelled by the thought of having to dispose of Chantha and Selena. But there could be no witnesses.

"It would be a little overwhelming, I think, for him to meet all three of you this first time. That much enthusiasm would be hard to keep bottled up . . ." Trisha winked. "So I'm going to ask you to vote and decide which one of you should come with me for this first meeting." And then she *pushed* hard.

The girls looked at each other, and then both Chantha and Selena looked at Nina. Chantha was the first to speak.

"We don't need to vote. It should be Nina. It's her bunny."

"I agree," Selena said, her face bordering on adoration for her *best ever friend*.

Nina's cheeks burned with both embarrassment and excitement. Everything was going right. The Money Bunny project was about to cease being a dream, and start becoming a reality. She would soon have a new home with the Millers. She would never have to consider using the bunny's pearl for anything except a heart. She looked at Chantha and Selena and saw not the slightest hint of disagreement. She finally turned to Trisha and spoke the one word Trisha had been hoping for.

"Okay." But even as she spoke, there was a nervous tickle deep inside, like when she had walked past the strange man who had stood next to Vice Principal Nedrickson. How had she described it to Chantha?

I feel like I just tripped on my shadow.

As Nina was agreeing to meet Trisha's European businessman, Valerie headed for a drive-up espresso stand she had spotted on her way into Langston. Following her district court success, she wanted to reward herself with a caramel macchiato.

Once she had her drink in hand, she turned off the main road, hoping to find some small neighborhood park where she could sit and peacefully enjoy it while working up the courage for a meeting with Clarissa.

What Valerie accidentally found was Langston High School. And parked in front of the school was a powder blue Mercedes with New York license plates.

CHAPTER SIXTY-SEVEN

Gunther left Seattle at sunrise on Monday, a day before Pieter requested, finally relieved of the fear that another restless night in Seattle would find him drawn to some rough-and-tumble neighborhood looking for action. And likely finding it. Jail time in America wasn't something he could afford to risk.

He was driving a blue Chevrolet Impala rental. At the top of Snoqualmie pass, he pulled off the freeway and drove to the back of the huge graveled parking lot that served skiers during the season—now vacant until winter snows returned.

With a knife he scraped off the bumper sticker which identified the car as a rental. He then unscrewed the license plates, carefully sliced off the tabs, and glued them onto plates he'd stolen from a gold-toned Galaxy 500 he'd found parked with two flat tires in a Seattle alleyway. Onto the Impala's bumpers went the Galaxy's plates, and into the bushes sailed the originals.

He arrived in Langston three hours later and discovered "Mom's Parkway Motel" on the outskirts of town. He requested a room as far as possible from the highway, telling the clerk he found it difficult to sleep with traffic noise. The one she offered was sufficiently away from the road to leave him undetectable through resonance.

He dumped his duffle bag on the bed, went back out to the car, took the rental papers and titling documents from the glove box, returned to his room and tore them into little pieces and flushed them down the toilet.

A few minutes later he was back in the car, driving through downtown Langston. Gunther consulted the GPS he'd bought in Seattle, and turned onto the East Lake Road.

Fifteen minutes later he reached Portage. He took a right onto Mellison and spotted the brass numerals "224" above the front door of the Torgerson house. There was a big black pickup parked in the short driveway, and a white Ford Taurus parked inside the open garage. But there was no resonance coming from the house. Gunther continued on up Mellison, circled the block, and headed back towards Langston.

CHAPTER SIXTY-EIGHT

Valerie was tempted to park her car behind the Mercedes and go into the schoolhouse to find Trisha. But she'd come to see Clarissa, and decided all of her energy needed to remain focused on that challenge.

There was one other reason she decided not to enter the school. As she sat in her Maserati, the engine idling with a smoothly powerful *thrum*, it felt as if someone was watching her. It was the same feeling Nina called "Tripping on your shadow." Valerie would later realize—too late—that she was feeling Nina's powerful resonance coming from within the building. She shifted her car into gear, cruised away from the school, and headed for Portage.

Ten minutes later, while driving up the East Lake Road, she had a similar queasy feeling for just a few seconds. She couldn't have known it was Gunther in his rental car, passing in the opposite direction. Valerie quickly dismissed it as a moment of apprehension for her upcoming meeting with Clarissa.

For Gunther, it was easy to recognize he'd just passed someone with resonance. As the red Maserati swept by, he had no chance to look and see who was behind the wheel. The Maserati's break lights didn't flash, so he decided to continue on down the road, greatly puzzled. It hadn't been Clarissa, for certain. He had experienced her presence at annual gatherings, and what he'd just felt was tame by comparison. It couldn't be the girl, because she, too, would be a powerful source. This was the resonance of a regular member.

I'll need to tell Pieter.

The closer Valerie got to Portage, the more nervous she became. When she finally pulled up in front of the Bosecker Inn she was actually shivering.

She found Clarissa waiting at the reception desk. Behind the desk, a young woman stood with a magazine in her hands, doing a poor job of trying to ignore the two women.

"Valerie," Clarissa said, with clear relief. "I'm so happy you came back."

"I guess I am too," Valerie said. But the only person she was fooling was Iris behind the desk. She nervously said, "Is there somewhere private where we can talk?"

"Certainly. My room is on the second floor." Clarissa walked to the staircase and Valerie followed, careful to avoid eye contact with the receptionist.

I'm already working to remain anonymous. Will it ever be otherwise? Valerie knew better.

The Bosecker's owners had restored Clarissa's room to its early splendor: lace curtains, Depression glass light fixtures, a freestanding white pine wardrobe with a matching chest of drawers, chintz doilies, and a handmade quilt spread across a brass rail bed.

An oval hand-knotted rug lay on the floor. Two comfortable overstuffed chairs faced each other across the rug. Clarissa sat in one and Valerie took the other.

"You must have many questions," Clarissa began, calmly.

Valerie's gut was churning. "Yes, I do," she said. "First off, you said the girl was in danger. You wouldn't have told me this unless you thought I could be of help. What exactly do you want from me?"

Clarissa had spent her life protecting the secrecy of the Order. That was now going to change. She found it surprisingly easy to speak the words that might finally lift the veil. It was a relief, actually, to finally commit to executing the plan.

"I have written out descriptions for each member of the Order. Their names, physical descriptions, everything someone would need to identify and find them. I want you to create a computer program capable of distributing this information across the Internet. Can you do that?"

"Yes," Valerie said, envisioning a fairly basic program that would turn the trick. "But why would you want this?"

"I plan to use the threat of its release as a form of extortion. If the Order doesn't feel endangered by the immediate disclosure of their existence, there will be nothing to stop them from attempting to kidnap the girl and removing her to some faraway place where they can control and indoctrinate her."

"And why would they do this?"

"Let's start with the fact that the Order and I differ on the potential impact of governmental collection of personal information like fingerprints, retinal imaging, facial patterns, and DNA. I believe this data will inevitably compromise the Order. Our members have so far chosen to put their heads in the proverbial sand. But the reality is that our days of living in a privileged and secret society are nearly over. If we don't begin to establish contact with select members of government and the scientific community, there will be no way to control how everything unravels when they discover we exist. We will be picked off, one by one, and it will not be nice."

Valerie's arms rested lightly in her lap, weighing the implications of what she was hearing. She nodded for Clarissa to continue.

"I hope to shape Nina Bea as the instrument by which that transition can be handled."

"Why don't you do it yourself?"

Clarissa had expected this challenge. And the answer wasn't a pleasant one to give. "If I thought I was going to be around long enough to complete the job I certainly would. But this may take several years, and I've not been feeling well of late."

Concern filled Valerie's face. Clarissa continued before she could ask the question.

"I don't know how long, if that's what you were going to ask."

Valerie nodded.

"I know my body well enough to understand that my time is limited. How limited, it's difficult to say. Maybe months. Possibly a few years. I'm hoping for the latter, but there's no certainty. The best I can do is to recruit a few members to become her teachers if I don't last long enough to do it myself. I hope you'll become one of those, Valerie. You are a product of the twenty-first century, and free of the weight of our traditions. Together with Nina Bea you could become a powerful force for reshaping much of what is wrong with mankind."

Valerie settled back in her chair. For a moment the room ceased to exist. Everything was gone except her beautiful mathematical mind—charting the permutations for what might be—and what might not be.

A few weeks ago I was a marketing guru. Now I'm asked to be a co-savior of the human race, partnered with a thirteen year old girl who presently has no clue that she might become the most important and powerful person on Earth.

One question now rose above all others. "Is there something special about the way *we* die?"

"No. it's much like when anyone dies. Except *we* usually have perfect health until the last few months. One day you look in the mirror and notice gray hairs, or you get a rash on your arm, maybe you catch your first flu. Time catches up rapidly after that."

"It must be terrible, to live for so long and then to fade so fast."

"Not really." Clarissa's eyes were calm; there was perfect clarity in their sapphire blue depth. "It's a relief, actually, when your time finally comes. We watch so many people die during our centuries. Some of them are so excellent in what they accomplish in much shorter life spans, and you find yourself wishing you could bestow your own longevity upon them. I never knew Albert Einstein, but I read about his discoveries at the time he was making them. I was able to understand his mathematics, his relativity. I've wondered how much more he might have been able to contribute to human knowledge if he'd been able to stay the same as he was in nineteen-oh-five when he published those first three papers, including the one that won him the Nobel Prize."

Clarissa paused, seeming lost in thought. After a moment of reflection, her focus returned to the present.

"Please understand that just because someone is born a member of the Order does not mean they will have the intellect of an Einstein or a Galileo. A member's natural human skills will be amplified, and they will become very good at one particular thing. They might be charming, a mathematician like yourself, good with animals, or a warrior."

"And what are you good at?"

"I am the rare exception. I was gifted with everything. But I've never been the intellectual equivalent of an Einstein." Clarissa paused. "So . . . what do you think about all of this?"

"Can I have some time before I answer that question?" Valerie asked, hopeful.

In answer, Clarissa stood up and walked over to the pine dresser, pulled open the top drawer, removed an inches-thick black scrapbook. She walked back and handed it to Valerie.

"It's all in there," she said. "You can, of course, take all the time in the world, if you wish. But the Order *will* send someone.

They might even arrive today. And once they have Nina Bea, the opportunity to place her in a position where she can work for the good of everyone will be lost. They might even tell her outright what she is and ask her to join forces with them. There's no guarantee she wouldn't agree. The Order will show her some wonderful things, incredible wealth, power. For a girl raised as an orphan the lure would be very tempting."

"I'll still some need time," Valerie insisted.

"Fine," Clarissa said. "You know where to find me." She reached to a small table beside her chair and lifted a pen, wrote a number on the pad, tore off the sheet and handed it to Valerie. "This is my cell phone. Call me anytime, day or night, when you have your answer, whether it is 'Yes' or 'No.' I'll be waiting."

"I thought you didn't believe in cell phones."

"Things change," Clarissa said with a wry smile, conceding to the inevitable.

CHAPTER SIXTY-NINE

The Wirtschaft Neumarkt restaurant was located on the ground floor of a medieval building in the heart of Zurich's old town, its courtyard sheltered from the summer sun by a canopy of ancient chestnut trees.

Pieter had asked Liesel to meet him here, promising important news. She arrived at the time they agreed, 8:30pm.

There was still heat from the day radiating from the whitewashed walls enclosing the courtyard. Tables were set out on the cobbles, with white linen tablecloths. A gentle breeze drifted through the tops of the trees and swirled amongst the diners who were conversing in quiet, polite voices.

When he finally did show—twenty minutes late—it came with no apology. He collapsed into a chair and didn't hesitate. "There's another member of the Order at this Lake Cascade, other than Clarissa and the girl." He said this matter-of-factly, as he grabbed a menu and began to scan the entrees.

Liesel stared across the table and realized there was only one way for him to know this.

"You've already got someone there!"

"Yes," Pieter confirmed, putting the menu down, raising a hand to attract the attention of a nearby waiter.

The waiter arrived before Liesel could speak again. He was dressed in formal black and white, standard livery in a city famous for its elegant dining.

"Sir?"

"Do you have the prawn salad with potatoes and olives this evening?"

"Yes, sir. A fine choice. With perhaps a glass of Riesling?"

"Yes. Excellent."

The waiter turned to Liesel. "And for madam?"

Liesel had a scowl on her face. "I've lost my appetite," she growled, sending the waiter in hasty retreat.

Pieter lamely tried to suppress a smile. "Too bad," he said. "The food here is excellent."

"Who do you have over there?" And then it occurred to Liesel who was unaccounted for. The group flying out tomorrow would be limited to herself, Pieter, Gunther and Hiroshi Nishikura. She had spoken with Hiroshi earlier in the day, to confirm he would be bringing the appropriate drugs to keep the girl sedated until they had her safe in the Bernese Oberland.

"Gott im Himmel! Pieter. You haven't—"

"Yes, I have."

"How did he travel?"

"Lufthansa."

"That breaks Order protocol."

"I know."

"And that also violates our agreement! Gunther was to travel with us on the Gulfstream, not by himself."

Diners at nearby tables had begun to throw furtive glances as the conversation escalated.

"Quietly *please*," Pieter said, his voice sinking to an urgent whisper. "I'm just trying to do what is best for the Order. There was too much uncertainty with Trisha. I saw no other way than to send him on ahead. It has already paid off. He's sensed another member."

"Who?"

"I don't know. It was someone driving a red Maserati. There can't be that many red Maseratis in such a backwater. You should warn Trisha to be on the lookout for this vehicle."

Liesel remembered Trisha's report that someone new had surfaced. *It must be the woman from California.* But if Pieter could have his secrets, so could she. More importantly, what directions had Pieter given to Gunther?

"You aren't having him do the kidnapping, are you?"

He looked instantly offended. "Of course not!" He had practically shouted. And now it was Pieter who received looks from nearby tables. His voice returned to a gentler level. "He's there for backup. That's all. I've made it very clear he is to keep a low profile."

"Will he be meeting us at the jet in East Wenatchee?"

"That is my plan."

"Have you bothered to tell Trisha of this change?"

"No."

"Why not?"

"Because," Pieter said carefully, eyes penetrating as he leaned forward, "I'm not certain she is worthy of being trusted." *And because the last time I called the bitch she hung up on me.*

"Is there anything specific she's done to cause you not to trust her?"

"No," Pieter lied, knowing she would sense the lie, but not caring. If she wanted to challenge him about it that was fine.

"Well, I trust her explicitly," Liesel said, deciding a fight was meaningless at this point. The damage was done. She finished, in an abrupt tone of voice, with, "So unless you have a good reason to doubt her, I'm satisfied."

"Of course you are," Pieter said. "She was your choice, not mine. And by the way, I think I see my wine coming. Are you sure you don't want some dinner?"

"Yes," Liesel said. All she wanted was to call Trisha and confirm that the woman she had met drove a red Maserati. "I'll see you tomorrow at the plane." She stood, sensing the relief of nearby diners—the unruly couple was parting and the evening could again relax.

"Fine," Pieter said, as the waiter arrived carrying his glass of Riesling.

CHAPTER SEVENTY

Trisha's successful morning with the girls took a nosedive when she reached her Mercedes and checked her cell phone for messages. There was just one. It had come in fifteen minutes ago. With a nine hour time lag between the continents that meant just past 9pm Zurich time. She thumbed the recall button and waited for Liesel's voice.

"Trisha?"

"Yes."

"We have a problem."

"Tell me," she said, as she turned the key and brought the Mercedes to life.

CHAPTER SEVENTY-ONE

After Valerie left Portage and arrived back in Langston, she detoured from the main road and drove by the high school. The Mercedes was gone. A sense of relief washed through her. She hadn't really wanted a confrontation.

There must be a logical explanation for why she was here.

Valerie *wanted* there to be a logical explanation. Her fondness for Trisha, and the friendship that seemed to flow so easily, was the one thing that had made her trip at least a little pleasurable.

She glanced at the scrapbook, lying on the front passenger seat, still unopened since she had received it from Clarissa. Wondering what secrets it held.

She reached with her index finger and gently lifted the front cover. Inside was a handwritten letter. She closed the cover and drove slowly to the end of the block, stopped at the intersection, almost pulled off to the side of the road to read the letter, chickened out, and turned in the direction of the highway with a momentary sense of relief.

Can I really afford to be such a flaming coward?

Before she turned onto the East Valley Highway she was again tempted to pull to the side of the road.

Go back to the hotel and hole up in the room. Take your time to digest it all.

Again, there was a feeling of relief, but coupled with a gnawing guilt, remembering what Clarissa had said.

You can take all the time in the world, if you wish. But the Order will send someone. They might even arrive today.

Remembering that Officer Johnson might be out there on the main highway with a radar gun, Valerie held the Maserati to the speed limit all the way back to the hotel—one of the most difficult things she had ever done.

She pushed open the door to her room and saw that the maid had been through and her bed was neatly made up, pillows tucked at the top. Fresh towels on the bathroom racks. With the curtains drawn open, the vast expanse of the lake beckoned.

Valerie yanked the curtains shut, sat down at the desk, switched on the lamp, laid the scrapbook square in the center, and lifted the black cover.

Dear V,

It may seem as though the world has collapsed upon you, but I promise that in time you will feel better about who you are, and about your future. At the moment, the focus must remain upon N.B., as she is in the greatest danger. This, too, will eventually be resolved, whether for the purposes I have explained to you, or in favor of the Order. Destiny often has its way despite the best efforts we make to control it.

If you wish to withdraw, I will understand, and not think less of you for it. Becoming involved will place you in danger, not just from the Order, but also from becoming known to mainstream humans. I only ask that, if possible, you come to a decision as quickly as possible.

If you decide not to join us, it may be wise for you not to read more than this letter. Feel free to destroy the book if you wish to go your own way. I have no one else capable of using this information in the way I have asked of you. Please note that I have elected to protect myself, you, N.B., and a friend of mine—C.D.—whom you have not yet met, by omitting them from my descriptions of the Order's members.

I wish learning about the Order had come to you in a gentler way, but that opportunity was lost when things got out of control due to my own lack of foresight in giving N.B. a bunny with my crest on its breast. My fault, and I now pay the price. I desperately hope N.B. does not also pay what would be a vastly greater price. I am sorry you must share the consequences of my shortcomings. I hope you will someday forgive me.

Yours, C

Valerie stared at the letter for a very long time before she finally laid it aside. At the top of the first page, in the same precise flowing script as the letter, Clarissa had entered a comment.

I am using only first names, since many of our members have chosen over the years to use different last names to disguise their identities. Most continue to use their first names out of pure convenience.

Halfway down the page, centered, was a single name, and for the next page and a half there followed a detailed description of who the person was and what she had done in her life.

Andrea

Born in 1841 in Bologna, Italy. Skilled in communicating with animals. A petite woman of 5'6" with dark brown hair usually cut just below the chin. Elfin features, lacking the classic "Roman nose" and instead has a small button of a nose slightly upturned. Brown eyes . . .

Valerie continued to read well into the night, finally pausing for sleep after finishing an entry that began,

Sandro
(A fourth great grandson of Dante Alighieri.) His skill is Charm. He is Italian, born in 1411. 5'10" wiry build, sandy blond hair, dark blue eyes. Very expressive, flamboyant, enjoys stylish clothing. Looks to be in his late 30's . . .

Valerie closed the book, head spinning, exhausted. Sleep came quickly and lasted far longer than she intended.

Had she continued to read, she would have soon reached a subject she would have recognized.

Trisha
The only American on the Council. Gifted with the Charm skill set. Medium length blonde hair with natural curls. Looks like Janet Leigh but not quite as pretty. 5' 11". Looks to be in her early 20's . . .

CHAPTER SEVENTY-TWO

Gunther spent Tuesday morning brooding in the motel room, feeling trapped. A sagging mattress, a thrumming wall-mounted air conditioner, a growing uneasiness, all contributed to a poor night's sleep.

I wish I were still in Wilhelmshaven, with a cool evening breeze off the harbor.

But he wasn't in Germany. He was in Washington.

He knew of at least four other members present in the Lake Cascade vicinity. Three of them—Clarissa, Trisha and the girl—could be identified. It was the mystery person driving the red Maserati that vexed him.

And are there more? How long will it be until I accidentally stumble across one of them and am found out?

This wasn't a bar brawl where he held the advantage. He was up against Clarissa. And there was Pieter Silberhof to consider—the stern Austrian warrior who currently chaired the Council. Someone who expected him to produce results. And definitely not the forgiving type.

But what could any of them really do to me? None would dare break the Order's rule against killing another member. Could any punishment they might impose make my life less meaningful?

Gunther burst out laughing, and felt better. For decades he'd been isolated, never welcome at annual gatherings, disallowed access to playthings other members freely enjoyed—yachts, jets, limos, a villa on the Mediterranean, luxury retreats around the world.

I will now prove my value.

Gunther stuffed his toilet kit and dirty shirt into the duffle and walked out to the parking lot and threw it into the Chevy's back seat, just in case he needed the trunk empty for the girl.

His senses were turned full up when he reached the little town of Portage. But when he reached 224 Mellison there wasn't the slightest hint of resonance.

Not that it mattered. The black pickup and the white Taurus were parked where they had been the previous day. The girl would eventually return.

Gunther drove to the end of the block, turned the corner, parked the Chevy in front of an empty lot, got out and walked back to the house.

I could still follow Pieter's game plan. I could go to my rental car and drive away, meet them at the airport, leave it to Trisha to do the dirty work.

The thought fled as quickly as it had come. Gunther raised his right hand, formed his fingers into a fist, rapped with his knuckles three times on the door. There were footsteps from inside. Gunther glanced around and no one was in sight. Looking back at the door he saw the knob turn. His hand bunched tight as it opened.

A surprised Dan Torgerson saw the quick jab at his head, felt the fist connect with his left cheek. His field of vision filled with sparkles as the back of his head hit the floor.

CHAPTER SEVENTY-THREE

Nina sat at the end of the dock on Portage Bay, fully aware of Charlie watching her from far down the shoreline, sitting on a bench near a tree.

Last night the dream about the colorful tents had returned. But instead of joyful faces, the people standing amongst the tents were angry—an anger directed towards her. They began to shout, to curse, and she woke up frightened.

When she found it impossible to fall asleep again, Nina turned on her bedside lamp, picked up a novel from her bedside table, and read until she heard Evelyn out in the kitchen beginning to prepare breakfast.

Now, perched on the end of the dock, toes dangling in the water, she fingered the black pearl under her shirt. More than anything, ever, she wanted the bunny project to move forward. With Chantha, Selena and herself running a company, making money, having a stake in the world.

That Selena could master so much software in just a few days held her thoughts for a moment. She had been wrong to think she was the weak link—the girl most likely to fall into the trap of boys before she was old enough. Yesterday morning, that revelation had come. Trisha's praise of Selena had triggered the it. This brought a final forgiveness of Selena's selfie with the bunny at the sleepover. She now realized that it was Selena who had first seen the true value of the bunny—as something to be loved, treasured, and sought after by so many girls.

And in that moment she finally knew the bunny's name. *He's my little Freddy Boy!*

Nina's thoughts drifted away from Fred, to Trisha. *I must do something special to thank her. Because without her we would just be three kids dreaming big but with no way to make our dreams come true.*

From the corner of her eye she saw Charlie backing carefully away from the tree, ducking behind a line of cars, and finally slipping back into downtown Portage.

Good. I'm hungry. Evelyn will have something in the refrigerator. And maybe she'll make Hungarian Goulash tonight.

She would miss the beef and vegetable stew, and a lot of other great food, after she moved out. Evelyn was lacking in many ways, but the kitchen wasn't one of them.

Nina stood up and brushed the bottom of her jeans, careful to check for wood splinters. She pulled on her socks and sneakers and paced the length of the dock, stepping in the middle of the wide planks to avoid the cracks. When she got to the end she turned and looked back out across the lake. The sun was sinking. The rippling water shimmered. Sun diamonds dappled the surface along a curve of drift far out in the bay.

For a moment she considered exploring the beach. There was almost always something interesting to find along the shore—a life vest, a fishing bobber, a Styrofoam float board. She had once found a twenty-dollar bill washing around in the rocks by the seawall. And there were always flat stones, perfect for skipping.

But I'm hungry!

The image of freshly baked bread slathered with honey and butter eased her desire to wander the beach. She glanced in the direction of the Bosecker, saw no sign of Charlie, and wondered if he might try to come and find her. Would he stake out the house? There was something vaguely attractive about this possibility, and for just a moment Nina wondered why it appealed to her. Her stomach grumbled, and she pushed the thoughts of Charlie aside and left the marina.

Four minutes later she reached the house. Dan's pickup was in the driveway, and the back end of Evelyn's Taurus poked out from the garage. And something didn't seem right. She paused, standing absolutely still, and felt that "shadow thing." She looked around, but there was nothing that looked out of the ordinary.

I'm just hungry. And maybe a little tired.

Choosing to ignore the voice of fear, she walked up to the front door, turned the knob, and pushed her way inside.

CHAPTER SEVENTY-FOUR

Valerie didn't wake up until noon on Tuesday, not having closed Clarissa's book until shortly before dawn. She lay in bed, stretching and yawning, replaying the stories revealed in those pages. A man who served in Napoleon's army. A woman who birthed twenty-seven children during a fifty year time span and watched them all grow old (from a distance) and die before she finally gave up hope that any would live as long as she. A man born in the thirteenth century who fled a French feudal village after being accused of sorcery and threatened with death by fire at the stake because he didn't age.

And these people are still alive! Imagine hearing firsthand from someone who had actually seen Shakespeare perform. Listening to how the black plague swept through Europe. Learning from those who experienced the Reformation as it rekindled art and science in the wake of the Dark Ages.

She glanced at the clock on the bedside table, felt hungry, decided to put off more reading until after lunch.

When she reached the pub she hoped to see Trisha, wanting to ask her what she had been doing at the school in Langston.

She ordered a burger and fries and ate slowly, hoping Trisha would show, but she never did.

After lunch, she walked down to the beach, in search of her new friend, and again came up empty. On her return, she noticed the blue Mercedes was missing from the parking lot. Finally, she went to the front desk.

The same receptionist who had told her the Mercedes belonged to Trisha was behind the counter. "Hi," he said. "How's your stay with us going?"

"Fine," Valerie said. "By the way, have you seen Trisha Peterson today?"

"Yes. She checked out early this morning. Is there anything else I can help you with?"

"No," Valerie said, "Thanks."

She didn't remember Trisha saying she might be leaving. This continued to puzzle her until that afternoon, when she turned a page in the scrapbook, and finally came to the entry headed by the name: *Trisha*.

CHAPTER SEVENTY-FIVE

Charlie realized he'd been seen by Nina and decided to move to a more discrete location, atop an old packing shed, three stories high and four blocks from the waterfront. It would make Nina less nervous. It also removed the chance that people in Portage would grow suspicious of a stranger who appeared to be stalking a teenage girl. He didn't want another encounter with Deputy Johnson.

When he was finally crouched behind the three-foot parapet that surrounded a quarter acre of roof, Charlie was rewarded to see Nina walking back up Mellison. She reached the end of the Torgerson's driveway, paused, walked up to the front door, paused once more, and then went inside.

With the pickup sitting in the driveway, and the back end of the Taurus visible in the garage, Charlie decided here was a chance to take a lunch break. He climbed down the ladder at the back of the shed and headed for the Bosecker, intent upon a sandwich and coffee, and to check in with Clarissa.

⊷⊶

A few minutes after Charlie left the rooftop, Dan regained consciousness. He saw Evelyn lying on her side, just a few feet away, hog tied like himself, and began to scream obscenities at the stranger who was standing and staring at the two of them. Evelyn began to bawl, and it just encouraged Dan's blue streak.

All of that swearing . . . it took a lot for Gunther not to give Dan a swift kick in the ribs. He instead found a roll of duct tape in the shop and tore off two long strips. Once their mouths were taped, Gunther slung them over his shoulder one at a time and carried each down the stairs and sat them on the couch in the den. He went back up to the kitchen, made himself a coffee, and sat down to wait.

He felt the girl's resonance long before she reached the front door.

When she finally entered the house, Gunther stood where the door would shield him from view just long enough to push it shut once she stepped inside.

He thought she might panic, maybe scream. But her first reaction was the opposite. She turned, saw him, froze, and what he got was a question.

"Who are you?" There was fear in her eyes, for certain, but it was a controlled fear.

She will make a great warrior someday.

"My name is Gunther," he said. In his thick German accent the name came out sounding like "Goon-tah."

"What are you doing here? Where are Dan and Evelyn?" Her gaze flicked around the room. She saw where Dan's nose had bled into the carpet. Her eyes flashed back to Gunther as quickly as they had looked away.

"They are safe," Gunther said in a flat, cold voice.

"Where?"

"Downstairs," he said. "I have them tied up and gagged, in the room where the large television is, but they have not been hurt." Actually, Dan had a swollen cheek and a partially closed left eye. To Gunther, "hurt" meant something was broken and wouldn't properly mend. So what he said was the truth, at least in his own mind. He saw disbelief register on the girl's face, and knew it was time to make his pitch.

"Nina," he said, showing he knew who she was—but he could have easily learned that from the Torgersons—"I know you've been talking with Clarissa." *That name* he couldn't have learned from the Torgersons.

Nina looked surprised. And here it got tricky. Gunther had no idea what Clarissa might have told the girl. If he offered her new knowledge, perhaps she might be swayed. He had to gamble.

"There are things Clarissa hasn't told you about who she is, and about the group she belongs to." Gunther paused, studying the girl's expression. "And about yourself."

Her face was a mask of confusion.

"I need to take you to meet some people."

Now, fear mingled with anger in her eyes.

"You are perfectly safe. I mean you no harm." It was the truth, and Gunther saw she was confused by it. No one her age should feel safe with a stranger who has tied up the adults she lives with.

But even at this young age, her instinct for the truth says I am not lying!

"Can't you just tell me about it here?" she challenged, resisting the urge to run. Gunther blocked the front door, and he would easily catch her before she could reach the back door. To even consider running was a waste of energy.

"No," Gunther said, realizing his first plan wasn't going to work. His darker warrior nature now took hold. "Do you value the people downstairs?"

Nina glanced at the door that led to the stairwell. "What do you mean?"

"I think you know what I mean," Gunther said, hoping the moment wouldn't turn into something unpleasant.

"Yes," Nina said, now with a thinly veiled fury. "I care about them."

Or at least I care about Evelyn. Dan? Not so much. But I still wouldn't want to see him badly hurt . . . or worse.

"If you want to keep them from harm you will come with me." Gunther followed this up with an insistent, "Again, I promise to keep you safe and not hurt you in any way." He smiled, but the struggle for politeness never came easy.

Nina thought of the many times she'd heard that one should never trust a strange man. To stay safe. To listen to the instinct of fear.

But I do have an option? The answer came easily. *Not really.* But there were points she might hope to negotiate on. *I need to see if he can be reasoned with.*

"May I see Dan and Evelyn to make sure they are okay?"

Gunther hesitated, remembering Dan's shiner. "Of course," he finally said. "But no talking. The less they know, the less I have to worry about."

"Agreed," Nina said.

When they reached the bottom of the stairs and entered the den, Dan was the first to see them from the couch. His eyes went buggy. Evelyn made a whimpering sound from deep from within her chest. Her body began to shake, eyes glassy with fear.

Nina turned on Gunther. "You said you didn't hurt them."

Gunther shrugged. "It's just a bruise. I would have felt it if any of his bones had broken."

Nina realized Gunther's idea of "hurt" was far different from her own. And that he was capable of worse. Her play for reasoning had quickly run out.

"Back upstairs," Gunther ordered. He ushered her up the stairwell, close enough to grab her if she bolted. Evelyn's whimpering continued until the stairwell door closed behind them.

When they were back in the living room, Gunther said, "I need to make a call." He pointed at the sofa. "Sit there."

Nina obeyed.

Gunther stood in the middle of the room, pulled out a cell phone and punched out a long number. When someone answered on the other end, Gunther began speaking in German. Nina couldn't understand what he was saying, but as the conversation went on, Gunther became more and more agitated. When the call ended, he said, "We must go." He kept staring at her as if she should know what he wanted her to do. When she continued to sit, he yelled, "Get up!"

Nina practically jumped off the couch.

"Where are the keys for the white car?"

"She keeps them in the kitchen," Nina replied quickly. "I can show you."

Gunther followed her into the kitchen. Nina picked up the keys from the end of the tiled counter and handed them over.

"We will go to the garage. Do you know what will happen if you try to run?"

Nina could easily imagine how roughly he might treat her. And downstairs, the Torgersons were helpless. "I won't run. I promise," she said.

"Good," Gunther said. Just the same, he took her hand before they reached the door to the garage. His fingers were thick and callused, and he did not let go until she was seated in the Taurus. When he finally released her there were red marks on her hand. He shut the door and walked quickly around and climbed into the driver's seat and turned the ignition and punched the lock button for all doors before he backed from the garage.

Once on the street, he didn't bother to drive around the block to check on his rental. It would likely be days before someone realized it was abandoned. The duffle in the back seat contained only his clothes and a toilet kit and they were no great loss.

"Where are we going?" Nina demanded, working to mask her fear.

Gunther almost yelled at her to shut up, but he recalled Pieter's warning: *Someday she will remember all of this.*

In a steady voice, he said, "To meet someone. Now please be quiet."

Nina sat and watched cars pass, wishing she could somehow signal her distress to other drivers. Wishing even more that she were still sitting at the end of the dock. Why hadn't Charlie followed her?

Gunther focused on driving, while replaying in his mind the conversation he'd had with Pieter.

"I have the girl," he'd said, expecting some sort of congratulation. Instead, Pieter had been livid.

"You *what?*"

"She is safe and unharmed. I will bring her to the plane." Gunther proceeded to give a brief description of how he had captured Nina, wanting to prove how careful he'd been. There was a moment of silence after he finished, and then the angry words began.

"This was not what we talked about!"

"I thought you wanted her to be at the jet. I thought you would be happy with this."

"You are wrong! You now risk everything!"

"I'm sorry. I didn't know—"

"Listen to me and listen carefully. If you deviate even the tiniest bit from what I am about to say, I swear that you will wind up in a weighted bag at the bottom of the Rhine. Do you understand?"

"Yes." Gunther suddenly felt very much like the fool he was certain they all called him behind his back.

"I will arrange for you to hand her over to Trisha. In the meantime, you will take her in one of the cars and find some safe and remote place to park and you will say the absolute minimum to the girl. Am I being clear enough?"

"Yes, Pieter. I understand."

"If she is in any way harmed, you cannot expect to hide. Someday she will have great power, and she will look back on the next few hours and she will remember. Understood?"

"Yes, yes, of course. I understand."

"She is a princess of the Order, so treat her as one. Now go and find a safe place. I will call you soon." The line went dead.

Even now, in the car, Gunther shivered as he recalled Pieter's fury. His idea of trying to curry the girl's favor by revealing details about the Order had been a miscalculation. Her kidnapping, another miscalculation. He could now only hope that Pieter would allow him to return to an obscure life.

She is a princess of the Order, so treat her as one.

He looked at the girl, and she returned his glance with one of her own. "I guess we're both in trouble," she said in a sage voice that invited no disagreement.

It took all of his willpower not to tell her that yes, indeed, they were both in deep.

CHAPTER SEVENTY-SIX

I rv Goodwin was hiding from the heat of the day in his home office, catching up on answering a handful of emails, when the phone on his desk rang. He reached and picked up the receiver, eyes still focused on the computer screen. "Hello?" he said, only half-listening while clicking the mouse to save the words he'd been composing.

"What's the name of the woman you said was helping you teach business principles?" Frank Miller sounded panicked. Irv's focus shifted to the phone.

"You mean Trisha?"

"And her last name?"

Irv thought for a second. "Peterson," he said, remembering how little he actually knew about the young woman who'd taken over the course. "Trisha Peterson," Irv repeated, trying to sound upbeat, hoping nothing had gone wrong. "Great gal for someone so young. In fact—" Irv realized the line had gone dead.

Frank was already dialing Clarissa's number. It barely finished the first ring before she answered.

"Yes?"

"Trisha Peterson," Frank gasped.

There was a brief pause, then, "Do you know where your daughter is right now?"

"Yes," Frank said, suddenly concerned. "She's over at Selena's house. Is she in danger?"

"I very much doubt it," Clarissa said. "But she may know something that will help us. Can you talk to her?"

"Of course. What do you need to know?"

"Ask her if Trisha Peterson was planning to do anything with the girls outside of the school."

"Okay. Should I call you back?"

"Immediately," she said, and hung up.

Clarissa had been on the phone for the past ten minutes, with calls from Valerie, to Charlie—who was back atop the old apple-packing shed—and to Frank.

Charlie reported the white sedan the foster mother always drove was gone. He'd not yet moved close enough to the house to check if he could feel Nina Bea's resonance. Clarissa now dialed Charlie's cell phone.

"Get down off the roof and check and see if she's there. Don't hang up." She listened to the sounds of Charlie climbing down the ladder and then his footfalls and heavy breathing as he ran towards the house. Her fears were confirmed when Charlie reached the Torgerson's front yard.

"She's not here. What do you want me to do?"

Clarissa thought for a moment. Charlie could knock on the door and confront the foster dad, presuming he was home. Dan Torgerson would have no idea who Charlie was and would probably try to call the police. Charlie could stop that. But what good would it serve?

If someone makes contact, it must be me.

There was no compelling reason to believe Nina Bea had already been taken. She could simply be with Evelyn, running errands. Clarissa needed one more piece of information before she took action. Charlie was still on the line.

"I'm expecting a call back from Frank Miller. He might have more information about Trisha and what she planned for the girls. Wait for my call. If the foster mom and Nina Bea return, call me immediately."

"Do you care where I wait?"

"Close to the house would be best."

"Good." Charlie began to walk towards the shade of the oak at the bus stop.

Clarissa realized her heart was racing. She sat down in a chair, taking deep breaths, trying to focus and relax—finding both difficult.

When the first call had come fifteen minutes ago, Valerie was in nearly a panic.

"I think the woman I met at the hotel is the same person you describe as 'Trisha' in the book. As soon as I read about her, I realized she gives off that 'resonance' feeling you told me about. I mistook it for the feeling you get when you meet someone you expect to become your friend. But it was always more than that. When I spotted her car up at the high school on Monday morning I should have put it all together. I'm so stupid. I should have seen it—"

"Valerie, calm down, and tell me everything you know about Trisha."

By the time she was through there was little doubt in Clarissa's mind that 'Trisha' was the American member she had met at gatherings. A quick call to Frank Miller brought confirmation.

How clever of them to choose her for the job. And she somehow managed to wrangle a position teaching the girls business principles for summer school. Brilliant!

Clearly, Trisha would know Valerie was a member. Did she also suspect Valerie was aware of what she was?

If she believes that, she would definitely know Valerie was in touch with me.

The cell phone rang and Clarissa saw the number was Frank's. "Yes?"

"I think I've got good news," Frank said. "Chantha says Trisha is taking Nina to the airport in East Wenatchee tomorrow to meet up with someone she described as a European business-man. She represented this man as someone interested in financ-ing the bunny business. The girls apparently voted on who they wanted to go, and Nina was their choice."

"Maybe we got lucky," Clarissa said. Still not ready to relax until Nina Bea surfaced, hopefully with her foster mom. Clarissa hung up and again called Charlie, and reported what Frank had told her. "Keep me posted," she said. "And let's hope the white car returns soon."

CHAPTER SEVENTY-SEVEN

Five miles south of Langston on Highway 97, Gunther turned onto a dirt road that snaked off into the sage brush. He continued for a couple hundred yards until a low hill left the Taurus invisible from the highway. At a wide spot he backed the car into the brush and turned around, shifted into park, and let the engine idle. He kept the air conditioner running full blast, staring straight out the window while he waited, armpits soaking his shirt with sweat despite the cold draft coming from the grill vents.

The girl had been quiet, but it didn't last.

"Why me?" she asked, staring at him. Pieter's warning about not talking to her rang in his ears. Gunther continued to stare out the front window.

It seemed as if the girl sensed his weakness.

"I know you're not a bad man," she said. "You're doing this for someone else. Someone who doesn't appreciate you. It's not too late for you to change your mind. You could take me back to Portage. If you let me go, the police might not even look for you. And if they caught you, I'd tell them you treated me well. That you didn't hurt me. I promise."

"Be quiet," Gunther said, eyes still riveted forward.

Nina was about to launch another salvo when Gunther's cell phone rang. He quickly pulled it from his pocket.

"Hello."

"Gunther?" It was Trisha.

"Yes?"

"You have the girl?"

"Yes."

"Where are you?"

"A few miles below where the bridge crosses the river."

"Where exactly?"

"I'm up a dirt road."

"I will have a hard time finding you. Can you come to me?"

"Yes. Where?"

"There's a little town called Orondo about twenty-five miles down the highway from the bridge. There's a brick school building on the river side of the road. Pull in behind the school. I'll be waiting." The line went dead.

Gunther shifted the car into gear and sped as fast as he dared down the rutted road, leaving a billowing trail of talcum fine dust. When he reached the highway the girl spoke again.

"Where are we going?"

Gunther turned left onto the highway, accelerated up to the speed limit, and continued to stare straight ahead.

Nina wasn't ready to give up.

"Can't you at least tell me where we are going?"

Gunther wanted her to be quiet. "To meet someone," he said abruptly, as guilt twisted his gut. He couldn't remember ever having taken advantage of a kid.

Nina finally had him talking, at least a little, and if she could keep him talking maybe she would learn something useful. Convincing him to let her go no longer seemed possible, but there seemed no harm in at least trying.

"I thought you promised to keep me safe and not hurt me in any way."

Gunther's hands felt sweaty on the wheel.

Nina pushed harder.

"I guess if you kidnap someone, a promise like that doesn't really mean anything, does it?"

"I haven't hurt you!" Gunther snapped, regretting it immediately. The girl had tricked him. But now that he'd said it, he wanted to defend himself. Pieter's words again echoed in his mind.

Some day she'll remember all of this.

Gunther tried to focus his attention on the road.

Nina kept at it, knowing it was her only hope. Whoever Gunther was taking her to was going to be smarter and not interested in any promises Gunther had made.

"What about keeping me safe? Are you doing that when you hand me over to whoever it is we're going to meet?"

Why did I have to tell her back at the house that I'd keep her safe? But the answer was simple. He'd wanted her cooperation. Making a promise to keep her safe seemed the best way to get it. It was true, at one level. The Order would never harm her. At least not physically. But they would work to change her thinking. Most certainly they would do that. He glanced at her. She held him in a steady gaze, her brown eyes pleading, and Gunther saw her fear, barely under control. He looked back to the highway. "I'm sorry," he said. "I didn't have a choice in this."

"You always have a choice," Nina pleaded. "That's what life is all about: making choices." She fell silent, as if she had said all there was to say.

After two minutes of nervous silence, Gunther found himself wishing she had kept talking. He tried to think of something to say that would make her think better of him. Nothing came to mind.

A few minutes later they came around a bend in the road and on the right was a brick building that looked like a school. The opportunity for talking seemed to be over.

Gunther slowed and turned off, circling the building. There was a parking lot in back, empty of cars except for a blue Mercedes. Nina's face took on a look of surprise that quickly turned to anger.

"Trisha," she said. She stared hard at Gunther. "Was it her all along?"

"Yes," Gunther said, happy to shift the blame.

He pulled to a stop behind the Mercedes and waited for Trisha to emerge. In those few seconds, Nina reached around her neck and pulled up the little pouch she had worn for the past two days. Gunther saw the motion and looked across.

"Here," Nina said, holding out the pouch. "I'd rather you have it, than her."

Gunther accepted the pouch just as the driver's door of the Mercedes opened and Trisha stepped out. Gunther stared at the girl.

"Take it," she said. "It may give you better choices in life."

Gunther took the pouch and pushed it into his pocket, pulled the keys from the ignition, opened the car door. "Stay here," he said, leaving the driver's door open.

Trisha stood beside the Mercedes. Gunther walked up to her, his face hard set. "Where do we take the girl now?" he asked.

"I will take her to the jet this afternoon," Trisha said.

"I thought we were meeting them tomorrow."

"*You* won't be meeting anyone! *You* will be catching a commercial flight back to Germany, where you will crawl back into your hole in Wilhelmshaven and stop causing trouble."

"But—"

"No!" Trisha shouted so loud it echoed off the nearby schoolhouse wall. "Your involvement in this is ended. You have caused enough trouble. Now, bring the girl from the car."

Gunther turned and walked back to the passenger door of the Taurus, opened it. Nina looked up at him in one last silent plea.

"I'm sorry," Gunther said, offering his hand to help her out of the seat. She took it and stood beside him. Turning her face away from Trisha, she whispered, "Clarissa would never treat you this way." The power in her words felt like the white heat of an explosion. Gunther almost buckled to his knees, and it took several seconds for him to recover, wondering what it was that he had just experienced.

Then he led her to where Trisha stood beside the Mercedes.

"Hello Nina," Trisha said, trying to sound pleasant.

Was that nervousness in the betrayer's face? Nina thought so. But not enough to make a difference. She glared back at the woman she had trusted.

"I'm sorry it worked out like this. Gunther wasn't supposed to be involved. If you and I had met the businessman tomorrow, like we discussed in class, you would have been given a choice whether or not you wanted to come to Switzerland to meet the rest of our group." She smiled—a smile that would have worked on anyone outside the Order. Nina saw the lie.

Trisha's smile dissolved. "So it must be like this," she said with resignation. She reached into her pocket and pulled out a yellow plastic vial. She twisted the cap and shook two oval blue pills into her open palm. "I'll need you to take these," she said.

Nina stared at the pills. "Will they hurt me?"

"No," Trisha replied. "They will only make you sleep for a few hours."

"You don't trust me?"

"I'm sorry, but I don't. I can't risk you trying to get away when we are near other people."

"Do you have some water for me to swallow them with?"

"Yes," Trisha said. She looked at Gunther, almost said something, then turned and took quick steps to the Mercedes, reached in and grabbed a water bottle.

Nina looked at Gunther. "You promised to keep me safe," she said, as tears welled in the corners of her eyes.

Gunther looked away, staring off into nothingness.

Trisha came back and handed the pills and the water bottle to Nina, who took one last look at Gunther, then put the two pills into her mouth and swallowed with three gulps from the bottle.

"Very good," Trisha said, taking the bottle from Nina. "Please go around and get into the front seat. You should recline the seat back so when you fall asleep you won't tip over."

Once Nina was inside the car, Trisha turned on Gunther. "This is your fault. You have set back the girl's rehabilitation by weeks, maybe months." She turned abruptly and got into the Mercedes, slamming the door shut.

After the Mercedes was gone, Gunther reached into his pocket and pulled out the small pouch, tugged at the string to open it. He turned the pouch upside down and stared at what fell into his hand. It was a piece of history. A part of the legend that surrounded Clarissa.

Caesar's black pearl!

CHAPTER SEVENTY-EIGHT

Charlie sat in the shade beneath the oak where Mellison joined the East Lake Road. A few minutes earlier he'd seen Valerie's Maserati zoom past. Finally, his cell phone finally rang.

"Have you seen any activity?"

"No."

"Something must be wrong. We're coming over. Meet us at the house." Clarissa hung up.

"We" turned out to be not just Clarissa and Valerie, but also Frank Miller. He had driven around the northern end of the lake. Valerie pulled up in her Maserati. Frank and Clarissa were right behind in Frank's Volvo.

"Any sign of the foster mom's car?" Clarissa asked Charlie, as they stood in the Torgersons' driveway.

"Nothing."

Clarissa began walking towards the front door and the others followed. With a nod from Clarissa, Charlie knocked. There was no response. He knocked again, harder. Nothing. He looked at Clarissa.

"Try it," she said.

Charlie reached out and twisted the knob. The door swung open. Charlie said in a challenging voice, "Hello?" After no reply, Charlie pushed the door wide and stepped inside, this time shouting loudly, "Hello?" He saw blood on the carpet, and heard a distant noise coming from behind a door off to one side of the room. He turned to Clarissa, who stood on the cement porch.

"Someone's crying."

When they reached the bottom of the stairs, they found Dan passed out on the couch. Evelyn was slumped against his shoulder, eyes red and cheeks stained with tears, sobs coming in slow, labored gasps through a snotty nose.

"Untie them," Clarissa said.

Charlie slowly pulled the masking tape first off Dan's mouth. After Evelyn's tape was removed, she began to bawl, snot running freely, her words jumbled and mostly incoherent.

Charlie cut the cords binding both of the Torgersons. Clarissa stepped forward and reached down and placed one hand on Evelyn's forehead, looking into her eyes. "Calm down, now. It will be alright."

Evelyn fell silent; the panic in her eyes replaced by the rapt attention one might expect from a well behaved six-year-old.

"I wish I could do that," Charlie said.

Clarissa gave him a dismissive look, then studied the reddened face of the woman. "Tell us what happened," she said.

Evelyn began to talk. Just before she finished, Dan came awake, cringing against the back of the couch like a beaten dog.

Clarissa said to both of them, "Listen closely to what I have to say." She told them that Dan had tripped, hit his face on the floor, and in the morning he should go and see a doctor about the bruise. She said everything else that had happened was just a bad dream. A dream they would now forget. Then she looked into Dan's eyes and gave one final command.

"After you have seen the doctor tomorrow, you will call the lawyer you hired for the adoption. Tell him you want to dismiss the petition."

She took a step back, looked at Dan and Evelyn, who clung to each other like lost and frightened bear cubs. "You are no longer interested in making Nina your daughter, or in keeping her in your home as a foster child. You will fully cooperate with Frank and Anna Miller in a transfer of custody. Now, you will sleep."

Dan nodded calmly, his eyelids slowly closing. Evelyn yawned and then looked at Dan with loving eyes. Within seconds, both were peacefully asleep on the couch.

"Back upstairs," Clarissa ordered.

When they reached the living room, Clarissa turned to Charlie.

"The man Evelyn described is a German named Gunther."

"I read about him in the book," Valerie added.

Frank looked confused. "The book?"

"I'll tell you later," Clarissa said. She looked at Valerie. "How quickly can you create a program to threaten them with?"

"The algorithm wouldn't take long. But the volume of information in your book would take several hours to enter. And then we would need to contact the Order. How do we go about doing that?"

Clarissa shook her head. The Order certainly didn't maintain a website. There was no telephone number she knew of to call, except for Liesel's. And calling her old friend presented its own risks, including endangering the one contact she had buried within the Order's ruling council. She hadn't told Liesel about the threat of disclosure and wasn't certain how she'd now take it.

"The only way I know of is to get on a jet and fly to Zurich and go to where they meet. But there's no guarantee someone would be there."

"So what do we do?" Charlie asked.

"The jet should arrive sometime tomorrow in East Wenatchee, if they go according to the plan Trisha arranged with the girls."

"And if they've changed the plan?" Valerie asked.

There was a long pause from Clarissa, and the look on her face betrayed what she was thinking.

Then we will have failed.

"I've got an idea," Valerie said. But as she was about to explain, there came the noise of a car pulling up to the house. A car door slammed. The front door opened, and there, standing in the doorway, was Gunther.

Charlie stepped in front to protect the others. Clarissa reached out and put one hand on his shoulder. "Wait," she said.

Gunther looked from face to face, extended his right hand, which was clenched tight, turned it palm up, and uncurled his fingers. In the middle of his palm lay the black pearl. In a choked voice, he said, "I want to help."

Clarissa stepped around Charlie. "Where is the girl?"

"Trisha has her."

"Where has she taken her?"

"To meet the jet from Zurich."

"So soon?"

"Yes. They moved up the time."

"Where are they landing?"

"Somewhere in Washington State. I think they may already be here."

Valerie now interrupted with, "I can find out."

Clarissa turned to her. "How?"

"The FAA tracks all aircraft. They had to file a flight plan coming from overseas, and they'll have to land at an international airport first, to clear customs. They can't come straight to the airport in East Wenatchee."

"Do it quickly," Clarissa said.

Valerie ran to the Maserati and pulled her laptop from the trunk and brought it back into the house. Within two minutes she was up on the Internet, and three minutes later she looked up from the laptop. "A flight from Zurich to Spokane landed earlier today. It was listed as a Gulfstream five-fifty. Does that sound right for something the Order would be using?"

"Yes," Clarissa said. "How far is Spokane by car?"

"Three hours," Frank volunteered.

Clarissa thought for a moment. "It wouldn't make sense that they have Trisha drive that far. They'll come to East Wenatchee with the jet." She looked at Valerie. "Can you tell us how long it will be before they leave Spokane?"

"Just a minute," Valerie said, tapping the laptop's keyboard. "Gotcha!" She looked up with a worried face. "They just filed a return flight plan from East Wenatchee to Zurich." Her face was solemn. "At the same time they activated a flight plan from Spokane to East Wenatchee."

"Activated?" Clarissa said.

"Yes. It means they're already taking off."

"Then we haven't much time," Clarissa said. "Valerie, we're going to see just how fast that car of yours will go." She turned to the others. "Charlie, you and I and Valerie are in the Maserati. Frank will follow with Gunther in the Volvo. He probably won't be able to keep up with us, but he shouldn't be too far behind."

Only Charlie appeared to hesitate. "Do you really want to take *him*?" He looked at Gunther.

"Yes," Clarissa said. "I think he's earned our trust." She flashed a quick look at Gunther, who nodded in agreement, finished with a half-grin.

Valerie had closed the laptop and was already headed for the door. Less than a minute later both cars were speeding down the East Lake Road.

Officer Troy Johnson was sitting in his patrol car just inside the city limits of Langston, at a point where the speed limit broke from 45 down to 25, when he saw his radar's digital readout jump to 85. "Holy Cripes!" he said, hitting the switch for the strobes.

Valerie saw the blue lights. "We're in trouble," she said, looking back at Clarissa. "Do you want me to try to run it?"

"No!" Clarissa smiled for the first time that morning. "It's perfect. Stop."

Puzzled, Valerie pulled in behind the cruiser. An equally puzzled Frank braked to a stop behind the Maserati.

Troy was out of his cruiser, right hand on his holster, having recognized both the car and the woman behind the wheel. It seemed a perfect opportunity to redeem himself with his sergeant. As he approached the driver's window he saw it was already down. As a surprise bonus, the Indian was in the passenger seat. Troy was about to order the Asian woman out of the car, at gunpoint if necessary, when a second woman, sitting in the back, spoke in a loud and commanding voice.

"Officer, we have a medical emergency and we need you to lead us at the greatest possible speed to within one mile of the East Wenatchee airport. When you reach one mile from the airport you will turn around and return to Langston. Do you understand?"

Troy stood transfixed as the woman gave orders, his face reduced to an observant mask. When she was finished, Troy simply said, "Yes, ma'am."

"*Then move it officer! This is an emergency!*"

Troy ran to his cruiser and left the strobes running. Charlie turned and looked back at Clarissa. "There's another thing I wish I could do," he said.

"Me too," Valerie added.

Clarissa reached for her seat belt. "Let's just hope he stays on the road." She pulled out her cell phone. When Frank answered, she said, "We've now got a police escort. Try to keep up, but don't risk your lives."

Officer Troy sped off through Langston with the Maserati and the Volvo in close pursuit.

Half an hour later, having topped one hundred and twenty on the straight stretches, the three cars entered East Wenatchee. As they closed in on the airport, Charlie turned around to ask Clarissa how she wanted to handle preventing the jet from taking off. She was leaned back in the seat with her eyes closed, her face a blank.

"Clarissa?"

Her eyes remained closed.

"Clarissa, we need you to wake up!"

No reaction. Charlie turned to Valerie, who was concentrating on the police cruiser doing 70 in a 35 zone as it wove through traffic. "Something's wrong with Clarissa," Charlie said.

Valerie didn't dare look away from the road. "What?" she said, continuing to focus on the cruiser.

"It's like she's gone to sleep," Charlie said.

"There's nothing we can do about it now," Valerie said. "She must have a reason."

Charlie looked again at Clarissa, praying it wasn't a stroke.

CHAPTER SEVENTY-NINE

The Gulfstream's starboard engine was left to run at low speed as Pieter carried the unconscious Nina from the Mercedes—now parked in the general aviation lot at Pangborn Field on the outskirts of East Wenatchee. He gently laid her on the single bed at the back of the cabin.

Hiroshi Nishikura took her pulse and felt her forehead and estimated it would be another three hours before the drug Trisha had administered lost enough strength in her bloodstream to bring her awake. He had brought along an additional sedative—this time a purely organic extract.

The two pilots remained in the cockpit, isolated from their passengers by a heavy security curtain. They had flown missions for this group before. They only knew of the Order as "those people" and never asked questions. What they did know was that the pay would be triple the standard rate and would be paid in Swiss Francs in a plain envelope.

As the hatch sealed and the port engine began to spool up, Trisha was staring out a portside window at the parking lot, hoping not to see a car racing up behind the fence. As she watched, a raven came swooping in over the tarmac and landed on the wing. Within seconds, another raven landed, appeared to screech at the first bird, then immediately launched back into flight in the direction of the front of the jet. Trisha turned to the other three, who were seated across the aisle. Her face was filled with concern. "Come and look at this."

Liesel crossed the aisle and looked out the next window. Pieter and Hiroshi crowded up to look over her shoulder. As they watched, dozens of ravens swarmed across the tarmac, some of them headed towards the front of the jet, others settling on the wing.

Liesel let out a long sigh, that ended with "*Clarissa!*"

"Is that possible?" Trisha asked.

"What else can explain it?" Pieter said, completely disgusted.

At that moment the security screen was shoved aside. The pilot, wearing a light blue uniform with four gold bars on each shoulder, said, "You need to come and see this."

They followed him to the cockpit and saw that the front windshield was covered in ravens, all of them flapping and jostling to keep from sliding off the curved plexiglass.

"I've never seen anything like it," the captain said. He turned to Pieter, whom he'd been told to consult only if a very serious problem arose. "We can't even see to taxi. If we came up to speed, they would peel off and get sucked into the engines." He raised his hands in surrender.

"We should at least try," Pieter said angrily.

"No," Liesel said. "She hasn't directed them into the engines yet, but I have no doubt she will if we force her to."

"She?" the captain said, puzzled.

Liesel said, "How this happened is not your concern, captain. Please keep the engines warm and ready if we should be able to take off, and remain in the cockpit." She said this in a charming way, but it was nonetheless an order. The captain reached for the throttles and pulled them back to the idle position, confused about what had just happened; and very glad he wasn't being commanded to fly a jet with birds literally hanging off the skin. One glimpse out the cockpit's side porthole confirmed the wings were now covered with birds.

The passengers retreated to the cabin, and the copilot pulled the screen back into place.

They sank into seats to await the inevitable, and no one looked at anyone else. And then, the inevitable occurred.

They all caught Clarissa's resonance at the same moment.

The police cruiser peeled off onto a side street a mile from the airport. Valerie floored the gas, worried the jet might have already taken off.

As the runway came into view, Charlie shouted, "Look! It's still there!"

Three hundred yards beyond the passenger terminal, a large private twinjet was parked just beyond the chain link fence.

Valerie was concentrating on her driving. "Is it moving?" she asked, as she veered onto the siding road that led past the terminal.

"I don't think so," Charlie said. "But there's something strange." He turned to look at Clarissa in the back seat. Her eyes were still closed.

As Valerie cleared the final hanger and screeched to a stop next to Trisha's blue Mercedes, she saw what he meant.

The jet was swarming with ravens.

Clarissa spoke from the back seat, her eyes now open. "I can't hold them for much longer." Her voice was shaky. "You need to go and get Nina Bea."

Even as Charlie opened the car door and ran for the chain link fence gate, one of the ravens on the near wing launched into flight and began to pump its way up into the air. Other birds took wing, and within seconds the jet was nearly free of fowl.

Charlie waited for the hatch to open, but instead, the engine on the far side began to whine a little louder. Charlie looked around for some way to stop the Gulfstream, but the tarmac was clear of anything he might use to block the wheels. The second engine began to spool up and the jet began to roll slowly away from him.

Charlie reached into the watch pocket of his jeans for the only thing that he might be able to throw far enough and accurately enough to do any damage. Three ounces of gold: the Crest of Clarissa.

He began to sprint towards the jet and managed to gain a few yards on the tail section where the engines were mounted. He slid to a stop and planned his right foot and took aim. The golden disc flew straight into the oval intake and there was a sharp *Bang!* of metal on metal. For a moment that seemed the end of it; but then the exhaust from the engine went from clear to a bluish color and immediately the whine from that engine took on a grinding sound.

Inside the cockpit the captain saw the readout for hydraulic pressure drop for the port engine. He pulled back on the throttle and began an emergency shutdown. Almost immediately, Pieter's head poked through the security curtain. "What is happening?" he demanded.

"The port engine has failed. We have to shut it down."

"Can't you take off with the remaining engine?"

The captain turned and looked at the man who was challenging him. Despite the fury and energy in those cruel blue eyes, the captain held his ground. "No," he said in a flat voice.

"Why not?"

"This runway is only fifty-seven hundred feet long. It is nearly one hundred degrees outside, resulting in what we call high-density altitude, which decreases the lift of the wings. We are carrying a full load of fuel, and we would never gain enough speed for takeoff." He paused, and when Pieter continued to stare at him, as if demanding a different answer, the captain asked, "Do you want to die today?"

What Pieter wanted to do was to scream. He wanted to pound his fists against the cabin walls. And most of all, he wanted to punish someone for what had happened. Instead, he said, "Alright. Shut it down, and the both of you stay up front until we have dealt with the situation."

The captain nodded in agreement, directing his copilot, "Take us through the checklist." The copilot reached for the second throttle, pulled it all the way back to shut down the remaining engine. The privacy curtain swished back into place.

Pieter returned to the others. "They have won the day," he said angrily. And then he went to the hatch and pulled the lever and pushed it open.

When the stairs were extended, a tall Indian appeared and demanded, "Where is she?"

Pieter silently led Charlie to the back of the plane. When he saw Nina fast asleep on the narrow bed, he turned on Pieter and said, "What have you done to her?"

Nishikura spoke up. "She's been sedated, but she's in no danger."

Charlie thought of a few choice words, but chose not to give them the satisfaction. He instead stared at the two men and the two women, memorizing their faces. Then he lifted Nina in his arms, cradling her head gently against his shoulder, and carried her from the jet.

As he stepped down onto the tarmac and walked toward Frank's Volvo, Gunther was hunkered down in the back seat, not wanting those onboard the jet to know it was he who had betrayed them. But at the same time, wishing that it was he who was carrying the princess to safety.

CHAPTER EIGHTY

As they drove back to Dartmouth Village from the airport, Clarissa listened to Gunther's explanation of what had happened to cause him to come to their aide. Even Gunther hadn't fully understood what Nina Bea had intuitively done. But Clarissa saw clearly that Nina Bea had sensed Gunther's lifetime of rejection, and then bestowed a gift so enormous, so seemingly undeserved, that it had turned Gunther completely around. He had never been totally loyal to Pieter Silberhof, or to anyone, really. He had only ever been loyal to himself. But he was now utterly devoted to Nina Bea. Clarissa suspected Gunther might even be willing to give up his life for her.

Clarissa now sat patiently beside the bed where Nina Bea lay, in one of the Miller's spare bedrooms, safely tucked beneath a sheet and a light blanket. *My brave little one. How ingenious you were. You unconsciously tapped into your potential, and used your ability to see into someone's heart and mind. You brought Gunther over to our side.*

Her eyes now fluttered open. "Where am I?" she said sleepily, seeing Clarissa by her bedside.

"Your new home," Clarissa replied.

"My new home?"

"You are at the Miller's, Nina Bea." Clarissa reached into her pocket and withdrew the black pearl, held it up. "I'm certain the bunny will appreciate having his heart returned."

There was sudden concern on Nina's face; she raised up on one elbow, a little wobbly but determined. "What happened to Gunther?"

And even after all she's been through there is still concern for him.

"He is safe here in the valley."

Nina lay back on the bed. Thinking of another question that would need to be asked. Not right now. But soon.

Why did all of this happen to me?

CHAPTER EIGHTY-ONE

The Council met in full session to hear a report from those who had gone to retrieve the girl. As the meeting came to a close, a vote was taken to form a special committee to consider how best to make a second attempt. Liesel would have voted "No" if she'd thought it would do any good.

But I must pick the battles I can win.

Her hand was begrudgingly raised in the affirmative with the others.

There was one positive for the day. Pieter Silberhof was removed from the ruling Council, as punishment for having sent Gunther ahead without first obtaining consent from the others.

Everyone accepted that the task of a second kidnapping would be far more difficult. Their opponent knew they were coming. And she was, after all, Clarissa of the Julii. The second daughter of Gaius Julius Caesar. Her existence lost to recorded history by reason of belonging to the Order. Clarissa had been gifted with powers far beyond those possessed any other living member of the Order. Until now. There was someone else who would soon hold all of the powers. Her name was Nina Beatrix Haas. She was just thirteen years old. And if she were allowed to continue on the path with Clarissa, there would eventually be no way of stopping her.

The next novel in this series will be *The Funny Bird*.

www.ingramcontent.com/pod-product-compliance
Lightning Source LLC
Chambersburg PA
CBHW070354260626

47161CB00001B/138